The Troika Belle

Ira J. Morris

HEINEMANN : LONDON

William Heinemann Ltd

LONDON MELBOURNE TORONTO

CAPE TOWN AUCKLAND

Printed in Great Britain by
Northumberland Press Limited
Gateshead

The Troika Belle

BOOKS BY

IRA J. MORRIS

NOVELS

A Kingdom for a Song
The Witch's Son
The Troika Belle

TRAVEL

My East was Gorgeous

In memory of my mother,

Frouma Mazower, *née Toumarkine*

for whose amusement in her last illness this
book was written, and whose high courage
gave me the heart to finish it afterwards.

Author's Note

All the words and actions of the historical personages who figure in this book are authentic, with the exception of a few lines of dialogue attributed to the Countess, later Princess, Lieven.

Historically minded readers may be interested to know that the incident of Napoleon's Cossack guest, who crops up in *War and Peace*, originated in the day-to-day journal kept by the Comte de Ségur, Napoleon's aide de camp in the Russian campaign. De Ségur vaguely refers to the Cossack as having been 'left behind by the enemy'—leaving novelists free to guess at the full story ever since.

Part One

Part One.

CHAPTER I

As long as the crashes reaching him from the private supper room had been of breaking glass. Shalash, the Tartar proprietor of the Balagan, did not worry. In that winter of 1811 the Balagan had all but established itself as the most fashionable of St Petersburg's island pleasure houses; and when the Tsar's Own Black Hussars entertained there two well-deserved reputations had to be maintained: theirs for wildness, the Balagan's for the lavish licence it offered its patrons, along with its famous gipsy girls and throbbing guitars.

Moreover, for that night's party the shrewd Shalash would have been happy to sacrifice his entire stock of glass, throw in the girls and foot the bill himself; because the Hussars' guest of honour was a very exalted foreign Royal Personage whose presence at the Balagan conferred upon it an almost official stamp of approval.

The Personage was in the last weeks of his State visit to Russia. An evening *en garçon* with some gay Guards officers was doubly welcome, since it also served to relieve the Tsar of the Prince's tedious company at supper. And the Hussars' choice of the Balagan to be graced by the royal spree was the sort of luck which Shalash's rivals sourly attributed to a personal pact with the devil.

Shalash had been up since dawn supervising every stage of the elaborate menu. The *specialité de la maison* on which the Balagan had built its reputation was fortunately available. She was the celebrated gipsy, Mila, whom Shalash had launched upon her glittering and scandalous career. Shalash, who heard everything, knew that she had recently left the protection of her Baltic millionaire for the arms of a handsome young rake in the Hussars named Sacha Arloff, the natural son of Count Arloff and the acknowledged leader of the fast set among the gilded young aristocrats of the Guard.

Since young Arloff was among tonight's hosts, Mila had graciously consented to appear—after no more than two hours of Shalash's coaxing and the conquering argument that a public triumph on such

A*

3

an occasion could not but enhance her charms in the eyes of her new protector.

Shalash had then hastened back to the hothouses for a wagon-load of Mila's favourite red roses. Later, carefully denuded of their thorns, these had been strewn to form a carpet for her royal —and barefoot—progress from Arloff's carriage to the supper room.

She was worth every rouble it had cost him, thought Shalash as he stood directing the service in the small buttery between the supper room and the kitchens. Once or twice he thought he could distinguish the Prince's braying laugh. The momentous evening was going well. He sent in the brandy and liqueurs. Then, as was his custom, he left the *maître d'hôtel* in charge and withdrew to his private cabinet across the corridor, where a cold collation awaited him.

Here the noise of the supper room was somewhat muted; but the roar of the toasts from four-and-twenty healthy, drunken young throats still set the lustres of the chandelier tinkling. Shalash calculated that another ten dozen glasses would probably be needed before the night was out and hospitality *à la russe* fully honoured. He sent for his *sommelier* and *maître d'hôtel*, arranged his saturnine features in an ingratiating smile, and, flanked by his acolytes, rolled to the door. All three froze at the pistol shots.

There were two, exploding in rapid succession, followed by some shouts whose import, Shalash prayed, might be merely the exuberance of youthful high spirits liberally laced with alcohol. But if it were not . . . ? For a moment the three eyed each other in silent consternation. Their relief at a burst of laughter from the supper room may be imagined. Shalash's frozen smile dissolved into an expression of furious indignation. Hitching his red satin sash round his bulky form, he kicked open the door and strode into the buttery.

'What misbegotten fool has let 'em get at their pistols?' he demanded of the huddle of cooks and lackeys. They parted to disclose a wilting young *chasseur*.

'So help me God, *barin*, it weren't my fault!' he wailed. 'Well, I ask you, sir, what's a fellow to do when this high almighty foreign Highness bellows "Hey—you there! My pistolets, at once. In my coach, dumpkopf!" And him I might've let stew, but when that young limb of Satan, Sacha Arloff, orders you to do something, you jump to it—as well you know, Stepan, for all that you stand there looking down your big nose now! *You* fixed up the cards on the mirror for them to shoot at—'

'The mirrors—?' moaned the *maître d'hôtel*.

'Smithereens,' the big-nosed Pavel opined with gloomy relish. 'It was like this, see, *barin*. This Serene Sauerkraut starts on about how the Emperor Napoleon and his Frenchies would have us on the run after the first volley if there's a war, because our guns weren't no good, and we're lucky if we get a few rusty English pieces through the blockade. "Well," drawls young Arloff, "I'd still back my rusty English Mantons to pick me out a fly on that mirror—or a French Marshal at full gallop." And 'fore you could turn round there's a wager on it and Oleg here is sent running for their pistols, while I'm told off to fetch a pack of cards. "Wait, though—" calls Arloff when I am at the door, "His Highness's concern was with our Army's *own* weapons. Waiter, my compliments to the sergeant of the escort, and tell him to give you two of his troopers' pistols." So I scoot out and get them, and the cards, and fix 'em up the four aces in the centre of the big mirror with candle-wax. Meanwhile Oleg's back with their own weapons. The Prince makes a great to-do over his loading. The girls start screeching and clapping their hands over their ears, but finally he blazes off. Two beauties. His first a bit low, but his second—'

Exploding through the recital and deafening them all, came the third shot.

'Everyone into the kitchens,' ordered Shalash. He himself took a deep breath, parted the red velvet *portières* over the door of the supper room and went in.

Inside, he nearly choked. A thick haze of powder smoke obscured the brilliance of the chandeliers. The acrid reek of powder mingled unpleasantly with the rich fumes of food and wine, and the overpowering scent of the roses massed round the walls. Shalash's eyes went instinctively to his precious floor-length pier-glass. Its centre was shattered into two jagged sunbursts of splinters. On either side of them, an ace of spades and an ace of clubs still dangled. If Shalash had looked among the mirror fragments on the floor, he would have found remnants of the wax that had attached the ace of diamonds—shot through cleanly by the Prince's second bullet—but no trace at all of the ace of hearts, of which, by some freak, a tiny corner had been left affixed to the mirror when His Highness's first bullet had gone slightly wide. Sacha Arloff had just shot off that corner.

The code of hospitality restrained the jubilant Hussars, so that no more than a gratified murmur from his brother-officers greeted his feat. But no obligations of the polite world hampered the glee of the gipsies. The guitars crashed into a wild triumph. The girls scattered about on the officers' laps rose like a flight of gaudy birds; and Mila herself sprang up from the cushions where she had been enthroned, shook back her magnificent black hair and whirled out on to the gleaming expanse of parquet before the mirrors.

Not even Shalash had ever seen her dance as seductively before. Despite himself, he joined in the roar of applause. Mila snatched up one of the pistols from the supper table and ended her dance with a triumphant, stamping swirl before the shattered mirror, the pistol held high. The Prince said:

'Fairground turn, no? And fairground shooting.'

There was a small, deadly silence.

Shalash, casting a swift glance at young Arloff, quickly moved forward. So did Sacha Arloff's half-brother, Count Paul, and the senior officer present, Major Lavrin, and a dark boy across the table, Prince Adam Ralensky, the heir to a great Polish house, who was serving with the Hussars and whose hero Sacha was. All of them noted uneasily that both Sacha and the Prince were angrier and rather more drunk than was at first apparent. Both had discarded their heavily-braided, gold-epauletted coats for the shooting. The Prince's florid countenance was now flushed a deeper pink than his rose brocade waistcoat. Sacha's handsome face was nearly as white as his fine cambric shirt. He kicked back his chair and rose, scattering the girls. Several locks of his straight, dark-streaked blond hair hung over his forehead. His moody dark-blue eyes glinted dangerously as he turned to the Prince.

'So His Highness thinks the Black Hussars do their fighting at fairgrounds?' he drawled. 'Gentlemen, we must not disappoint our guest. So let's show him a real fairground turn, shall we? With a live target, eh, Mila?'

'Sacha, don't be a fool!' urged Count Paul in an undervoice. 'Recollect whom you provoke—'

'Gentlemen, gentlemen, you'll ruin me!' whined Shalash, already foreseeing the inevitable scandal.

'Champagne!' ordered Major Lavrin sharply. 'Sacha, dear boy, you're foxed. Sit down.'

'No such thing!' yelled Sacha. 'Mila, my girl, are you game? Then stay where you are, and we'll show the Prince what he and his master Napoleon can expect if they ever venture on to our fairgrounds!'

Drunk or sober, Sacha Arloff could load his silver-mounted Mantons in thirty seconds. The soft click as he drew back the hammer sounded loud in the hush that held the room. Mila had stood absolutely still, leaning indolently against the mirror, while he loaded. Now, as if some invisible thread between them were directing her movement, she laid the pistol she still held on to a console and returned to exactly her previous position at the centre of the mirror. Every eye in the room moved with her. Then, again as if she were drawn there by his hand, she took one pace forward and stood facing him, her hands on her hips, her lovely head tilted insolently back on its smooth column of neck. Still he did not move. Her hand came up, made a minute adjustment to the red rose she wore in her hair just above her right ear, and returned to her hip. Sacha fired. When the smoke cleared, Mila stood there smiling. She no longer wore a rose in her hair.

This time no *politesse* could hold back the Hussars' triumph. The guitars rang out. Every man was on his feet, the Prince with the rest. Sacha leapt up on to the table, holding up his glass.

'Hussars, I give you a toast—Mila!'

'Mila!' thundered the Hussars.

'*Hoch!*' cried the Prince.

They drank. The glasses crashed. Sacha sprang down and waltzed across to Mila, a brimming glass of champagne held aloft. The Hussars roared again as he swung her up in his arms and kissed her as she held the glass to both their lips. Then the other girls were upon him, whirling him into their wild dance. Spurs rang and chairs flew back as other young officers joined in, laughing and yelling, deafened by the clashing tambourines. Everyone began to clap and stamp to the throbbing rhythm, except Shalash and the Prince; Shalash because he was professionally immune from the intoxication of tzigane music, the Prince being unfortunately tone-deaf. Moreover, the royal mind was at best unable to entertain more than one thought at a time; at the moment it was still intent upon the novel target apparently in use with Russian regiments.

'It is only for your Horse Guards—dis shooting practice at live tzigane females, or also for Infantry?' he enquired of Major Lavrin, 'And you are losing how many girls a week?'

The Major choked into his champagne but assured His Highness that the Hussars prided themselves on never losing a girl.

The Prince's slightly glazed eyes widened.

'Ach so. Then it is perhaps not so difficult, dis liddle shot. It is a question of de nerve, yes? Goot. I will try it. Please to call the tzigane here.'

'Sir, I'm afraid—'

'No, no,' cried His Highness jovially, clapping the Major on the back, 'Do not fear. *In vino veritas. Je suis un maître.* The tzigane shall haf a fine *douceur*, and I shall haf my liddle souvenir—hic!—of your Russian hospitality.'

Without waiting for the Major's services, the Prince gripped the table, swayed to his feet and threaded his unsteady way through the dancers to Mila.

She had returned to her throne of cushions to sulk because Sacha was dancing with the other girls. She cast the Prince a smouldering look and went on tearing the petals off a rose. When, however, she had comprehended his request, she hesitated and looked around for Sacha, who chose this unfortunate moment to collapse laughing into a chaiselongue, with a girl on each arm. Mila's round chin came up. She plucked a fresh rose for her hair, flounced over to the mirror and stood again, arms akimbo, smiling insolently at the Prince.

He puffed happily back to the table; and with surprising deftness for one so deep in liquor, re-loaded one of his pistols and cocked it.

'Sir,' said the Major, rising, 'I must earnestly beg you not to proceed with this. It was but a—'

'Poof!' said the Prince.

Count Paul Arloff had also risen and was looking round anxiously for Sacha. The guitars stopped in mid-bar. The officers released their girls and crowded round the table. The Prince waved his loaded weapon.

' 'Way there! I make de aim.'

'Your Highness—Mila, get away!'

'Poof! Not to moof, woman!'

Mila, abruptly emerging from her pique, looked down the length of the brilliant room into a wicked black muzzle wavering at her in the Prince's unsteady hand. Her limbs locked in terror. She could not move; but she screamed.

Fortunately her voice was a powerful one and its urgency pierced Sacha's alcoholic daze. He sat up, and then leapt off the chaiselongue, scattering bottles and girls.

'Moof ze head a 'lil to de ri',' crooned the Prince, peering along the barrel.

'Mila—*down*!' roared Sacha.

But with half the room between them he could not hope to reach her in time. Instead, he flung himself at the console where Mila had laid the pistol of her triumphal dance, praying that it was loaded. He did not remember cocking it or taking aim, and the shot—since it was desirable not to kill the Prince—was an impossible one even for a crack marksman, in cold blood. The two weapons seemed to explode simultaneously. The Prince's bullet buried itself harmlessly in the ceiling. Sacha's, knocking the pistol out of the Prince's hand with minimal bloodshed—a powder burn and a graze —went on to wreck another of Shalash's mirrors, but this was not immediately noticed. What the horrified Hussars saw to the exclusion of all else, was a very exalted, foreign Royal Personage sprawling across their supper table after being shot by one of his hosts.

CHAPTER II

Early next morning, news of the night's disaster began to seep through Count Arloff's great mansion in the Nevsky Prospect.

The first intimation the household had of it was when Count Paul's coachman returned at dawn, requiring the young Count's valet to accompany him back to the Palace, where his master and Major Lavrin were endeavouring to dissuade the Prince from any of the violent courses His Highness had mooted during their return from the Balagan.

Unfortunately it had been out of their power to prevent rumours of the night's events from spreading. The Prince had not shared their optimistic view of his injuries and had required four stout lackeys to carry him from the carriage, enjoining them at each step to recall that they were bearing a wounded man.

A surgeon was immediately sent for. Finding nothing else to do, he decided to bleed the Prince, and was engaged in the cupping when a harassed Imperial equerry arrived to discover what was amiss.

Count Paul's coachman had heard all the backstairs rumours both at the Balagan and the Palace. He imparted the chief of them freely to his round-eyed kitchen audience, between refreshing draughts of *kvass*, while Count Paul's valet put together a cloak bag.

After their departure the news spread rapidly; first to the upper servants, then to Master Sacha's old nurse, Akoulina, in her retirement on the attic floor, and finally to such household dignitaries as the Italian chef and Count Nicolas's English tutor, Mr Tickell, when he came to discover what had delayed the service of breakfast to his charge, whose appetite and volatile spirits were in no way impaired by being confined to his bed with the measles.

None of the foreign elements could be expected to share the Slavonic extravagance of the household's devotion to Master Sacha. Mr Tickell went on to confirm everyone's worst suspicions of *perfide Albion* by pointing out that if you shot people you were liable to justice, and that he had always known that Master Sacha would go his length one day.

With that he returned upstairs, bestowing a calm 'good morning' upon a weeping maid whom he encountered taking her washing water up to Mademoiselle Lise de Montargis, the young émigré French girl who was being brought up by the Countess.

The Countess herself was of French origin, though, unlike Lise, not quite of the *haute noblesse*, and Lise's position in the household was somewhere between that of unpaid companion and dependent niece, according to her ladyship's humour. That is to say, she was permitted to call the Countess *'ma tante'*, since her ladyship was not averse to assuming kinship with the Montargis; the Countess had hired nursemaids and a governess for her, and then allowed Count Nicolas's tutor to continue her instruction, but had never scrupled to disrupt her lessons whenever she required Lise's attendance. And that autumn she had abruptly terminated any further education and introduced Lise into society at a magnificent ball for which her ladyship had required a novel distraction.

Lise, at barely sixteen, was a thin, pale little girl whose sole claim to beauty were her huge, brilliant, and very expressive dark eyes, marigold-fringed with a tangle of black lashes under extravagantly arched brows. For the rest, her small head always seemed to be drooping on its long, childishly thin neck, and her dark hair, unless expertly dressed, tended to tumble out of all the ribbons into which she ruthlessly scraped it back from her face. The face itself was piquant but childishly unformed, with a soft, full, pale mouth, a lifted upper lip, a blunt little nose and an expression of friendliness and faint surprise, perhaps at harbouring the astonishing eyes. She was also blessed with an enchanting laugh.

Lise was still much more at home sharing Nicky's schoolroom than being quizzed by modish bucks in the salons. But she was a stoic child, who had of necessity learnt to take life as it came, without pretension to having her own wishes consulted.

So she thoroughly enjoyed the possession of three pretty, new dresses which marked her debut. She was gratified if anyone spoke to her at the routs and receptions to which the Countess's caprice took her, and overjoyed whenever these outings brought her a glimpse of her own and Nicolas's idol, Sacha, on one of his occasional appearances in the polite world.

Once, he had actually danced with her; and several times she had been privileged to watch him dancing with the Princess Nina

Volkonsky, the raison d'être for his presence at any ball that year.

For some unaccountable reason, the spectacle always had a lowering effect on Lise's spirits; although he and the peerless Nina were commonly allowed to be 'the handsomest pair in Petersburg' and both danced extremely well. An engagement was confidently mooted, if once the scruples of Nina's parents could be overcome. *Their* objection was to Sacha's wild ways. His irregular birth was not held to be an obstacle, since his mother had been a noted society beauty and her liaison with Count Arloff one of those connections which are recognised in the highest circles.

No member of the Count's household could muster the courage to disturb his slumbers, whatever the emergency. Finally, however, Nurse Akoulina settled her chins and marched in, armoured in her old retainer's privileges and ready to brave the Tsar himself in defence of her nursling.

The Count manifested neither surprise nor dismay at her news. Long experience of his favourite son had taught him to believe the worst at once and to waste no energy on repining. But instead of proceeding to the breakfast parlour when he came downstairs, he turned into his cabinet and shut himself in, curtly instructing that no one but a messenger from the Palace be admitted to him.

It was then barely eight o'clock on a bleak February morning. About an hour later, her maid drew back the Countess's nattier-blue satin bed curtains and informed her ladyship that the Count wished to be received at her earliest convenience, adding that his visit was probably to do with 'Something awful Master Sacha's got himself into this time, milady.'

Her ladyship also knew better than to take it lightly. The Countess sat up, commanded her *maquillage* and the attendance of her resident spiritual adviser, the abbé Jacquot, and sent for Ton-Ton and 'Oupette, her two poodles, and Lise. Thus reinforced, she despatched her Turkish page to the Count to announce that madame would receive him directly.

When the Count had first met her, Anne Amélie, the second Countess Arloff, had been living in Brussels; the handsome relict of a Flamand banker and in no hurry to end her independence or place her ample jointure at the disposal of one of the needy aristocratic émigrés who had flocked to Brussels after the Revolution in France.

Nevertheless, she entertained them freely and opened her purse to Royalist funds. Among her benefactions was one that gave her peculiar pleasure since its recipient had once been her schoolfellow in Paris. To be sure, Julie de Rohan had then barely deigned to acknowledge Amélie's existence; but in Brussels, as the Marquise de Montargis, newly-widowed and at the end of her slender resources, Julie and her children owed their survival to her schoolmate's charity, for Amélie had descended upon their attic after the news of the Marquis's death in the Vendée fighting and removed the whole family to the luxurious shelter of her mansion.

In the course of a few months, Mme de Montargis' spirits revived sufficiently to make a continued sojourn as Amélie's pensioners intolerable. She elected to remove to England, where an elderly cousin was already established. Her two older children, Marie-Louise and Armand, travelled with her; the new-born baby, Lise, was to remain with her wet-nurse until she was robust enough to support a sea voyage. But Mme de Montargis had never conceived a fondness for her youngest, and she spared few lamentations from her own unhappy lot when the renewed war presently put it out of question for the child to join the straitened household in Yorkshire.

It thus came about that Lise was a recognised if little regarded member of the ménage, when Amélie's decision to end her widowhood disrupted the whole household.

Count Arloff had descended in Brussels on his way home to Russia from a diplomatic mission. Neither he nor Amélie made their decision at the promptings of a suddenly-conceived passion; but both exactly fulfilled what each wished for in a second partner.

Amélie had been determined that her second alliance should remedy the bourgeois stigma of her first, with no sacrifice of income. Both these conditions could be amply guaranteed by the match. Count Arloff might strike terror into his colleagues and dependants, but he was a man of magnificent presence, then in his late prime, and he knew how to make himself agreeable when he wished. He was also extremely rich, and, like Amélie, widowed, but in circumstances which might have given pause to a less determined bride.

For Serge Arloff had long ago used up the heart which a woman may expect to be offered with a man's hand in marriage. He needed a hostess. His houses needed a mistress. His young sons might be thought to need a mother. Above all, Amélie satisfied his main requirement in that he judged her affections to be as little engaged as his own.

His first wife had been a dim, clinging creature, devoted to the enjoyment of ill-health. It is to be hoped that this proved adequate consolation when, within a year of their marriage, her husband fell violently and irrevocably in love with one of Petersburg's reigning beauties, whom her parents' ambition had forced into a resplendent but distasteful marriage.

He and the lovely Hélène were of the same circle; and since Society chose to countenance their liaison, it was expected that their wronged spouses should view it with equal complaisance. Hélène's husband had understood his rôle but it proved beyond the powers of Countess Arloff. Finally, after staging many deathbeds, she had succumbed to a minor ailment and died—practically unnoticed by her husband and her world, since her demise took place within three weeks of Hélène's death in childbed.

The baby lived. Count Arloff had him brought up at Hélène's dower-estate of Volnoya, near Smolensk, where she had removed for his birth, frequently visiting him there and finding the only consolation for his grief in the little boy's lively resemblance to his mother.

When the child was eight, the special Royal dispensation necessary for his official adoption by the Count was forthcoming, and little Alexander—or Sacha, as he was known—was transferred to St Petersburg to be brought up alongside his step-brother, Paul, the Count's legitimate son and heir.

At the time of the Count's sojourn in Brussels, Sacha had recently begun his sensational career as a cadet at the Royal Military Academy, where, as the Count told Amélie with a fond smile, 'I have placed him in the faint hope that their discipline will take before the young rascal is spoilt to death.'

Amélie thought it an opportune moment to mention her own intention of carrying the five-year-old Lise with her into her new life. The Count did not appear as edified by her benevolence as she was herself. He gave his approval to the scheme with little more deliberation than he would have accorded to the addition of a pet monkey to the new Countess's household; a letter was sent to Mme de Montargis by diplomatic bag, and Lise was added to the formidable cavalcade which presently set out for St Petersburg.

In the event, the new Countess Arloff's relations with her two step-sons were fixed by a development which she had envisaged as little as the Count—the birth of her own son within a year of their marriage.

Little as she was inclined to strong affections, Amélie could not avoid a certain maternal resentment of his father's perfect indifference to the child. It was small consolation that this indifference extended equally to his heir; but, as the years went by, it disposed her to do more justice to Count Paul's amiable qualities—and of course, it inflamed her just disapproval of Sacha's existence, extravagance, morals and mode of life.

Nevertheless, she could not help being amused by him, nor wholly resist the appeal of a handsome young rake to a woman of the world. But the whole household sensed that no reliance was to be placed upon her complaisance in the periodic emergencies that tested their own loyalty to their favourite; and in the crisis to which everyone awoke that bleak February morning, no one, above or below stairs, counted on the Countess as an ally.

CHAPTER III

By the time she arrived in the Countess's bedchamber, Lise had heard three garbled versions of the night's events, and the dictates of her complete, unquestioning devotion to Sacha were to rush immediately to his rescue. A vague project of interposing her own trembling body between him and an equally vague doom was forming in her mind, when the summons to attend the Countess brought her sharply back to realities—and to the sensible reflection that, at such an early hour, it meant that the crisis had been taken in hand by authority.

Her ladyship was sitting up against a bank of monogrammed lace pillows. Her maid held a gold handglass as the Countess quickly but skilfully applied powder and rouge, talking all the while to the abbé who had discreetly withdrawn to the fire.

Lise curtsied.

'Bonjour, ma tante. Bonjour, M. l'abbé.'

'My chocolate at once,' said the Countess.

In the upstairs kitchen, Lise found one of the conclaves taking place all over the house that morning. The Countess's chocolate was boiling over unheeded. Lise snatched it from the stove and looked round for the croissants from Leblanc, the French *pâtissier* who served the Court and all fashionable Petersburg.

One of the footmen turned to shrug. The croissants had been forgotten in the crisis. Her ladyship was reduced to the pitiable choice of yesterday's croissants or one of the nine different kinds of rolls, milk breads, sweet breads, scones, pancakes, vatrushki, kalachi, ponchiki, rogaliki and bulochki whose delicious, new-baked smell was wafting all over the house.

A rack of them had been sent up from the main kitchens. Lise selected a flour-dusted milk roll, dug a generous lump of butter into its warm middle and popped it whole into her mouth.

'How some people have the heart to eat when they're dragging my innocent lamb off to prison or worse, I *don't* know,' observed Nurse Akoulina sourly.

Lise choked, partly from emotion, but also at the vision of Sacha as an innocent lamb.

'But Nania dear, it won't help Sacha if we starve!' she protested. 'Come, try and swallow a bulochka yourself; just to please him.'

The old woman accepted a buttered bulochka, but halfway to her mouth her hand dropped.

'Dry bread and salt herring, if he's lucky—that's what he'll have in Siberia,' she wailed. 'Pasha, Igor, get me a linen basket, quick! Olga, run down to the larders and fetch a ham; salmon, caviare—the black, zernistoye kind, mind!—and some foie gras and game pasties and sturgeon; and maybe a brace of pheasants; and have them send round to the hothouses for . . .'

Lise picked up the Countess's tray and fled.

The Countess was too preoccupied to spare a glance at her breakfast tray. The Count had arrived. Clad in his scarlet brocade morning gown and gold-worked Turkish slippers, he looked no whit less impressive than in full Court uniform. He stood bestraddling the marble fireplace, flanked by his great mastiff, Sgobar, and, to all appearances according as little attention as his pet to the Countess's diatribe. Her ladyship paused for breath.

'*Ma chère*, you will do us both a favour if you will drink your chocolate before it gets cold, and send for a cup for me,' drawled her husband. 'No, Lise, you will not make it your errand. I am persuaded that this household boasts a sufficiency of housemaids. Abbé, you have not yet had an opportunity to favour us with your views. What is your advice on our best course to extricate my deplorable son from his just deserts?'

The abbé coughed deprecatingly.

'I would not venture to proffer your lordship *advice*—' he began.

'My dear Arloff, how may the abbé say anything to the purpose?' the Countess broke in. 'As well ask Lise, or—'

'An excellent idea. Lise, what is your counsel?'

'I—Oh, sir, has Sacha *really* shot someone? Count Paul's man says—'

'For once he probably does not exaggerate. Sacha has indubitably shot, not just someone, but a Prince of the Blood—mercifully not one of ours—and the fact that the bullet did no more harm than to prevent the Prince from committing murder need not flatter our hopes. His Highness is the guest of Russia, and I have already this morning been privileged to hear from two high sources of the clamour he is raising. The consideration that Sacha drew in defence of a notorious gipsy *fille de joie*, his current mistress, is also unlikely to lessen the scandal. The Tsar-Emperor is gravely displeased.'

The measured words fell on his listeners' ears with stony finality. A silence in which the mastiff's heavy breathing and the soft crackle of the fire sounded loud, enveloped the room. Her ladyship was the first to recover her powers.

'I trust, monseigneur, that you will now see fit to acknowledge the justice of my warnings all these years,' she observed, biting strongly into a milk roll. 'Time after time have I represented to you the unwisdom of your indulgence to M. Sacha. Repeatedly, I have pointed out—have I not, abbé?—that the scandals arising out of his mode of life would one day not only precipitate his own ruin, but endanger the family he disgraces!'

Seeing that her ladyship's agitation of spirit was about to endanger her breakfast tray, the two poodles and the various *articles de toilette* scattered over the bedclothes, Lise hastily removed them in turn to safety. The Count observed her activity with an amused eye.

'Everyone aspiring to such dramatic sensibility should have a Lise in attendance,' he remarked, pinching her cheek. 'Compose yourself, madame. I am tolerably certain that your comfort at any rate will not be touched by this affair. But I will not disguise from you that it is going to take every ounce of my influence to extricate Sacha or even to mitigate the consequences of his rash act. So spare me your histrionic talents, Amélie, and recollect that you have a good head on your shoulders. Who of our acquaintance can we count on? And which of the dragon dowagers I encounter in your salon is closest to the Empress-Mother? She wields a lot of influence with His Majesty.'

The Countess sat up.

'Useless,' she snapped. 'Sacha is no favourite *there*. Of my female acquaintance, there is certainly Nathalie Pavlovna and the Duchesse de S—., but you will hardly expect them to acknowledge *their* attachment to M. Sacha. Of the men . . .' Her pale blue eyes, whose abstracted gaze had been directed at Lise's efforts to keep the poodles from annoying Sgobar, abruptly focussed on the girl.

'Lise, go outside,' she ordered. 'You may take 'Oupette with you. *Elle m'énerve.*'

Lise's second attempt to run to Sacha's rescue was again frustrated by the Countess's summons, some half hour later; but this time Lise found herself the prime object of attention from the three persons in the bedchamber. The Count had gone. His place by the fire had been taken by Count Paul, as neat as ever in a plain blue coat, but shewing on his pleasant face some traces of his recent tribulations at the Palace.

The Countess seemed in no hurry to give her orders. At last, she said impressively:

'My child, it is in your power to show some of the gratitude you must feel to myself and monseigneur. I am referring to the flattering offer which, despite your total lack of advantages, the Honourable Councillor Niebling has discussed with me on behalf of his son. The Councillor has the ear of very highly placed persons; indeed of His Majesty himself—'

Count Paul had been observing Lise's growing bewilderment. He held up his hand.

'Your pardon for interrupting you, madame, but is Lise *au courant* with the offer you speak of?'

'Naturally not,' snapped the Countess, 'since the young man has very properly left it to his father to ascertain my wishes first.'

'But then Lise may not like the match.'

'Twenty thousand a year and a position in the first circles—when she has not a sou to recommend her! My dear Paul, this is no time for frivolity. The only problem we face is whether the Councillor will *now* be willing to see his son form an alliance with this unhappy family; since he himself must then engage his influence on our behalf. I presume I have no need to question my dependence on *you* to use all your interest with M. Adolf Niebling, Lise?'

'No, *ma tante*. But—Oh, madame, I do not understand! That fat, German young man with the pince-nez, who spilled the sorbet on my pink dress? M-marry him?'

The abbé in his corner smothered a small sound in a discreet bout of coughing. Count Paul frowned.

'Madame, I beg you will reconsider,' he urged in an undervoice. 'The child is no more fit for marriage than—than Nicolas. I am persuaded that Sacha would not relish help by such means.'

'M. Sacha is not my prime consideration,' retorted the Countess. 'Nor have I ever observed him to have any scruples in pursuit of his interest. As to the other, you must give me leave to be the judge of what is fitting. Lise, I shall expect you to be ready to receive M. Adolf Niebling presently—if the note I have sent him prompts him to prevail with his parent. You may go and change your gown now.'

Lise managed to curtsy and get herself outside. She stood for a few moments in the ante-room, trying to compose her spirits. That—that pink porker to wish to marry her! And his offer—if she heeded *ma tante*—to put her in power to be of use to Sacha in the present crisis! Feeling an overwhelming need of someone to talk to in her bewilderment, Lise fled to her bedridden ally upstairs.

As always, Count Nicolas managed to look angelic, although his cherubic face under its mop of dark curls was currently spotted with measles and flushed with frustration.

'You *will* remember what the doctor said about not bringing on a spasm, won't you, Miss Lise?' enjoined Mr Tickell at the door.

'Leeze, like E-lee-zabeth,' corrected Lise mechanically. 'All right, I'll remember—though anyone less prone to spasms than Nicky. . . .'

'Gudgeon,' growled Count Nicolas, 'I'll *have* a spasm if he don't leave us. Shut the door, Lise. You've been an *age*,' he grumbled. 'I have nearly burst, I promise you, with everyone bidding me lie down and not fret myself. Now tell me all of it. Tickell says Count Paul has returned from the Palace. What are they deciding about Sacha? Is he arrested? Is my father—'

'Lie down and I'll tell you everything,' said Lise, curling up in her usual place at the foot of the bed. She was assumed to have had the measles at some point in her early childhood, so as to be eligible to amuse the invalid.

She poured out her tale, ending with her own dilemma.

'Mm-mmm,' commented Nicolas, nibbling his thumb. 'Well, *I* think this offer-thing is all a hum. How could such a slow-top as old Councillor Niebling get Sacha off? I 'spect he doesn't hold with Sacha anyway. So what would be the use of you marrying a fat German sausage like his Adolf?'

'Oh, Nicky, that's just what he *is*! The pumpernickel kind with a pink skin.'

Nicky puffed out his cheeks in a fearsome imitation of the pompous Adolf.

'*Gnädige Mam'sel*, you haf the honour to be chosen by me—'

'Don't,' cried Lise. 'You'll have me in whoops. But. Nicky, if *ma tante* says—'

'I daresay maman don't know Sacha like we do.' His eyes flashed. 'Can *you* see him seeking help from a Niebling?'

'N-no. But . . . Nicky, if you'd *heard* the Count! This isn't just an ordinary scrape. The Tsar-Emperor is gravely displeased. Maybe someone important and—and *heavy*, like the Councillor—'

'Fiddle! Even if he agreed, you couldn't be sure that the Tsar would be in the mood to listen to him; and then you'd be stuck there, married, with no gain to Sacha. And what would happen to our Escape Plan? Oh, Lise—!' He broke off and suddenly bounced up in the bed like a jack-in-the-box, his mouth an O of wonder and discovery.

'What?' cried Lise breathlessly.

'I've got it! I've got it! Our Plan! Well? Don't you see?'

Lise shook her head. The great Escape Plan was a long-standing compact between them, dating from an evening when Lise, in disgrace with the Countess, had tearfully confided to him her dream of running away to her mother in England. Nicky had improved upon it by adding his company and the final aim of joining Lise's brother Armand, who had followed M. de Talleyrand to America, and the three of them seeking their combined fortune in the New World. As she grew older, the project had become half jest to Lise, though they still talked of it and collected all possible information about the habits of Red Indians. It seemed remote from their present troubles.

'But don't you *see*?' demanded Nicolas, continuing to bounce wildly on his pillows, 'We must all three go! I mean Sacha must escape and come with us. We must contrive his escape!'

For a moment Lise was too entranced with such a vision to reflect on its feasibility. Then her five years of seniority spoke.

'How?' she asked flatly.

Count Nicolas subsided, digging his fists into his chin. Presently his brow cleared and he smiled angelically.

'I shall think of something,' he promised. 'F'rinstance, if we—'

'Cavé!' hissed Lise as someone scratched at the door.

'Beg pardon, miss, but you're wanted downstairs. The Honourable Adolf Niebling, in the yellow saloon with her ladyship.'

'Oh,' cried Lise, clapping her hands to her skirts, 'and I haven't changed my gown!'

'*Gnädige Mam'sel*, I haf the honour—What is the matter? Haf I said something humorous?'

'N-no,' spluttered Lise, 'I—I was not laughing at you, truly. I—er —choked.'

'You wish me to ring for some hartshorn?' enquired her suitor, peering over the rim of his pince-nez. 'I know young ladies are prone to be overcome on such occasions. Especially in the delicate situation we haf been placed.'

'No, I thank you. I am quite recovered. But, please M. Niebling—'

'You may address me as Adolf. Yes, from now on that is your privilege. But I will not disguise from you, my dear Mlle Lise, that our felicity was in grave doubt. Yet I am here. Does that not amaze you? But Mlle Lise you haf not yet the privilege of knowing my parent! Just as I am about to renounce my hopes, papa says to me: "Adolf, you are a fool; but these Russians are bigger fools than you. They haf no logic, no common sense. If you haf married this little girl a week ago, everyone would say 'what imprudence to marry an émigré girl without a *dot.*' But if you marry her *now*, when the family is under a cloud, everyone cries: 'What a romance!' 'What a generous heart!' The Tsar himself sheds a tear as he signs the order for young Arloff's exile to Siberia; you become the hero of the salons; your career is advanced. That is Russia." So you see, Mlle Lise—'

Lise had stopped seeing or hearing anything at the fatal words 'exile to Siberia'. Their dreadful import lent her a desperate courage.

'M. Niebling, pray tell me one thing. If—if I agree to marry you, will your father intercede with the Tsar for Sa—on behalf of Captain Alexander Arloff?'

M. Niebling came to an abrupt halt. He did not look for a powerful understanding in his schoolroom bride, but such want of sense bordered on simplicity.

'*Liebchen,*' he said gravely, 'you cannot haf been listening to me.'

Lise jumped up, her black eyes snapping.

'I have! But you mistake the matter. I was only going to marry you if your father got Sacha off. And Nicky is right; why should the Tsar listen to your father if he's at all like you? And he probably is, because he sounds a perfect Beast!'

Every feeling now demanded a flood of tears and a slammed door to crown her outburst; but her suitor was barring her path, openmouthed.

'There is nothing more to be said,' he announced hollowly, after due reflection.

Unfortunately there was, for he was obliged to request Lise to ring for his hat. He did so with awful dignity and stalked out, passing the Countess in the hall with a stiff bow.

Indignation buoyed Lise up for the first ten minutes of her subsequent interview with her ladyship; then she took refuge in tears. The Countess raised her voice. Lise sobbed louder, and the Count walked in.

'I collect that Lise has turned down her fat suitor. Do I also assume that you wish to apprise the whole house of your displeasure, Amélie?' he enquired icily.

The Countess bit her lip.

'You must allow me to be the judge of what tone I use to an insolent, selfish, ungrateful girl.'

'Then Lise must learn to cry less disrespectfully. By the by, is this list of her qualities à propos of her refusal of young Niebling?'

'How else would you term her action at this juncture in our affairs?'

'I would term it natural, madame, at any time.' He turned to Lise. 'My poor child, there is no need to look so stricken! Sacha will not be consigned to the salt mines but for the intervention of Councillor Niebling! His voice would have been a useful one; but I promise you that we have no need to enact a boulevard tragedy here, with you as the innocent heroine forced into a hateful marriage for her starving brother's sake. If I know anything of my Sacha he would not starve under any circumstances.'

'For her *brother's* sake—no,' murmured the Countess with a lift of her pencilled brows. Her cold eyes held Lise's. The Count's piercing blue eyes also swooped down on her. The awkward moment was fortunately interrupted by a footman. The Count went out. Her ladyship said:

'I do not know if you are aware that M. Sacha's position is grown graver every hour. In your shoes I would be thinking of what I could say to induce M. Adolf Niebling to come back. Go to your room and reflect. You may present yourself to me when you have composed your letter to him.'

CHAPTER IV

Fortunately for Lise, her ladyship had even graver matters than her protégée's defiance to preoccupy her during the harrowing four-and-twenty hours that followed.

By the evening the whole household knew the worst: Sacha Arloff was to be dismissed with ignominy from his regiment and exiled at the Tsar's pleasure. The Count had resigned all his offices in protest and sent back his orders and decorations.

In recognition of the Count's services to the Crown, Sacha's exile was to his own remote estate at Volnoya, and he was permitted to journey there under his own parole to report to the authorities at Smolensk. But this was the only mitigation.

Lise crept back to her room, flung herself down on the bed and gave herself up to utter dejection.

She did not at first hear the soft scratching at her door. Opened, it revealed little Count Nicolas's footman, Igor, who produced a much-folded billet from his sleeve.

'From the young Count, miss. I am to wait your answer and get it to him secret-like.'

Lise blew her reddened nose and took the missive over to the candles on her dressing table. The note read:

'Do not dispare. The Plan goes forward. We must escape by Sea. Tell Sacha, Igor has been down to the port and Discovered a ship for us to Stoway on to England. She sales the day after tomorrow. Bring my fishing rod and skates and air gun and Plenty of biskits. Tickel may be dificut. Bring some Stout Kord.'

In her tribulations Lise had almost forgotten her young ally's solution to their troubles. She stared at his note, divided between amusement and an immense, unreasoning lightening of her spirits.

Yet was it so unreasoning? Ever since the previous December, when the Tsar had opened Russian ports in defiance of Napoleon's Continental System, English ships had been running the blockade into St Petersburg. Count Paul had good-naturedly driven Nicky and

24

Lise to see the first of them at anchor in the port and Nicky had talked of nothing else for days on end. No doubt it was the powerful impression thus left upon his infant mind which had now combined with his fiendish ingenuity to produce the Plan; and while her fellow-conspirator's spelling might invite her smiles, his dazzling stratagem fired Lise with almost his own faith in its genius.

Had she not seen the English ships with her own eyes? In three weeks they could be sailing up London river! Sacha freed and both of them safe with her mother in England! All her base ingratitude over M. Adolf forgotten and forgiven to Sacha's rescuer! An entrancing picture of the two families' ultimate reunion in London, with herself as the heroine of the hour, inflamed her ready imagination. She rapidly added the Tsar's pardon for Sacha and her brother Armand's return from the American wilds to complete the blissful vision, and sat up with a bounce, her mind made up. All that remained was to inform Sacha of his rescue and convince him of its feasibility.

Some lingering remains of sanity warned her against embroiling Nicky further into the plot. She jumped up, seized a sheet of paper from her *escritoire* and sat biting her pen. Igor coughed.

'Beg pardon, miss, but could you see your way to letting me come along with you to England? I'll go my length to help Master Sacha, but I'd just as soon not be here when her ladyship discovers the little Count is missing—and him sick with the measles too.'

'The measles!' cried Lise. 'But of course!' and leaving Igor to his puzzlement, she quickly wrote:

'Dearest Nicky, it is a famous plan, but you have forgot one thing. No shipmaster will have us aboard if you come, for fear of the Infection to his crew. Indeed, Nicky, he would put back at once and Sacha would be Undone. Once we are safe in England and your spots are gone, we shall devise a way for you to join us; but now you must stay here and Cover our Traces. Destroy this. Your affec. Lise.'

'Give this to Count Nicolas as soon as you can do it privily,' she charged the lad, 'And not a word of it to anyone, if you want to help Master Sacha.'

'Cross my heart, miss,' he promised, sliding out.

In the morning, Lise decided to venture down to the Countess as usual. She encountered Count Paul coming upstairs four at a time.

'Good morning, Lise. I am come to make my farewells. Is her lady-ship ready to receive anyone?'

'Your farewells?' cried Lise. 'Why, Paul, where are you going?'

'Have you not heard? Don't look so scared, child. I'm not to be banished like Sacha; merely consigned to a temporary, cushioned exile in Moscow, where I shall enjoy looking up all my friends. Could you discover if her ladyship will see me? I leave within the hour.'

Lise, to whom the morning had brought many misgivings, had formed a vague design to make Count Paul her confidant; but this was now out of question. She ushered him in to the Countess and retired to her favourite refuge in the winter garden.

There she spent an uncomfortable half-hour reviewing all the enormities she was about to commit—ranging from running away, to lèse-majesté and High Treason—or whatever was the awful term for stowing away a fugitive from Royal justice aboard a foreign ship.

She rose from this appraisal considerably refreshed. Beside such heroic sins the immediate outrage of playing truant and venturing unchaperoned into Sacha's bachelor quarters paled to insignificance.

Count Nicolas's harassed attendants were very ready to surrender the task of keeping the invalid amused for a while. As soon as Mr Tickell had withdrawn, Nicky bounded out of bed, bolted the door and hurled himself bodily on Lise.

'Well? Have you been to Sacha? Don't he think it a famous plan? How will he join you? And, oh, Lise, may I not come too? I swear the spots are many fewer already, and by tomorrow—'

'No, they're not. I can see at least six new ones. Anyway it's all a hum because I have not seen Sacha yet. What I came to tell you, if you give me a chance, is that I'm off to see him directly. Nicky, will you get back under the covers! What in heaven's name are you doing down there?'

Count Nicolas, hanging practically upside down over the edge of his bed, turned up a suffused but triumphant countenance.

'Getting the Escape Pack,' he hissed, straightening up. In his hand he clutched something bulky knotted up in a red cotton kerchief.

Untied, it disclosed a crumpled brown half-wig, a pair of steel-rim spectacles, a loo mask, a miniature of the Tsar-Emperor and a much-folded sheet of paper.

Count Nicolas contemplated his trove with modest pride.

'The wig and spectacles are for Sacha's disguise. I stole them from m'tutor. The mask is for you; maman forgot it here once before a rout. And on here, Lise, I've written the name of the ship. "The London Lass"—is that not a fortunate name?'

'Yes, yes,' nodded Lise eagerly, succumbing to escape fever. 'But what is the Tsar's portrait for?'

'Silly. Supposing you're challenged on the quayside by some official? You show him the miniature and he realises at once you're someone 'stremely highly-placed and lets you go.'

'Nicky,' said Lise, suddenly sobered, 'I recognise it now. That's the portrait His Majesty presented to the Count on his last name-day. How did you come by it?'

'I went down last night and took it from its case in my father's cabinet. Do you imagine my father would grudge it to save Sacha?'

The force of this argument quite dispelled Lise's qualms. She quickly re-tied the Escape Pack and concealed it under the coverlet.

'Now listen, Nicky. You know nothing, nothing at all, if anyone questions you. If—when—we reach England, I shall write of course, and so will Sacha. All I shall do before we go is to leave a note for *ma tante* to tell her I am safe with Sacha, so that she may not be troubled about any harm having come to me. But no one must even suspect where we are gone, or about the ship, or *anything*, lest they try to pursue us.'

'Do you think they would?' cried Nicky, his eyes sparkling. 'With a fast armed frigate of the Fleet and boarding parties standing by?'

Lise blanched. 'Oh, Nicky, suppose they did—'

'What a lark! No, don't look so, silly, I was just funning! I forgot you're only a female. Lise, you *aren't* going to turn all missish and cry off *now*? Oh *why* am I stuck in bed here—'

'Hush, you'll fret yourself into a fever. I promise I won't cry off, come what may. Now lie down again.'

'Honour bright, you'll stick to Sacha through thick and thin?'

'Through thick and thin,' she repeated, with a queer lurch of her heart. She stood up.

'Shake on it?' said Nicky. They shook hands solemnly. Nicky entrusted her with the Escape Pack.

'You—you'll tell Sacha I helped?' he asked in a small voice.

'Of course I will! It was all your idea. And I'll try to send you word with one of Sacha's servants when we're safely off.'

'Oh *yes*! He can come by the back stair and I'll tell Tickell I feel an awful pain coming on and he'll go rushing off to fetch the doctors and—'

The unsuspecting victim of the crisis rattled at the door, and the conspirators hastily parted.

Lise's letter to the Countess presented even more difficulties than is usual for a fugitive's parting words. In the end she wrote rapidly as follows:

'*Ma chère tante*, pray forgive me for the Anxiety I must cause you. There is no need for it, because I am gone with Sacha and so am quite Safe. I am sorry to have disobeyed you over M. Adolf Niebling; but indeed dear Madame, he would Not have engaged to Serve us as you Thought. By the time you read this Sacha and I will be far away, and I beg that no one try to discover our direction. Later you and Monseigneur will learn Why and forgive All to your affec. Lise.'

This fatally misleading missive she swiftly sealed and ordered her maid to deliver to her ladyship's dresser 'not a minute before noon tomorrow'.

Then, having assembled the few necessities she could accommodate in the largest of her bandboxes—making due allowance for the Escape Pack—she tucked the bandbox ribbons over her arm and tripped downstairs with such a guilty air that she must have at once aroused the suspicions of anyone encountering her. But beyond a half dozen bored footmen there was no one about.

She was the second agitated young lady the grizzled porter of his lodgings had admitted to Captain Arloff that afternoon. The first one had astonished him too, because he had recognised her as the Princess Nina Volkonsky, known to all Petersburg for her beauty. 'Come to take her farewell of him,' the porter had decided, knowing that young Arloff was said to be paying her court. 'And now here's another young ladyship, hurrying up on foot if you please! Ah well, young blood . . .'

He beamed paternally at Lise and shepherded her up to Captain Arloff's rooms on the first floor.

'You'd best go straight in, miss, they're all in there. Don't stand on ceremony.'

The front doors stood open. Loud male voices floated out into the vestibule. Lise stood hesitating amid a confusion of valises and portmanteaux, piles of corded books propping up several sporting guns in their leather cases, and the carelessly piled cloaks, swords and black-plumed *shakos* of Sacha's visitors. Their voices were issuing from the high doorway directly ahead. As she eyed it, trying to muster up her courage to knock, the doors flung open and Prince Adam Ralensky came out, shouting:

'Danilo! What the devil do you—'

He broke off abruptly and stood staring at Lise open-mouthed. Then, being a very well-mannered young man, he swiftly crossed to her and bowed over her hand, saying in his soft voice:

'Mlle de Montargis! Have those rascals of Sacha's left you standing here unattended? I'm afraid the household's in an uproar, but this is too bad! You have come with a message from madame la Comtesse?'

'N-no. That is . . . Prince Adam, I—I have come to see Sa— Monsieur Arloff. It is *very* important. Please will you take me to him?'

Prince Adam was a *very* well-mannered young man. Not one of the thoughts chasing each other through his head was permitted to show on his face. Taking Lise's arm, he quickly shepherded her into the cabinet and closed the door.

'You will be more comfortable in here. Let me set down your bandbox and tell me how I may serve you. But Mlle Lise, will you be advised by me and let me escort you home? This is no place for you, and Sacha would not thank me for letting you stay. Is your maid below? Let me send for my carriage and—'

Lise shook her head. She knew Prince Adam for a friend of Sacha's but she was not quite prepared to risk confiding the secret of the great Escape Plan to him. She said earnestly, 'Thank you, but I *have* to speak with M. Sacha. Please, Prince Adam, I may not tell you about it, but he—he will be glad I have come, and . . . Oh, it is so *very* important that I see him!'

The effect of this ingenuous declaration was to achieve her end; though for reasons unsuspected by her innocence.

The young man looked at her, his eyes narrowing a little. Until now, if he had thought of her at all, he had considered Lise a child, thrust into the great world at the Countess's idle whim, when she ought to be still at her schoolbooks. The unlikeliest object in the world to fix a brilliant rake's interest. Every feeling was revolted by such a connection; but the girl was here, alone, with a bandbox—and how well did he really know his hero? Or any Russian?

'Pray be seated, mademoiselle,' he said coldly. 'I will inform M. Sacha Arloff of your presence.'

He bowed and left her; his romantic Polish soul filled with sadness and disillusion.

Lise did not avail herself of the chair Prince Adam had placed for her. All through her exchange with Prince Adam she had been aware of a buzz of voices. The secret of their penetration she quickly traced to a door masked by a jut of bookshelves and a Persian hanging. The recessed door behind it had been left wide open, and Lise found that she could by no means close it without stepping into the room beyond and betraying her presence to the occupants whose conversation she was overhearing.

Having done her best to draw the *portière* shut, Lise retired to the farthest corner, resolved not to distinguish another word of her involuntary eavesdropping. Then her heart jumped as a girl's voice sounded above the men's in the room beyond.

It was, normally, a charming voice, used to commanding the undivided attention of any gentleman within range. This was so far from being the present case that the Princess Nina actually sounded a little shrill.

'This,' she announced, 'is the last straw.'

In the circumstances this statement evinced a rare degree of self-restraint. Few young ladies who had risked coming to a bachelor's apartment to take farewell of their ruined love would care to find him hedged about by a grim-faced guard of brother-officers. Fewer still would have refrained from a tearful scene on discovering him drunk, dishevelled and totally insensible to their self-sacrifice, however picturesque he looked in that situation. And the Princess Nina was surely unique in not falling into strong hysterics on being confronted with his gipsy mistress.

Mila had come in carrying a blue riding coat to replace the dishonoured Hussar jacket which, roughly stripped of its epaulettes and medals, was still flung round Sacha's shoulders. She was, as usual, barefooted, and the extravagance of gipsy sorrow had precluded such mundane cares as washing or combing her hair for the past two days. At the sight of the Princess she folded her arms and smiled insolently. Nina, her magnificent eyes flashing, whirled round on the embarrassed gentlemen.

'So this is what you've been trying to hide! *This* is why you're all so anxious to get me out of here! Would not leave me alone with him! And I thought it was his care for my reputation! I thought at the least that I was dealing with a *gentleman*. Oh, what a fool I've been—'

'Precisely,' cut in a cold voice Lise barely recognised as Prince Adam's. 'So now, Nina, perhaps you will spare us any more of your vapours and go. You know you've no business to be here—'

'Adam, dear boy—'

'Ralensky, this is hardly the tone—'

'Well, what did she expect in coming here?' cried Prince Adam angrily. 'A drawing room to play out a romantic farewell? Listen to me, Nina. Three hours ago he was marched out before the whole regiment, had his sword broken, his medals torn off: dismissed, disgraced before us all—and you flounce in here all airs and graces and pout because he doesn't make you a pretty speech for your pains!'

'I don't! I don't! Oh, how odious you all are, when I've risked everything, yes, everything, to come to him. To find *this*! Fool that I was, I'll be well-served if all the old cats ring a peal over me when it gets out. Oh, *why* did I come here—'

The spoilt, furious young voice ceased abruptly and there was a tense pause, though Lise could not know it was because Sacha had lifted his head from his arms for the first time since he had slumped at the table some two hours ago.

'Why did you come here, Nina?'

Lise froze, not only with the horror of her eavesdropping but with uneasy recognition of the mannered drawl blurring Sacha's normally crisp voice. It meant that he was drunk: the only perceptible signal but one not to be ignored, according to household gossip at the Arloff mansion. Sacha's friends, who knew him rather better, knew that there were various stages in his drinking, and this was the deep and dangerous stage when a wanton devil danced behind his moody eyes and he was capable of anything. The Princess Nina was not of course attuned to this storm warning. She merely felt a natural satisfaction in having his attention once more properly focussed on her.

'Why did I come?' she repeated in thrilling accents. 'Because I *thought* you loved me. Misguided, trusting fool that I was—! When you don't care if we never see each other again, as long as you're left with your odious friends and—and your gipsy *creature*!'

There came a sharp crack of laughter.

'At any rate she is willing to face exile with me. Are you, my sweet Nina?'

'Oh, you—you Beast!' gasped Nina. Lise, her eyes like saucers, heard the slam of a door, a sharp tattoo of heels on the parquet; and then the outer door into the cabinet flung open and she was confronted with the raging young goddess in person.

Both young ladies stood transfixed, too astonished to pay any heed to the demands of civility. As often happens at such dramatic moments, Lise became aware of the entirely trivial circumstance that the pile of sables on the ottoman were the Princess Nina's *shuba* and muff—which doubtless accounted for her intrusion. Nina was the first to recover. Casting a scorching look at Lise, she swept across the room and threw the furs round her shoulders. Unfortunately this brought her within sight of the communicating door, and its mortifying significance was quickly grasped.

'You have been waiting for me to leave?' she enquired sweetly. 'Do pray go in, since *delicacy* need not deter you.'

She jerked the *portière* apart, propelling the unfortunate Lise before her into the salon, and, after all, had the last word:

'Another candidate,' she announced.

CHAPTER V

Four of the gentlemen in the salon stared at Lise thunderstruck. Then Major Lavrin started forward. Sacha, in the process of being coaxed into his coat by the kneeling Mila, glanced round indifferently and returned to his moody contemplation of the glass before him. Mila also ignored the newcomer. Prince Adam swore under his breath and swiftly interposed himself between the pair and the trembling girl on the threshold.

'Lavrin, allow me. Mademoiselle de Montargis, may I present Major Lavrin? Mademoiselle has called—that is, I was obliged to leave mademoiselle to wait in the cabinet while. . . . Get that damned gipsy out of here,' he hissed to the Major.

This was easier urged than done; since Mila, having ousted one rival, was by no means disposed to leave the field clear to another. Finally it took the combined exertions of all four officers to shift her from the room.

They returned to find Lise installed in her place.

She knelt by Sacha's chair, guiding his arm into the sleeve of the blue coat while she poured into his ear the great Escape Plan, in a breathless whisper of which barely a syllable penetrated his clouded understanding. But no amount of alcohol could impair Sacha Arloff's ability to grasp that here was that recurring factor in his life: a desirable girl offering to run off with him.

His friends took in the tableau they presented with varied degrees of misunderstanding. Sacha said:

'Pour me a drink,' and when Lise had swiftly complied, closed his hand round hers on the glass she held out.

'You're a poppet. Shouldn't be here though. Shouldn't want to go off with me, should she, Adam? Picture my step-maman's face!— and all the rest o' the salon-pussies—'

'Oh pray do not regard them!' cried Lise. '*Ma tante* has said she washes her hands of me, because she quite despairs of my making a respectable alliance the way I am going,' she quoted with fatal accuracy.

Her audience exchanged glances. Sacha tilted his glass.

'A fellow-outcast, eh?' He swayed to his feet. 'Give the tattle-mongers a real field-day, shall we?'

He began to laugh softly; Lise stared up at him, half-frightened, half-entranced. His major-domo, a flat-faced, shaven-headed Kulmak, came in, dressed for the road, carrying his master's fur-lined black riding cloak, hat and gloves, and the long-thonged Cossack whip called the *nagaika*, favoured by Petersburg's young bloods.

'The carriage is below, sir, and all the baggage stowed.'

He cocked an eyebrow at his master and said in a low voice to Major Lavrin:

'I've had them bring round Galant as he ordered, sir, but—'

'Sacha, you're never going to ride in your state?' asked the Major sharply.

'O' course I am. Think I'm going to slink out of town in a closed coach? Danilo, I'll be down directly! It's only a question of who comes with me. Well, gentlemen? Which one of 'em shall I take?'

He stood, rocking a little on his heels, very bright-eyed, smiling as he had smiled over the sights of his pistol at the Balagan and looking from Lise to Mila, who had appeared in the doorway behind the servant. Lise, obscurely conscious that something was going very wrong with the great Escape Plan, opened her mouth to speak. Prince Adam caught Sacha's arm.

'*'Garde à toi*. A girl of your father's household—'

'Set the cat well 'n truly among the pigeons, won't I? Danilo, my cloak! Lavrin, where the devil are the papers I'm to present to my jailer in Smolensk? Countersigned by the Tsar-Emperor himself—with a flourish for every year I'm to rot in my village. Never do to forget those—'

'I have them here. You'd best give them into Danilo's charge till you've sobered. Now come on down.' The Major lowered his voice. 'And stop playing the fool. The girl's a child. Take the gipsy if you must—'

'Oh no, not "must". *Must* go. *Must* report. *Must* rot away at the Tsar's pleasure. But I go to the devil my own way, and no one says "must" to me over a woman!'

'The horses are waiting, your honour,' said a voice at the door.

'Another "must"! Mustn't keep the horses waiting—'

He shrugged himself into the cloak held out by Danilo, crammed a high, Cossack fur hat at the back of his head and flicked the thin, wicked whip over his shoulder.

'Danilo, charge the glasses!' he roared. 'Come on, my lads, a last toast! Here's to going to the devil our own Hussar way—with a new girl and a tried horse under you and no heel taps!'

The familiar ring of a hundred regimental toasts on a hundred wild nights, had a magical effect on the spirits of the male company. Even Major Lavrin joined in the roar of laughter with the rest. Trust Sacha Arloff to finish up with a true Hussar swagger!

'Bravo, Sacha!' yelled one of the others. 'But which girl do we drink to?'

'Sir, the horses—'

'Lord, yes—I'm coming! Yes—but which girl? Can't have Nina. Tired of Mila. . . . So here's to you, my pretty! Up you come!'

The glasses crashed. Lise, dazed, deafened and increasingly dismayed, found herself flung up over a hard shoulder to a roar of approval from the Hussars. She gave a small, outraged squeak and clutched unavailingly at her bonnet. It sailed off. Flushed, laughing faces swung dizzily up at her through a cascade of tumbling hair and hairpins. The fur of Sacha's cloak tickled her nose; and few things in her life had proved as acutely uncomfortable as her first taste of a man's arms round her when Sacha chose to take the stairs four at a time in belated consideration of the waiting horses.

The whole company followed. Behind them, on the upper landing, Mila shrieked and rather halfheartedly produced a dagger. Danilo ordered a footman to bring down miss's bandbox and himself presently followed, carrying the magnificent sables cloak in which Mila had swept into the Balagan for the Prince's party.

Outside, the lamplighters had not yet come, so the busy scene was illumined only by the carriage lamps and the bobbing lanterns of the postillions, shining palely in the famous, milky blue-green Petersburg twilight. The bustle of departure was complicated by the usual last-minute hitches.

Sacha's cherished Galant chose to take a sudden dislike to the human race, shying and showing foam-flecked teeth at the approach of anyone but his master. Servants scurried to and from the house. The postillions cursed. No one had any eyes for Lise, hanging forlornly out of the window of the chaise. Danilo pushed his way through to his master.

'If your honour's set on taking the girl, she'd best have this or we'll have her sneezing by nightfall,' he remarked, holding up the sable cloak. 'T'other won't miss it, with all you've given her.'

B*

'Good man. Hey, Adam—!' Sacha leant down from the saddle, caught the cloak and tossed it over the crowding heads to Prince Adam.

'For my pretty,' he shouted. 'It's Mila's, so get her another from me, won't you? Are you up, Danilo? All right, stand away then— and we're off!'

'With God, off and aaa-way!' came the postillions' answering yell.

The long whips cracked and the chaise leapt forward, throwing Lise into a heap on the floor. Fortunately it was one of the Count's own travelling carriages, luxuriously padded and sprung, so that she sustained no injury except to her already sadly dishevelled appearance.

She picked herself up and found that the cushioned seat was wide enough to accommodate her bodily; so she curled up on it and composed herself to wait. Now that they were off, the bewilderment and doubts of the past hour could be dismissed. She was well used to the inexplicable, sometimes cruel whims of grown-ups. But now, England, home and glory awaited her; and Sacha would surely lose his frightening humour once he had sobered up, thought Lise drowsily, snuggling down into a gipsy courtesan's furs as the speeding chaise bore her irrevocably down what the Countess was to describe as her Road to Ruin.

Her ladyship did not learn of Lise's flight until the following evening. And until then, the mystery of Lise's disappearance was totally eclipsed in household gossip by conjecture about a far more important development.

This was no less than an equerry in royal livery bearing a peremptory command for the Count to attend His Majesty that evening at Peterhof, the Tsar's country Palace outside the capital, where, in the ordinary way, only favoured intimates were received.

Her ladyship was too well acquainted with the Imperial temperament to be more than amazed to learn next morning that the Tsar had received Count Arloff with every mark of cordiality and attention.

But reading eagerly between the lines of the Count's billet, she perceived that this was something out of the common run, even for the Tsar's habitually wild oscillation between opposites. To force a high dignitary's resignation and banish his son one day, and then receive him as if nothing had happened the next, was inconsistency on a truly Imperial scale.

'Never, never will I understand these Russians,' sighed Amélie to the sympathetic abbé.

'But perhaps His Majesty's—er—volte-face might presage a mitigation of his displeasure with M. Sacha?' he murmured.

'I would doubt it. This facility of the Emperor's character has its limits, never going beyond the circle he has traced for it—and that circle is of iron. I wish I might be sure that Arloff's blind partiality for Sacha has not led him into some imprudence on that score! I am told that the Prince informed the Tsar that he could not remain the guest of a country where the very officers of the Monarch's Guard were untamed barbarians. Alexander will not easily forgive or forget that.'

But her ladyship's fears were wholly eclipsed in the various gratifications brought by the Count's return. The first of these was the sight of him once more wearing his stars—whose return he had been persuaded to accept from his sovereign's own hand. The second was the news which quickly convulsed all Petersburg, of his appointment to the coveted Inspectorate-General which had been the goal of many exalted ambitions for months past.

It involved, he informed the Countess, his immediate departure to look into the affairs of the Finnish provinces, as soon as he had selected his staff; 'I shall send for Paul as my chief aide. He can join me in Finland. Will you have them hold dinner a while? I have much to do.'

'Willingly, since I wish to sit a little with Nicolas. They tell me he has been fretful all day; his tutor even sent down to me to beg that Lise might attend him, as he was forever enquiring about her absence. And that reminds me—' she added with a smile, reaching for the bell pull. 'The child has been confined to her room in disgrace since yesterday; well-deserved as you know, but your news shall earn her her pardon.'

The Count smiled too.

'*Ma chère*, I am persuaded that your sponsoring will soon procure her a husband whom both of you will like better than the egregious Adolf. Excuse me now. Tell Lise I am glad that my new Office can at least help to end *her* exile,' he added with a sigh.

To please him, the Countess sighed too, though only with her heartfelt relief that Sacha's exile could no longer threaten the disgrace of his family; and the Arloffs parted with complaisance on both sides.

The hour that followed demonstrated to her ladyship once and for all the folly of entertaining any such comfortable hopes in connection with Sacha.

Her first impulse was naturally to confound the Count with the news that his son had crowned his scandalous conduct by abducting her ward; but as the various circumstances of the affair came to light she grew more and more wary.

The conquering reason for her caution was of course Count Nicolas's involvement. His mother did not believe a word of the Escape Plan, which he had painfully been made to disclose; Lise's damning letter made the object of her flight all too plain. But her cherished Nicky, now sobbing his heart out into his pillows, must be dragged in once the Count started probing the affair.

Her ladyship looked very thoughtful as she sat mechanically strok-
ing the curly head buried in the pillows. Nicky shook off the maternal
hand and sat up.

'I hate you,' he announced tearfully, 'I hate everybody 'cept Lise
and Sacha. We promised *honour bright*—and now you've made me
tell on them! But whatever you do, they've gone and it's too late now
for any of you to stop them!' he ended on a more robust note, and
dived back into his pillows.

His mother had just been struck by the same thought herself, from
a different viewpoint. It was indeed too late. Nothing could alter
the fact that Lise would have spent at least two nights in Sacha's
company before anyone could catch up with the fugitives. So to gallop
post-haste after them now—as the Count would surely insist on doing
regardless of all its attendant evils of publicity—would achieve
nothing except to ensure the scandal.

Her ladyship smoothed the coverlet over her now sleeping son and
rose with a strong swish of silks, her mind made up to the heroic
task of saving the day alone.

The plan already vaguely forming in her head had the simplicity of
genius. It was to do nothing; for her powerful understanding had
quickly grasped that though it was too late to save Lise from the consequences of her folly, it was *not* too late to avert the scandal, if the
affair could be hushed up.

Mercifully, Sacha's own servants would have gone with him, and
in such a matter she could count on the discretion of his dissolute
friends. But there was still the problem of putting about some plaus-
ible story to cover Lise's absence from the drawing rooms.

Well, thought the Countess, staring down at her flushed, sleeping
son, the girl could have . . . but of course! The girl could have
easily caught the measles from her playmate; and what more natural
than for her to be sent to the country to recover? A protracted recovery. Then, when all curiosity had died down and the Count was
returned from Finland, they would decide quietly what best to do.
Or Sacha might even have solved the problem by marrying the chit.

The Countess thought this highly unlikely and decided that her
next letter to Mme de Montargis in London must prepare Lise's
mother for the Worst.

CHAPTER VII

Towards dawn, Lise was awoken by the shout of 'Horses!' rousing the sleepy ostlers of the posting-yard. After a moment's bewilderment, she recollected where she was, and, as the prospect outside looked singularly uninviting in the cold, greying darkness, settled herself back into her nest of furs and was asleep before they pulled out of the yard.

By morning Sacha's recent excesses had begun to take their toll even of his iron constitution.

He permitted one of the outriders to take Galant on a leading rein, fell across Lise into the coach and went to sleep.

After a while she ventured to arrange his cloak more comfortably round him and to tuck a cushion under his head. He stretched luxuriously, murmured 'Thank you, darling' to his pillow and slept on.

Lise curled into a ball in the small corner of the seat left at her disposal. Resolutely she transferred her gaze to the monotonous straggle of bare woods and fields past the window, and tried to concentrate upon the many dilemmas of her situation.

But neither her eyes nor her thoughts would obey her. Her gaze strayed irresistibly back to Sacha's tousled head on the cushions, while her spirit struggled in vain against the overwhelming sensation that all was right with the world and she herself entirely happy for the first time in her life.

Sacha slept on and off for the next sixteen hours. This seemed to occasion no surprise or concern in his servants.

'When we've been in deep doings for three days and nights, miss, we *sleep*,' Danilo grunted. 'You leave him to us, missie, we're used to his ways. Just eat up your dinner and get to bed. We'll need to be away at first light to make Vilensk by evening.'

Lise had to be content with that, and later, with such repose as she could find in the *kibitka*, drawn up in the yard of the peasant hut

40

where Danilo had served her dinner on porcelain and silver plate. Lise was well used to these vagaries of travel in Russia, where a carriage full of cooks, hothouse fruit and delicacies, kitchen utensils, silver, napery and even a butler, always preceded the journeying of a noble household. An abrupt departure into exile had not permitted of the usual preparations, so that but one *kibitka* and that piled with baggage, followed the chaise. Nevertheless, the dinner Danilo set before Lise in the peasant's hut had still carried several dishes to each course, and she slept in the *kibitka* on crested linen and down pillows.

Their start at dawn found her tolerably refreshed but sadly conscious of having lacked her maid for three days to make an adequate toilette.

Sacha, wide awake, washed, shaved and breakfasted, ruffled her hair by way of greeting, remarked that she looked charmingly and went off whistling to find Galant, promising her better entertainment in Vilensk.

Thus encouraged, Lise forgot her disarray and settled down to enjoy the present. The chaise bowled along, its superb English springing making light of the potholes and slush of the road; and though the landscape continued bleak and featureless it was considerably improved by a clear sky and some pale sunlight.

Even the monotonous jingle of the horses' bells sounded more cheerful; Lise let down the window and leant out, taking deep breaths of freedom and the sharp, clean air. Sacha sketched her a gay salute; she waved back and then returned to the soft embrace of her sables. By wriggling a little on the seat, she found she could obtain a clear view of Sacha's profile whenever Galant ranged alongside the chaise, which left little more in the world to be desired.

A light snow fell in the afternoon, so that it was dark by the time they reached Vilensk. It make the well-lit hostelry to which they drew up look even more inviting. But Lise had only time to gain a confused impression of noise, bustle and warm, rich smells before she was whisked upstairs with Danilo and a chambermaid in attendance.

By contrast with the public rooms below, the bedchamber to which she was conducted was dimly lit, and its chill was only slightly dispelled by the newly-lit iron stove at its centre. Danilo at once sent the maid to procure candles and more logs. The girl returned followed by a small procession. The chamber's furnishings began to look more inviting in the glow of many candles. The stove too was

persuaded to emit a cheering crackle. Lise looked with longing at
the steaming jugs on the wash-stand and at the vast four-poster, now
being laid with their own snowy linen and a high featherbed in a
white worked-linen cover. She allowed Danilo to divest her of her
furs and went across to a chair by the stove until the servants should
have finished their business.

'His honour said to serve supper up here,' Danilo informed her.
'I'll have 'em bring it up directly. You get miss's box unpacked and
look sharp about it,' he bade the chambermaid. 'She'll want to
pretty up. Ivan!' he barked at the valet who was busying himself over
Sacha's valise. 'What are you doing with that shirt?'

'Just laying it out, Danilo.'

'After it's been folded in the valise all day, numbskull? Give it
here. You, girl, what's your name?'

The maid giggled.

'Afdotia, sir.'

'Down to the kitchens with you to put me on an iron. Got a gopher-
ing iron in the place? Wait though—' He dived bodily under the
bedclothes and emerged brandishing a warming pan. 'Cold!' he pronounced with grim triumph. 'You, laddie, don't stand there gawp-
ing at your betters, fetch me another, double quick! His honour's
slippers must be in the other bag, Ivan. Afdotia, give me miss's nightgear and be off with you.'

Afdotia gave her customary giggle.

'She ain't got none. Unless you'd call *that* a nightgown!' she
added, holding up a wisp of a chemise.

Lise, who had been observing the servants' bustle with growing
disquiet, jumped to her feet.

'Put it down. Danilo, there—there must be some mistake! Is this
not my bedchamber? Then why are you laying out his honour's
things in here?'

The company gaped at her and then exchanged speaking glances.
Danilo's flat face became a mask.

'I couldn't say, miss. His honour's orders.'

'Then you must have misunderstood him. Where is his honour?'

'Below, miss.'

'Well then, pray ask him—No, I will go down myself. There has
been some stupid mistake.'

'I wouldn't do that, miss—'

But Lise was already running down the passage. Halfway down
the stairs she was arrested by the din surging up from the public

rooms. The evening was well advanced, the hostelry popular, and a wedding party was adding its raucous merriment to the clamour of drunken voices, the clash of glasses and cutlery and the shouts for service. Lise shrank back; then, squaring her thin shoulders she marched on down into the mêlée. After some difficulty she discovered the porter and ascertained from him that the *barin* was playing cards in the private parlour.

'With our boss himself in attendance; so the word's been passed not to disturb 'em on any account. What's to do, *barinka*? Something you need?'

'Yes, yes, please. A—a room. You see, our servants have made some mistake, and there must be another bedchamber bespoken for me. If you would please discover which it is and—'

'As to that, I wouldn't be knowing. But I tell you what, missie, I'll ask the boss as soon as he's finished in there. Meanwhile, do you go on back upstairs; this ain't no place for a young lady like you.'

The wisdom of this advice was plain to Lise too. She re-entered her former chamber reluctantly; but at least it was now empty of all save Danilo setting out a copious supper on a round table by the stove. Danilo stood back and cast a professional eye over his preparations; he adjusted a fold of his master's silk nightshirt laid out on the bed, and favoured Lise with one of his stiff-necked bows.

'Supper is served, miss, whenever his honour is ready.'

'Pray inform him that I am waiting,' responded Mlle de Montargis with as much dignity as she could muster.

CHAPTER VIII

Lise was still waiting when the stables clock struck midnight outside.

All was now silent. Her little watch on the table beside her ticked on. The ill-made candles guttered and smoked. The stove emitted an evil odour and a thin, persistent haze of smoke. The quiet and fatigue combined to make Lise drowsy and she nodded off; but her discomfort and the increasing cold precluded real repose. She awoke presently to acute hunger. She rose and poked dispiritedly among the congealed supper dishes, her appetite evaporating at the sight of them. Then she glanced at her watch and saw that it marked a quarter of two. Surely, she thought, Sacha will not come now. . . .

But so far from adding the last touch to her dejection, this conjecture suddenly presented itself as the solution to all her trouble. For of course Sacha had never intended to come! And why indeed should he have done so, having seen her safely disposed and supper sent up to her? It was the stupid servants who had misunderstood him and assumed . . . and, yes indeed, she herself who had dared to harbour doubt and suspicion! Her cheeks flamed at the thought of her unworthy fears. She ran over to the bed, removed Sacha's nightgear and carefully folded it on a chair by his valise, mentally abjuring Danilo for the discomfort his master must now be suffering in some other part of the hostelry. Most of the candles had guttered out. She quickly snuffed the rest, gabbled her prayers and dived into bed, snuggling blissfully down into its softness. She was fast asleep within minutes, with one dark plait and the tip of a small nose alone visible above the featherbed.

She was awakened by the crash of a spurred boot that sent the door swinging back on its hinges to admit Sacha, perilously balancing two bottles of champagne, a silver bucket of ice and a tall, branched candlestick. He kicked the door shut behind him with another crash, and, at Lise's frightened gasp, waved the bottles by way of apology.

'Your pardon for my unmannerly entrance, poppet, but I felt it 'cumbent upon me to bring the wine up myself, after the job I had

44

to get it! Obliged to go down to the cellar myself, I swear, after the rogue downstairs tried to fob me off with non-vintage. Lord, what a fug there is in here! I don't wonder you haven't touched any supper. Have you the head-ache? My poor girl, what a miserable start to things! Ne'er mind, *chérie*, let me just get this window open and give you a glass of wine, and then we may be comfortable.'

'Sacha—'

'Shhh-h! Not a word. You are about to forfeit your unique distinction of not uttering one syllable of reproach for my lateness, neglect, lack of consideration et cetera. Don't do it, darling; just because every other woman would in your shoes. Tell you how it was—'

He had been busying himself as he talked, and now came over to seat himself casually by her on the bed, having aired the room and drawn up a small table to the bedside for the champagne, a candelabra and two glasses from the supper table.

'*Voilà*, I was going to come straight up, honour bright, as Nicky would say, after just a glass of vodka; but there was this game in progress down there and one of the men asked me if I'd care to take his bank while he drank a glass with some wedding party. So I sat down. Well, I had the devil's own luck, hand after hand; when he came back I couldn't well leave without letting the locals have their chance of revenge, now could I? So I took the bank after him; and damme if my luck didn't hold! I just could not lose, try as I would. Lord, you should have seen those bleary little provincial eyes fairly popping with suspicion that I was sharp! Well, at last, when I am nearly dead of boredom, I 'ssure you, one of 'em manages to win a few roubles and I am free to go, honour satisfied.'

He sent the champagne cork flying, poured two glasses and picked one up; but made no move to drink it or give the other to Lise.

'Honour satisfied,' he repeated softly. '*My* honour—'

He flung to his feet, ripping a long tear in the linen bedcover with his spur, and stood staring before him with over-bright, narrowed eyes.

'My honour. *Merde!*'

The stem of the glass in his clenched hand snapped and the glass shattered into splinters on the floor. Champagne and blood spattered the white coverlet. Lise gave a smothered shriek. Sacha laughed.

'A thousand pardons, m'dear. Messy thing to do. Conduct unbecoming to an officer and gentleman of the Tsar's Own Black Hussars. Disgrace to the regiment. Disgrace to Holy Russia. Disgrace to an honourable name—or would be if I weren't a bastard! And so on and so forth, for at least an hour. . . . All of which your undoubted charms are going to help me to forget for tonight at least, eh my girl?'

His face, fitfully lit by the wavering candles, changed and softened; yet strangely seemed the more frightening to Lise.

'Such very sweet charms,' he said with a note in his voice she had never heard before. 'Outcasts have their compensations it seems. Come here. Show me how to forget . . . everything.'

Cold fear gripped the foolish child of sixteen who had so lightly agreed to run off with Petersburg's most eligible rake. She huddled bolt upright in the farthest corner of the bed, her dark eyes, huge with fright, wildly searching the man's face above her for the Sacha of her childish devotion. He frowned.

'What is it, sweetheart?'

'Oh Sacha, please—' She licked her dry lips. 'Please—I—I realise now how very wrong I was, but—oh, please, I beg you, do not be angry! I—I know how it must look to you—' Then it all came out in a rush, in her eagerness to explain matters '. . . and—and then it was so late and I—I thought suddenly how *idiotish* I had been to pay any heed to the stupid servants . . . so I went to bed.' She choked on a sob and for lack of breath, but rushed on: 'But I do see how it must look to you . . . finding me here like this—and, oh, Sacha, please d-don't think me a cheat . . . r-running away with you . . . oh, please—I—I'd do anything for you—'

For a few minutes there was no sound in the chamber but Lise's convulsive sobbing. From where he stood above her, all Sacha could see was the back of her dark head, a dark plait and one childishly thin, bare shoulder sunk into the billows of the featherbed. It was as if he really saw her for the first time: saw her and knew who she was.

Lise. *Lise*—whom he was used to find trotting at his heels along with Nicky whenever he went to his father's house.

Neither Sacha Arloff's tastes nor vices included the raping of children. More than the clouds of the liquor he had imbibed since the fatal night at the Balagan cleared from his brain.

'Oh my God,' he whispered. 'Oh my God, what have I done?'

That tried and true remedy, a pillow to cry into brought Lise its well-known relief; and presently, worn out with manifold extremes of emotion, she fell into a deep sleep. Having assured himself of this, Sacha moved swiftly around the room, ruthlessly stowing all Danilo's unpacking pell-mell into his valise, while his thoughts raced.

It was too much to hope that with all Petersburg buzzing with the Prince's shooting, his assailant's latest escapade would not be regaling every dinner table in town. To send Lise straight back with Danilo in the morning, as had been his first impulse, was obviously to feed her whole to the gossips—and unthinkable. Briefly he considered breaking his parole and turning back with her; but a moment's reflection sufficed to shew the futility of such a gesture. It would hardly add to Lise's credit to come upon the town in the company of her supposed seducer. No, there was only one thing to be done, little as he relished it.

He glanced over at the small, dark head buried in the pillows and decided to postpone all discussion of the future until the morning. Sleep would do more for the child than any words of his. He twisted a handkerchief round his cut hand, snapped the locks of the valise shut and turned to go. Lise stirred, raising a tear-stained face, and sat up, blinking. He went over to her, carefully keeping his distance.

'Back to sleep with you, Lise. In the morning we'll talk about how I am going to get you out of this mess. But now you'll be my good, brave Lise and go to sleep and not worry about anything. I'll see you downstairs at breakfast. Goodnight, my chicken. Sleep.'

The door closed, softly this time, behind him, and Lise listened to the ring of his spurs recede down the corridor. In the silence that now settled over the room she heard the faint hiss of the dying bubbles in the champagne; and unaccountably she began to cry again.

CHAPTER IX

The chaise rolled between interminable pine and birchwoods, whose branches retained a thick powdering of yesterday's snow; although the road itself was tolerably clear and the sky blue again.

To her surprise, Lise had slept soundly and had found herself able to do fair justice to the ample breakfast Sacha had ordered her to consume. Now, snugly settled in the chaise beside him, the tone of her mind was so far restored that she was able to offer a spirited protest to his plans for her future.

Sacha was also somewhat restored to his usual self.

'Now we'll have no more argument from you, my child,' he told her crisply. 'I've made up my mind what's best to do, and you will allow that I know our world a trifle better than you. But you yourself have been enough into Society this winter to know that I am right. We could stay in different towns from now on, and it'd make no difference. As far as Petersburg is concerned, you have eloped with me, or I've abducted you—and I dare swear the gossips would prefer the latter—and there's only one way to mend it, as I've told you. And that is to brazen it out and get married; like it or not.'

A muffled voice from the depths of the sables was understood to say that Mlle de Montargis did not care a fig for St Petersburg's opinion of her, hated every member of the polite world from the Tsar down, and was solely concerned with taking her departure to England there and then.

'Which way does mademoiselle propose to go—through the forests?' enquired Sacha politely. Then he smiled, a kind smile that lit his handsome, moody face. 'There, it's too bad to quiz you! But my dearest child, even if you could take wing and fly to your mother on the instant, I doubt if your arrival in London would greatly anticipate the news of your scandalous conduct. Madame my stepmother will have seen to it that the diplomatic bag even now carries a full justification of *her* conduct towards you, and *your* base ingratitude in thus flouting her careful guardianship. No, Lise, however little you may relish it, there's nothing for us but marriage as quickly as I can arrange it.'

48

There was a small sound from the opposite corner. Sacha's mouth hardened.

'Dammit, girl, it's not my wish either! Believe me, I am fully conscious of my current ineligibility. Disgraced; exiled; no future; I make a fine *parti* for any girl! And I tell you to your head, Lise, that in my situation one does not saddle oneself with a wife. But that's nothing to the purpose. What matters is to get the news of our nuptials back to Petersburg as quickly as we may, to confound the gossips. Then, as Madame Arloff, you may travel safely to England or anywhere. Lise, are you listening to me?'

'Yes, Sacha.'

He frowned and then leant over and lightly brushed his fingertip across the corner of her cheek visible among the furs.

'My poor chicken, how bleak it must sound! But no tears. With me you take gambler's luck, my dear; and gamblers don't cry when they're dipped. Never fear, we'll come about—both of us—and you'll laugh looking back at this when you're dancing at Almack's, with all the London bucks at your feet. Meanwhile—' He hesitated and then said harshly: 'One thing I can promise you. There'll be no repetition of last night, now or ever. Apart from bearing my name, you'll be free.'

It appeared, however, to be one thing to resolve upon a runaway marriage; quite another to put it into effect.

At each succeeding town, the civil and religious authorities looked equally askance at the fugitive couple and demanded a host of tedious documents whose very existence Sacha had overlooked in making his lofty gesture. Totally unused to being crossed by pettifogging officials, Sacha's temper grew vile. Nor was it improved by his new régime of drinking far into the night with whatever company was to be found at their halts, and then, as often as not, stretching out in the chaise whilst Lise cried herself to sleep upstairs at the inns or in the *kibitka*.

Her tears were for Sacha, whom, in her own estimation, she had so miserably failed and was now putting to such trouble and vexation. For herself, though the night in Vilensk had demolished her dreams of escape, she found that it had been powerless to destroy her happiness in her new life.

She loved it all; the silent woods, the misted fields, rolling away into the vast stillness of the sky; the straggling villages with their huddled, wooden houses and painted churches. She loved the coachman's sad songs and the horses' bells that were the haunting voice of this inscrutable land where Sacha was at home. She had traversed its monotonous landscape many times before; but now there were no lapdogs to mind, no *ma tante* with her arbitrary whims, no constant reminders of her own dependence. Instead, every morning brought the genial bustle of the posting yard, the glossy horses, the trampling men, loading up, shouting orders, inspecting hooves and harness, quizzing the yard wenches. It brought Sacha, devastatingly handsome with his cossack hat pulled down over one eye, lifting her over the slush into the chaise, before swinging up into the saddle as the ostlers stood away from the horses' heads; and then the crack of the long whips and the postillions' yell, as they whirled off to another day of peace and freedom under the vast sky.

Usually Sacha spent most of the day in the saddle, but whenever he felt that Galant needed resting, he would come with Lise in the coach. These times were the peak of her felicity. Sacha's ill-humour was quickly forgotten as he made her recount the saga of the Niebling proposal or told her stories of his childhood at Volnoya, which was so soon to be the confine of his exile. He also initiated her into the mysteries of picquet on the folding card-board they found in the chaise. One afternoon, after a hand where she had acquitted herself with fair credit, he looked up and said:

'Poppet, I think I could make a card player of you yet. You're even beginning to learn not to let every card in your hand show on your face. A pity I'll not have time to complete your education.'

Lise's face, which had indeed been expressive of nothing but adoration, blanched slightly.

'But why will you not have time?'

'Because tomorrow morning I hope we shall reach Smolensk, where I am to report to the Governor. He is an old acquaintance of my father's, and I can count on him to cut through all these plaguey formalities and get us married. Then I'll hire you a good maid, give you Danilo and put you in a coach for Petersburg. My father will make all arrangements for your passage to London and direct my man of business about the settlements. I am tolerably rich, you know, from my mother's inheritance; so you will not need to regret your mésalliance on that score.'

He stirred restlessly.

'Don't look like that, Lise. I'm as conscious as you could wish of how ill I serve you in sending you off with only servants to escort you. But *you* know the conditions of my exile. And at least you'll be well rid of me.'

She watched his strong, fine hands clench on the cards, and bit back her tears. Of what use was it to explain the cause of her stricken look, when their parting was not even an object of regret with him? Nevertheless she faltered:

'Sacha, perhaps—that is, could I not remain with you for a little? I—I could see to the household at Volnoya and you would teach me to play picquet better, and we would be so comfortable!'

He shouted with laughter, put a finger under her chin and turned her face up to him.

'How old are you, poppet?'

'*Fully* sixteen, and *madame ma tante* says—'

'That you are ready to receive the addresses of an Adolf Niebling. I take leave to differ. But it would not answer for all that. I'd be enchanted to have your company, dear Lise, but I am only human. So you'll have to go.'

Snow began to fall again in the night, so that they saw the dark red walls and the gilded onion domes and steeples of Smolensk through the softly falling flakes, silhouetted on a white landscape.

Despite his hopes of engaging the Governor's support, the prospect of having to report to the authorities did nothing to improve the black mood that had descended upon Sacha as his exile drew nearer.

He left Lise at the house of a former steward of the Count's from one of his southern estates, and rode off to the Governor's residence.

Lise had never seen the like of the household she now entered. Their host held to the good old ways, and everything about her bed-chamber in the women's half, from its painted chests to the triple, gilded ikon glowing darkly above its candles in a corner, engaged her interest. She was an equal novelty to her hostess and her three daughters.

'Mama, imagine! The *barinya* is sixteen like me, for all that she's such a slip of a thing.'

'And she has the Tsar's portrait on a ribbon—'

'And wears no stays and but one petticoat—'

'And stands in sore need of a clean one!' laughed Lise, examining its mud-splashed lace with dismay. 'Oh, and if it were possible to take a bath—!'

For some reason this seemed to cause her hostesses exquisite amusement. The girls whooped, covering their faces with their brightly embroidered aprons. Their mother laughed too; but then set her hands on her ample hips and demanded:

'And why shouldn't she—like any other good Christian before the Lord's Day?' She turned to Lise. 'We're not like some folk in this town, *barinya*, forever aping their betters with baths in their bed-chambers. The village *bania* was good enough for us once, and it's good enough for us now we've come up in the world and can afford to have one for our own household. There it is, out there in the yard, miss, clean and decent as you could wish, and the fires already kindled for all of us tonight.'

She drew Lise over to the window, pointing out a small wooden structure, whose chimney was belching a tall column of white smoke.

Lise had seen many such in the Count's villages, and the ritual of the peasants' Saturday night communal bath was known to her with the academic remoteness of other primitive customs. A vision of the Countess's face on learning that her ward was about to try it out for herself made her giggle delightedly—and decided her at once to do it.

'Thank you, Elena Pavlovna, I would love to try your *bania*,'' she said firmly. 'And perhaps while I am in it—'

'But of course!' cried her hostess. 'Luba! Nadia! We'll have every stitch of miss's clothes off to be washed and brushed while she's in the *bania*. Sonichka, fly down and tell 'em to set out my best towels. Luba, your new red boots for miss to wear back to the house! Run, girls! Now, miss dear, you just relax and let Elena Pavlovna take care of you.'

The *bania*'s outer room was small and scrupulously scrubbed from its wooden floor to ceiling. A strapping old peasant woman in a white kerchief was pouring water into one of its several wooden tubs. These and a couple of scrubbed benches completed the furnishings. Lise sniffed appreciatively at the aromatic tang of birch wood in the warm air; but she barely had time to take in her surroundings before energetic hands had all her clothes off her and bundled out to the kitchen, and old Pelagia was soaping her from top to toe, hair and all, with the kindly ruthlessness of a nurse bathing a baby.

Lise emerged, spluttering but happy, feeling all the inadequate washing of the past ten days more than made up for; but she was to learn that this was only the first step to cleanliness in a real Russian *bania*. Pelagia swished one last tubful over her and stood back.

'There, missie, we'll do now. In you go,' she ordered, opening a door in the far corner.

The secret of the *bania*'s warm air was at once revealed in the cloud of aromatic steam that billowed out of the inner 'hot room'. Her mentor was already enveloped in it and a firm hand drew Lise in and shut the door behind them. A white mist of heat engulfed her, but presently she distinguished another white-clad form in the steam. She also made out a huge, flat-topped brick stove, built out from one wall. Pelagia's twin shovelled a generous armful of logs into the stove's open, red-glowing heart. As the flames roared high, she seized two buckets of water and sent them hissing over its flat top. Vast billows of hot steam blotted out everything. Lise shrieked, and then joined in the old women's laughter.

'But I shall be boiled alive like a lobster! Pelagia, where are you? I cannot see a thing!'

'No, you won't. Over here, dearie, and now stretch out for us.'

A scrubbed bench received her; and if Pelagia's soaping had been thorough, the scouring that followed made it seem perfunctory. After a few moments Lise surrendered to it, stretching like a little cat under the skilled, kneading hands, feeling herself deliciously adrift on the birch-scented steam. Then, just as she seemed about to melt, the kneading changed to a tattoo of brisk slaps and with a cry of 'Up you come. Shut your eyes tight!' two tubs of ice-cold water descended over her.

When she had got back her breath, Lise shook herself all over like a puppy, crying:

'Oh, wonderful! First I'm a melting blancmanger and now I am simply a tingle all over. Oh, and I've never felt so clean! Oh, thank you!'

'Out with you then to be dried and dressed,' ordered Pelagia, red as a lobster herself. 'We don't want you taking a rheum now, with standing around without a stitch.'

Back in the warm ante-room, Lise was towelled into such a glow as to preclude any possibility of taking cold even if she had ventured out as she was into the snow, as the peasants did.

'Which I'll have to do, it seems,' she giggled. 'For all my clothes are gone and there is nothing here to put on but Luba's red boots.'

A hurried conference with the lad whom Elena Pavlovna had stationed outside, yielded the intelligence that all miss's garments were still being frantically waved before the kitchen fire to get the damp out.

The *bania* party settled down to wait. The old women produced glasses of tea. Lise worked off her overflow of glowing energy by donning the red boots and performing a spirited Cossack dance across the springy floor. In high glee, Pelagia and her acolyte began to clap and stamp their feet in rhythm, with shrill 'Ai-ai-ai-*ya-yas*!' of encouragement; and the fun was at its height when there arose a violent commotion at the outer door and a furious voice demanded to know where was the young *barina* and what the devil was going on in there?

The dance stopped abruptly. Lise ran to the door of the porch but recalled just in time that she was in no state to open it.

'Sacha! Oh, I am so glad you are returned early! Only I cannot join you yet. I am having a *bania*.'

'You are having a— Are you out of your mind? Come out of there at once!'

'But . . . But, Sacha, indeed I cannot! I am not dressed and—'

'And I suppose this lout out here is going to dress you! In a peasant *sarafan*! I warn you, my girl, it'll be worse for you if I have to come in and fetch you. Open up before I break this door down.'

The old women set up a terrified wail; but Pelagia, with admirable presence of mind, snatched up a towel—unfortunately the smallest— and threw it round Lise just as Sacha's patience gave out.

He flung in like the north wind, scattering snow from his cloak. A glance calmed his main fear of finding Lise sharing the *bania* with a gaggle of crude peasant girls. But the outrage of her venturing into one at all paled before his feelings at being confronted by his charge in the *déshabillé* of red boots and little else, affected by Petersburg's most expensive cyprians for the delectation of favoured clients.

After an instant's scorching appraisal he jerked off his cloak and bundled it round her. Then, in grim silence, watched by several pairs of frightened eyes at the windows, he strode back with her to the house and dumped her across the threshold of her room with a curt injunction to get some clothes on and be ready to receive him within the half hour.

Lise's clothes were still imperfectly dried. Elena Pavlovna and the daughters got in the way and wept, while Lise did her nervous best to dress and coil up her wet hair, with one eye on the door.

Exactly on the half hour, it opened after a decorous knock. Sacha had cooled down somewhat. His temper was not a sullen one; a period for reflection had enabled him to recognise the injustice of visiting his fury over his reception at the Governor's upon the innocent folly of his young charge. And the doleful sight of her all but melted his resolve to take her to task.

'You'll catch your death of cold walking around with wet hair,' he grumbled. 'Come over here to the stove and let's take the pins out. Good heavens, child, your dress is damp too—look at it steaming! Has Elena Pavlovna taken leave of her senses? Take it off at once and put on your dressing gown or something.'

'I—I am sorry, Sacha, but I do not have a dressing robe. You see, with not wanting to crush the wig in the Escape Pack, there wasn't room—'

Sacha clutched at his head.

'The Escape Pack! Good God, for which of my sins did I have to abduct a brat out of the nursery!'

He subsided into a chair by Lise's stool and laughed himself entirely out of his annoyance. Lise peered at him nervously past her curtain of hair and then laughed too with the relief of seeing his ill-humour dispelled. He said lazily:

'Sunlight on diamonds. You'll learn to value your enchanting laugh, poppet, when a few more gentlemen have told you that. Now I'll leave you to get yourself into something dry before we dine—and I *quite* understand that a lady travelling with an Escape Pack may well find herself reduced to a peasant *sarafan* for a change of clothing.'

'Now you are quizzing me! And it is a great deal too bad because you must know that it is perfectly *comme il faut* to dress up as a peasant if one so pleases. My mother frequently recalls in her letters how she and our martyred Queen's other *demoiselles d'honneur* used to don little caps and aprons *à la bergère*, and even milk cows at the Petit Trianon.'

Sacha suppressed his retort as to the price all Europe was still paying for Marie Antoinette's frolics, in the ravages of the power-drunk Corsican who now lolled in the Tuileries. To madame la Marquise de Montargis and her kind, the clocks there had stopped in 1789, and no doubt she had imbued Lise with her own notions. He rose, tweaking one of the drying black locks.

'Very well then, you shall dine with me *à la bergère*. But I beg you will not outrage Danilo's susceptibilities by your toilette when we leave tomorrow. He is such a stickler for decorum.'

'When we leave tomorrow?' cried Lise. 'Oh Sacha, does that mean that I am to go on with you to Volnoya?'

'You are fortunate in finding the prospect pleasing,' he said drily, turning away.

Lise jumped up and timidly touched his arm.

'Please, Sacha, I'm sorry. Please tell me what went wrong?'

'Nothing. Everything. The Governor is away taking the waters at Carlsbad. His Deputy is a jumped-up jack-in-office whom I wouldn't admit to my Sergeants' mess. I told him so. He then had the impudence to require me to report again tomorrow so that he may "formulate the dossier". I told him what he may do with his dossier.' Sacha's smouldering gaze lit with a reminiscent grin. 'His Excellency ordered me to stay. So we shall leave in the morning.'

Lise nodded sagely.

'It is the only way to deal with such *canaille*. How long will it be before the Governor returns?'

Sacha shrugged.

'I didn't ask. You will understand that we were not long bandying civilities. And the Governor's presence is no longer an object with me. If once I am resigned to having to drag you to Volnoya, I have my own priest there in the village who'll despatch our business without more ado. It only means another three days' journey for you before you can join the Petersburg road here.'

'Yes, Sacha.'

Around them the daylight was waning fast. Lise stared out at the steadily falling snow through the small portion of the window panes left clear of frost. It looked as bleak as her future.

'But I shall see Volnoya,' she said stoutly. 'And how I shall enjoy being on the road again! Sacha, if you would permit Luba to give me her boots, could I perhaps ride one of the postillions' horses for a while?'

'Certainly not. But I might take you up on Galant, if you are a good girl and get into no more scrapes whatsoever.'

'Oh, I won't,' promised Lise fervently. 'Oh, Sacha, how good you are to me! Now I am perfectly happy.'

He made no reply. The small, snowbound room was now lit only by the rosy glow of the stove and the candles under the ikon. In its soft shadows the gaudy chests shimmered like dark jewels. It was so silent that they could hear their own breathing and the stir of the candleflames. Sacha was neither so dissolute nor so blasé as to be proof against the moment's magic; nor against the appeal of a pair of melting dark eyes gazing up at him in frank adoration. He turned on his heel, saying brusquely:

'Have them serve your dinner as soon as you are changed. I'm going out. I'll see you in the morning.'

CHAPTER X

Lise did not attain the supreme felicity of a ride on Galant. The late snowfall, lying soft but deep made their next days' progress difficult, and the men were too preoccupied with clogged wheels and foundering horses to think about joy-rides. However, every other happiness—on her undemanding scale—was hers, with the additional charm of the enchanted white forest that now received them into its silent depths.

The third night found them pulling up at a lonely posting yard that seemed to be the only habitation in the whole vast, snowbound landscape.

To their surprise they found two other travellers installed in the public room, although they had observed no carriage in the yard.

Sacha wished the pair a civil 'Good evening' and despatched Danilo to rout out the service. The two occupants watched his every move. One of them, hunched by the stove, was a plump, rabbity man in a pince-nez, wearing a greenish-black frock coat and a shawl round his shoulders. The other was a lady of middle years and formidable aspect, clad in what appeared to be some form of riding habit and a high-crowned beaver over a white cap. She sat bolt upright in a hard chair. The pair did not seem to be acquainted but shared two singular characteristics: both were obviously foreigners and both seemed to be in the grip of some strong and mutually unpalatable emotion.

The station-master appeared. Sacha ordered punch and supper and obligingly offered to fill in the station-master's road book, bidding him go speed the meal. As soon as the door shut on his bowing back, both strangers turned to Sacha and started to speak. The lady's strong bass prevailed.

'Sir,' she boomed in robustly Anglo-Saxon French. 'You appear to be a person of some influence. Perhaps you would care to exert it to see justice is done; since it is beyond my power to make the station-keeper understand his responsibilities.'

Sacha rose politely.

'You are in difficulties over horses, madame?' he enquired.

'Horses,' announced the lady in accents of doom, 'are the least of it. I am speaking of robbery, sir; barefaced, daylight robbery of the trunk containing my life-work for the Royal Geographical Society. And of cow-hearted chicanery that makes me despair of the German race!'

The shrinking representative of it by the stove gave a goaded mumble and drew his shawl bodily over his head. Lise suppressed a giggle. Sacha, his eyes snapping with amusement, said gravely:

'At all costs the Royal Geographical Society must not be deprived of your life-work, madame. I collect you are English?' he asked, switching to that language. 'Permit me to make myself known to you. Sacha Arloff, entirely at your service. Now if I may know—?'

'My card,' boomed the lady, diving into a capacious reticule. 'Oh drat it, no. I recollect that I gave the last to a very obliging yak-driver in Uszbekistan. He required it for putting the evil eye on an enemy. Highly interesting, the procedure involved; remind me to tell you about it. I have my notes of the whole ritual. *Had*,' she corrected herself bitterly. 'All in the trunk! All God knows where by now! However, to business. Name's Honoria Smith. *Miss* Smith, and I am returning to London from a year's visit to your benighted country, studying the flora and fauna of your Asian territories and Outer Mongolia.' Miss Smith said it with the nonchalance of one completing a tour of the Lake District in her homeland.

'I should say I *was* on my way home, but that was before I had the misfortune to encounter Herr Whatsisname—'

'Schmitt,' snapped the rabbit and popped back into his shawl.

'Herr Whatsisname, at the post house by the Nikolaevsky gate in Smolensk. It was late and they had but the one troika left. Rather than wait, I decided to take it and share it with this individual, as he had bespoken it first. I will not speak of the trials of our route— what with your Russian roads and a companion who was persuaded that a bandit lurked behind every tree. In the event he was proved right of course,' she added gloomily. 'At least twelve of 'em, mounted, armed and yelling like dervishes. Their leader masked and flourishing a pair of pistols in what I did not scruple to tell him was a highly dangerous fashion, straight under my nose. He had the grace to apologise and draw off. By this time I had recollected my gift of a pistol from the Khan of Kurdistan and located it inside my cloak-bag. Fortunately it proved to be loaded, but it was too late to afford me anything but a parting shot at our assailants as they galloped off.'

c

'You are no doubt accustomed to handling weapons, madame?' murmured Sacha, who by now would have learnt with little astonishment that Miss Smith was a crack shot.

'I grew tolerably proficient with a Gurkha knife during my sojourn in India. But pistols are regarded as unsuited to females in our effete age, so I have had little practice,' admitted Miss Smith. 'I shall hold myself lucky if I so much as winged the ruffian. To continue. As you might expect, my shot, instead of heartening my companion, merely set him howling to high heaven. The robbers had left him sitting in the middle of the road. Our coachman was lying trussed and senseless in the ditch. By the time I had quieted the one and roused the other, it was too late. My trunk was gone and the rascals miles away. Fortunately they had assaulted us reasonably near here—where you might think all efforts would be made to appraise the authorities of the outrage. Hah!' Miss Smith gave an embittered snort which caused the post-keeper, entering with the punch, to jump nervously.

Sacha bespoke another round at once and took a glass to Miss Smith with his most engaging smile.

'A restorative, ma'am, before you continue your shocking tale. And you must blame its interest for my neglect to present Mademoiselle de Montargis to you. An ardent botanist like yourself,' he added, as a first step to the wild plan beginning to stir vaguely at the back of his mind. Miss Smith glanced at him suspiciously but encountered Sacha's gaming table face.

'How de do,' she barked, sipping the punch. 'Little more to tell, that's the rub. The bumbling idiot in charge here either cannot or, more likely, *will* not understand me; and my fellow victim, so far from making any push to recover his property, turns out to be in league with the robbers!'

Having delivered this broadside, Miss Smith devoted herself to her punch.

Lise and Sacha turned to examine the object of her strictures with new interest. 'But I do not understand,' frowned Lise. 'Were you not robbed too? Surely you must be anxious to have the robbers caught?'

Herr Schmitt took to his shawl again and from its depths vouchsafed that he was a peace-loving man. Miss Smith gave vent to another sinister snort and accepted her third glass of punch.

'I am a musician,' Herr Schmitt suddenly burst out. 'I hold the medal of the Leipzig Conservatoire, second class. I haf played before Governor Count Rostopchin in Moscow. Now I am—was—on my way to take up a post in a great house of these parts, where I was to conduct the household orchestra and instruct the *barin*'s daughter in the pianoforte and geography. That is not nothing, I suppose?'

'Indeed not!' Lise assured him. 'Are you then perhaps afraid that you may endanger your post by any delay? But I am sure that— Why Sacha, what ails you?'

'Incipient hysteria. I *must* know—why geography?'

Miss Smith quelled him with a look.

'You will observe that this paragon of respectability says "*was* on my way", "*was* to conduct",' she snapped. 'His respectability and his virtue are not proof against the ten thousand roubles the robbers slipped into his pocket to cover their traces while they get away with my trunk!'

'It is not true!' shrieked Herr Schmitt, jumping up. 'There was no compact between us. I haf not any idea why the rogues bestowed this money on me. I do not even recall her wretched trunk!' He turned to Sacha. 'Picture it, *mein Herr*, I am left lying in the road, more dead than alive. I stagger to my feet. I feel myself. *Gott sei dank*, no bones are broken. I feel for my wallet. It is gone! All my papers, my letters of recommendation, my diploma, gone! But I feel something else. I bring it out. I cannot believe my senses. It is a *rouleau* of thousand-rouble assignats. Ten of them, all new. It is a miracle, a dispensation from Providence!'

'In new notes too,' murmured Sacha. 'Providence, or the robbers, must set a high value on your credentials.'

'My credentials are impeccable, sir! But not even a Russian could be mad enough to think them worth ten thousand roubles. But I appeal to your honour, in my shoes, would you stay to question this miracle? Or thank the *lieber Gott*, keep quiet and get back to Leipzig by the first coach, as I mean to do?'

'Poltroon!' hissed Miss Smith.

Herr Schmitt made a dash for the door.

'Renegade! Mountebank!'

The door closed with a devil-may-care snap of its bolt.

'Supper,' said Sacha firmly.

CHAPTER XI

Food, wine and an attentive audience had the mellowing effect upon Miss Smith which Sacha had carefully calculated.

He had been observing her closely ever since she had pronounced the magic word 'London', and he had come to certain conclusions about her which made his wild plan almost feasible.

After the meal, he quickly despatched Lise to bed, settled Miss Smith in the only comfortable chair and commanded coffee and brandy. Then he stretched his long legs to the stove and resigned himself to listen to yet another recital of her woes.

Miss Smith regarded him over the rim of her glass with a disconcerting twinkle.

'Now then, young man, you have not fed and wined me and bought me this excellent cognac to discuss my trunk. Nor, I'll wager, is it your normal habit to countermand your horses in order to engineer a midnight tête-à-tête with an *old* woman. Out with it. What do you want?'

Sacha grinned and sketched a rueful gesture of surrender.

'Rompé'd by God! Horse, foot and guns! Miss Smith, you see me at your mercy. I'm after . . . well, if not precisely your money, then certainly your life. No, I assure you I am cold sober; so you must ascribe my impertinence to the devil's own mess into which I've landed myself—and Mlle de Montargis.'

'Ah,' breathed Miss Smith. 'I thought as much. Well, you'd best explain yourself. . . . You ran off with her, I collect?'

'Worse than that,' said Sacha sombrely. 'But give me leave to tell you the whole story.'

Miss Smith listened to it, sipping her brandy and occasionally twitching her long nose in a manner that reminded Sacha forcibly of a mare he had raced the previous summer. The resemblance ended at Miss Smith's fine, shrewd grey eyes. They appraised him frankly throughout his recital; and their owner found no difficulty in picturing the wild, drunken mood in which he had chosen between Lise and the gipsy; nor why either of them should have come at his nod.

But she also found herself dimly perceiving some reasons for the loving trust which the child obviously reposed in her ravisher despite her shocking experience.

Sacha ended his tale and sat back with a faint shrug.

'So you see why I said "your life", ma'am. I can plead not the smallest reason why you should take Lise under your wing to England. Her plight and her future are my concern. But when I heard you name London as your destination it seemed, to quote our departed friend, "a dispensation of providence". To know her in safe hands for the journey! To have her spared the ordeal of Petersburg! To rely upon you to smooth her meeting with her mother!' He turned to Miss Smith. 'I could not but ask you—after I had put you in possession of all the discreditable facts. Now you may rebuke my impudence as it deserves.'

'First things first,' growled Miss Smith. 'Carrying the girl with me to England is nothing. The point is, how do I get you both out of this pickle? For it'd be an odd mother who would thank me for delivering her daughter to her with a wedding ring but no husband.'

'What else can I do for her?' he said sullenly.

Miss Smith never rushed her fences, so she merely grunted:

'Not the marrying kind, are ye? That the rub?'

He shrugged. 'In my present pass, ma'am—no! Once . . . But I don't deal in might-have-beens. Where Lise is concerned it is the only way to right things, as you'll allow.'

'I'll allow you nothing but the most damnable arrogance!' retorted Miss Smith roundly. 'So you'd bestow the inestimable privilege of your name and your money on a girl you've so cruelly wronged, and consider yourself honourably quit of her! Upon my word, I don't give much for your notion of honour!'

Sacha flinched and for an instant looked murderous.

'We'll accept my honour as forfeited, ma'am, along with my sword,' he said between his teeth. 'But you'll permit me to correct *your* notion of Lise. When she came to my rooms it was with the charming design, agreed between her and her fellow-conspirator of eleven, to smuggle me out by sea disguised in his tutor's wig. Until the night in Vilensk she had about as much understanding of what she had gone into as—as Nicky. And not much more after it.'

He gave a bitter bark of laughter, flung out of his chair and began to pace restlessly up and down, reminding Miss Smith in her turn, of an elegant and highly dangerous young panther she had viewed at a rather safer distance during her visit to the Court of Seringopotam.

Sacha sent an inoffending tabouret in his path crashing against the wall.

'I'd give a year of freedom to undo that night in Vilensk!' he flung over his shoulder. 'Do you think I *want* to tie her to a ruined man? Or shackle myself to a child in this mockery of a marriage? But there's nothing else will answer. And by your leave, madam, I do not rape children—with or without a wedding ring on!'

'Nor do *I* discuss such matters with children,' snapped Miss Smith. 'Sit down, you foolish boy, and stop treating me to a display of your slavonic temperament. There, that is better, is it not? Now we will discuss our problem rationally. You may give me another glass of brandy. A quite remarkable bouquet, is it not, for a remote provincial post-house?'

Warily, she gauged the measure of relaxation in the stormy face opposite—and regretfully discarded any present possibility of suggesting that happiness for Lise and himself could lie together. But there are more ways of killing a cat—or even a panther—she thought, and said briskly:

'Very well; so you marry her now and scotch most of the scandal. And what happens when she is eighteen or twenty and falls in love with a man who can make her happiness?'

His tone was as cool as his reply.

'I imagine matters could be arranged. Both my Church and hers recognise the possibility of annulment where a marriage has not been consummated. *You* will be able to vouch for that, since we shall part at the church door.'

'And in your own case?'

'Lise need have no fear that such an application will ever come from my side. Something I decided in Vilensk.'

He raised his glass with a mocking smile.

'A toast, ma'am, to the elastic bonds of matrimony!'

Miss Smith set down her glass.

'Young man, your tone is as improper as your sentiments. Now you will listen to me if you please, and to some English horse-sense. As you rightly said, encountering me was a dispensation of providence. And now that *I* am in charge, we'll have things shipshape and Bristol-fashion, and no hare-brained marriages! Tomorrow you will write to apprise your father and step-mother of the following *facts*.'

She gave her favourite snort and sat forward, ticking off the points of her discourse on an admonitory finger.

'One: that you encountered me at your first overnight stop in

Vilensk. I give you leave to have me an English Duke's aunt if that will help. Two: that my carriage had suffered a mishap and I accepted a seat in your chaise, having taken a strong fancy to Mademoiselle Lise. Three: that she has been under my close chaperonage ever since and I have undertaken the charge of her to London.' Miss Smith leant back.

For several moments Sacha could only gaze at her in awed admiration. Then he burst into a shout of laughter, sprang up, kissed her on both leathery cheeks and raised his glass again.

'Now I *will* have a toast. To your bandits, God bless 'em!'

Miss Smith, a trifle pink, quite failed to rebuke his unseemly behaviour. They clinked glasses. Sacha promptly refilled them and lounged back in his chair. His companion discovered that the devastating, moody eyes could sparkle with schoolboy mischief.

'You have forgot one other very material *fact*, ma'am,' he informed her. 'Obviously you are disposed to do all this because you are acquainted with Lise's mother in London. I believe that Mme de Montargis' straitened means do not permit her to go much into Society, so it is unlikely that a Duke's aunt would have her acquaintance. Could you perhaps bring yourself to be the aunt of a mere baronet?'

'By no means. My acquaintance with the Marquise was formed through my warm adherence to the Bourbon cause, which brings me frequently to honour émigré circles with my august presence. I collect that Mme de Montargis is of the *ancien régime*?'

'To her fingertips. So be it then, and—Oh bless you, ma'am, from my heart!'

'Fiddle,' growled Miss Smith. 'Do ye think I do this for nothing? It is now up to you to recover my trunk, young man—intact—before I move one step to England.'

CHAPTER XII

The nearest approach to official authority at hand was the post-master; so, as soon as they had breakfasted, Sacha had the man summoned and ordered him to set down a complete report of the outrage, in official form, to be carried at once to the justices in Smolensk.

The post-master had barely covered a page, however, when he laid down his pen and coughed discreetly.

'Begging your honour's pardon, but we've no call to be sending to Smolensk with this. It's what you might term a local job, for un-doubtedly these foreign folk were set upon by our young Charsky. Observe, sir; neither was harmed, and the musical party even had his money returned to him, he was telling me. Well, that's young Charsky for you, all over. He never robs but from the rich and the Government.'

When Miss Smith, whose Russian was rudimentary, had been acquainted with the magnanimity of her despoiler, she gave a mam-moth snort; but Lise was agog to hear more of the local Robin Hood and begged the post-master for details of his exploits. Sacha, who had been frowning abstractedly, suddenly snapped his fingers and exclaimed:

'I knew the name was familiar! Is there not a large land-owner of these parts named Charsky? Never tell me he has turned bandit?'

'Well, fancy you being on terms with him, sir, so to speak! It is indeed young Charsky's father who is one of our big *barins* round here; and a shocking tale it is how his only son came to take to highway robbery. They say—'

'When do we get to my trunk?'

'Directly, ma'am, I promise you,' smiled Sacha. 'For with Vladi-mir Charsky as its ravisher, we certainly have no need of the gendarmes. The young rascal was once my most faithful follower up every high tree in Volnoya woods. Let me once get my hands on him and your trunk is as good as found. He is—or was—a most amiable lad. How he came to take to banditry—'

66

'But that is what the post-master was about to tell us,' complained Lise. 'Please, Sacha, may we not hear the story?'

Thus encouraged, the post-master again launched into his tale.

'A *most* shocking business,' he intoned with relish. 'I had it all from the Charsky steward. It seems that for years it had been understood between old M. Charsky and his neighbour, General Mirnoff, that Vladimir would wed the Mirnoff daughter when he was returned from his education abroad.'

'Mirnoff?' said Sacha. 'Yes, I believe I remember him too. A pompous old fool with a passion for all things Prussian. I do not recall any daughter, so she cannot have been pretty.'

'But she may be much improved,' urged Lise, whose romantic soul could not suffer a heroine to be less than handsome.

'As proper a young lady as I ever saw,' affirmed the post-master. 'And not at all high in the instep, for all that she's the biggest heiress in the province. So you may imagine what a set-to there was when the young sprig flatly refused to marry her! Within a month of setting eyes on her after he came home! And that was not the worst.'

'Oh pray go on,' begged Lise as he paused for dramatic effect.

'Well, miss, if I hadn't had it from the Charsky steward's own lips—'

'Get to the point, man. We haven't all day.'

'At once, your honour. I was only attempting— But to make no bones about it, there young Charsky stood, bold as brass, telling his father that he could not wed the lady because he had fallen in love with a peasant girl on the Mirnoff estate and proposed to marry *her*!'

The post-master sat back to enjoy the just reward of serving up such a sensation. His audience gratified his expectations. Sacha pursed his lips in a long whistle. Lise gazed at him open-mouthed; and even Miss Smith had been in Russia long enough to value the full outrage of a landowner's son proposing to ally himself with one of his neighbour's serfs in preference to the daughter of the house.

'So then the fat was in the fire. The steward said his master near took an apoplexy and had to be bled. At the end of two days young Charsky was out on his ear, as the saying goes, cut off without a penny and bidden never to darken his father's eyes again!'

'So then he took to the highways?'

'Not directly, no. His design was to carry off the peasant girl with him; and there came the rub, for she could not be found. Young Charsky had gone to Livno, a shooting box he owns, the steward said, and his peasants there were ordered to snoop around the Mirnoff

c*

villages for news of her, while he himself haunts the woods where they were used to meet. Well, this gets around to old Charsky and, next thing young Charsky knows there's a troop of gendarmes at his door with the justices' order to dispossess him of Livno. The steward held that he must've had warning of it, for he had the Livno men all armed and there was a regular pitched battle fought, before he fired the house and all of 'em took to the woods. And there he has been ever since with his band, living off the country, as they say. They've even had the militia out, but no one has caught so much as a hair of him.'

'But that was before he had the misfortune to decamp with Miss Smith's trunk,' said Sacha, rising. 'Horses, post-master, as fast as your men can harness 'em! Lise, if you have lost your gloves *again* I shall take you across my knee. What in God's name have you got there, Danilo?'

'The English lady's *shuba*, your honour.'

'Mongolian goat, dear boy,' boomed Miss Smith transforming herself before their eyes into the abominable snowman of Himalayan folklore. 'Presented to me by the Emir of Baluchistan. I am told your Imperial family have all their bed coverlets made from it, and I can vouch for it being excessively light and warm—as well as stunning,' she added with a twinkle.

Her audience recovered their manners and Sacha protested that he had never seen its equal.

'Jackanapes!' said Miss Smith amiably. 'But I'll still let you off helping me into the coach. It moults.'

CHAPTER XIII

It was inevitable that as Volnoya neared and the landmarks grew familiar, they should recall to Sacha's mind the bleak purpose of his return to his childhood home.

He rode beside the chaise in grim silence, his face half-muffled in his cloak, staring sombrely ahead into the swirling snow. It was not much better at their midday halt nor when he joined them after it in the coach, except inasmuch as Miss Smith robustly chose to ignore his gloom and regaled them with an unceasing flow of anecdotes from her travels.

Good manners forced Sacha to make a show of listening, and insensibly her stories lightened his mood. By the time they were rolling through Volnoya woods in the gathering dusk, he was sufficiently enlivened to point out the river through a break in the trees and the lime avenue Hélène's great-great-uncle had planted up to the gardens of the house.

No one was surprised to find the house shuttered and barred for the night. It was now too dark for Lise to distinguish its features, but by craning out she was able to ascertain that Volnoya was a rambling, white-washed, two-storey structure, much over-grown in creeper, with single-storey wings thrown out at each side. Straggling on to embrace the wide lawns, came a line of low outbuildings of which Lise could pick out the stables and a pigeon loft. For all its lack of welcome, it was the first house in her life to give her a sense of home-coming.

As the coach drew up, a cautious light appeared at a side door; by the time the postillions had let down the steps the front door was open and candles were being hastily fetched into the hall.

Nevertheless, their young master's arrival seemed to have caught the household in considerable disarray and to plunge everyone in it, from Ahripoff, the dignified, white-haired steward, to the youngest of the curtseying maids, into abject confusion.

After listening for a few minutes to the old man's trembling explanations of why nothing was ready for his honour, Sacha said brusquely:

'Very well. Get the maids preparing their rooms for the ladies and send in a grog at once into the dining saloon, whilst you fix up a meal. Through here, Miss Smith.'

'Oh not in there, sir! I—it's—that is . . . the—the fire is not kindled in there, sir. If your honour would be so very obliging as to use the breakfast parlour—?'

'Your pantry, man, if it will get us refreshment! Have the fire lit immediately in the dining saloon. And bring some more lights. The place is like a morgue.'

'Sacha—if I might just go up and tidy myself a little first?'

'Of course. 'Dossia will take you upstairs. You too, Miss Smith? And you'd like your baggage—Well, 'Dossia, *now* what is it?'

Theodossia Ivanovna, the normally placid housekeeper, was wringing her hands.

'If you please, Master Sacha, the—the rooms . . . Well, it's not fit for the ladies upstairs. That is to say—it's . . . Well, sir, it's not fit. If their ladyships could but wait till I've run up to see . . .' She trailed off uneasily.

The effect of these representations on Sacha was what might have been foreseen. He ran his eye round the ring of embarrassed servants and said:

'There's something damned—I beg your pardon, ladies—but *damned* smokey going on in this house, and I—'

A fairly hefty crash upstairs appeared to confirm his prognosis. Sacha smiled.

'As I was saying before the interruption, something damned smokey going on, and I am going to find out what it is. Miss Smith, you and Lise will forgive me if I leave Theodossia to conduct you to the breakfast parlour? The rest of you back to the kitchens. Ahripoff, you shall have the pleasure of lighting me upstairs.'

He disappeared rapidly into the darkness above. Lise gripped her hands together.

'Oh Miss Smith, if he should walk into some ambush—!'

'Fiddlededee, child. He is far more likely to discover an illicit still in the master bedchamber. Or . . . If I did wing the rascal . . . Well, we shall see shortly. Now you will kindly direct this good woman to show us into the *dining* saloon. I too am curious to see what is going on in this house.'

Theodossia Ivanovna received the command with Slavonic fatalism and threw open the high oak doors of the dining parlour.

The room beyond was bathed in a mellow glow from the still

healthy fire in the grate and two tall silver branches of candles on the dining table. It also hinted at its recent occupation in the remains of a copious supper set out on the fine white cloth.

Miss Smith manifested no sign of surprise beyond a trumpeting snort.

'*Just* as I suspected,' she boomed, marching up to the table. 'Of *all* the infernal impudence!'

She picked up a crystal decanter of red wine, poured a little into a glass, sniffed at it, rolled it round her tongue and gave vent to another triumphant snort.

'Château Margaux! The best in the cellar, I'll be bound!'

She finished the rest of the glass and swept out into the passage, bearing Lise with her.

'So. We progress. Now we may repair to the breakfast parlour. Dear child, if you could bring yourself to suspend your natural wonder—and your present imitation of an astonished goldfish—I promise you we shall not have long to wait on the explanation of our mystery. Ah, here is a good fire and a cosy enough apartment. And I think I can hear enough disturbance upstairs to announce Mr Arloff's return.'

Her words were lost in Sacha's explosive entry, followed by a trail of quaking domestics.

'Now!' he roared, '*Now*, Ahripoff, and all of you—Miss Smith, you cannot conceive what these rogues— Do you know what I found upstairs?'

It was a rhetorical question, but Miss Smith chose to answer it.

'Let me guess,' she offered. 'You discovered evidence of recent occupation in the bedchambers? And probably signs of a precipitate withdrawal within the past half hour?'

Sacha joined Lise in her portrayal of an astonished goldfish.

'But—but how do you know—?'

'Someone has been sleeping in your bed,' continued Miss Smith placidly. 'And without wishing to sound like the tale of the three bears, let me add that someone has also been sitting at your dining table, and drinking what I would hazard to be your best claret.'

'But how in God's name did you guess?' cried Sacha. 'How could you know—? And who the devil—?'

'Perhaps I can elucidate,' said a voice at the door.

They all swung round. The newcomer framed in the doorway was not alone. Supporting his slender form on either side were two villainous-looking individuals dressed in an assortment of rough

clothing. He himself, in other circumstances, might have been considered a very pretty young man, favouring the dark, poetic style
lately made fashionable by the English Lord Byron. At the moment,
with his coat slung round his shoulders, no neckcloth and his open
shirt imperfectly hiding a bandaged chest, he looked every inch a
Corsair—if one comprehends in the picturesque the presence of a
levelled pistol in each hand.

Miss Smith could move with surprising celerity. Before Sacha
could react to their presence she had interposed her ample bulk
between him and the stranger.

'I was wondering when you would join us,' she told him cordially.
'No, no, M. Arloff, monsieur and I are acquainted so you will allow
me to perform the introductions. Lise, may I present to you—'

'Vladimir!' yelled Sacha.

'—my recent assailant, M. Vladimir Charsky,' continued Miss
Smith, beaming. 'M. Charsky, Mlle de Montargis. M. Sacha Arloff I
believe you know already.'

M. Charsky, faced with the choice of discharging his pistols or
acknowledging the introduction, sullenly lowered his weapons. Sacha
was anyway already clapping him on the back, calling him a string of
affectionately abusive names and demanding to know what the devil
he meant by bivouacking in his house without a by-your-leave? M.
Charsky winced.

'I would have you know . . . Ouch! Mind my shoulder. I would
have you know, sir— Oh curse you, Sacha, if it is not like you to turn
up out of the blue! But do not blame your servants. I'll explain how it
was—'

'It strikes me that you have a vast deal of explaining to do, young
man,' snorted Miss Smith. 'But you may do the rest at your leisure
when you have made yourself fit for ladies' company. For the
present one answer will suffice. Where is my trunk?'

'Trunk?' he repeated vaguely. His slightly fevered eyes roved over
Miss Smith as if he suspected her of being a figment of his imagination. 'I do not know, madame. Wha—what trunk?'

'What trunk! Now you listen to me—'

Miss Smith advanced to do battle, but at a closer view of her
opponent her tone changed abruptly. Sacha had also perceived
that something was wrong. He wrenched the coat off the boy's
shoulders to disclose a dark stain seeping through his shirt at the
right side of his chest. He was also in time to steady him as he swayed
forward.

'Whoever bandaged you knows nothing of applying a tourniquet,' he said severely. 'Dizzy, ain't you? All right, I've got you. Easy now. One of you—take his legs.'

'I have them,' boomed Miss Smith's voice from below. 'Lise, I shall require boiling water, towels, linen and the sharp scissors from my reticule. M. Sacha, pray desire one of his ruffians to remove his pistols from underfoot. They could cause a serious accident.'

'Very good, ma'am,' responded Sacha, all but saluting. 'I was proposing to stretch him out on the sopha here—unless you would risk having him carried upstairs?'

Their eyes met.

'The bullet?' asked Miss Smith in an undervoice.

'Precisely, ma'am.'

'The sopha then. And some brandy.'

'I am quite allri',' mumbled the invalid, striving feebly to impede their progress to the sopha. 'Levko! Pavel! Get the horses. Where's my coat? What the devil—'

'You'll pipe down and save your breath, my lad,' Sacha ordered, laying him down and throwing to the floor the cushions Lise had piled up for his head. 'You—' he flicked his fingers at the two for-lorn desperados lurking in the doorway. 'Tell me this: is the bullet still lodged?'

Disconsolate mutters yielded the intelligence that some unspecified elder of the band had endeavoured to extract it, with sanguinary results. It had been their intention to resort to the kidnapping of the nearest surgeon if their next attempt—for which their patient had so unwisely sought to fortify himself with Sacha's best claret—also proved abortive.

'That of course is all we need—a bound and gagged sawbones to complete our house-party,' snapped Sacha. He turned to Miss Smith.

'Well, ma'am?' he challenged softly. 'I'll wager we'll do as well by him as a peasant cut-throat with a rusty knife.'

Miss Smith glanced up from her inspection of the medical supplies being brought in under Lise's anxious supervision.

'Needs must,' she replied with a wry grin. 'And as it is my bullet lodged in the young rascal, I suppose it is up to me to recover it. Fortunately you will observe that it is but a flesh wound.'

She draped herself in an assortment of towels and screwed her quizzing glass firmly into her eye. Sacha took off his coat and rolled up the sleeves of his shirt. Lise, who had been observing these preparations with growing alarm, manfully held out a basin for him to wash his hands.

'Thank you, poppet. Now off you go to the dining parlour to brew us the strongest grog you ever tasted. Hurry, for we'll be ready for it in no time at all.'

'Yes, Sacha; at once.'

She nodded importantly and ran off. Sacha grinned.

'I'm learning to deal famously with children, ain't I? Now, ma'am, if you would swab the wound as clean as you can—'

M. Charsky gave a groan and opened his eyes.

'Wha' the devil you doin'?' he muttered, struggling to sit up. 'Sacha, must 'pologise . . . 'splain sometime . . . Got to go now—'

'Lie down, you fool, we're going to get your bullet out. Drink this.'

'Never put brandy 'top o' claret without port between, m'father says. Got to go now.'

'Drink it!' rapped Sacha, with an ungentle hand under the boy's head and the brandy glass at his lips. M. Charsky drank and spluttered.

'Don' unnerstan' . . . Got to *go*, I tell you. 'Spected two days ago at Mirnoff's.'

Sacha shook his head.

'Raving.'

The patient sat up.

'No, I am not,' he announced with the owlish clarity induced by a powerful shot of alcohol. 'En-tirely master of my fate. I was fixed to join the Mirnoff household two days ago. Well, not I precisely, but the new music master. Same thing. How else am I going to find out where they have hid my Anichka?'

Having made his point, he relapsed again into Miss Smith's arms and closed his eyes. Sacha motioned her to bring the candles closer and bent over him.

'How indeed?' she murmured, seating herself beside the patient and taking his hands. 'Now, dear boy, hold on to my hands hard and keep quite still. That's right. Very still. There's my brave boy. Only a little while longer. We'll find your Anichka for you, never fear. Ve-ry still now . . . There! All over.'

'He has fainted,' said Sacha, stepping back rather white himself, and wiping his brow. 'I trust, dear ma'am, that he did so before he had fully digested your rash promise.'

CHAPTER XIV

The habit of the road caused Lise to wake early next morning. She stretched luxuriously, flinging her thin arms wide on the pillows, but even then they could hardly encompass all the joys ahead. The action brought into view her one impediment to perfect happiness: her clothes.

The wear and tear of the road had taken a sad toll of the gown and ribbons she had been wearing on the fateful day of her flight. If only she had thought to choose something more hardy! But what, after all, did her appearance matter beside the miracle of being freely with Sacha at Volnoya instead of jogging back to Petersburg to face the Countess as his unwanted wife?

She pattered across to the window and threw back the starched linen curtains. Outside the sun was glinting on the snow, on Galant's glossy flanks and on Sacha's bare head as he cantered up the drive on his way back from visiting the *starosta* of Volnoya village.

Volnoya had been built to accord with the great-great-uncle's imperfect recollection of a French château he had visited on his Grand Tour. The local Russian builders' limitations had lost all the grandeur of the original, but were more than compensated in the charm of the result.

The house plan was simplicity itself. One stepped out of a tiny vestibule straight into the grand salon, known as the hall, a handsome apartment which ran the full depth of the house and ended in a row of tall french windows opening on to the river terrace. The staircase mounted directly out of the hall, which all the household were obliged to cross a dozen times a day. The breakfast parlour was also most inconveniently placed for the kitchens. However, Hélène had chosen it to command a prospect of the rough-cut, tree-shaded lawns descending to the river, with the morning sunlight sparkling on the water and the dark woods beyond. Over the years, the sun had bleached the oak furnishings to a golden-grey and faded the chestnut leather of the chairs and sopha to the mellow russet of autumn leaves, just as she had intended.

Hélène had spent two happy periods of her life at Volnoya: the first as a child with the maternal aunt from whom she had inherited the estate; the second when she had removed there to await the birth of her child by the man she loved.

It had been her elegant whim to preserve the little château's quaint rusticity, and she had amused herself during her months of waiting by enriching the simple house with the choicest purchases of her foreign travels. Now, a fine set of Ingres drawings kept the aunt's water-colours company in the breakfast parlour; Sèvres, Meissen and Wedgwood flanked traditional Russian enamel and malachite bibelots on the carved chests. In the cabinet, a Fra Angelico madonna faced the medieval Kazan ikon; and a superb Romney of Hélène dressed for hunting glowed among the dim family portraits in the grand saloon.

The indifferent mistress of palaces in Petersburg and Moscow, Hélène had taken an almost childish pleasure in embellishing her childhood home; and her fastidious caprices still ruled its well-ordered household. Miss Smith and Lise exclaimed over the tall branches of white lilac whose scent mingled deliciously with the fragrance of coffee that greeted them in the breakfast parlour.

'From the hothouses,' Sacha told them. 'It has been white lilac in that pedestal vase ever since I can remember, at this time of year. A little ham, Miss Smith? Our patient tells me that he has already been honoured with a visit from you. I thought he seemed fairly stout. What is your view?'

Miss Smith was able to support this comfortable report. M. Charsky's fever was abated. All that threatened his recovery was his impatience to pursue his search for Anichka in the Mirnoff stronghold where he was persuaded she was held.

'In durance vile,' murmured Lise, saucer-eyed.

'Indubitably,' agreed Sacha. 'Do you know, ma'am, that I am fast beginning to doubt the existence of this Anichka? She sounds too poetic by half. Every peasant girl *I* have ever known has been all too strongly in evidence any time after one has distinguished her.'

Miss Smith cast him a quelling look. Lise said anxiously:

'Oh, you do not suppose some harm may have come to her? General Mirnoff must have been excessively angry to have one of his village girls preferred to his daughter.'

'Mm-mm. More likely to have sold her quietly to the mines though, to stop any more talk.'

The Englishwoman glanced from one to the other of them and hunched an exasperated shoulder. That such barbarism should seem nothing out of the way to these gently nurtured children! A devoted adherent of Mr Wilberforce's crusade against the African slave-trade, Miss Smith had found much to distress her in serf-owning Holy Russia. She determined to take Lise firmly in hand during their voyage to England. It would never do for the child to outrage some English country host by referring to his sturdy tenant-farmers as 'serfs', through the innocently held tenets of her upbringing in this barbarous land.

Miss Smith was aroused from her reverie by hearing the one word warranted to gain her instant attention.

'. . . still carrying the trunk,' Sacha was saying. 'By this time, as you may collect, they were in a fair way to panic: what with their leader bleeding over his horse's neck, the night coming on and twenty versts to go to their nearest hide-out. It was then that one of the ruffians you saw last night bethought him of the fact that Ahripoff was his wife's uncle. Volnoya was near and known to be untenanted. It was decided to pin their hopes to the claims of kinship—with the results we found. As I told Ahripoff, I wish I might picture any one of *my* uncles cherishing such family feeling! So here we are with a houseful of bandits as guests. It should enliven my exile.'

'Sacha!' cried Lise. 'What if that horrid Deputy in Smolensk gets to hear of it! Or the justices—'

'Why then we can expect yet more uninvited guests. Shortly, I would hazard.'

'Not if my patient has his way,' snorted Miss Smith. 'His sole object is to get himself conveyed to General Mirnoff's on the instant; and presumably his band will then take to the hills or your Russian equivalent. What, I must confess, teases me is not only why, but *how* he intends to pass himself off as a Leipzig music master, when everyone in these parts must know him.'

'He informs me that he has provided himself with a false beard,' said Sacha drily. 'Something *you* never thought of, poppet! As to being known, you might be out on that, ma'am. Recollect that he is but newly returned from five years abroad and has met the General and Mlle Mirnoff only once since his return, he tells me. Of course that still leaves the problem of sustaining the character

of a Herr Schmitt, of which I'd give him an hour's lease at the
outside; but he says that for his Anichka he could be inspired to
anything. And he is convinced she is immured somewhere around
the house at Zacharovo—that's the Mirnoff estate—because he first
encountered her in the company of Mlle Mirnoff's maid.'

'Oh pray, how did they meet?' asked Lise eagerly.

'Romantically enough to satisfy you, I trust. He was riding alone
in the woods at dusk, as befits a poet, when he heard distant sounds
of a balalaika and singing. He followed a bridle path and came into
a village, to find it en fête for a Saint's day. She was dancing in one
of the girls' rings; and if one is to believe him, one glance of her
blue eyes sufficed to draw him in and transform his life. This cold
sober! Have you ever attended one of our village fêtes, ma'am? It is
vastly pretty I assure you. The whole village in its best embroidered
shirts and scarlet boots, and the girls gaudy as maypoles in their
ribbons and beads and *sarafans*. First there's church, then a feast
with enough vodka and home-brews to float a house, and then the
dancing in the rings, boys and girls, while the elders get drunk as
lords. And later—'

'Most enjoyable I'm sure,' boomed Miss Smith. 'And in the case
of M. Charsky the acquaintance also progressed rapidly?'

'And poetically. Within a week he was reading her his poems in
the woods. Within a fortnight he had taught *her* to read 'em, and
love-letters were being left in a hollow oak. Then came the dénoue-
ment with his father and he implored his Anichka to flee with him.
She promised and vanished.'

Lise, listening raptly, let out her suspended breath in a long
sigh.

'Oh Sacha, is it not the most romantical thing you ever heard? How
I wish we could help him!'

Sacha grinned.

'Miss Smith has anticipated your wish. She offered our services
last night.'

'Cawker! You know very well it was but to soothe him while you
performed your grisly task. However, one must always keep one's
promises to children. So what must I do—don the false beard and
claim *I* am Herr Schmitt, before I get back my trunk?'

Sacha clapped a hand to his head.

'The trunk! How could I thus forget the prime object of our
existence! But ma'am, I hardly know how . . . Lise, some black
coffee if you please.'

He laced it liberally with some cognac from the sideboard and carried the cup to Miss Smith.

'Drink this, ma'am,' he urged, 'and Lise shall ring for some hartshorn to—'

Lise, after a fearful glance, gave a smothered giggle.

'A pox on the pair of you!' spluttered Miss Smith. 'And if you do not wish me to burst a blood vessel, tell me plainly what has befallen my trunk.'

'The worst, ma'am,' announced Sacha hollowly. 'I had thought to soften the blow of your bereavement, but you are right. Where there is no hope it is but cruel to be kind.'

'I'll cap you. More matter with less art. Where is my trunk?'

'Brevity being the soul of wit, ma'am . . . In the river.'

'Oh do not say so!' cried Lise. 'The bandits dropped it?'

'Threw it in as they neared the house; their rude cunning informing them that they'd stand a better chance with Ahripoff minus their loot.'

The bereaved owner took a large gulp of the laced coffee. But not for nothing had the Emir of Bokhara quailed before Miss Smith.

'Then you will have to drag the river for it, will you not?' she said sweetly. 'What a good thing the robbers are still here to point out where it sank!'

In Sacha Arloff she had met her match.

'Providential, ma'am,' he drawled. 'And as the spot is quite near, *you* will be able to come and give the operation the benefit of your advice—whenever General Mirnoff can spare you from your musical duties!'

Neither Sacha nor Miss Smith gave their lighthearted challenges another thought. Both would have repudiated as nonsensical any suggestion that they would shortly find themselves in the throes of these harebrained undertakings.

After luncheon, M. Charsky greeted enquiries as to how he did, with an impatient shrug.

'Oh Lord, I'm well enough; and if some officious idiot had not removed my clothes I'd be on my way now, sparing you all this embarrassment. Sacha, you know my well-meaning fools. Bid them stop fussing and bring my clothes; they'll have to obey you.'

'I depend on that; since I ordered them to remove 'em. Pray have a little sense, Vladimir. Much as I would welcome your instant removal, you cannot go as you are. It'll take at least another week to get you on your feet, even if you obey orders and lie quiet.'

'Lie quiet! A week! Whilst the German poodlefaker sets every justice in Smolensk by the ears and has 'em swarming down to Mirnoff's with enquiries! My sole, my best chance of wresting from Mirnoff the secret of where he has hid my Anichka—Ouch!'

His agitation had betrayed M. Charsky into a violence of gesture that dislodged Sacha's tourniquet. The resultant pain and Sacha's ruthless renewal of his handiwork left him considerably subdued and without strength to do other than lie quiet on his pillows with closed eyes. In this situation he looked so absurdly boyish and disarming that Miss Smith, actuated as she later averred, by senile folly, was moved to say:

'Now let that be the end of your nonsense, my lad! I told you last night that we shall find your Anichka for you; but not one step do I move to General Mirnoff's if I have another of your wild starts.'

She seated herself beside the bed and felt the boy's pulse, while he fastened incredulous, eloquent dark eyes to her face.

'You—you really mean it, ma'am? You'll go to Mirnoff's and discover what they've done with her?'

'*If* you rest now, eat the gruel I shall order for your dinner and refrain from moving your shoulder one inch during the next two hours. And if I can devise a means of taking Mlle de Montargis with me.'

'I was wondering when that aspect of your difficulties would strike you, ma'am,' said Sacha softly. 'Almost as awkward as being of the wrong sex to be Herr Schmitt . . . Why, poppet, what ails you? Just think of the glorious hazards of the adventure ahead of you! It is even better than smuggling me out of the country as a ship's stowaway.'

'Ye-yes, Sacha.'

M. Charsky found all this beyond him and devoted his depleted energies to gripping Miss Smith's hand.

'You are an angel,' he stated huskily. 'Who are you?'

Sacha choked; but Miss Smith, disengaging her hand, placidly patted the tousled black head on the pillow.

'Later, dear boy. We shall leave you now to rest until I come up with your gruel.'

'You will . . . be sure to come back?' mumbled the patient, closing his eyes again. 'I'm sorry 'bout your trunk . . . ma'am.'

'You may call me Miss Smith.'

'Miss . . . Smith. Herr . . . Schmitt. What a . . . c'incidence.'

Sacha, who had been rifling through some papers on the night table, looked up with a shout of laughter. Miss Smith shushed him indignantly and shepherded the party out.

'We should have a doctor to him,' she said, frowning. 'He is considerably fevered. I will see how he does after his rest. And no more visits from you, my boy. I fear yours is too restless a presence for a sickroom.'

'My apologies for laughing, ma'am, but I had just come upon Herr Schmitt's letter of recommendation. It occurred to me—merely a passing thought—that you might wish to familiarise yourself with —er—your new self.'

Miss Smith snorted.

'You're out if you think *I* am proposing to figure as that Schmitt, in *any* respect. A poor sort of creature with no bottom. Not my style at all.'

'But then—' Lise knitted her brows. 'How may you pass yourself off as him, ma'am?'

'The false beard,' murmured Sacha irrepressibly, but it was lost in Miss Smith's boom.

'Perfectly simple, dear child. I shall not become Schmitt. *He* shall become Smith.'

It was dusk by the time Miss Smith joined Lise and Sacha in the small saloon for the promised discussion of her plan of campaign.

They had been playing picquet, and the board was still set up on the card table by the fire where they had left it when the light had discouraged further play.

Sacha had sprawled back in his chair, a hand deep in his breeches' pocket, his booted legs stretched out to the fire. Lise had slipped down to a footstool beside him, to sit contentedly staring into the flames, while he idly curled a lock of her hair round a lazy finger. Snowflakes fell silently against the double windows. The occasional soft hiss and splutter of the fire served but to emphasise the room's quiet. Miss Smith stood for a moment in the doorway, taking in the picture the two of them made, before Sacha rose and Lise bobbed up to curtsy at her entrance.

Miss Smith's eyes met Sacha's; but as far as she could tell in the soft gloom, his face betrayed no consciousness.

'We were too lazy to ring for lights,' he said, stifling a yawn and reaching for the bell rope. 'Sheer indolence—the curse of rural life in this country. Thank God you are come to rouse us from our sloth. Especially if you will engage to explain how Herr Schmitt becomes Miss Smith. Lise and I have contained our curiosity as best we may; but we refuse to wait a minute longer for its satisfaction.'

Lise looked up with a dreaming smile; but it was plain to Miss Smith that nothing outside the enchanted circle of firelight in the quiet room had existed for her during that afternoon. Sacha too glanced down into her bemused little face and looked away with a slight frown. He rose and took some papers from the bureau to Miss Smith.

'You disclaimed any interest in Herr Schmitt's credentials, ma'am, but you must indulge me by perusing his letter of recommendation. It is from General Mirnoff's nephew in Moscow, and I'll hazard a guess that choosing a musical instructor is *not* his forte.'

Miss Smith scanned it rapidly and sat up, her eyes snapping.

'Hah! You will have doubtless observed that here is not one word to indicate the *sex* of the bearer.'

'Let me see—Good God, you are right!' cried Sacha after a hasty re-perusal. 'Not a "he" in it!'

'One might almost say that it was designed to prepare the General for my arrival,' continued Miss Smith pensively. 'The little matter of spelling my name as "Schmitt" is easily overcome. Lise, dear child, you will be so good as to order our packing. We will remove to the General's tomorrow.'

'You have thought of a story to cover her presence with you?' asked Sacha in a worried undervoice, as Lise departed sadly on her errand.

'Not a story, no. I have always believed firmly in sticking to the truth as far as it is practical in this life. The truth will serve very well in the present case, with the small omission of your part in it. So . . . Lise shall have been on her way to join her mother in London in my care, as far as our way lay together. We were obliged to leave her maid behind in Smolensk—no doubt the woman fell ill—and the robbers accounted for Lise's baggage as well as my trunk. You will have come upon us on the road after the robbery, just as you did, more or less, and kindly carried us to Volnoya, before putting one of your own carriages at our disposal. The rescue of two ladies in distress may also help to restore your credit in the neighbourhood.'

'If they swallow it,' said Sacha grimly. 'I imagine the tale of my disgrace and exile must be known, or we'd have half the province leaving cards by now.'

'Particularly the matchmaking mamas, eh?'

Sacha shrugged, wrinkling his beautiful nose.

'You know the provinces for *that*, ma'am! I swear there is something in country air that makes 'em breed daughters. Confoundedly plain ones as a rule.'

'Is Mlle Mirnoff perhaps an exception?'

'Believe me, ma'am, there *are* no exceptions. Charsky describes this one as a simpering miss, dripping with false curls and diamonds. Enough to disgust one even with an heiress; though there was no need to go to the length of preferring a bride from the village! By the by, ma'am, if you really are intending to find the wretched girl for him, how the devil do you propose to do it?'

'A scheme will doubtless occur to me. M. Charsky confided to me *his* plan of entering the General's bed-chamber at dead of night and extracting her whereabouts from him at pistol point. But that was to be if all else failed, of course.'

Sacha raised his eyebrows, his eyes dancing.

'The impropriety, ma'am!' he urged. 'Entering a man's bedroom!'

'Jackanapes!' said Miss Smith, rising. 'I'll thank you to remember the respect due to your elders—even if they have succumbed to their second childhood.'

He grinned and held the door for her.

'But you're an engaging rascal, I grant you that,' she growled. She stopped in the doorway and looked steadily for a moment into the dark-blue, moody eyes from which the laughter was already fading. She said abruptly:

'Exile is hardest on your sort. Lise was telling me that Volnoya means "free" . . .'

He stiffened.

'Yes, ma'am,' he replied expressionlessly. 'There is a country saying: "*volnoya ptitsa*", meaning roughly "free as a bird".'

'You will be. Oh my dear, you will be!'

She gave a trumpeting snort and blew her nose on an incongruously delicate lace handkerchief.

'Meanwhile try to refrain from breaking every woman's heart in the province, if you can,' she told him severely. 'I'll be off upstairs. That foolish child will have had ample time to cry her eyes out by now and should be ready to benefit by the consolations of common sense.'

CHAPTER XVI

Lise's uncertain status somewhat reduced the period which General Mirnoff would have normally kept a music master cooling his heels. The butler's extraordinary report that the new tutor had turned out to be of the female sex and had driven up in the Arloff carriage, also required investigation. So it was a mere forty minutes before the ladies were conducted to the General's cabinet.

The apartment was handsome and gloomy. Like all the public rooms of the house, it served as a repository for memorials of every aspect of the General's military career. The cabinet was devoted to portraits and statuary of the horses which had borne him since his commission in the Dragoons some thirty-six years before. Some depicted the General in the act of charging the enemy; a particularly vivid representation caused Lise to jump nervously as she crossed the room behind Miss Smith.

General Mirnoff, looking startlingly like his portraits—since he still affected military dress in his retirement—bobbed up from behind a vast leather-covered desk and ran round it to confront them. On his feet, he was revealed to be a much smaller man than he appeared on horseback. A choleric flush suffused his normally florid complexion to a full-blooded purple, and his sweeping mustachios and side-whiskers, which he wore à la Blucher, bristled with suspicion.

'What's this?' he barked, darting all round the ladies. 'Who the devil are ye? I'm expecting a tutor. Are *you* the tutor? Why are you a female? Why are you rolling up in Arloff's carriage? And who are *you*, my girl?'

Finding the General at her back, Miss Smith slowly pivoted round and looked down at him from her full six feet.

'If you will speak English or French, sir, remain stationary, and address yourself in a proper manner to Mademoiselle de Montargis, we may conceivably arrive at an understanding.'

Perhaps it was Miss Smith's resemblance to several of the noblest animals round the walls that caused the General to moderate his tone. At any rate he came to a halt and obediently switched to French.

'I do not understand. Kindly explain yourself . . .' He paused and then threw in a 'madame' to be on the safe side.

'That,' replied Miss Smith, 'will take a little time. First, allow me to present Mademoiselle de Montargis to you.'

Lise curtsied; the General, under Miss Smith's compelling eye, gave a jerky bow.

'And I am Honoria Smith, come to take up my post in your household. Here is my letter of recommendation from your nephew, M. Anatole Mirnoff.'

The General snatched it.

'But . . . you're a female! How the devil can a female conduct my *musique militaire*, eh? Answer me that! And why—' he stabbed the letter with a triumphant finger, '—does this letter say "Schmitt" if you're Smith?'

'I cannot imagine, sir,' said Miss Smith composedly. 'You had best ask M. Anatole Mirnoff.'

'Be sure I will, my good woman!' cried the General, beginning to fidget again. 'Be sure I will! My nephew is a flibberty-gibbet, but this is doing it rather too brown! There's something fishy here. I smell it. Where are your papers, eh? Your diploma or whatever? Your passport?'

'I was coming to that, and when you have heard me out, sir, you shall form your own judgment as to which of us has the right to suspicion! You—or I who took up your nephew's offer in good faith, only to be set upon, robbed, abandoned to my fate in the snow with this innocent child . . . Words fail me, sir! And then this reception!'

She turned to Lise.

'Mademoiselle de Montargis, I was obviously deceived in my assurance to you that a gentleman's household awaited me. The Governor of this district must be informed at once of your plight so that he may render you the courtesy due to your rank. I believe our rescuer's carriage may still be here—'

Several minor eruptions from the General had failed to interrupt her flow; but now his pent-up emotions exploded in full force to vent his bewilderment, dismay and righteous indignation at the slur on his hospitality and gentlemanly instincts.

Miss Smith boomed back at him, at point-blank range. The General roared. Lise edged towards the door. However, when the rumblings of the last exchanges had died away, the party was found to be seated, Miss Smith had been so far mollified as to accept an offer of refreshment, and Lise found herself the object of every civility the General could muster.

This included his daughter's immediate attendance—if Mademoiselle de Montargis could bring herself to put up with the hospitality of a rough soldier's household until her baggage were recovered?

Mademoiselle, who had been hoping against hope to be summarily returned to Volnoya, accepted his offer with just the right degree of polite indifference. Mlle Mirnoff was sent for; and Miss Smith favoured Lise with a triumphant wink when the General presented her without question as her new tutor to her future charge.

The young lady glanced at her in surprise; but it was as nothing to the astonishment she aroused in both her new acquaintances.

Where were the false curls, the affectations and rouge of the simpering provincial miss who had so disgusted M. Charsky's poetic soul? For a moment Lise wondered if the girl plying Miss Smith and herself with eager questions could be a younger sister? But the General presently put her identity beyond doubt by his injunction to Miss Smith to exercise firm discipline with his spoilt, only child.

Mlle Mirnoff giggled all over her charming, round, rosy face, which was innocent of any suspicion of rouge, and tossed what were indubitably her own golden curls.

'Papa is forever trying to make a soldier of me! But *dear* Miss Smith, you will not set me too many horrid scales and lessons while Mlle de Montargis is with us? Oh, it will be famous to have you at Zacharovo!' she cried, impulsively taking Lise's hands. 'You cannot conceive how flat I have been since . . . I hope it may be *months* before they recover your baggage from the robbers. Oh—!'

She broke off and stood staring at Lise open-mouthed.

'Oh could it have been. . . ? Oh pray tell me, did you get a sight of the bandits?'

Miss Smith snorted.

'We saw enough of 'em. I winged their leader, a rascal called Charsky.'

Mlle Mirnoff's plump little hands flew to her mouth.

'He—he was not badly hurt?' she stammered.

'Did ye, by God!' roared the General. 'More than our fool gendarmes have managed in six months of chasing him, the young ruffian! Saw fit to find me daughter here less to his taste than a village wench; but a prime young gamecock for all his poetic falals. As good a seat on a horse as I ever saw. Pity you could not contrive to tempt him, miss, even with all your mother's jewels on you!'

Lise looked to see her new friend thrown into a flutter by this indelicacy; but though Mlle Mirnoff blushed and looked conscious her lowered lashes imperfectly concealed a flash of mischief.

'Indeed, papa, it quite sank me with chagrin.'

'Chagrin! Poppycock! Ten thousand acres and at the least two thousand serfs—*that's* what you should be regretting, my girl. *And* my lifelong friendship with an old comrade, which you've cost me between you with your fancies! In my young day . . .'

In her pretty boudoir upstairs, Mlle Mirnoff settled Lise on a buttoned blue chaiselongue, plumped herself down on a stool and cried:

'Oh, do tell me about Arloff! It is all over the neighbourhood that he has been exiled here in disgrace by the Tsar-Emperor himself. Did he really rescue you? They say he is excessively handsome and a shocking rake. Oh, if you are not the luckiest of females, Lise! Charsky *and* Arloff! What is he like?'

'An arrogant, spoilt rakehell, with a good heart and an ungovernable temper,' came the unexpected reply from Miss Smith at the door. 'And far too much charm for his own good. You'll do well to forget him, the pair of you, and stick to masquerading as peasant girls for the undoing of pretty boys like your headstrong Charsky!'

The effect of this broadside was foreseeably to rob both young ladies of all power of speech. Miss Smith took advantage of their thunderstruck silence to develop her theme.

'I might have deduced the truth from your own lips when you were thrown into such a pother at hearing that I had shot M. Charsky,' she told the unhappy Annette. 'But in the event, no rational process was needed. During the afternoon I spent at his bedside, M. Charsky favoured me with a lyrical portrait of his peasant love; and this, making due allowance for poetic licence and his fevered state, presented me with a speaking likeness of you, miss! *Now* what have you to say?'

A small sob issued from behind the culprit's clasped hands. Lise's warm heart could stand it no longer. She jumped up and threw her arms round Annette's drooping form, saying imploringly to Miss Smith:

'Oh pray do not scold her, ma'am. See how wretched she is already over the affair! I am sure she is truly sorry for it.'

'No, I am not!' said Annette fiercely, raising a pink, tear-wet face from Lise's shoulder. 'It has all gone awry, and I would not have Charsky a bandit and getting shot, for the world! But I am *not* sorry I dressed up and pretended to be a girl from our village and—and used to steal out to meet him in the woods, because it is the most wonderful thing that ever happened to me!'

Recollection of the wonder produced a renewed flood of tears. Lise murmured comfort and presently Annette found strength to continue.

'You see, everyone has known forever that our fathers wished Charsky and me to marry. The day he came home, papa was dining with old M. Charsky at Svetlovo—that's their estate—and he . . . well, you will come to know his bluff ways. It all came to a head over a toast papa proposed. The Svetlovo butler told our coachman how young M. Charsky went quite white and deliberately put down his glass, saying he'd be d—d if he'd drink to marrying eight thousand acres, five villages and an iron foundry. Only I believe the word he used was even more shocking than that, for all three were well in liquor by this time . . . When papa returned next morning, he was still very incensed; and for *weeks* the least thing was enough to set him off about brash young puppies, and poets, and foreign education. But the worst was that I was forbidden to receive M. Charsky, when every girl in the neighbourhood had contrived to meet him, and even my maid Pasha had danced with him when the Svetlovo cook's son married one of our coachman's daughters. It was hearing about their wedding party in Svetlovo village that gave me the idea . . .'

Annette gave a ghost of her giggle; but it was succeeded by a small frown and a troubled look in the china-blue eyes.

'*Everyone* else I had been in love with knew me for papa's heiress, you see.'

The oddly forlorn note in her voice caused Miss Smith to glance at her keenly. So the chit was not entirely the fool she looked. Lise was too absorbed in the tale to examine the character of the teller.

'Oh, Annette, were you not afraid?' she cried. 'How dreadfully poor M. Charsky would have felt if your deception had been discovered to him.'

'That is precisely what happened,' replied Annette tragically. 'Not that *he* unmasked me; the case was far worse than that! Papa and old M. Charsky suddenly made it up.'

Lise duly gasped.

'Never shall I forget that day,' Annette went on with a shudder. 'Papa sent for me in the morning, on his return from Svetlovo, and directed me to look my prettiest since I was to meet my bridegroom at dinner! My prettiest—when I was ready to sink! It was my maid Pasha who saved me. Just before the Charskys were due, she said to me: "Miss, you look pale as a ghost. Why don't we use a touch of the rouge your last governess left behind?" Well, I was too *énervée* to care *how* I looked, but I let her go and fetch Fräulein Schiller's old box.'

Annette unsuccessfully stifled a reminiscent giggle.

'Oh, Lise, you cannot conceive what a sketch I looked when I came downstairs! *Full* balldress, gloves and fan, and *all* my mother's diamonds; rouged to the eyebrows and the Schiller curls bobbing . . . And throughout dinner I spoke only French, in the most die-away, lisping tones, with my eyes demurely cast down. Even papa was put out; but I assured him afterwards it was all the crack. Oh, it was so droll when Charsky next morning in the woods told me in what disgust he had taken the heiress!'

She bit her lip and added mournfully:

'Well, it *seemed* droll then. How could I foresee the dreadful outcome? *Why* are men so provoking!'

'The nature of the beast,' grunted Miss Smith. She leant back in her chair. 'Well now, the first thing we have to do—What in heaven's name is that?'

The cause of her exclamation was a rousing trumpet blast resounding through the house with the urgency of a call to arms. Lise also jumped up in alarm. Annette, however, was able to reassure them that this was merely the General's preferred form of signalling to his household that dinner was served.

Glowing with robust health, in a freshly-starched stock and with her skirts hitched high over shining top-boots, Miss Smith entered the breakfast parlour next morning, breezily declaring herself ready to take up her musical duties.

On their way to Zacharovo she had made Lise laugh in spite of herself when she had suddenly clapped a hand to her head, exclaiming: 'Good God, Lise, I had clean forgot—I don't know a note of music!' Could she have forgotten that salient fact again? Lise thought wildly, as she listened to the General outline his militant ambitions for his household orchestra.

No possibility of a private word presented itself. After breakfast Lise watched with dismay Miss Smith's departure to put the orchestra through its paces. At the door, Miss Smith paused; but it was only to issue a brisk command to the young ladies to enjoy a healthful walk until she was ready for them.

However, no exposure of their conductor's inadequacy resulted from that first or subsequent sessions. On the contrary, the Mirnoff orchestra appeared to gain a new lease of life. Miss Smith, when applied to for the secret, merely grinned and boomed:

'The principle of constitutional democracy, dear child. Nothing like it for encouraging enterprise in the lower orders. My troop now has an elected leader from their own ranks, who drives them far harder than I'd dare to, even if I knew a note. All *I* have to do is admire and take the credit. Did I not say we would push through?'

Following Miss Smith's lead proved even more puzzling in the matter of Annette. There Miss Smith seemed to have no other design than to make up for the years of that young lady's neglected education. And Lise herself, discovered mooning by a window, was summarily restored to the schoolroom in deference to an obscure British proverb about Satan finding mischief for idle hands.

The General too found himself taken in hand.

The mealtime call to arms was abolished. The General's bark became modulated to a mere shout; and several of his more discomforting habits, such as darting like a ricochetting bullet round any person he was addressing, were undermined to a degree that would have amazed his household if they were not beyond any astonishment over Miss Smith's capabilities.

In fact, a simple secret lay behind the apparent miracle of their master's reformation. The General, in losing a tutor, had gained a crony. One moreover of his own age and autocratic habit, but equipped with a well-informed mind and an endless flow of travel-lore and gossip of European politics and personages. When she was found to add to these advantages a knowledge of horse-

D

flesh to match his own, the General's surrender was complete.

His need of eligible company was even greater than his daughter's. The Charsky contretemps had merely deprived her of a clandestine lover; *he* had been robbed of his oldest friendship, with all that this comprehends of constant intercourse and steady esteem.

There had been no contact between the two neighbours since the fatal night of young Charsky's quarrel with his father. Both parents' injuries had been exacerbated by all-too-faithful reports of their animadversions on each other, from their acquaintances and servants. Miss Smith did not underestimate the problem facing her in her determination to reconcile them; nor indeed the practical difficulty of being admitted to a sight of old M. Charsky, who had let it be known that anyone connected with Zacharovo would have the dogs set on them if they ventured on Svetlovo land.

Nevertheless it was essential to press forward with her plans. A note by the hand of one of Sacha's footmen warned her that young Charsky was making alarming progress and could not be restrained at Volnoya much longer. In a characteristically casual postscript, Sacha gave the news of his father's elevation—if she had not already heard of it—adding that he was now in a good position to gauge the astuteness of the neighbouring gentry from their alacrity in calling at Volnoya. 'By this criterion,' he wrote, 'your General must be either stupid or proud; probably both. Or have you forbid him to come?—since rumour has you firmly in the saddle at Zacharovo. But I beg you will not let your new protégés displace my little Lise with you, ma'am.'

Miss Smith despatched a brief reply. Then she sat gazing down at the sheet of Hélène's hotpress covered in her son's sprawling hand, with a smile that belied her thoughts. She remembered so well the suddenly softened note in Sacha's voice which sounded in the last sentence of his postscript. She also recalled its effect even upon her own unimpressionable heart and sourly wondered if the young scapegrace were not well aware of it. Nevertheless, it would be unfair to rob Lise of the happiness which Sacha's thought for her would assuredly bestow; so, on her way to her morning ride with the General, Miss Smith made a detour to give Lise a cautious version of M. Arloff's concern for her welfare.

The General, with whom punctuality had been a religion for some fifty-five years, gave vent to nothing more than a muted growl in response to Miss Smith's greeting.

'I must apologise for my delay,' said Miss Smith calmly. 'I was engaged in casting up my accounts. To date, sir, you owe me 203 roubles, 9 kopecks, for my wages and out-of-pocket expenditure on the journey here. Also a day off.'

Her employer was so far disconcerted as to relapse into his rico-chetting run around the cabinet. Recollecting Miss Smith's warning of what it did to his spleen, he reined in before the mantel while his never-powerful understanding struggled with the complex assault upon it.

First of all, tutors did not have days off.

But then, was Miss Smith a tutor?

And if not, who was she and where was the tutor?

These uncomfortable questions had been tacitly shelved during the past weeks. To reopen them courted the risk of losing his new crony. After several minutes of unaccustomed mental exercise, the General admitted to himself that he did not greatly care whether she was the tutor or not. All that mattered was to ensure her remaining fixed at Zacharovo. So if a day's furlough was a condition of it, a day's furlough she should have. He asked, a trifle wistfully, what she intended to do with her holiday?

'If you will let me have a mount, I fancied to take a look around the neighbouring country. To a botanist, the turn of the year yields much of interest; and now that the snow is gone, I am told that the roads will shortly become a mire. I will desire the cook to put me up a pique nique. The girls may have a holiday too, after they have rehearsed their lesson. I believe I may go tomorrow.'

Several times during the day the General returned to the subject of her furlough, and only Miss Smith's tact prevented him from proposing his company. Lise and Annette frankly demanded to go with her.

'But it is to give myself a rest from the pair of you that I am going, you goosecaps! And I give you leave to get up to what mischief you please until I return, as long as it does not disturb your papa's peace, Annette.' Miss Smith smiled. 'One of my nephews once took that as a licence to climb an eighty-foot tower, on the plea that if he fell it would not be on the side of the house commanded by his papa's library windows.'

Lise at once begged to hear more of the escapade, but Miss Smith brusquely turned the conversation.

When the household retired, with no bugle-call now, Miss Smith found a neat package on her dresser. It contained 203 roubles, 9 kopecks, a sketch-map of the neighbourhood drawn by the General's own hand and his own silver campaigning flask filled with his best cognac.

Lise, Annette, the housekeeper, the head groom and the elected leader of the orchestra all waited on her early next morning, proffering comforts for her excursion and rather forlornly enquiring her orders for the day. The General kept to his rooms, whence a series of muffled explosions warned the household of storms to come.

The two girls retired to the schoolroom to apply themselves dispiritedly to Mercator's projection of the globe.

However, a few minutes saw a mercurial change in their demeanour when a breathless maid bobbed in to announce that M. Sacha Arloff was below, enquiring for Miss Smith.

'Oh!' cried Lise, turning as pale as she had been flushed at hearing his name. 'Oh, Annette, he will assuredly go away on learning that Miss Smith is from home all day! Unless the General . . . But you know how short he was at breakfast—'

Annette smiled with superior worldly wisdom.

'La, my dear, have you forgot the news of Count Arloff's great new Office? It is true papa said that *he* would not be among the toadeaters now flocking to Volnoya, but common civility will oblige him to offer his felicitations now M. Arloff is here. Oh, I quite long to see him at last! I believe—yes, I really believe you are trembling! Dear creature, have I uncovered your secret? Oh, but I should have guessed; for how could you help falling in love with such a rescuer? Tell me at once: did you know of his shocking reputation? And now he is here! Oh my dear creature, let me at least furbish up your ribbons!'

Lise had been steadfast in her refusal of Annette's generous offer of the run of her wardrobe. At first this had been no hardship, since Miss Smith had noted the necessity of procuring her charge some clothes; but she had not pursued the matter and Lise had been too proud to recall it to her notice. Consequently she was still wearing the dove-grey gown of her flight, freshened up as best she could with clean ruffles, and the coqueliquot ribbons which were now sadly limp with constant ironing. She gently repulsed Annette's eager hands, saying stoutly:

'Thank you, but my ribbons are past repair; and I am not in love with anyone.'

She turned away and spun Mr Mercator's globe on its axis, staring fiercely at the mass of the Americas through a blur of tears.

'And in any case, M. Arloff has not asked for me.'

'But papa must send for us, knowing that you are acquainted. Oh, he must! It would be too cruel to let us pine away of curiosity up here! Let me think. Supposing I were to trip down to the cabinet to consult papa about our lesson—being *totally* unaware that he has a visitor? Then I could make sure that papa asks him to stay to dinner.'

But by the time the little coquette had changed her gown and rejected two sets of ribbons to achieve a toilette worthy of a famous rake, the object of her interest was cantering out of Zacharovo, having politely but firmly resisted the General's persuasions to stay to dinner.

Had Sacha looked back, he might have seen a small, tear-stained face pressed to an upper window; but as it was the one face in Zacharovo he had determined to avoid seeing, it is doubtful whether the sight would have moved him.

Annette too dissolved into tears—of sheer temper over her disappointment. So all in all it was a sorry household to which Miss Smith returned that evening.

Her first charity was to hear out a full recital of the day's woes, above and below stairs. Then she went into action. Annette was swiftly restored to cheerfulness by a hint of exciting events in store for her on the morrow. The General required nothing more than the fact of his Smith's return.

Lise was a more delicate matter. Miss Smith reserved her till last, and it only lacked a half hour to supper when she scratched at the door of Lise's bedchamber. As she suspected, the child had been sitting in the dark, huddled in the window-seat with her chin sunk on her knees. Miss Smith hardened her heart, lit all the candles and plumped herself into a chair, exclaiming:

'Well, what a day I have had of it! With parents like M. Charsky and the General one can hardly wonder that their offspring take to crime and imposture! And though such extravagant folly may have a certain charm in the young, it is beyond permission in the old, as I told M. Charsky. *When* I finally got within speaking distance of him.'

'You went to Svetlovo, ma'am?' cried Lise, startled out of her dejection. 'Oh pray tell me what happened? Did M. Charsky refuse to receive you?'

'He set the dogs on me,' said Miss Smith simply. 'Fortunately I am fond of dogs and well accustomed to having numbers of them around me. Getting on terms with *them* was a simple matter beside reaching an understanding with their master; although he does look singularly like a bloodhound I once owned. One of your choleric and melancholy natures, who always think their servants are cheating them and the post-master giving them the worst nags in the stable. Usually they are right of course.'

She brooded on this truth for a few moments and then chuckled. 'As in this case; for it seems that when young Charsky flung out of his father's presence it was with the rather hackneyed threat that he would rob purses on the highway rather than betray his love. This of course, he proceeded to do, thus fulfilling his father's worst fears. And this now affords M. Charsky a certain melancholy satisfaction which I fear he will sadly miss in the felicity awaiting him.'

Lise gurgled, her tears forgotten.

'But will he not be consoled by deploring Annette's shocking behaviour, ma'am?'

'*You*, miss, remind me that the young should not be tempted into shewing their natural disrespect for their elders! However, strictly as between fellow-conspirators—I have determined as far as possible to keep both fathers in ignorance of the facts behind the happy outcome of their troubles. There is only one person in this coil whose sense of humour I would trust to relish the whole story, and that is M. Sacha Arloff.'

She spoke the name deliberately and duly noted the clouding of the expressive little face opposite. She permitted her own features to fall into lines of deepest dejection and heaved a sigh for good measure.

'The General tells me he was here today.'

'Yes, ma'am,' agreed a small, colourless voice.

'You must wonder at his apparent want of civility in not waiting on you, Lise. Alas, his errand here must excuse any neglect. It was to apprise me—' She broke off and, to Lise's dismay, dabbed her eyes with one of her absurdly delicate lace handkerchiefs. 'Dear child, forgive me, I can scarce bear to speak of it.'

All thought of her own disappointment vanished from Lise's mind as she threw herself into the task of comforting her mentor and seeking the cause of her distress. Miss Smith grinned behind her handkerchief and said brokenly:

'My life-work. All my notes. My specimens. The fruits of a year's toil . . . Yes, you have guessed it. They have succeeded in raising my trunk from the river bed. It has leaked. The plant specimens are green porridge. The ink of my notebooks has run. M. Arloff has all of it being dried on special racks. But it is a question of how much can be saved from the wreck of my hopes before the ink quite fades.'

'Oh, but ma'am we *will* save it!' protested Lise, clasping her hands. 'Only let me think . . . Oh ma'am, if both of us—and Annette—were to set ourselves to transcribe it and trace the drawings . . . Oh, we must start at once!'

Miss Smith looked thoughtful. She had been embroidering her theme at random, intent only upon taking the sting out of Sacha's neglect for the girl. In fact, she had already more or less resigned herself to the loss of her notebooks. Her nonsensical task at Zacharovo was almost done. It remained but to arrange the reunion of the lovers. This accomplished, she and Lise were free to set out for England. But the girl's eager notion of rescuing the Smith contribution to the anthropology of botany hit its author at her weakest point. It also answered the unease she felt over leaving Russia without making a push to reconcile Sacha to his fate.

'Exile is hardest on your sort,' she had said to him, knowing it out of her experience not of him but of another wild boy, who had been infinitely dear to her. He was now only an anguished memory and a blackened wooden cross on a Spanish hillside; but it was because Sacha had recalled him to her that she was here.

Lise was anxiously studying her abstracted face. Miss Smith smiled.

'Child, I believe you have hit upon the solution! I shall wait on the General tomorrow to seek his permission to visit Volnoya, so that I can ask M. Arloff if we may depend on his renewed hospitality. But we will not count on Annette as a copyist; the next few weeks should see the Mirnoffs fully occupied with their own affairs, if all goes to plan. Dear child, you will not object to being fixed at Volnoya for the duration of our task?'

Lise's answer was a bear-hug. Moth to the flame, thought Miss Smith, and heroically resolved to curtail the transcription of her notebooks—and their stay at Volnoya—to the minimum. Lise would soon get over her childish adoration of Sacha in the normal process of growing up; it would be a different matter if some action of his were to touch off the hair-spring that would plunge her into love with him. True, the girl had emerged untouched by the night in Vilensk. But the elderly spinster who had never known love, knew a great deal about the secrets which the human heart can conceal even from itself. She knew that neither Lise nor Sacha were the same after that night; she also realised wryly how firmly both had ensconced themselves in her own heart.

That'll teach me to lend myself to nonsensical adventures on the road, thought Miss Smith, rising and bestowing a peck on Lise's forehead. She then gave a complex snort and bade Lise wash her face before joining the party downstairs.

Miss Smith herself sent down her excuses to the General and supped in her own quarters, having much to do.

First, she wrote a billet to Sacha. Then, smiling a little, she dashed off an appropriately melodramatic enclosure to young Charsky, bidding him ask no questions but present himself at Zacharovo by noon (how she regretted being unable to make it midnight) if he would be united with his Anichka.

She rang and directed to have a trusty man ride over to Volnoya with her missive that night.

Her supper was grown cold beside her; but Miss Smith made a hearty meal, enjoyed a nightcap with the General and retired to sleep as soundly as her fellow-master of strategy, Napoleon, was reputed to do on the eve of battle.

CHAPTER XVII

The Zacharovo breakfast table, bathed in spring sunshine, looked vastly peaceful for a battlefield.

The General readily acceded to Miss Smith's request to visit Volnoya. They would all go, he declared, since it would enable him to repay Arloff's call while Miss Smith assessed the damage to her life-work. Miss Smith made no mention of fixing herself at Volnoya; time enough for that blow when the General had his reconciliation with Svetlovo to divert his thoughts.

The day being clement, it was decided with only the gentlest prompting from Miss Smith, to set out directly after breakfast.

Annette, for all that she had been primed about the thrilling event awaiting her at home, could not forbear a pout as she listened to the Volnoya scheme. Lise hastily nudged her friend into recalling her rôle.

'Oh! Oh—er—Papa, will you excuse me from accompanying you? I—I believe I have the head ache coming on.'

'Eh? What's the matter with you? You look healthy enough to me. Eaten something, has she?'

'More than likely, sir. The *kuliebiaka* last night was perhaps a thought rich. I have already spoken to the cook,' lied Miss Smith. 'Annette shall have an infusion of camomile and a plain dinner and be right as rain on your return. The drive, however, might overset her digestion for several days.'

'You hear that, miss? And none of your sweet-nibbling between meals either, or this will not be the only young man you'll miss a sight of. Well, you'll excuse me now to see that my rascals have put some decent cattle between the shafts. Y'r servant, ladies.'

'I do not see why I should have to be afflicted with the stomach ache as well,' complained Annette as soon as the door had closed. 'And I really could wait till tomorrow to—'

'Tol-lol, Miss Contrary, but you will fidget yourself into a real head ache at this rate; and then you will look sickly and M. Charsky will not recognise his Anichka in you after all,' boomed Miss Smith.

D*   99

'But now you will favour me with your full attention. As you know, Annette, M. Charsky is even now setting out for Zacharovo. With love lending wings to his steed, or even at a mere gallop, he should be here well before noon. How you settle matters between you I leave to your romantic souls; but as soon as you have emerged from your raptures I beg you will despatch a note to Volnoya, simply informing the General that M. Charsky is here and asks to see him. Is that quite clear?'

The first fresh green was showing in the trees and meadows along their route.

Comparison of the shocking neglect of the roads obtaining in various European countries provided a ready theme for Miss Smith and the General. Lise asked for no other employment than to hang out of the window and exclaim over each landmark that brought them nearer to Volnoya.

Only once did her elders' conversation engage her attention. This came naturally enough at the mention of Sacha's name.

The General was recalling the days of his service under his great compatriot, General Kutuzov (for in military matters the General was staunchly Russian and held no brief for the German, Beningsen and the Scotsman, Barclay de Tolly, appointed by the Tsar to High Command).

'But mark my words, Miss Smith, we shall see the Grand Old Man back in the saddle if ever we find ourselves bang up against Bonaparte,' he growled. 'The best thing I know about young Arloff is that old One-Eye stood godfather to him—unofficially of course.'

'Oh?'

The General glanced at Lise and carefully lowered his parade ground voice to normal speaking tones.

'Yes; it came about because Kutuzov was a devoted admirer of *la belle* Hélène and a friend of Count Arloff since his Army days. You know the story of course?'

'In sum. *La petite*—' she nodded at Lise's back, 'made some mention of M. Sacha's irregular birth—as an accepted thing in high circles, I gather. And the housekeeper at Volnoya pointed out to me a magnificent Romney of his mother. This, I collect, would be "*la belle* Hélène"?'

'Lovely woman,' grunted the General, leaning back against the squabs.

He cast another wary eye at Lise, who glued herself to the window, and proceeded to regale Miss Smith with the whole scandalous story.

It was the first time Lise had heard it in full. And naturally the tale did nothing to dispel the halo of romance already glinting round Hélène's son's handsome head.

Despite six well-found horses, the progress of the lumbering barouche was slow; but at last the great lime avenue offered its prospect of the friendly, whitewashed house and overgrown lawns. A flock of plump geese scattered with outraged squawks before the horses. Lise could have embraced the feckless geese and the sprawling fruit trees and the rabble of rosy yard children who skipped unrebuked around the carriage; but instead she curtsied sedately enough to the owner of these delights, before he upset all decorum by swinging her high in his arms and declaring that she had grown at least an inch and sadly needed a new dress.

He himself, in country rig of russet grey coat, buckskins and mud-splashed top boots, with a carelessly knotted silk kerchief round his throat, looked no less elegant than in full regimentals. But he hastened to apologise for his attire, explaining with a speaking look at Miss Smith, that he had this moment come in from riding round the estate farms; had he but known of the honour of their visit, etc. etc.

This civility was at first lost on the General, who was still grappling with his host's extraordinary welcome to Mlle de Montargis. Miss Smith glowered at Sacha, and the General, recovering his manners, barked:

'No need to apologise, my boy, no need at all. Like to see a young feller taking an interest in his place. As for us, we're here on business. Mighty sad business too, my good Miss Smith tells me. Her trunk, you understand . . .'

- He trailed off, breathing heavily with the effort of pursuing two trains of thought at once.

'Upon my soul,' he burst out. 'It's beyond my understanding! Thought you first met Mlle de Montargis when you came to their rescue on the road? There's something havey-cavey here—unless it's Petersburg manners to make so free with young ladies after one meeting! In which case I take leave to inform you, sir—'

Lise turned scarlet. Miss Smith made a hasty move to intervene;

but Sacha, who had utterly forgotten the ins and outs of the con-spiracy when he greeted Lise, had been doing some extremely rapid thinking.

'General, you are right!' he cried. 'Your acumen makes all disguise useless. I see that there is nothing for it but to tell you the whole story and leave the verdict to your own rare discernment. Come, sir, allow me to escort the ladies and yourself where we may be comfortable, and then you shall judge the whole matter for yourself.'

All this, delivered in Sacha's most persuasive tone and with a gently propelling hand under the General's arm, had them installed in the sunlit drawing room with a glass of madeira at the General's elbow before he well knew what was happening. Finding himself somehow committed to hearing out the tale, the General made the best of it, drank his wine and growled to the effect that his young officers had always been able to rely upon a fair hearing from him.

'That is all I ask,' declared Sacha. 'Your health, sir!'

Lise took a nervous sip at her glass. Miss Smith drained hers like one whose health could have done with the toast. She caught Sacha's eye and turned her own up to heaven. He grinned wickedly.

'Well?' barked the General.

'Before I begin, sir, may I trespass further upon your good nature to ask your advice on a matter which your knowledge of affairs can best judge? This morning I have received a most impertinent communication from the Deputy-Governor, requiring an account of all horses and arms in my possession and a roster of all able-bodied men on the estate. Does the fool think I am going to start a revolt with my handful of peasants? Surely, sir, the fact of being exiled does not require me to put up with such indignity?'

Miss Smith looked her congratulations, since the diversion bril-liantly coupled the General's *bête noire,* the Deputy-Governor, with his other hobby-horse: the sacred rights of landowners. Miss Smith listened complacently to the General launch himself upon his favour-ite themes, punctuated every now and again by a lazy 'Indeed, sir!' from Sacha.

In a low voice she bade Lise touch the bell-pull. Danilo was also well used to tight corners. Correctly interpreting his master's signal of distress, he announced that a nuncheon was served whenever his honour was ready.

'*Zackouski* and vodka for His Excellency and your honour are waiting in the cabinet, sir.'

'They'll have to wait—unless of course. . . ?'

'Well, well, I daresay your tale won't sound any worse after a bite to eat,' conceded the General. 'You were used to keep a tolerable cook at Volnoya, as I recall.'

'Your memory is remarkable, sir and Anastasi's cooking has only improved with the years. Danilo, send Theodossia in to the ladies. This way, sir, if you please. Now, as you were saying about guard drill . . .'

The General's trenchant views on the subject died away down the corridor.

'Until now I have always deplored the Russian custom of leaving the men alone *before* dinner, so that they arrive at the table drunk instead of only leaving it in that condition,' remarked Miss Smith. 'However, in the present circumstances I begin to see some merit in it. But is it not somewhat unusual to indulge in this habit before a nuncheon?'

'Well, yes it is, ma'am; but I expect Sacha ordered the *zackouski* and vodka to try to put the General in a good humour for when the message from Annette arrives.'

'Hah! His complaisance is going to be needed earlier than that, thanks to M. Sacha's imprudence! He underestimates the General's persistence. Mark my words, we shall have the whole story out of the bag—when my entire strategy was based upon surprise and the argument of the *fait accompli*, whose power Bonaparte has demonstrated sufficiently, I hope, during the past twenty years!'

'Yes, ma'am,' agreed Lise with awe. 'But I am sure Sacha did not mean to cross you. I—I think he just forgot.'

'Forgot!' snorted Miss Smith. 'Forgot! Tell me,' she continued, watching the girl more narrowly than the case warranted. 'Is M. Sacha apt to forget any dependence placed upon him?'

Lise's chin came up.

'No, ma'am. It—it is just that he is a little careless.'

'And reckless and fickle and negligent—and always forgiven, eh?'

Lise glanced up in surprise at the gentle note in the booming voice, belying its words. Miss Smith's fine grey eyes stared past her with an abstracted look.

'As if you were speaking of someone else,' said Lise impulsively. 'Is he like Sacha? Are you very fond of him? Oh, I beg your pardon, ma'am. I did not mean to pry.'

'You're not prying and you are right. I was fond of him,' replied Miss Smith gruffly. 'And he was like Sacha—another of your gay blades who're no good to anyone. Ride straight, speak the truth and never show fear—that's all you can depend on 'em for. That and your life in a tight corner. Well, well, here is Theodossia. Since the men will be a good half hour over their vodka, I think I shall profit by it to inspect the state of my notebooks. Pray desire Theodossia to take us to them.'

On their way upstairs, the housekeeper was able to reassure them that young M. Charsky had set out for Zacharovo without even waiting for breakfast.

'In fact all would be going swimmingly if M. Sacha had not chosen to greet you as if he had known you since you were in leading reins,' grumbled Miss Smith.

'But he *has*, ma'am.'

'I beg you will not try my patience further, any of you, or I wash my hands of all your affairs!'

Liberal sampling of Volnoya's collection of vodkas brought the General to the nuncheon table less inclined to question his host's credentials. Miss Smith's notebooks occupied them through the meal. After it, the General bluffly announced his intention not to stand on ceremony with them but retire at once to the cabinet for his siesta. Sacha saw him comfortably bestowed, with a red silk handkerchief over his face, and waited for his guest's first snore before quietly letting himself out.

Another, more delicate snore from Miss Smith greeted him in the drawing room. Chuckling silently, he and Lise tiptoed out, and by common consent sought the sunshine on the river terrace.

'But it looks quite different now,' exclaimed Lise. 'Look, the blossom is already in bud on the cherry. Oh Sacha, may we perhaps walk down to the river?'

'All right, but the grass is a foot high, still wet, and you do not go without a shawl. Wait here, I'll have them find you one.'

He returned presently to wrap an exquisitely fine Kashmiri shawl around her. It smelt faintly of jasmine and of the sandalwood chest where it had lain. Lise smoothed it against her cheek, wondering whether it had last been worn round Hélène's lovely shoulders.

Their exchange of news brought them down to the river. Here, the ground beneath the high grass was indeed a morass underfoot and Sacha lifted her over it to the safety of a big fallen log which he bestrode casually beside her.

They fell silent, listening to the river. Presently the small creatures of the river bank, disturbed by their coming, again joined their soft chorus of chirps and twitters to the murmur of the water. A jewel-bright water-bird flew up out of the reeds immediately ahead of them and skimmed along the surface, flashing in the sun. Lise laughed with delight, and her laughter was the very sound of the glittering flight. Sacha smiled, ruffling her hair.

'No playing truant by the river when Miss Smith sets you to work, poppet. I only desire that I may not be roped in to the task! Up you come now. We shall pay a call on Galant, and then we must go back to support Miss Smith, lest the General awakes with new energy to resolving the mystery of our acquaintance. It was curst careless in me to forget that I am supposed never to have set eyes on you until my chivalrous rescue of two ladies in distress.'

'But Sacha, what are you going to tell him if he *does* return to it?'

'I have no idea. But—ah, trust the devil to look after his own! Here, if I am not mistaken, comes succour from Zacharovo. Volodya has made quick work of it with your Annette.'

A groom in the General's military livery was indeed dismounting in the stable yard. Sacha bore him back with them to the house and had him conducted to his master.

They had not long to contain their suspense in the drawing room. In a few minutes, rapid-fire footsteps sounded down the corridor and the General entered at a militant run, flourishing an opened letter in his hand and fairly bristling with surprise and suspicion.

'Odd! Most odd! Remarkable!' he ejaculated. 'Can't think what's possessed the feller! Listen to this, my boy. Here's my daughter sending to tell me that the old curmudgeon Charsky, after all these months at daggers drawn, has turned up at Zacharovo asking to see me! What d'ye make of it, eh? Eh, Miss Smith?'

'Impossible!' cried Miss Smith, fairly naturally. 'Pray let me see the letter, sir.'

She snatched it up, and there in black and white, in Annette's unformed hand, was the note of her own dictation—with one fatal omission. Either from natural folly or in the carelessness of rapture, Annette had simply written 'M. Charsky'—and the General had naturally jumped to the less unlikely conclusion of a visit from the father rather than an invasion by the outlawed son.

In the same bitter moment the impossibility of correcting his error was also borne upon Miss Smith. She turned a look of urgent appeal on Sacha, who appeared to be having some difficulty in keeping his countenance. Nevertheless he threw himself at once into the common task of getting the General to Zacharovo.

'You should go at once, sir! No need for an old neighbour to stand on ceremony at Volnoya,' he urged. 'But such a singular mark of M. Charsky's desire for reconciliation as to wait on you in person surely calls for a like response! Civility, generosity, the claims of your long friendship demand it! Permit me, sir, to send a fast rider to Zacharovo to say you are on your way.' He reached unobtrusively for the bell-pull. 'Miss Smith, do you not endorse this view? Ah, she is already off to write a note to Zacharovo for you, sir. Danilo, have my groom saddle immediately and send in a tray of meats. His Excellency has to be on the road in half an hour.'

'But—I—damme, I haven't yet decided whether I want to see the feller—!'

'Oh, but sir, think how cast down M. Charsky must have been at finding you from home, when *he* has swallowed his pride to come to you!' cried Lise, joining in the crusade. 'And think of poor Annette near distracted with wondering if she has done right to admit him!'

'Admit him? My oldest friend? I'd take a whip to the chit if she'd had him turned away from my door! Of course she did right!'

'Of course, sir,' soothed Sacha. 'I knew your understanding would go to the root of the matter. Depend upon it, Mlle Mirnoff will have done everything that is proper, pending your return. Now if you will excuse me—?'

Miss Smith met him crossing the hall and after one glance at each other, both dissolved into helpless laughter.

'But I believe we may yet save the day,' gasped Sacha, wiping his eyes. 'I have left Lise nobly holding the fort; but you'd best go back, ma'am, to see that he does not weaken, while I get off a groom with your note. I wish I might be there to see *mon général*'s face when he is confronted with Volodya and his daughter locked in each other's arms, instead of his old friend come to make amends.'

'I will engage to describe the full disaster to you tomorrow,' promised Miss Smith grimly. 'That is, if you are prepared to have us back?'

'The house is yours, ma'am, for as long as you wish. No hospitality could repay my obligation to you.'

'H'mm. I'll cut our stay as short as possible, for the child's sake—but we will not enlarge on that now. Here is the note for Annette.'

'I'll get the man off and order your carriage. There's some goodish claret coming up to the drawing room, ma'am.'

When he returned, Lise and Miss Smith were descending the staircase into the hall, dressed for their journey. Sacha detained them for a moment, saying plaintively:

'By the by, ma'am, to save me from committing any more gaffes, will you tell me now just what is supposed to be our footing when I next see you both? Just in case the General is again in attendance.'

'I propose to tell him the truth, as ever,' replied Miss Smith blandly. 'But it will require to be adjusted to his understanding. So I think it will be as well if Lise is at least a distant cousin of yours, and I had better be her aunt. A family party at Volnoya will in any case be more generally acceptable. You may call me Aunt Hon, child, as my nephew is used to.'

'The one who climbed the tower, ma'am?—I mean, Aunt Hon? Shall I meet him in England?'

'No,' said Miss Smith fiercely. 'Not the one who climbed the tower. That gay lad was first up the walls of Badajoz, from which only a handful of his regiment returned. So it is his brother who now . . . lives in the house with the tower. As to meeting him, I daresay you will, for what that's worth.'

She stalked off. Lise and Sacha exchanged glances. But they had little time to puzzle over the hints of mystery attaching to Miss Smith's life in England. With the promise of an early engagement for dinner, the Zacharovo party was off at a gallop to the cheers of the yard children.

Sacha turned back into the house. But for some reason he could not settle either to his dinner or his book. Postponing the one and throwing down the other, he went out into the gathering dusk and again made his way down the lawns to the river.

A light rain was falling. He splashed up to his knees in mud and the river breeze shook cold wet flurries down his neck from the trees. He turned up his collar and stood staring across the darkening water. To someone invisible he said grimly: 'For the child's sake, eh?'

Then he laughed and went back to the house to take a hot bath and do full justice to Anastasi's cooking and the claret.

CHAPTER XVIII

'But I still fail to see why you cannot have all the notebooks and stuff transported from Volnoya and do your copying or whatever here,' complained the General to Miss Smith for the fourth time, since the augmented house party at Zacharovo had sat down to breakfast.

For her part, she had even forgiven old M. Charsky the ill-timed access of sentiment which had smitten him after her visit and sent him hotfoot to Zacharovo to bury the hatchet with his old friend.

The discovery of his estranged son already in possession of the citadel, with the bride he had scorned firmly clasped in his arms, and then the shock of learning that she was the peasant Anichka when in fact he knew her very well to be the daughter of the house, had for a time seriously threatened to unseat his reason. The happy pair had been in no state to furnish him with a rational explanation and complete confusion had reigned. Fortunately the manifest advantages of the situation were soon uppermost with all three. By the time the Volnoya party returned, the future was their prime object, with young Charsky declaring himself happy to lay aside brigandage for his Anichka's sake, his father happily prophesying woe to come when such a flighty pair set up house-keeping, and Annette engrossed in her trousseau.

Toying with her second helping of smoked ham, Miss Smith glanced round the faces at the breakfast table and mused again on the power of the Napoleonic *fait accompli*. The General and M. Charsky had been no more proof against it than the crowned heads of Europe. Had she been inclined to vanity, she could have been gratifying it now with the fact that the General was willing to swallow all of it except her removal from Zacharovo. To this he had objected with all the force of some fifty years of autocratic rule; and to it he kept returning with the booming monotony of a battle-ship going down with one gun still firing. Miss Smith sighed.

'But my dear sir, we are agreed that I have already shamelessly imposed upon you with my masquerade as your tutor. I could not in conscience encroach further upon your hospitality now that—'

'Not at all. Happy to have you stay a twelvemonth,' boomed the minute gun.

'—now that I have accomplished my mission here, which must be the excuse for my imposture. Moreover, M. Arloff is naturally anxious to have his young relative back under his roof and—'

'. . . not *his* aunt.'

'—and Mlle de Montargis obviously cannot dispense with my chaperonage. It is my hope that Annette may spare time from her trousseau to cheer Lise and myself at our labours. And of course you yourself, sir, would be the most welcome of—'

'Well, it is true I am engaged to dine at Volnoya,' admitted the General irritably. 'But that is not to the purpose. The point is that I cannot see why your notebooks and stuff should not be brought to you and you do your copying or whatever *here* . . .'

Miss Smith closed her eyes. Annette emerged from her blissful daze to say:

'But dear papa, will you not in any case be off to Smolensk with papa Charsky to see the Deputy-Governor about . . .' She made expressive eyes at her bridegroom to indicate the delicate object of their mission.

'Eh?' barked the General. 'Ah yes, to be sure. The chit's right, Alexei Ivanitch, you and I will have to put our heads together and our hands in our pockets, I'll be bound, before this rascal of yours can show his face in the neighbourhood again. A good thing we've both got long heads and long pockets, eh?'

'Papa, please!' begged Annette, noting her beloved's smouldering look.

'I am not a schoolboy caught robbing an orchard, sir!' announced Vladimir with awful dignity. 'The fat purses I took went to the poor, and I'm damned if I'll skulk here whilst the pair of you—'

'You'll do as you're bid, sir, and keep a civil tongue in your head to your elders!' yelped his father. 'As if it were not disgrace enough—'

'Papa Charsky, *please*—'

'. . . licking the Deputy-Governor's boots and oiling palms. I'd rather—'

'What's this? You young puppy, have you the impudence to—'

'Damned if I'll have my daughter—'

'Papa, *please*—!'

'Silence!' roared Miss Smith.

When it was achieved she said severely:

'I do not know which to deplore most—your want of conduct, young man, or your father's want of sense, not to speak of your future father-in-law's crotchets! Heaven preserve me from the Slavonic temperament! General, when you and M. Charsky are open to rational advice, I shall be pleased to proffer you some in the schoolroom. Annette, your papa will excuse you if you remove your firebrand now. Lise, you may accompany me to order our packing.'

'Oh, I am so happy, so happy, so happy!' carolled Lise, 'Here I am at Volnoya, Volnoya, Volnoya, we're going to stay at Volnoya and no one's ever been so happy in the world!'

'Has the child entirely taken leave of her senses?' demanded Sacha. 'Take care, you whirling dervish, or you'll knock into the furniture.'

'No I won't, not at Volnoya! Oh, Sacha, can I have my former room? Can I come with you to see Galant tomorrow? May we take a boat on the river? Imagine, Danilo actually said he was pleased to see me again! Oh, Aunt Hon, is it not wonderful to be back? Oh, you are all so good to me!'

Miss Smith received the whirling dervish full-tilt into her ample embrace and held her close, thinking about the girl's cold, unloved childhood in the great mansion in Petersburg. No one to run to with joys or tears, she thought; a spoilt brat for company and a gazetted rake to worship as a beau ideal of all the virtues! She met the unsuitable idol's eyes over Lise's bobbing head. He gave a faint, rueful shrug and turned on his heel, saying carelessly:

'You'll have to obtain your Aunt Hon's indulgence if we are to fulfil this programme of pleasure, poppet. I thought you were bent on salvaging her life-work?'

'Oh!' cried Lise, stepping back with stricken eyes. 'Oh ma'am, I did not mean . . . pray let us go up at once and make a start on your notebooks.'

Miss Smith had had every intention of resting comfortably in her room with a book until dinner; but Sacha's moody look had to be taken into account.

'Tol-lol, tomorrow will be soon enough,' she said easily. 'But you may come up with me now to hear all about my plans for Annette and Charsky.'

Lise's delight in being restored to Volnoya was not easily clouded. But as the weeks went by it became increasingly plain how ill its placidity accorded with Sacha's restless temper.

'You are drinking too much,' Miss Smith told him bluntly. 'I warned you that exile was hard on your kind; you are doing your best to make it harder. The estate runs itself under Ahripoff. Get yourself something to do.'

'What would you suggest, ma'am? A course as a copyist with you? Or should I try my hand at running a private peasant army like the General?'

'You could do worse than either,' snapped Miss Smith. 'In fact you *are* doing worse. And do not be too quick to sneer at our friend's eccentric hobby; Russia may well need even her peasants in arms if Bonaparte moves against you in force.'

'*Guerilleros*—like your Wellington is using in Spain?' asked Sacha, with the first gleam of interest in his eyes she had seen there for weeks. 'But it's a far cry from the Sierras to the Pripet marshes, ma'am. Our serfs are not bred to think—or fight.'

'They are born *men*, which you seem to forget in Russia! And I was not speaking of the Pripet marshes. Your German generals will engage Boney *there*—probably with as much success as they had at Austerlitz! And then you will have only your steppes and your peasants against the might of the *Grande Armée*.'

'No, ma'am. We shall still have the man who can save Russia if the Tsar will let him: Kutuzov.'

'Your unofficial godfather?'

'The unofficial godfather of every officer in the Army with a head to think beyond parade drill and dressage! Our present covey of Germans at Headquarters are past-masters at manoeuvring troops—for Reviews! But when it comes to . . . Well, I must not bore you with my Hussar "shop".'

'I am not bored.'

'I am though; especially just after I've lapsed into forgetting that it is no longer *my* "shop". Bored enough to wish that I had let Lise inveigle me into her harebrained escape plan.'

'I beg you will not tell her so! Her devotion to your interests will instantly set her to devise another.'

'God forbid. Be easy on that score, ma'am. I am maturing my own plans in that direction.'

'In your cups?'

'I admit my plan looks better in the evenings. But it is not very heroic. I had it in mind to turn up at my godfather's Headquarters in Besarabia and beg his influence to let me enlist in the ranks of his army against the Turks. Between them he and my father might persuade the Tsar to condone it. In my sober moments, I agree that it might be as well to write to my godfather first.'

'At least promise me that!' broke from Miss Smith before she could stop herself. Then she compressed her lips and swallowed various manifest objections to the scheme. Instead she said lightly:

'Well, now you can expand the scope of your letter to mention your alternate intention of training a force of *guerilleros* on the estate. I'll wager it will interest him more than the other.'

'Taken. Your stake, ma'am?'

'A new dress for Lise. Like this she will get it either way.'

'No bet; for it is a great deal too bad to make the child wait so long. I've been meaning to do it this age. I shall send Danilo into Mogilev tomorrow to buy her a whole new set of furbelows.'

It was typical of Sacha that having bethought him at last of Lise's wardrobe it became an object with him to furnish it with all speed and style. Danilo was despatched at dawn next morning, provided with a fat purse and strictly enjoined to remember that this time he was outfitting a respectable female. He also carried Sacha's letter to General Kutuzov.

Miss Smith waylaid Sacha after breakfast. He was considerably put out when she insisted upon reimbursing him in full for the sum laid out to Danilo. Sacha had never enquired into Miss Smith's finances and he wondered uneasily whether he had committed her on a scale beyond her means. But it was done, with his usual carelessness; and now he could not but yield to the force of Miss Smith's strictures on the impropriety of his paying for Lise's dressing.

In the event, he need not have worried. Miss Smith had no notion whatever of the price of clothing, regarding it as a boring necessity to be renewed once a year from Saul and Wesson, where they had kept a *toile* of her habit for thirty-five years and had not yet sent in their bill.

It was not to be expected that a mind of so lofty an order could enter into Lise's feelings over the long-delayed replenishment of her wardrobe. She went quite pink with pleasure and excitement. A whole new set of dresses! Ribbons galore! Shawls, bonnets, hats, petticoats, shoes, chemises, gloves, stockings . . .

Miss Smith let her chatter on, allowing the drawing she was tracing to lie idle on the table before her, while she herself, equally idle, considered the problem of Sacha.

To depart, leaving him to ruin himself with his wild scheme of escape or to drink himself to death with boredom, was equally unthinkable. Yet how to prevent either, when it lacked only a se'nnight at most to see her work finished and him left to his own dangerous devices? Miss Smith gave a snort of exasperation. Between the folly of the child opposite and the vagaries of her would-be ravisher, she herself was in a fair way to be saddled for life with their problems. The snort brought Lise back to attention with a guilty start.

'I'm sorry, Aunt Hon, I'll get on with the tracing.'

'Take your time, child,' said Miss Smith absently, preoccupied with grand strategy.

First, being a realist, she acknowledged her personal surrender. She *was* prepared to turn her life upside down for the chance-met, ill-assorted pair of them. Doubtless she would not have been so ready if a gay lad had not been first up the bloodstained walls of Badajoz. But there was no denying that Lise and Sacha had come to fill the empty place he had left in her heart. Both of them equally. Which brought her back to the present dilemma : Sacha's immediate need of distraction and his long-term need of conformable occupation, if he was to endure his exile.

Well, the immediate distraction was certainly at hand; needing only a word to run to provide her idol with her engaging companion- ship. And perhaps the long-term occupation could arise out of the gleam of interest in Sacha's eyes over the *guerilleros*? If she won her wager on General Kutuzov's good sense, it could yet push his godson into the scheme; and then she could leave for England with a quiet mind. All of which meant extending their stay, and for this her notebooks provided an ever-ready excuse. With another, valedictory snort, Miss Smith rose to launch Sacha's reclamation.

'The ink deteriorates every day, or my eyesight is doing so! I believe I must start to dictate you many passages from memory, Lise. It may take many more weeks; but *festina lente*, as with all scientific method.'

As Miss Smith suspected, Lise had never heard of Suetonius or scientific method; but from then on she was prepared to be their staunchest adherent.

'There will be no need for you to attend me while I make my first notes, dear child. You have been the most faithful of amanuenses, but now you must get outdoors and put some roses back in your cheeks. Starting today.'

'You are really, truly sure I cannot be of use to you, Aunt Hon?'

'Just now you'll be of far more use to me out in the garden,' observed her Aunt Hon after a glance out of the window. 'Be off with you.'

Sacha broke off his conference with the ancient who ruled—or rather, misruled—the Volnoya gardens, and came across the lawns to meet Lise when she appeared on the terrace.

'What's this, poppet? Playing truant?'

Lise explained the new, scientific method of working; and Miss Smith, watching them set off for the river, had the satisfaction of knowing Sacha provided with a distraction for the rest of the afternoon. She was taking a risk, but it was a nicely calculated risk; for she rightly defined Sacha's present craving to be for company, amusement, occupation, rather than love. And she shrewdly guessed him to be neither too old nor too dissolute to throw himself whole-heartedly into the country joys he opened to his little companion.

Spring had come with a rush of warmth and abundance. The newly green branches formed a sun-dappled canopy over the grass rides in the woods. 'Listen,' Lise would command, reining in the skittering little blood-mare Sacha had acquired for her use. 'Just listen to everything growing!'

She had never seen a country spring before, since the Countess always spent the season in Petersburg; but no spring could ever have been like this one. And no birdsong could ever have trilled with such sweetness as the dawn chorus under her window when it was joined by a low whistle and Sacha's enquiry whether she meant to lie abed all day?

Miss Smith watched them both with demure satisfaction. The

evenings still presented a certain problem; but even there the activity
of the day advanced the claims of healthy fatigue against any exten-
sive brooding over the brandy decanter. She herself began to take
longer and longer over the scientific method. As the days grew really
warm, she discovered that it could be practised just as effectively out
of doors on the terrace; and, after nuncheon, frequently with the
eyes closed.

Lise's pale skin acquired a light powdering of freckles and warmed
to a colour Sacha defined as brown country egg.

Annette, descending upon them in a whirl of trousseau planning,
exclaimed in dismay over her friend's ruined complexion and coun-
selled nightly applications of strawberries, and a parasol at all times.

'She'd look a sketch trying to steer the boat with a parasol clutched
like a sail,' remarked Sacha, raising himself lazily up on his elbow
from the cushions where he lounged on the grass. 'And I will not
dispense with my helmsman, since it enables me to lie back and
think great thoughts.'

'Well, at least she could be permitted to wear a sun-bonnet I
suppose, if you must use her as a galley-slave!' exclaimed Annette
indignantly.

Like most of the neighbourhood, she had quite got over her first
romantic conjectures about Lise and her host. Miss Smith's presence
and Sacha's own attitude to his 'young relative' discouraged all but
the most determined gossips. So the young ladies of the district,
deprived of Vladimir Charsky, were free to sigh over Sacha Arloff
all they pleased, and agree among themselves that in Lise's shoes
they would be making more of her opportunities.

Fortunately for the conspirators, Annette's bridegroom had not
yet managed to stem her flow of chatter for long enough to satisfy
her curiosity about his first encounter with Lise and Miss Smith.
He himself was now fully restored to society and eligibility. He sat
on the grass beside Annette's chair, gazing up adoringly at his pink
and white darling as she debated the rival merits of a chip bonnet
against a leghorn straw for keeping the sun at bay.

Lise hung her head, touched at the still sore spot of her wardrobe.
She was able to forget about it for days at a time now, but the
evening of Danilo's return from Mogilev would always rank as
one of the most dismal in her sixteen years.

There had been all the excitement of untying and unwrapping her new possessions from their layers of silk paper. And then, one by one, they began to emerge . . . Somehow Lise had swallowed her tears and remembered her manners for long enough to thank Aunt Hon for her new clothes. Then she had begged her Aunt's permission to retire and had fled upstairs to weep as one can only weep at sixteen over a wardrobe of purple crape.

Sacha's taste in dress had been formed by some of the most elegant females in Petersburg, respectable and otherwise. The first time Lise had worn one of her purple dresses he had stared and begged to know whether she was setting up as a dowager? As this took place in Miss Smith's presence, Lise had stoutly declared herself delighted with her aunt's choice; and Sacha, for all his irreverence, was far too well-bred not to recognise her obligation to be pleased—once he was reminded of it.

Good manners also prevented Annette from questioning her friend's strange taste in dress. Out of the generosity engendered by the possession of a brand new trousseau, Annette determined to present Lise with a conformable gown in which to attend her wedding.

For Annette to think a thing was to say it. She jumped up and drew Lise to her feet, passing an arm round her waist.

'Dear creature, I have had such a famous notion! Oh, but here come papa and Miss Smith. Be sure to remind me to tell you later. Why, papa, what have you and Miss Smith been doing to yourselves?'

The source of her astonishment was easily traceable to the Volnoya cherry trees, just on the turn of their brief flowering, after a vintage year. Drifts of their blossom lay underfoot and wafted across the lawns on each stir of the breeze. Miss Smith and her escort had been strolling under their shade and a sportive zephyr had crowned both of them with a rich powdering of pink and white petals.

'For all the world like wedding crowns!' exclaimed Annette. She gave a crow of laughter. 'Oh, would it not be a good joke if . . .'

Miss Smith said composedly:

'Impertinence belongs in the schoolroom, dear child, where it can be fittingly corrected. You cannot wish Vladimir to be put to the blush by the tone of his wife's mind.'

Annette retired, suitably crushed; but not before the whole party had observed that it was not M. Charsky but the General who was blushing. He gave vent to some indefinable growls, breathing heavily. Then he brushed his sparse hair free of the offending petals and barked:

'Place is going to ruin, Arloff! The plantations have not been thinned in years, I daresay, and as for the hothouses—'

'They are more like a jungle are they not, sir? Lise and I have had some splendid sport cutting our way through the undergrowth when she had a fancy to taste the peaches. But I believe I shall keep the plantations to their present wildness. Their condition should provide an excellent terrain when I start the training of my recruits. I had just begun outlining my scheme of raising a company of irregulars to Volodya. I should be honoured to have your opinion of it.'

'Eh? What's this? Recruiting? In *your* situation? Well, if that don't beat the band for effrontery! Come and sit down and tell me all about it, my boy. The ladies will excuse us for a while.'

The *young* ladies were happy to do so, perceiving little to interest them in the scheme. Miss Smith, watching Sacha with narrowed eyes, said sharply:

'So I have won my wager on your godfather's interest?'

'Handsomely, ma'am. And now you may remind me that we neglected to fix *my* stake, so little did I expect to lose! So you now have *carte blanche*.'

CHAPTER XIX

The payment of Sacha's gaming debt remained a standing joke between him and the lady he termed his 'honorary Aunt Hon' but the project which had occasioned the wager advanced apace. Miss Smith preened herself as she watched the formation of his Volnoya Irregulars absorb more and more of the exile's unwanted time and attention. And as word of it spread, several of the more dashing young blades of the province, summering in the country with their families, neglected their prime duty of falling in love with the local young ladies in favour of spending days and nights at a time as volunteers at Volnoya.

Rumour of their mysterious activity there duly reached the Deputy-Governor, who fell upon it, convinced that the subversive tendencies he had noted in young Arloff were now erupting into militant political conspiracy. His Excellency laid his plans carefully and no more than half the villages en route knew of his proposed surprise descent on Volnoya.

Reinforced by his escort of militia, he galloped up the lime avenue in fine style and burst upon the lawns—to find Miss Smith instructing a dozen mettlesome young Russians and some thirty of their stout serfs in the rudiments of the English game of cricket.

It was a peaceful scene. The brilliant July day was hot without being oppressive. Some rustic seats under the shade of a spreading oak served as the pavilion, where Lise and Annette presided over a table of cool drinks for the gentlemen, while several rosy maids supplied foaming tankards of kvass and homebrewed to the thirst of the 'players'.

Only Miss Smith was aware of the suspicious discrepancy in the number of the cricketers; but the Deputy-Governor, though unversed in foreign sports, still viewed the scene with rightful suspicion and demanded furiously to know what was going on.

Noting Sacha's dangerous look, Miss Smith, grown suddenly obtuse and garrulous, took this as an invitation to initiate His Excellency into the mysteries of cricket. She expounded them at length, resisting all attempts at interruption and ending with a homily upon the virtues of keeping a straight bat. By now, her team of young gentlemen were almost openly applauding. Sacha, sufficiently cooled to relish the absurdity of the situation, drawled:

'Had Your Excellency apprised me of your coming, I would have made sure of having my gyves upon my wrists as well as these cricket pads on my legs. Your Excellency is come to make another convert to England's national sport?'

'You may take it that my errand is not one of pleasure!' snarled the Deputy, wishing that he had not dismounted.

It placed him under a double disadvantage. A small man in every respect, he had rashly resolved to recoup his complaisance over young Charsky by ignoring all worldly considerations in his treatment of Count Arloff's delinquent son. Now he found himself envisaging all kinds of uncomfortable consequences—and perceiving immediate danger in the contemptuous dark-blue eyes a good twelve inches above him.

'I—I would have you know that I am here on a serious matter—' he began.

'Then, my dear sir, you cannot do better than to join in our game. No one playing it for five minutes could doubt that cricket is a serious business. I am sure that Miss Smith—'

'You are pleased to be insolent, sir—which you may live to regret when the Tsar-Emperor sees my report! And I should be failing in my duty if I did not warn all here—' the Deputy raised his somewhat piping voice '—that their consorting with an exiled subversive does not go unnoticed. It may entail serious consequences, very serious consequences indeed, to their own future! I bid you good day, gentlemen. And you, madam, will have the goodness to accompany me into the house and show me your papers.'

Sacha whitened under his tan.

'You will cross the threshold of my house uninvited at your peril.'

'The terms of your sentence license the authorities to inspect—'

'Move just one step—'

'Help!' shrieked Lise.

Everyone, including the Deputy's escort, who had edged their horses closer, swung round. Sacha leapt across to the tree. Miss Smith prayed that her inspiration would not desert the child.

'Sacha! Aunt Hon! Help!' wailed Lise like a banshee. 'Oh, I—I have been stung! Help!'

'Where? Show me. What was it, a wasp?' demanded Sacha, clasping the capering sufferer.

'No, a—a huge bee! Oh Sacha—!'

'Hush, easy now, poppet, easy now. Show me the bite.'

'Oh! Oh! AwoooO!'

'Dear child—give her to me if you please, Sacha. There, my love, there. It stung you inside your dress, did it not? I thought so. Come, let me get you into the house and we shall have you to rights in no time. Your Excellency will excuse me while I attend to my niece? I shall not keep you above an hour, if you would care to wait?'

But the anti-climax was too much for the Deputy. Darkly enjoining everyone present to watch what they did, he mustered his force and departed in fairly good order.

Miss Smith and Annette tenderly supported Lise into the hall, where Miss Smith abruptly withdrew her arm and darted to a window to watch out the Deputy's departure. Then, to Annette's bewilderment, she collapsed into the nearest chair and laughed till she cried.

Lise ran to her, crying: 'He's really gone, ma'am?' Obtaining a choked affirmative, she whirled round Annette in a dance of triumph as Sacha strode in from the garden.

'What in God's name—?' he demanded.

'They've both run mad!' wailed Annette.

Sacha looked from Lise to the whooping Miss Smith and completed Annette's confusion by promptly joining them in their inexplicable mirth.

'I could not have done it better myself!' Miss Smith gasped. 'Masterly, dear child, masterly.'

She cast a wary eye at Sacha and saw that it was now safe to tease him.

'I verily thought you were about to run him through with your cricket bat, dear boy.'

'So I was like to do; though not with a cricket bat,' he responded grimly. 'But for mademoiselle's *tour de force* . . . Poppet, from now on you are appointed an honorary ensign of the Volnoya Irregulars. Come on outside and be toasted by your regiment in the claret cup.'

'But I still do not understand,' bleated Annette. 'Did Lise not get stung by *anything*?'

'Charsky shall explain it all to you, dear,' Miss Smith told her. 'Now you may go outside with your friend. Half a glass only, I beg you, Sacha; our heroine is already dizzy with excitement alone.'

She rose, 'I shall compose my spirits with a little work, I believe. You stay to dine with us, Annette? I shall see you all then.'

But she had barely settled herself to her notebooks upstairs when Sacha strolled in, after a perfunctory knock.

He swept a corner of the table clear of papers and lounged against it, looking down at her.

'So Lise too has appointed herself my watch-dog, ma'am,' he said silkily. 'May I know whether her dramatic intervention was agreed between you?'

'Not a bit of it, dear boy. Pure inspiration,' boomed Miss Smith genially, choosing to ignore the storm warnings.

'Then I should be obliged to you both—'

'You have reason to be so! I tell you to your head that black temper of yours needs curb and bridle if you're to ride out your misfortune! And kicking against the pricks is the most futile of all. What can it profit you to set the whole pack of these local bumblers by the ears?'

'Pure amusement,' he retorted coolly. 'Exiles must find distraction where they can, you know! But I beg you will not make a piece of work of it, ma'am' he went on in a more rational tone. 'The Deputy is nothing but a jack-in-office, puffing himself while he may until the Governor returns. And if I know anything of Prince Ulanoff, he will soon send him to the rightabout.'

'I wish I may be sure of it! What sort of man is the Prince? I collect you have met him?'

'Any time these past twenty years—without ever suspecting that my comfort would one day depend on him! He is an old acquaintance of my father's; very rich and, as he puts it himself, "a monument to a mis-spent life", being a martyr to gout and dyspepsia. And now I come to think of it, we shall have something in common apart from our penchant for brandy; our taste in women. Ulanoff, for all his grey hairs, was an assiduous member of Nina's court.'

Miss Smith started. Sacha had never referred to the Princess Nina. The full tale of his attachment she had had from Lise. Well, Sacha Arloff was demonstrably not a man to wear the willow for any woman. But if this Nina still attached him—and there was no one as faithful in his fashion as a rake—then it would explain why Lise could touch everything but his heart.

'The Prince was your rival there?' she asked, feeling her way.

'Hardly that. More the sort of elderly admirer who is a required appendage to a gazetted beauty. My Nina knows what is due to her position! So you see, the Governor and I should deal famously together.'

Such easy optimism was not for Miss Smith. But the authorities seemed in no hurry to cross swords again with their dangerous charge. As the weeks went by, her vigilance relaxed and the sight of horsemen or an equipage sweeping up the lime avenue no longer caused her any qualms, even when these arrived in the thick of one of Sacha's more spectacular manoeuvres of his troop.

The Volnoya Irregulars had grown into a tight-knit, resourceful fighting force; loosely disciplined, and, to the General's sorrow, lacking any pretention to parade ground smartness, but up to every trick and skill of the fighting Sacha was training them for. It was a proud night for Sacha—if something else to his startled ladies—when a newly recruited cadre 'ambushed' the chaise, postillions and all, without a sound, on their return journey from attending Annette's wedding ball at Zacharovo.

Next morning, Miss Smith lay in bed sipping her chocolate and tenderly feeling the bruises where she had been bumped by the ambushed carriage. She told herself sternly that it was high time to review the whole situation; a resolve formed regularly every week for the past two months.

She gave her night-cap an admonitory tug and settled more comfortably on her pillows. The action brought into view the balmy prospect of Volnoya woods in the faint heat-haze of a perfect August morning. Miss Smith emitted a small snort of content. But now, out of the corner of her eye, she could also see a portion of the night-table beside her, and on it the cause of all her procrastination.

It looked innocuous enough: a well-thumbed copybook, with a row of sharpened pencils beside the burnt-out candle. But Miss Smith knew it now for her Downfall.

How innocently it had started! She could pinpoint the very day when, tempted by the fine morning, she had decided that the Smith version of the scientific method might just as well be practised in the sunshine of the terrace. A cushioned cane chair had been placed for her. Her writing and drawing implements had been laid out on the low table; a bowl of Volnoya's rosy-white cherries waited beside her for refreshment during her labours. Lise and Sacha had tiptoed past her to the waiting horses. The maids had been sternly enjoined not to shake anything out of the windows on that side of the house. The yard children had been shoo'ed away. An untimely cricket had ceased in mid-whirr. The perfect peace of a writer's dreams had enwrapped Volnoya.

Her pen had flown.

No galloping fever could have advanced on its victim more swiftly than the fatal facility which, from that day on, drove Miss Smith to cover page after virgin page with her forceful script. By the end of that week there could no longer be any doubt: Miss Smith had been well and truly bitten by the writer's bug.

Coy visions of The Book began to tease her imagination. She could see it plain: a modest volume in sober mottled board covers, simply entitled 'A Traveller's Journal. The Record of. . . .' And there of course had lain the second snare; for why confine it to the record of her year in Russia, when all the untapped riches of her other travels lay waiting to be explored?

On the morning after Annette's wedding ball, as she lay in bed reviewing the situation, Miss Smith's pen was still in Russia; but the story of her adventures there had already been placed within the framework of the grand design which she now envisaged for the whole book.

Her gradual immersion in it had come to be accepted by Lise and Sacha as tacitly as it had absorbed herself. *He* was too preoccupied with his own ploy to refine on it; Lise was too accustomed to grown-up vagaries and only too happy to lend herself to any device for extending their stay at Volnoya.

To make a piece of work over stretching it a trifle further, to cover the month or so needed to complete her Russian chapters, seemed mere quibbling. But *could* it be August already? Waking to day after perfect, cloudless day, it seemed as if time as well as weather had stood still. How much she was going to miss this strange, enchanted life at Volnoya! Nevertheless she determined that Lise should write to her mother that very day to put a period to it.

E

CHAPTER XX

The excitement of Annette's wedding and her removal from Zacharovo left the General sadly at a loss to occupy his time.

He considered driving over to Svetlovo or Volnoya, but the Job's comfort he would find at the former and his friend's curst scribbling at the latter deterred him. Besides, more than an afternoon's or even an overnight absence was needed to see his household back to its decorous routine. He had reached the stables in his aimless promenade when the happy notion struck him to spend a few days in Smolensk, choosing the phaeton he had promised Annette for her bride gift.

No business could have occupied him more pleasantly for the next six days. Moreover, the happy accident of his presence in Smolensk enabled him to be among the first of the local gentry to wait on the Governor, at last returned from his travels, and certainly to be the first to bring back to all the neighbourhood the surprising news of His Excellency's marriage.

The General's first call was at Volnoya. The ladies were as interested as he could wish in his choice of Annette's equipage, and they quite startled him by their reception of his other news—when he mentioned the name of the Governor's bride.

It was out of his power to surprise Sacha with it. Prince Adam, Major Lavrin and several other friends, as well as the Countess, had already written to inform him of the Princess Nina's marriage; and for the past four days it had been his study to keep the news from showing on his face. The only particular Sacha did not know until the General's coming was that the new Princess Ulanoff had waived any honeymoon voyage, insisting, to her husband's surprise, upon the claims of his Governor's duties to require their immediate removal to Dubrovnoye, his estate in the province which lay within only three hours' hard riding from Volnoya.

Lise and Miss Smith discussed the news far into the night in the latter's bedchamber, lowering their voices, mindful of the glowing end of Sacha's cigar still visible below on his endless pacing to and fro along the terrace.

Both ladies woke and went down to breakfast in the liveliest appre-hension of Sacha's mood. He appeared, however, his normal self, made no reference to the shattering news and proposed a river pique-nique to dispel the head ache Lise confessed to as the cause of her lowered spirits.

This precarious complaisance lasted until the evening. Lise dis-pensed tea on the terrace, as had become their custom during the very hot weather. Sacha joined the ladies earlier than was usual. He accepted a glass of tea and pronounced Lise to be looking more pros-perous. Miss Smith sought his help over a puzzling Kurdish custom in her notes, and was reminded by it of a deplorable marital habit obtaining among the hill tribes of Kabul. Sacha laughed heartily at the story. The crickets' evening concert got into its swing. Lise leant back with a sigh of content, feeling Volnoya restored to its serenity.

Her relief was shortlived. Danilo was crossing the terrace with a hurried tread and bearing a sealed letter on a salver.

'A special courier from the Governor at Dubrovnoye, your honour.'

Sacha put out a hand for the letter. The candlelight showed Lise his suddenly still face as he saw the superscription. He remained for a moment motionless. Then, with a violent movement, he pushed back his chair and without a word strode off into the house, carrying the unopened letter in his clenched hand. The three on the terrace held their breath, as if anticipating a sequel. It came with dramatic apt-ness in a flash of summer lightning in the sky accompanied by two shattering crashes inside the house, which just forestalled the subse-quent clap of thunder.

'A fairly heavy vase, I think,' said Miss Smith. 'And I would not vouch for the hinges of the cabinet door. Perhaps you had better bespeak the carpenter for tomorrow, Danilo.'

'We'll be lucky if there's no more to mend than that, ma'am,' res-ponded Danilo darkly with the voice of experience.

By the following afternoon Sacha felt the need of company, and the young gentlemen of the Volnoya Irregulars were all too ready to hand. Sacha's version of their manoeuvres for that evening revived the ancient Cossack custom of leaping their outraged horses over a deepish gorge on the outskirts of Volnoya woods. Few of them would have attempted it sober; mercifully all of them negotiated it

safely drunk. Sacha therefore presently pronounced this hazard too
tame for sport, and ordered a large bonfire to be kindled on the lawn
before the house. None of the young gentlemen or their mounts
cared to follow Galant over the flames, and Miss Smith arrived in
time to prevent the conflagration from spreading to the house.

Being then privileged to overhear Sacha's plans for their further
entertainment, Miss Smith quickly returned indoors, locked Lise in
her room and herself retired to bed with both ears plugged with
wadding. Early next morning she ordered the curricle to convey her
and Lise to Svetlovo on a return of Annette's bride-visit.

At Svetlovo, Miss Smith readily yielded to her former pupil's
persuasions to stay the night, and next day to partake of a nuncheon
before starting the journey home to Volnoya.

There all seemed restored to its normal serenity. The setting sun
bathed the house in its usual mellow glow and only a charred patch on
the lawns bore witness to the recent havoc. The young gentlemen had
ridden or been driven back to their homes. The dancing bear, the
balalaika players and the shameless fairground girls, who had
variously contributed to their entertainment, had been cleared out by
Danilo. Indoors, the broken glass and crockery had been swept up,
the furniture righted and polished clean of liquor stains. Fresh bouquets replaced the wilted roses that had seen out the revels. Volnoya
was itself again, as it had been after many another such bout of
Slavonic temperament and extravagance in the past. Only its master
was missing.

'Rode off an hour ago to Dubrovnoye, ma'am,' Danilo informed
Miss Smith out of the corner of his mouth.

She sent Lise on upstairs and beckoned Danilo into the breakfast
parlour. Between their two phlegmatic and resourceful natures there
had grown up the confidence of allies. She said without preliminaries:

'He had sobered?'

'Yes and no, ma'am, seeing it's as reckless as jumping that bonfire
for him to be riding to *that* house tonight—with the Governor still in
Smolensk. Why that bi— that Princess Nina has to come and set him
off again, the devil in her only knows! She had her chance of him
in Petersburg, didn't she?'

'The letter was from the Princess then?'

'I twigged it as soon as he clapped eyes on it—and could have cut
my hand off for bringing it to him! What's to do now, ma'am?'

'Little enough, since the young woman is apparently prepared to go
to the length of marriage for the sole aim of establishing herself in

his neighbourhood. Such tenacity of purpose is not easily discouraged! And you will not tell me that any man could be insensible to such a compliment. Especially, as I collect, from a Beauty, and after he has led an exemplary life for months. I shall of course remove Miss Lise as soon as—' she hesitated, '—as soon as a selfish old woman can bring herself to move. Meanwhile—'

'Begging your pardon, ma'am, you will be sadly missed by all of us—*and* him. Never shall I forget how you stopped that bonfire turn-up t'other night— You wouldn't see your way to letting things ride for a bit, ma'am? Being busy about your writing and such? It was hoped below stairs that little missie might. . . . She's full young but a game 'un. I beg your pardon, madame. Will I serve dinner now?'

'Hold it a while yet, if Anastasi will not burst a blood-vessel. I must go up to Miss Lise. Even game 'uns need a little help over their fences now and again.'

She found Lise having her hair dressed; or, more accurately, sitting before her dressing table while her maid held a comb and regaled her with the tale of the revels. Lise quickly dismissed the girl and turned to Miss Smith.

'Aunt Hon, where is Sacha?'

'He is gone to wait on the Governor.'

'You mean he is gone to see the Princess Nina.'

'I mean he is gone to see the Princess Nina, if you wish, since she is the Governor's wife and therefore resides at Dubrovnoye,' said Miss Smith steadily.

She placed her hands on the girl's shoulders and held her lightly at arms' length.

'Do you dislike it, Lise?' The dark, troubled eyes did not waver under her scrutiny.

'I dislike it very much,' said Lise stoutly. 'I have *no* opinion of the Princess Nina, even though she is a Beauty. *Ma tante* used to say that her influence might prevail upon Sacha to reform; but as you have seen, Aunt Hon, it appears to do just the opposite! And it is surely *very* improper for a married lady to be sending him billets to come to her.'

'*Most* improper—if that were the case,' boomed Miss Smith. 'But we must not be too hasty to accept facts vouched for merely by servants' gossip, dear child. We ourselves have no evidence that Sacha's letter was from the Princess; or, if it was so, that it held anything more particular than the common run of civility between old acquaintance.'

'No, Aunt Hon,' agreed Lise dubiously, but with some of the troubled look clearing from her expressive eyes.

'No judgement without the evidence is a first principle of English law and a very sound precept in life.'

'Yes, Aunt Hon.'

'So now you can forget the whole foolish episode, eh, dear child? What a piece of work servants will make of the least household flurry!' she added genially.

Lise looked a trifle surprised by this triumph of understatement, but nodded wisely.

'I had observed Sacha to be spoiling for mischief these past two weeks,' Miss Smith went on, judging her audience's suspension of disbelief to be now almost complete. 'We must not forget how much his exile chafes him, for all his brave show of spirits.'

Lise looked up.

'Oh Aunt Hon, he *is* brave, is he not?'

'An admirable character in parts—like most of us,' was as far as Miss Smith was prepared to go; but she offered it with a beaming smile that was entirely a tribute to her own relief at having the troublesome matter so comfortably settled. The completion of the Russian chapters could proceed with a more or less clear conscience.

It is difficult however to be the possessor of a brilliantly unscrupulous mind and only a more or less clear conscience. That awkward member gave Miss Smith some uncomfortable qualms when events quickly showed just *how* over-sanguine had been her hopes of Nina's discretion and Sacha's conduct.

He did not return from Dubrovnoye till well after dawn; and by breakfast time this fact was known throughout his household.

Miss Smith entered the breakfast parlour looking more equine than usual. However, Lise greeted her and Sacha with equal lack of consciousness, and her mentor breathed more easily. Nevertheless she found herself unable to settle to her writing afterwards, and presently gave up all pretence of concentration upon anything but the situation at Volnoya.

If this flagrant lack of discretion was but the start, what folly might not follow? And how long before Lise understood all too clearly what was going on?

Miss Smith snapped her copybook shut, closed the standish and rose with a warlike snort. Action was essential. The first thing to do was to see the Princess Nina.

CHAPTER XXI

Miss Smith had a ready pretext for her call at Dubrovnoye in a foreigner's desire to observe all civilities due to the returning Governor. For her passport to the Princess Nina's presence she had all that was required in her visiting card, fortunately discovered undamaged in her trunk, across whose printed London address she had written 'at Volnoya'. It would be a lofty turn of mind, even in a Beauty, that could resist discovering what kind of unmarried lady claimed residence at Volnoya.

Her choice of conveyance fell upon a light *linée*. The day was hot and Miss Smith did not hold with parasols. The four-hour drive under a broiling sun brought her to Dubrovnoye considerably flushed and devoutly hoping that honour would not forbid her to accept refreshment.

The *linée* entered imposing, gilt-pointed gates between stone pillars carved with the Prince's arms, and then rolled beneath the grateful shade of a well kept park. Zacharovo and Svetlovo were both handsome properties, but Dubrovnoye was a palace. The great house which presently came into view was stuccoed the pale green of the Hermitage in St Petersburg and ornamented in the same lavish extravagance of baroque taste. Fortunately Miss Smith could not be oppressed by grandeur, and was able to admire freely and judge without awe.

A footman in powder and silk stockings took her card. Her Excellency was at home and would be pleased to receive the English lady. As Miss Smith followed him up the wide marble staircase, she wondered whether Sacha had left by it some hours earlier that morning and from the very apartments she was now about to enter.

The Princess Nina's private drawing room, had not yet been refurnished to her taste; but its satin, marble, mirrors, gilt and buhl, the commonplaces of luxury, seemed to her visitor's eye exactly suited to the opulent beauty of the young woman who rose languidly from a striped satin chaiselongue to greet her.

A Beauty the Princess unquestionably was. Beside her Lise

129

dwindled to a little girl with big eyes. But whereas Lise, in or out of looks, could never be commonplace, Miss Smith was pleased to detect about her voluptuous hostess a kind of blatancy: an obviousness of perfection that could disgust—in time.

Meanwhile there was no underrating her formidable armoury as an opponent; for it was no stupid woman who said sweetly:

'*Two* visitors from Volnoya within two days! And how doubly remiss of Sacha to tell me nothing of you—and doubtless forget to inform *you* of His Excellency's absence. You must give him a good set down when you get back! But now pray sit down and let me offer you some refreshment. This heat is quite *énervant*, is it not? Do you make a long stay at Volnoya?'

Miss Smith lowered herself gingerly into a spindly gilt armchair. Her hostess sank languorously back on to rose satin cushions. A Mameluke page ushered in a table of *liqueurs blancs*, iced lemonade and sherbets. The demands of hospitality occupied both ladies for long enough to give Miss Smith time to ponder her reply. She decided upon a frankness as bland as that of her hostess.

'I had formed no intention of staying at Volnoya at all,' she told her. 'My sojourn in Russia is finished and my niece and I were on our way home to England, when—'

'Your niece?'

'—by marriage, through the cadet branch. She has been living in Petersburg. It may well be that you are aquainted with her through the Arloffs: Mademoiselle de Montargis. Well, as I was saying. . . . Dear me, Princess, is something the matter? Did you perhaps swallow a sip the wrong way? Pray let me ring for a glass of water—'

Nina, unbecomingly flushed, waved aside these attentions.

'So he did take her!' she gasped. 'The cunning little snake! Oh I might have known—! And that Arloff harpy, cool as a cucumber—! Measles indeed!'

'A distressing complaint,' boomed Miss Smith, baffled but pursuing.

Her hostess, who until now had held her in great complaisance for being elderly and plain, rounded on her in sudden suspicion.

'And may I ask where *you* come into it, madam? Am I to understand that Mlle de Montargis, who was given out as recovering from the measles in the country, is in fact doing so at *Volnoya*?' she demanded with awful sarcasm.

'She is at Volnoya, and she has certainly had the measles,' replied Miss Smith, truthfully as far as she knew. 'But it is in my power to relieve your anxiety as to any lingering effects of the ailment. My niece's health, though not robust, gives me no present cause for anxiety.'

'But her character might well do so! Madam, I do not know—'

The Princess stopped, biting her lip. The whole trouble was that she did *not* know anything for certain; and even in her seething indignation she felt a twinge of doubt about accusing the formidably respectable personage before her of being privy to Lise's elopement.

Controlling her agitation of spirit as best she might, the Princess continued on a considerably lowered note:

'It is possible, madam, that you have been grossly imposed upon. The young woman of whom we are speaking, be she your relative or not, was last seen, unchaperoned, in M. Sacha Arloff's lodgings on the day of his departure into exile. No one in Petersburg has set eyes on her since, but all natural suspicion was lulled by the Countess Arloff's report of her succumbing to an infection and being sent to convalesce at one of the Count's country houses. I need not tell you—'

'That it was you yourself who saw her in M. Arloff's rooms? Tol-lol, Princess, but it would appear to be a case of the pot and the kettle—if you will admit of such a homely comparison! And as we are on the subject of proverbs, perhaps you have a Russian equivalent of our old English saying that people who live in glass houses should refrain from throwing stones? So true! And so particularly apt when these fragile dwellings are Governor's palaces! Their structure can so easily be shattered, especially by a reckless visitor leaving at dawn.'

Miss Smith sat back and gave her full due of admiration to the Princess Nina, risen to her feet with flashing eyes and heaving bosom, and rendered temporarily speechless with indignation. Miss Smith rose too, taking advantage of the pause to say briskly:

'Now that we understand each other so well, it will not be encroaching in me to be plain with you. Consider me your ally as long as you conspire with *me* to spare my little Lise any distressful knowledge. *You* may well find it useful to have a conformable connection with Volnoya to show to the world. My visit is a first step; it will enable you to engage our whole party for dinner as soon as your husband is in residence. A big dinner is the poorest sort of nourishment for gossip! No, do not say anything now—' she boomed, seeing the Princess about to recover her powers of speech. 'You may thank me when you have had time to reflect; or it can wait until you observe

E*

the benefits of my advice. And now, *chère princesse*, if you will kindly have my carriage called, I really feel . . .'

On Saturday, an elaborately crested missive was delivered by special courier to Volnoya at midday; the packet disclosed a prettily worded invitation for the whole Volnoya party to dine at Dubrovnoye the following Tuesday.

Sacha, who had been in louring mood all week, looked across at Miss Smith with immediate suspicion; but Miss Smith merely remarked that she had not looked for such extraordinary civility on the strength of one formal call. Sacha sat up.

'*You* have called at Dubrovnoye?'

'Naturally, dear boy. I hope I know what observances are due to His Excellency from a foreign visitor! I confess I did not look for an advance of the acquaintance to follow so promptly,' she admitted with perfect truth.

The two of them were lingering over their coffee beneath the spreading oak which had figured as the cricket pavilion during a previous crisis in their affairs. Lise had left the table to change into riding dress, before the invitation came to hand. Sacha looked from it to Miss Smith for another fulminating minute and then threw down his napkin and fell to his restless pacing.

'Well, it is quite impossible for Lise to go,' he flung over his shoulder.

'Dear boy, I have had occasion before to deplore your prowling habit. It would not be so uncomfortable if it put me in mind of a *caged* panther. . . . Now do pray sit down again, let me pour you some more coffee and tell you that I honour your sentiments but cannot agree with your policy. The child could not avoid falling a prey to surmise if she were left behind. And you know well that servants' gossip is never wanting to supply such a need.'

'So you would rather have me introduce her to—'

'—to the Governor's household,' said Miss Smith smoothly. 'Ah, here she comes. Dear child, Sacha and I have such an agreeable surprise for you! On Tuesday we are all bidden to dine with the Governor.'

Sacha had risen again at Lise's approach and stood leaning against the tree trunk, watching her narrowly. He stepped forward, lightly caught her arm and turned her to face him.

'What is it, poppet? You don't want to go? Tell me.'

'Oh no. It's only— Oh Sacha, it's just that I have nothing to wear!'

He shouted with laughter from sheer relief; Miss Smith threw him a speaking look—and Lise went to dine at the Governor's in her usual purple crape, the only other choice being the dove-grey gown which the Princess Nina might remember all too well.

After that dinner, so reassuring to all parties, Sacha became a household figure at Dubrovnoye.

CHAPTER XXII

The end of summer saw the completion of Miss Smith's Russian chapters; but, like the balmy weather that seemed reluctant to let the season go, so did she linger over them, revising and polishing with a true author's fever for the impossible perfection.

However, there dawned at last the morning when she pronounced her labours finished. Sacha called for a celebration and delayed his departure for Dubrovnoye by a whole hour to crack a bottle of champagne in honour of The Book.

Lise cheered up at once. She and Sacha vied with each other in their extravagant forecasts of the masterpiece's reception by a waiting world, Lise greeting every capping of hers with peals of her enchanting laughter. The General arrived. Sacha sent for another bottle. Danilo brought two. The genial magic of Volnoya was at work again.

It was only after Sacha had left that Lise recalled what the end of the Russian chapters portended.

Sacha gave a passing thought to it too, riding back from Dubrovnoye next day, and was pleased to reflect that he carried some exciting news to cheer his poppet.

The Governor was to give a ball; the first real Imperial Governor's Ball the province had enjoyed for over two years. And now the felicity of receiving a card for it would not only admit the fortunate to a sight of Her Excellency's vaunted beauty but privilege them to observe at first hand the progress of the province's favourite theme of gossip, thought Sacha grimly.

For while Miss Smith's strategic advice had suppressed scandal, it was too much to expect it to silence gossip. Her achievement was to arrest the gossip at conjecture and to divide the gossips into two camps.

'Those who believe me deceived, and those who suspect I am not,' said the Governor to Miss Smith, in whose confidence he was in a fair way to displace the General.

'*Believe* and *suspect* are the pastimes of the provinces the world over,' she shrugged. 'No provincial society could do less for such a promising combination as a handsome, exiled rake and the Governor's beautiful young wife, under any circumstances.'

'H'mm. Well, thanks to you, the circumstances are . . . gentlemanly. I like the young scapegrace, there's the rub! Dammit, I've known him since he was in short coats! And it was careless in me not to enquire into Nina's sudden complaisance towards my suit. Unpardonably, I imagined splendour and position to be her sole concern.'

'I fancy they would prevail.'

'My good Miss Smith, I do not do my wife the injustice of suspecting her capable of love in a cottage! Or in exile. Neither does Arloff. Therein of course lies my main hope for the future.'

'You will need patience,' she told him.

'Our Russian virtue—or vice. But I wish I might persuade you not to take your charming little girl away from Volnoya.'

'*That* would be testing the virtue of patience too far. She is at an age when one can grow up overnight; and she shall not do so in Sacha Arloff's vicinity if I can prevent it.'

'You mean you are not gambler enough to risk it. A pity. The result might have been diverting. I shall miss *you* too. The pleasures of rational conversation do not often come the way of a provincial Governor. Ironic, is it not, that I shall be obliged to depend upon young Arloff for such? He is very sound on the subject of our parlous military situation.'

Prince Ulanoff was not the only gentleman to view Miss Smith's iminent departure with dismay. The General resolved upon desperate remedies.

His agitation of spirit continued unabated for several days. The news of the Governor's ball relieved him of some immediate anxiety, since Miss Smith had readily acceded to Lise's plea to stay for it; but even so, his household was thankful to see him set off to Volnoya.

There he found Sacha missing as usual and Lise and Miss Smith given over to ball fever.

Theodossia had turned up an attic-ful of old finery. She, the two ladies and quite half the maids were now up there, knee-deep in brocades, laces, wigs, hoops, panniers and plumes, examining and exclaiming over their finds.

Miss Smith had been doing so only to please Lise. When the General was announced she took his arm and escaped thankfully with him to the stables.

Lise, who had suspected the nature of her aunt's interest all along, was thus freed to give her whole mind to pouncing upon such treasures as remained fit for conversion.

To that task she set the whole of the Volnoya *devichia*. Their combined dressmaking skill was not great, as witnessed by her purple wardrobe, but at the end of five days of concentrated toil Lise was the joyful possessor of a ball gown.

The creation comprised a tunic of only slightly yellowed French lace, over an under-dress of rose silk, and a train. True, the hemline was less than even and the puff of one sleeve obstinately fuller than its fellow; but with fresh roses in her sash, an elegant *brisé* fan and the finest of kid gloves—only perished in two places—Lise felt entitled to be pleased with her reflection for the first time since her adventures began.

Her humble vanity had so long been deprived of its due that on the afternoon of the ball she was a creature transformed. Capricious, exigent, nervous and elated by turn, she drove the maids and Miss Smith to despair of her ever being ready to set off. However, the *grande toilette* was at last accomplished.

Miss Smith, standing already cloaked, was then obliged to remove her wrap so that her gown might receive its share of admiration. The tribute was at first one of stunned silence. Then Theodossia deposed in awed tones that it put her in mind of the ikon in the breakfast parlour.

'A trifle more Oriental than that,' boomed Miss Smith, smoothing her rich folds complacently. 'Scarlet of course is a favoured colour with the Hindus, and green with the Moslems.'

'Oh ma'am, I never saw anything to compare with it!' cried Lise truthfully. 'Do not, I beg you, resume your cloak, but let us go down directly and show ourselves to Sacha. 'Dossia, my gloves! Olga, you may carry my cloak and reticule. Shall I let my train trail or pick it up over my arm? Oh Aunt Hon, do but listen to the way my skirts *shu-ussh* as I walk! Sonya, run and tell his honour we are coming down.'

Unfortunately only Danilo was awaiting them in the hall; and with the ominous news that his honour was still down in the stables where Galant was suspected of croup.

'Best if you were to go on, ma'am. He's not even dressed yet.'

'Hmm. Very well. Lise, do you proceed into the carriage. I might just look in at the stables; there's a remedy we use at home— No, no, bless the child! We shall go. In with you! I daresay Sacha will do all that is needed. Drat these plumes! I always forget how high they make me.'

'But Aunt Hon—we cannot go like this! Suppose—suppose Sacha does not come at all?'

'Then you will still have an excellent ball without him. But do not fret yourself, dear child, I will vouch for it that Sacha will arrive sooner or later. Danilo, inform his honour that I will make his excuse to their Excellencies.'

In Lise's heightened state of sensibility it was but a step to sulks and a shorter one to tears. Her misery endured until the full splendour of Dubrovnoye *en fête* burst upon them.

Even Miss Smith sat up and fixed her quizzing glass; at sixteen and a half, no mere personal chagrin could dim the glory of a ball in such a setting.

The great house was ablaze. Light streamed from its high, opened windows. Lights wreathed it in a glittering necklace at each storey from the tiers of *flambeaux* that formed part of its baroque façade. They shone on the plumes and satins and brilliant uniforms of the groups of guests who had strolled out to admire the splendid prospect, after being received. The house was the first object of their admiration; but the lawns wreathed with coloured lanterns and the cunningly illumined fountains and statuary had to be given their due, while a fleet of gay gondolas on the lake, complete with lanterns, beribboned gipsy gondoliers and guitars, quickly claimed the wonder of the younger guests.

Lise had not lacked balls or splendour in St Petersburg; but no ball, however glittering, could hold magic when attended in *ma tante*'s wake. Now, reassured by Miss Smith's promise of Sacha's arrival 'sooner or later', there could be no bar to enchantment.

Inside, to Lise's charmed eyes, the formal magnificence of the mansion had transformed itself into a fairyland palace. The staircase balustrade was a bank of roses running with a miniature cascade. Tiny, brilliant birds fluttered among the floral bowers of the winter garden; while the supper room and its open terrace had become a fabulous tent, under a blue silk canopy supported by gold-swagged pilasters and lit by innumerable chandeliers.

The dancing was already in full swing upstairs. The whirl and stamp of a mazurka resounded out of the ballroom as Lise and Miss Smith slowly mounted the grand staircase in the wake of other late arrivals. Lise's feet began to tap irresistibly inside their new satin slippers and she impatiently counted the couples ahead of them in the receiving line.

The Governor was also covertly counting the heads to come. For the past half hour he had taken to a chair, and he greeted each guest with a wry apology for the claims of his gout. The Princess Nina, upright and dazzling in the full splendour of bared white shoulders, white satin, plumes and diamonds, stood beside his chair with a smile that did not falter even at the sight of Lise and Miss Smith unaccompanied by their escort. To be sure, it grew a little fixed when Miss Smith explained the cause of Sacha's tardiness, and for once Lise found herself in perfect charity with her hostess when Nina said pettishly:

'And I suppose if the wretched animal coughs all night Sacha will forget he was ever engaged to come to a ball. Oh, how provoking men are!'

Miss Smith's snort all but convulsed the Governor, and Lise hastily drew her aunt across to the ballroom. Here, their entry did not go unremarked. Miss Smith's toilette caused the sensation it deserved; but Lise also aroused quite a stir of interest. She was at once accosted by Annette, enchanting in blue, and her friends of the Volnoya Irregulars quickly claimed several dances.

Once on the floor she was in her element. Several local beaux, who had formerly regarded her as a thin little girl, now found her worthy of their notice. Miss Smith beamed upon them and presently judged her protégée sufficiently launched to permit of her own retirement to the card room.

Lise barely remarked her departure. She had not sat down for a single dance. The Governor's household orchestra was inspired by a Viennese conductor, and she could not be less than happy as long as she could go on twirling, light as air, to the frenzy of the mazurkas and the intoxication of the new, dizzying, dangerous, Viennese waltz.

The Princess Nina, freed at last from her receiving duties, came into the ballroom on her husband's arm. Her practised eye soon noted Lise's modest success. So on the ballroom floor the chit must be considered a rival! She herself was at once duly surrounded; but like Lise she obstinately kept the supper dance free against Sacha's coming.

The supper dance was announced as a waltz, to the enchantment of all the young ladies provided with an eligible partner.

'Ze Vinter Palace valse,' intoned the orchestra leader, kissing his fingers in anticipation.

Polite applause and a buzz of talk followed his announcement, creating a pause in the business of the ball. If Sacha had planned his entrance to arouse the maximum of comment, he could scarcely have timed it better.

The flunkeys at the open doors of the ballroom moved forward to announce him, but he waved them aside and paused at the top of the shallow marble steps to distinguish his host—or perhaps his hostess —in the crowd below. For a moment he stood there, completely unconscious of the figure he cut on the sweep of white marble, in the severe elegance of his black and white, with sunbleached hair and darkly tanned skin. The whole shining expanse of floor before him was emptied of dancers. He saw Nina at the far end of the apartment, unhurriedly descended the steps and strolled towards her.

Every feminine eye in the room followed his progress. Male and female eyes alike observed the Princess Nina stop in the middle of the sentence she was addressing to the Chief Justice and take two quick steps forward, before she checked herself. They were quite small steps; but if she had run across the length of the ballroom floor to Sacha, and he seized her in his arms instead of formally kissing her gloved hand, the effect upon her guests could not have been more electrifying, nor their hopes of the evening more amply fulfilled.

A few of the spectators were also privileged to note the Governor's fleeting frown as he took in the scene. Only one person noticed Lise's hands clench on her fan and the sudden dimming of her excited little face. That person was Sacha, who had caught sight of her as he bowed over Nina's hand. He straightened up, apologised for his tardiness and moved on to make his excuses to the Governor. As soon as he had discharged this task he made his way to Lise.

The dancing recommenced and Lise's partner came up to claim her. He stayed talking a few minutes to Sacha. Lise did not retain one word of the conversation; but she took her place in the set with her slippers once more treading on air, because Sacha had bespoken the supper dance with her.

He took both Lise and Miss Smith down to supper, to the General's and the Princess Nina's chagrin. After supper he danced with Annette, Lise again, and any other girl who took his eye. The Princess Nina developed the head ache and denied herself to all

aspiring partners. By one o'clock, when the much anticipated fireworks and transparencies were due to start, her head ache had become
a raging need to express her grievances and demand an explanation
to which she determined she would not listen: in short to create the
sort of scene for which privacy and the undivided attention of its
object is a prime necessity.

Everyone streamed out at the burst of the first rocket. The fireworks were given in the gardens at the back of the house, with the
tree-fringed lake as their setting, and some of the prettiest effects were
obtained when the showers of descending stars fell over the water.
Cries of delighted appreciation greeted the set-pieces; a transparency
of the Tsar-Emperor and Empress being particularly admired.
Guests scattered to various vantage points of the gardens to watch,
and it was not long before the enterprise of the young people
launched a regatta of boats on to the lake. There, the gondolas made
a charming spectacle in themselves, with the coloured lanterns at
their prows reflected in the dark water and the girls' bright dresses
sporadically lit up by the fireworks.

Few of the young ladies were bold enough to venture into the boats
tête-à-tête; but several promising flirtations prospered nevertheless
and it was generally voted the most popular feature of the ball.

Lise and Annette were among the first to embark, escorted by
Vladimir and Lise's favourite among the Volnoya Irregulars. Their
boatman guided their craft into the centre of the lake where they
could command an unimpeded view of the fireworks. Here it was also
quiet enough to enjoy a serenade, and the girls were soon plying him
with requests for their favourite gipsy melodies.

Lise discarded her gloves and lay back against the cushions, letting
her arm trail in the silky water. The warm night air was like a caress
on her face and bared shoulders. Sacha had danced with her twice.
The gipsy sang of lovers' farewell and lovers' meeting, far away and
long ago. Annette leant her head on her husband's shoulder and
moved closer within his arm. An indefinable ache, a longing for she
knew not what, at once painful and sweet, quivered through Lise.
She wanted to cry because all this beauty would so soon be gone; she
herself would be gone. Nothing lasted; nothing was safe. Yet with a
part of her she was impatient to be done with the present, because
she was ready and eager for the mysterious next step to which all
this night's magic whispered invitation and warning.

She stirred restlessly on the cushions. Whatever the mystery was,
the amiable youth trying to capture her hand beside her held no key

to it for her. She sat up. The sky above them suddenly exploded into arabesques of white, gold, rose and purple on its blackness, and they drifted through a shower of multi-coloured falling stars. Lise laughed with delight, craning perilously over the side of the boat, trying to catch one as they descended into the water.

'Ahoy there, you mermaid, be careful or you'll have us all over-board,' called Vladimir.

'No, I won't; but pray tell the man to row, Volodya, because we are drifting close to the island.'

'An island? I did not know the lake was big enough to hold one.'

'Oh, it is but an islet, with a little bridge to it from the park. The Princess showed it to us, and there is a pretty little folly on it, built like a Grecian temple. But now it is all overgrown; and if we get in amongst the weeping willows we shall not properly see the next firework.'

'We'll turn back then. Hey, boatman—'

'No, wait, let him finish his song,' begged Annette. 'The last verses are the prettiest. Sing it to the end,' she bade the gondolier.

He put aside his oar and took up his guitar again, and then went on with his lay of a faithless *chela* and of the revenge jealousy took among the gipsy camp-fires. The boat drifted on inshore past the willows. A magnificent set-piece, the final glory of the display, ex-ploded slightly off-course directly above them, illuminating the islet and its Grecian folly in a burst of pink and white light. For a few seconds the white-pillared little temple ashore was as brightly lit as a stage. At the centre of it, they saw a man's tall black back with a pair of bejewelled white arms locked around his neck. They could not see his face, but they saw the Princess Nina's: rapt, blind, beauti-ful, turned up for his kiss.

CHAPTER XXIII

Now it was Lise who urged Miss Smith to speed their departure and Sacha who cast about in his mind for means to delay it.

He was determined that Lise should not leave Volnoya the silent, listless ghost of herself which she presented since the ball. He did not suspect the cause of her distress, but he was willing to believe *any* evil of that ill-starred night. Galant was now mercifully on the mend, and he had almost forgiven Nina for the scene she had attempted to make him in the island summerhouse; but the memory of it, and of her callous dismissal of Galant's danger, lingered as distastefully as the thought of the figure her indecorous move had made him cut in the ballroom.

In Sacha's world, the dangerous game he and Nina were playing had its strict code; and the Petersburg great ladies who played it knew the rules.

He signalised his displeasure by staying away from Dubrovnoye for a week on end, which afforded him the satisfaction of watching over Galant's progress, but also served to bring Lise's distress to his notice.

For once Miss Smith was of little help, declaring herself out of patience with the pair of them and too busy with the packing of her notebooks to withstand all possible hazards on their journey to London.

In fact she was too busy blaming herself for whatever lapse in her care had exposed Lise to the shock she must have sustained at the ill-fated ball.

The second miserable week was dragging to its close when Sacha received a summons to Dubrovnoye from the Governor. He returned from his visit cheerful for the first time since the ball. The probable cause of his improved spirits might reasonably have been calculated to depress Lise; but as it was well-nigh impossible to withstand Sacha in his gay mood, the tone of the whole Volnoya household was swiftly raised.

Over a late supper, Sacha gallantly attributed his improvement to

an extension of the ladies' stay with him. The Governor had discovered that Miss Smith's passport would require his Kiev colleague's
endorsement before she could travel to Odessa.

'So I can count on your company for at least another two weeks.
Thank God for officialdom! Now, mesdames, we shall plan a continuous dizzy round of pleasure that'll set the whole province by the
ears! But the chief item is already settled and it is to be a surprise
for Aunt Hon. Lise, if you take a vow of secrecy, and your aunt
will excuse us for a few minutes, I *might* be brought to impart it to
you.'

Outside, he took her arm and lowered his voice confidentially.

'The endorsement is all a hum of course. But imagine, poppet, in
examining her passport the Governor discovered that it is Aunt
Hon's birthday in a few weeks! Now you cannot celebrate a birthday jogging in a coach, can you? Besides, picture the General's feelings if he were robbed of such an occasion to show his esteem! And
the Governor is determined to outdo him. That is what he summoned me to discuss—the nature of the celebration. Well, I have told
him my idea, which *I* believe little short of genius, but it must have
your approval. So listen to it and tell me what you think . . .'

The Governor had certainly fastened upon Miss Smith's impending birthday to delay her departure; but, as with Sacha, the happy
event was serving him to excuse a more pressing necessity. In his
case it was to re-establish contact with Volnoya. The Princess Nina's
sulks since the ball had aggravated his dyspepsia to a point where this
was preferable to their continuance. He and Sacha understood each
other perfectly on that score and the birthday project promised well,
being so exactly suited to the interests of each party to it.

Nor was Lise so sunk in her trouble as to be indifferent to her
Aunt Hon's pleasure. She was delighted with Sacha's scheme to stage
—as nearly as they might from Miss Smith's frequent reminiscences
—a true Indian Gymkhana in honour of her birthday. It was to be
given at Dubrovnoye. Sacha had already charged himself with the
supervision of the jumps and handicapping. The stewards would be
drawn from the officers of the Smolensk garrison and Miss Smith
herself would present the prizes. But Lise must at once set herself to
the task of deciding what these should be, and to schooling her mare
to take part in the Ladies' Race.

'But Sacha, I have never done any jumping—'

'Nonsense. You've followed me over every hedge and ditch in
Volnoya. You've got good hands and plenty of pluck. The rest is

practice, and I'll see that you get it, my girl! But of course you *might* find yourself up against Aunt Hon.'

'Well, I'll not find myself pulling my horse to let her win!' laughed Lise. 'Oh Sacha, it is a famous scheme! Nothing could please Aunt Hon more, for she's forever talking about the gymkhana she attended in India. And *we* shall go one better, if you will give your display of Cossack riding.'

'Now what the devil do you know about that?'

She gave a crow of laughter; the first time he had heard her laugh since the accursed ball, and his heart smote him for whatever failing of his had made his little companion so unlike her cheerful self for the past two weeks.

'I have my spies,' she chortled. 'And I watched your bonfire jump from my window upstairs. Can you do it sober, too?'

'You are an imp and I suspect you of a growing disrespect for your elders! For your private ear alone—I have never attempted it sober, but I might in honour of Aunt Hon. Come on back to her now—and not a word! Tomorrow we'll ride over to the General's and Svetlovo to tell them all about this.'

They left the General brooding deeply over his present to Miss Smith, and went on to Svetlovo where Annette delighted Lise with the private intelligence that *her* dinner for Miss Smith would also serve to celebrate some news of which she and her dear Charsky were almost certain. Her father-in-law contented himself with prophesying that the weather would not hold for outdoor junketings and that Annette was mistaken.

His second prognosis was happily proved wrong, but his first was fulfilled that very night. The Indian summer broke with dramatic suddenness in a thunder storm and torrential rain, ushering in the autumn with the excess of all things Russian.

Nevertheless, preparations for the gymkhana continued apace. Dubrovnoye presented a scene of constant activity and restored content. The Governor had issued a standing invitation to all aspirants to come and try their mounts round the course; while the construction of the hazards quite naturally required Sacha's constant presence—to the great relief of the Governor's dyspepsia.

Nor did Sacha neglect Lise's training for the Ladies' Race, undeterred by her own and her mare's refusal to surmount the smallest obstacle presented to them in cold blood. As he justly pointed out, both of them had sailed over every obstruction of the Volnoya and Zacharovo landscape without making a piece of work of it. Now, just because they knew that four brushwood fences and a trifling ditch awaited them. . . .

But it was the sight of the Princess Nina going faultlessly round the course by Sacha's side that finally spurred Lise to emulation.

By the end of the week, she had the satisfaction of completing the Dubrovnoye Ladies' course without baulking at a single fence and only brushing through two of them. Sacha grinned and had the brushwood raised a foot.

By now hardly an estate throughout the province was without its quota of aspirants practising jumps and dressage. Miss Smith preserved an appearance of ignorance by becoming virtually a recluse, so that plans for the various birthday festivities might be safely discussed by her friends and her household. Her intercourse with Lise too was severely limited by the latter's inability to fix her mind upon anything but horses and fences. Miss Smith smiled and cryptically informed Sacha that he should have been put into the Diplomatic.

At last only three days remained before the gymkhana. Excitement mounted to a happy fever pitch. Even the weather fell in line with the general festive mood, and a fine October morning saw Lise ready to do a last full practice round of the course. She went round in one of her best timings yet, and arrived at the winning post in fine style to collect congratulations from the group of aficionados and grooms gathered to watch the entrants.

The obstacles were raised for the men's races, and Sacha mounted to try out the new water jump. He took Galant over it with that perfect harmony of horse and rider that made it look so maddeningly easy. Then he pulled Galant up within his own length and joined the other riders at the side of the track.

'So low it's a dead bore,' he shrugged. 'Constantin, I told you yesterday it would not serve unless you had them build up the wood. Why the devil has it not been done?'

'I'm sorry Sacha, but—'

'It was not done because I forbade it, sir,' broke in the fat Major who had constituted himself acting-Chief Steward.

He edged his mount forward, determined not to be intimidated by these idle and dissolute aristocrats who had nothing better to do than try to break their necks.

'I forbade it,' he repeated with some relish, 'in my capacity as acting-Chief Steward for my Colonel. We serving officers—' he drew himself up and had the satisfaction of seeing a muscle begin to twitch by Sacha's mouth '—are not at liberty to hazard life and limb for nothing, since these are at the sacred service of our country and the Tsar-Emperor! And I would have you know, sir, that your so-called authority here—'

'Extraordinary people they admit to these provincial Messes,' drawled Sacha, looking straight through him. He flicked Constantin's horse with his whip. 'Come on. Let's go up to the house and have a drink to get the taste out of our mouths.'

The boy laughed nervously and turned his horse to follow Sacha, but one of the older men in the group wheeled his mount sharply and barred their way. He caught Sacha's arm in a hard grip.

'Arloff, for God's sake—! This is no way to talk,' he urged in an undervoice. 'Major Shuskin is right. Also he is twice your age, with a family to support. He cannot afford to challenge you for your insult. Get back and apologise.'

The moody, dark-blue eyes flared dangerously and then wavered. Sacha shrugged off the restraining arm and pulled Galant round so sharply that he went back on his haunches. But when he faced the Major again he was smiling.

'It seems that I might be misunderstood about your Mess, sir. My apologies. But I still hope to persuade you that *you* are wrong about my fence. Come, try it for yourself and you shall see that a child could sail over it. Yes, by God, I'll show you— Hey, poppet! Lise!' he called in his Petersburg parade-ground voice.

She waved in reply, touched her spur to her mare and came tearing up, still a little flushed with her recent success.

'Poppet, I want you to go over the water jump again for me. Want me to pace you over it?'

'N-no, Sacha.'

'That's my girl! Off you go.'

She had cantered off to get her run at it before the group by the fence fully realised what was happening. The Major was the first to recover his powers.

'You are out of your mind! That fence is a good two feet higher than it was for the ladies—'

'Sacha, are you sure she—' began Constantin.

'Don't be a fool, Arloff—'

'I tell you, sir, you are risking—'

'Nonsense. The fence is child's play and she's been over the ditch a dozen times. Come on, Lise! you can do it!'

She heard him faintly above the drumming of hooves and blood in her ears. The fence ahead of her loomed like a wall. She knew that she must not think of it. Simply soar up and over. Let your horse do it. Throw your heart over and follow it; up and over. *Let your horse do it*. And then she felt herself give a tiny, uncontrollable, unforgivable movement of terror in the saddle—and saw the black sky and ground rushing up at her. . . .

CHAPTER XXIV

It took some time to persuade Sacha that no more than mild concussion and a broken leg threatened Lise. When finally the combined efforts of Miss Smith, the Governor and Annette had succeeded in convincing him, the effect upon him was a sad disappointment to Annette's romantic hopes.

Once again the Slavonic temperament defeated logic and expectation. Sacha relaxed sufficiently to discontinue his vigil by Lise's bedside, but relief and remorse *à la russe* then found expression in a carouse at Volnoya whose wildness scandalised the whole neighbourhood. Miss Smith was not as outraged as most; but even she could not be expected to know how much alcohol it took to drown out the echo of your own voice saying 'Come on, Lise! you can do it!' Nor how closely the girl's unconscious face on the pillows had resembled the same face, white with fear, on another set of pillows in Vilensk.

On the fourth day of the riot, Danilo came to Dubrovnoye to beg Miss Smith's intervention.

'An astute man, Danilo,' said the Governor. 'I should like to endorse his plea; for I will not disguise from you that I cannot afford a scandalised province on my hands. My wife's folly has already provided gossip enough to be heard in Petersburg; and both Count Arloff and I have our enemies there who will not be slow to profit by my laxity towards his deplorable son. Sacha's treatment in exile has not been precisely according to Imperial Regulations, you know! My Deputy has a dossier a foot long, I promise you, of irregularities and subversive activities.'

Miss Smith smiled.

'Ah yes, His Excellency's ill-starred descent on the Volnoya Irregulars. I collect they would constitute "subversive activity" in exile?'

'Certainly. One which I wish a few more of our landowners indulged in this year! I also think it represents Arloff's best chance of recouping himself. As you know, I share your view that we shall

148

be at war soon. In war, much may be forgiven to a born fighting leader.'

'When he is dead, for preference!'

'I would put young Arloff's powers of survival high, if he does not succeed in drinking himself to death meanwhile.'

'So you would have me discourage his present attempt? You realise it will bring him back here if I succeed?'

'Undoubtedly,' agreed the Governor cheerfully, '—to devote himself wholly to our little patient, in his present remorseful mood. I do not think that Nina has quite allowed for this.'

It certainly did not appear so when the Princess Nina added her plea for Miss Smith's intervention, later that afternoon. Miss Smith, who was not often malicious, smiled sweetly.

'Very well, I shall go to Volnoya. There is but one thing likely to make him stop and bring him here—which I take to be your object —and that is to tell him that Lise has asked for him.'

'Has she?' asked Nina quickly.

'Oh, but of course,' beamed Miss Smith. 'Almost as frequently as yourself. Upon my word, I sometimes wonder that Sacha is not more impossible than he is! However, my patient will undoubtedly benefit from his presence and the riot at Volnoya must be stopped. So if I may give Sacha *carte blanche* to visit our invalid—?'

'My husband has already begged you to treat this house as your own,' said the Princess coldly. 'Pray make whatever dispositions you see fit to promote mademoiselle's recovery.'

After watching Miss Smith's dispositions at work for a fortnight or so, the Governor had compassion on his wife's nerves and carried her off to Moscow.

Their Excellencies' return some six weeks later found a charming domestic routine established at Dubrovnoye. The Princess Nina walked in upon the cosy tableau of Lise tucked up on the sopha before the library fire, with Sacha beside her and only a chessboard between them, while Miss Smith nodded over her notebook opposite.

She closed her notebook with a snap on the morning after Princess Nina's return. The Governor's wisdom in removing his wife from Dubrovnoye had won only a qualified approval from Miss Smith. In her view, remorse and relief were flimsy safeguards against the enchantment lent by absence to a conquering Beauty. Nor had she been so drowsy the previous evening as to miss the dazzling effect of the Princess Nina's entrance, wrapped from head to foot in the darkest sables, her alabaster skin glowing even whiter in the frame of her fur hood and her eyes and cheeks brilliant with the cold and excitement.

The discomfort the vision had induced in Miss Smith took the form of violent indigestion later in the night, and her trip to the kitchens for a soothing draught had brought her back upstairs in time to observe her hostess let herself quietly out of Sacha's bedchamber. In the morning Miss Smith sent to Smolensk for Lise's doctors.

Their consultation had the full benefit of Miss Smith's advice; they pronounced Lise fit to be removed home to Volnoya.

And how truly by now it was home! Lise took her first faltering steps since her accident across the hall, firmly supported by Sacha's arm. That afternoon she sat in the place of honour at the festive dinner-table, with all her well-wishers around her and Sacha proposing the toast to her recovery. The world had no greater felicity to offer.

Miss Smith raised her glass to the hope that every evil of the Russian winter might rapidly descend upon the road to Dubrovnoye.

CHAPTER XXV

Count Nicolas's natural talent as a conspirator had made possible a fairly regular secret correspondence between him and Lise since her flight.

There had been a break in it of nearly six weeks after Lise's accident, causing Nicky some anxiety. Her first letter informing him of it was also the first to be intercepted, unfortunately, by the Count himself.

On his return from Finland, the Countess had not thought it necessary to trouble her husband with Lise's flight, merely informing him that the girl had been despatched to join her mother in the care of a respectable Englishwoman travelling home to London.

Confronted by her husband brandishing Lise's intercepted letter and furiously demanding to know what it meant, she had still managed to keep her head against a strong impulse to deny all knowledge. Instead she gave him the brief explanation she had prepared against just such an emergency, stressing how her own actions had been guided solely by her desire to obviate further scandal.

'Which you will confess I have achieved,' she ended. 'Not a word of gossip about the girl's elopement has been heard; and the happy accident of them encountering this Madame Smith terminated the necessity of further concern on our part. But as to why the two of them are still fixed with M. Sacha, I am as much at a loss as yourself.'

The Count heard her out in grim silence. Then he began to pace about her pretty room with a violence that threatened the bric-à-brac.

'So you abandoned the child to her fate and gave out that she was recuperating from illness in the country,' he drawled. 'Infamous, but undoubtedly effective. I have always admired your utter lack of scruple where your comfort is concerned, Amélie.'

'*My* comfort may not be an object with you, Arloff, but I am persuaded that you would not have wished your son's exile transferred to Siberia,' snapped his wife. 'And that is what the least noise of the affair would have invited—with no accruing benefit to the little hussy, who is as guilty as her ravisher. She was beyond anything fortunate in acquiring this Madame Smith's protection and her chaperonage to London. Where—' cried the Countess, inspired by a sudden recollection '—I had every reason to believe her creditably established by now. It appears that her brother Armand—'

'The one who, along with posses of Red Indians, figures so largely in Nicky's plans for his future?'

'Nicky's plans? What *can* you intend, Arloff?'

'Nothing to alarm you. Pray proceed, *ma chère*.'

The Countess shrugged.

'My informant was the newly-arrived American Consul, who waited on me on her brother's behalf. Our understanding was limited by monsieur's barbarous accent; but I was able to collect that the brother had sailed—or would shortly sail—to England, to do his duty by his mother and sisters. So why I should have been any further concerned for Lise. . . . Nor can I conceive why she and Madame Smith continue to linger at Volnoya, when—'

The Count swung round in his pacing and came to throw himself into one of the delicate *grisaille* chairs, which creaked protestingly.

'Can you not? I would have thought an imagination as ready as yours would have furnished you with a dozen possibilities. Let me give you but two. One: that their lingering is as innocent as this letter suggests, with the girl's accident as its cause. The other possibility is that your convenient Miss Smith is not quite as respectable as you would have her. Sacha is rich, handsome, unattached; and he is still my son. He might well appear a very good match to the chaperone of a girl he has compromised—even if she is not looking to her own advantage. After all, what do you know of this Smith? Who is she? What is she doing travelling in Russia? What does the English Ambassador have to say of her?'

'Nothing,' replied the Countess truthfully, since she had not asked him. 'But I am satisfied that she is perfectly *comme il faut*. She is the aunt of an English *duc* and an old acquaintance of Julie de Montargis.' She frowned, trying to recall the rest of Sacha's letter. 'It appears that she travels to collect fossils or flowers or some such thing—mad like all the English, but obviously of the first respectability. Rest assured we need have no scruples about having confided the girl to her care.'

'I wish I might think so,' responded the Count sombrely. 'Just as I wish I could be easy about the thing being an elopement and not an abduction. But knowing my Sacha, I can imagine only too well the mood in which he left for exile.'

He lapsed into silence, staring down at the crumpled sheet in his hand. Her ladyship leant forward.

'Pray let me see her letter, Arloff, for in any case I must punish Nicky for his deceit. And to have our innocent child involved in such a correspondence—'

The Count grinned.

'Calm your maternal fears, Amélie. I daresay the little monkey is in it up to the hilt, but the tone of her letter hardly makes one tremble for his innocence. Read it.' He watched her frown as she scanned it. 'Well, Amélie? Sitting by her bedside, reading to her, carrying her out for airings. . . . A man in love, you would say— but not with his mistress if I know aught of such matters!'

Her ladyship smiled thinly.

'You forget that Sacha has no need of Lise to fulfil *that* function now. Prince Adam Ralensky was telling Count Paul that the Princess Nina did not even delay for a honeymoon to install herself at Dubrovnoye.'

'A ramshackle business,' grunted the Count. 'Still, when a man of almost my age marries a girl of two-and-twenty and a Beauty to boot, he may look for trouble! But it is not a connection I like for Sacha; and it makes this—' he tapped Sacha's letter '—even more of a puzzle.'

He rose and held the letter out to his wife.

'You'll do as you see fit with this, but don't go plaguing Nicky with useless questioning. This is a puzzle I shall resolve for myself.'

'How?' she demanded, already fearing his answer.

'Very simply. By arriving at Volnoya unheralded and seeing for myself what *kind* of scrape Sacha is in this time. It is unfortunate that the disturbing news from France makes it impossible for me to absent myself at present. I shall go as soon as I can be spared.'

'Arloff, I beg you will not do this!' broke from her ladyship. 'Do —do but consider the state of the roads,' she urged somewhat faintly.

'I'm sorry, my lord, but we're stuck fast. Both the wheelers over their bellies. Looks like a bear-trap; though what anyone's doing digging a bear-trap in the middle of the highway, I can't—aaaAAHH!'

Suddenly, silently, from the snowladen branches above came the answer.

Sacha's Irregulars had learnt their lessons in winter skirmishing all too well. The present patrol, led by an ex-bandit now translated into a sergeant, was perhaps a trifle influenced by his former vocation. All they needed was the chance to put their skill to the test, and here it was. Their patriotically inflamed imagination all but *saw* the arrogant French Marshal lolling on the cushions of the imposing equipage below them. Each of the white-clad defenders of Holy Russia concealed in the trees picked out his man from the Count's entourage and now hurled himself upon him with admirable, ferocious precision. Their fellows, crouched in the snowdrifts at the side of the road, leapt for the horses' heads, and had succeeded in slashing their traces before the Count's enraged roar brought mutual, horrified recognition. A terrible silence fell.

Some half hour later, the Count's cavalcade continued its journey through Volnoya woods at the cautious pace enjoined by the hastily mended traces. It was followed by a rueful posse of *guerilleros* marching under the eye of the Count's outriders. As the procession entered the lime avenue the outriders prodded their charges forward, none too gently. By now these were a sorry sight; his lordship's animadversions on their character and probable future in the salt mines having been scrupulously passed on to them by their guards. They arrived at the edge of the lawns at a shambling rush—and there froze, along with the rest, at the sight which met their eyes.

A shallow ditch ran like a scar across the snow of the lower lawn. Crouching in it at an interval of some four feet were a line of men holding muskets at the ready. A couple of them turned to look at the newcomers, but their attention was immediately returned to their front, as indeed was everyone's present.

The fascinated silence was abruptly shattered by a blood-curdling Cossack yell. Charging round from the stables side of the house came six horsemen at a gallop, standing up in their stirrups with drawn sabres. They swerved across the upper lawn, to bring them into straight line ahead as they topped its rise and came thundering down on the men in the ditch.

These did Sacha proud, holding their fire until the last hair-raising second and then discharging their weapons point-blank at the maddened horses overhead, before flinging themselves flat into the safety of their trench.

Everyone survived. The Count lowered his quizzing glass and permitted two stout footmen to help him from the coach. He received his gold-topped cane, and leaning on it strolled unhurriedly towards the riders. Sacha's progress towards *him* was impeded by the Count's prisoners, who now rushed forward to fling themselves in the snow at his feet, filling the air with their lamentations. Over their heads Sacha met his father's cold eyes. Cutting through the hubbub, he heard the one voice in the world he revered, say gently:

'No doubt you will wish to consider your explanation of this outrage carefully. Meanwhile you must allow me to congratulate you. I had not imagined it still possible for any exploit of yours to astonish me. You have surpassed yourself.'

The young gentlemen with Sacha sensed that this was no time to stand on the forms of civility. They made hasty bows to the Count and beat a swift, strategic retreat to the stables, agreeing among themselves that they would not be in Arloff's shoes for a million during the next few hours.

Inside the house, the appalling news had spread. Lise found her aunt in their workroom, surrounded by various agitated relatives possessed by the Volnoya Irregulars among the household.

'Sapskulls every one of you!' she was saying. 'Nobody is going to be sent to the saltmines—unless by me for setting a ruined dinner before the Count! Back to the kitchens with you at once! And you, Ahripoff, pull yourself together, man, and get you down into the hall to attend on his lordship.'

Her Russian, though vilely accented, was now sufficiently confident to convey the force of this to her listeners, and they obediently dispersed. Miss Smith turned to Lise.

'Dear child, if you are come to tell me that I am shortly to make the acquaintance of your former guardian, I must warn you that this entire household is already buzzing with the news.'

F

'Oh Aunt Hon, what are we to *do*?'

'Do? Why, go down and greet him with the normal usages of civility due to his age and rank. The Count is not an ogre, I presume, despite the panic into which his appearance seems to have cast everyone in this house. I must confess I do not envy Sacha the next few hours, but that is not to the purpose.'

Nevertheless it had the desired effect of immediately detaching Lise's mind from her own situation as she followed her aunt downstairs to the hall.

All the confusion of panic reigned there. It had been Miss Smith's confident hope that her admonition would return the afflicted relatives of the Irregulars to their posts, but they had got no farther than the hall. There, joined by the culprits themselves, they now wept like children at the Count's feet and besieged their own master to intervene for them. They had also been reinforced by most of the remaining domestics, who had spontaneously assumed the rôle of a Greek chorus, wringing their hands and commenting freely on the drama.

Pausing on the stairs, Miss Smith surveyed the scene below with a crescendo of snorts among which phrases like 'Oriental slavery', and 'evils of despotic rule' were audible but entirely inexplicable to Lise, who took the servants' behaviour for granted and was concerned only with watching Sacha and the Count.

The former stood as ramrod-straight as if he were on parade, with his face as rigidly set. The Count had subsided into a deep claw-armed chair, round which pools were beginning to form from the snow melting off his furs and boots. Suddenly he cut across the clamour with a roar to have both removed, and two valets sprang forward. Shrugging himself out of his *shuba* brought Miss Smith and Lise into his lordship's line of vision. His eyes narrowed.

'Out!' he commanded the domestic assembly. 'And you'll none of you let me hear one more word of this farrago if you want to save your skins! Not one word, d'ye hear?' he thundered.

Tears and laments ceased as if by magic; for this was not only reprieve but forgiveness and restoration to grace and favour. The staff trooped happily off to their duties.

The two ladies finished their descent. Sacha took two stiff steps towards them and said expressionlessly:

'Sir, will you allow me to make my guest, Miss Smith, known to you? Lise you will of course recall. Miss Smith, my father, Count Arloff.'

'Your servant, madam,' drawled his lordship, bowing coldly and measuring her with his fierce, narrowed eyes. He turned to his son. 'Sacha, I do not believe it can be anything but painful to Mlle de Montargis to meet me until you have explained her presence here. You may attend me to your cabinet. The ladies will excuse us.'

Sacha stood rigid.

'You have my word, sir, that you may meet Mlle de Montargis on the same footing as at any time during the years she lived in your house.'

Miss Smith, with a warlike snort, advanced to do battle. The Count raised his quizzing glass.

'I am happy to hear it; but I will still postpone the pleasure till we have had our talk. Your obliged, madam! Sacha, you cannot intend to keep me waiting.'

'Proud, arrogant, self-willed, selfish—and very like his son, if you could but be brought to see it!' snorted Miss Smith as the ring of Sacha's spurs and the Count's heavy tread died away. 'What a country! What a crew! I vow you'll be well rid of the lot of 'em, child. But if Monseigneur thinks he can permit himself such manners towards us, he does not know Honoria Smith! And I'll wager you'll find him in different trim by dinner time, unless I've vastly over-estimated Sacha.'

The conclave in the cabinet was not, however, progressing on the lines Miss Smith envisaged. She had not overestimated Sacha, but she had done less than justice to the Count's powerful understanding.

'I beg you will not insult my intelligence, Sacha!' he growled. 'I did not imagine that you were attempting to present me with your mistress. What I wish to know is whether I am being asked to notice a girl who should be your wife? And if not, just what is she doing here?'

'I must remind you, sir, that you had my word on the propriety of admitting Lise to your presence.'

'Don't be a stiff-necked fool. Your honour is not in question. Your future is—which is my concern. I want an answer, Sacha. And you owe it to the girl, if her credit weighs with you.'

His lordship let it sink in, contemplating his well-kept hands as he spread them to the fire.

'Very well then,' said Sacha between his teeth. 'There is no reason for Mlle de Montargis to feel constrained to marry me. And she is here as my guest, with her chaperone.'

'Ah yes, the so-convenient chaperone who turns up out of the blue to pull both your and Amélie's chestnuts out of the fire. Forgive me if I am at a loss to account for her function now! How did she come to change her mind about removing her charge from your improper company? Was it perhaps after due reflection as to the advantages you might still have to offer? Or after hearing of my new honours?'

'The answer is no, sir; and I must take leave to tell you—'

'That my suspicions are odious and cast an unwarranted slur upon this sterling character? Pray give me leave to inform *you* that I have had slightly wider experience of human nature than yourself, despite your colourful past! However, I shall not refine on the subject further at present; though I will go so far as to tell you that I acquit the girl of aught but innocent complicity—which can be the most dangerous of all of course.'

He watched his son's handsome face darken and grow rigid, and smiled grimly.

'My compliments on your self-command. Now you may relax your guard. Sit down and tell me how an exile contrives to keep a private army.'

The Count had arrived at Volnoya with no other design than to resolve its puzzle and extricate Sacha from whatever toil had been set for him. He had long buried the hurt of Sacha's exile too deep to permit himself to think of how much he missed his favourite son and what joy he would know in their reunion. And he had certainly given little consideration to the furore which his coming would cause in the province.

From the moment when every servants' hall in the neighbourhood got wind of the Count's arrival, Volnoya became the focus of every civility the province could muster—from a deputation of village elders, to the Governor calling in person with his wife.

The Princess Nina herself had urged the propriety of this gesture and declared herself ready to brave the winter roads. Her reward came when the Count insisted on retaining his old colleague for the night, and carried him off to talk politics as soon as the tea table was brought into the drawing room.

The party there broke up early and the ladies retired upstairs. At her bedchamber door, the Princess hesitated.

'I believe I must go down again and remind Ulanoff of our early start. You know what men are! Do not disturb yourself to accompany me, ma'am, I beg you. Nor you, mademoiselle. I know my way about the house.'

Nevertheless she found it necessary to pause in the dimly lit hall until a tall figure had detached himself from the shadows of the far windows. She walked quickly down the moonlit length of the floor towards him, until she too was lost in them.

Lise had cried herself to sleep long before the Princess Nina's delicate slippers tiptoed back upstairs.

Towards the end of the month, Miss Smith declared herself quite hagged with the press of society at Volnoya and took herself off to spend the day with the General. She returned looking extremely thoughtful; and to Lise's enquiry as to whether she had passed an agreeable day, made the cryptic answer that there was no fool like an old fool.

Lise's mind was too distracted to refine upon her aunt's mysterious utterance. She had all but forgotten it the following morning when Sacha found her sitting listlessly in the saloon in an interval between callers.

'Get your furs and come out. I've got such a gem of news to tell you that you'll never heed the cold. Hurry, before the next batch descend on us.'

The frosty air on the terrace caught her breath, but she stepped out briskly on Sacha's arm, lifting her face to the rosy winter sun.

'Good, isn't it? Poppet, such news! I've been trying to get you alone since breakfast. The General has done it!'

'Done what?' she asked blankly.

'Why, made an offer to Miss Smith, of course! *En forme* with flags flying and a salute of guns for all I know.'

'Made an offer to *Aunt Hon*? Impossible! How—who told you?'

'Danilo, who had it from the Zacharovo butler, so you can depend on it. Moreover, both servants' halls have already accepted,' he added, for the pleasure of hearing her laugh.

'Oh Sacha, you are roasting me! The General and Aunt Hon—why—why they are *old*!'

'Shocking ain't it? But it seems Cupid's darts are no respecter of age. The General at any rate . . .'

Lise was not listening. Amazement and disbelief gave way to one overwhelming thought: if Sacha's startling news was true and the General's proposal accepted, Miss Smith would be fixed in Russia. And then perhaps—

'I would not need to go away!' she blurted, 'Aunt Hon would live here at Zacharovo and I could remain too! Oh, Sacha . . .'

Until then their parting had been an inevitable doom, to be postponed as best she might but inexorably awaiting her. Now, in a single confused rush Lise acknowledged all her dread of it, all her fear of England, all the impossibility of a future in which Sacha had no part. The realisation set her trembling from head to foot. He said curtly:

'Before you quite settle your plans, pray recall that it is *Miss Smith* the General wishes to marry. Come indoors, you're shivering.'

He left her at the door and himself returned to pace the icy terrace, oblivious of the cold, while he in his turn confronted some unpalatable truths about the situation he had allowed to develop at Volnoya.

It was partly due to Lise's accident of course; he had been too thankful to have the child emerge whole and healthy, and—as he now acknowledged with some surprise—too pleased to have her back, to worry about the implications of her continued stay. But the real truth of the matter lay elsewhere: he had shelved the question of Lise's departure, as he had shelved all else, because life at Volnoya was coming to an end anyway.

With what astonishment Lise would have learnt that the period of her happiness was being decided in the secret war councils of the Tuileries, in the muster rolls of the *Grande Armée*, in the speed at which gun caissons, *fourgons* and fighting men could be moved across Germany! But to how many of the thousands whose lives and happiness were forfeit to the giant shadow moving daily closer to Russia, was the connection plain? Sacha Arloff was one; but this was because to him the coming of war would offer the desperate gamble upon which he had determined to stake his future.

The Count had been agreeably surprised to find his exiled son in such good heart. Had anyone informed his lordship that the improvement had come at the prospect of danger and action, he would have found the change entirely explicable, however thoroughly Sacha's plan earned his horrified prohibition. This, and how it might be overcome and his father's support enlisted, was the main object exercising Sacha's mind; and it was with some effort that he switched it to Lise's trouble. *His* trouble there was that he could not now imagine Volnoya without her chatter, her enchanting laughter, her adoring eyes and ugly purple dresses. But even his selfishness baulked at ruining her happiness for the casual pleasure he took in her company. Her 'I could remain here too!' had been a cry from the heart. One did not break children's hearts. He turned sharply and went back indoors, his mind made up.

CHAPTER XXVII

'What's this preposterous talk I hear of Mirnoff offering for Miss Smith?' the Count asked Sacha as they took their vodka and *zakouski* before dinner.

Sacha smiled.

'Preposterous was the word the lady used to me herself, sir.'

'H'mm. She will accept him of course. The woman is an adventuress.'

'Your pardon for correcting you, sir: an adventu*rer*. And I had flattered my hopes that you were beginning to like her!'

'Certainly. I have liked many adventuresses in my time and so have you, though I doubt if one has called any of them "Aunt". Still, I grant you, a likeable rogue and a lady—even if she is no more a Duke's aunt than she is yours.'

Sacha swallowed a hasty glass of vodka.

'As to that, sir, I may be responsible. It is possible that I—er—prodded Miss Smith a trifle to that height of respectability.'

'Ah, I thought the ducal nephew was doing it rather too brown,' remarked the Count with satisfaction, spearing an *ogurchik*. 'Some day you must regale me with the whole story, dear boy. But this folly of Mirnoff's makes it even more incumbent upon me to have my explanation with Miss Smith.'

It proved impossible to do so, however, because Miss Smith was found to have barricaded herself in her bedchamber against the household's and neighbourhood's warm efforts to press the General's suit. When the Count's valet scratched at her door to say that his lordship requested the favour of an interview, Miss Smith's patience snapped and she desired the man to inform his lordship that she had succumbed to a strong attack of the vapours, as became a bride. She then bolted her door and laughed till tears ran down her weather-beaten cheeks, so that she might not cry in earnest over the first marriage proposal of her life.

By morning she was feeling steadier and somewhat contrite, and she devoted the chief of it to composing a letter expressing her obligation to the General. She ended with her dependence on her Dear Friend to visit her in England, and promised him an inscribed copy of the Book as well as her unfailing regard, gratitude and esteem.

This missive, signed with a flourish, she bore downstairs herself. In the hall she found Danilo and Ahripoff deep in conclave with a travel-stained servant. Portmanteaux were being brought in from a troika outside. The conclave broke up at her approach. Miss Smith detained Danilo.

'What's this? Guests?'

'No, ma'am. A courier for the Count. Young Graf Nureyn; we know him from Petersburg. Driven day and night, his man says. His honour took him straight in to his lordship in the cabinet.'

Booted footsteps sounded and Sacha came in. He checked at the sight of Miss Smith.

'Good morning, ma'am. Danilo, where's the Graf's baggage?'

'I've had it taken up, sir.'

'He requires some papers from the dressing case or the cloak bag; he's too sleepy to remember which. Better have the lot brought down to him. Oh, and send in some black coffee. You've heard of our flurry, ma'am?'

'Yes. Sacha, is it—war?'

'No. That is: not yet. But the guns are being moved up; Napoleon has left Paris for the East.'

Miss Smith never despatched that particular letter to the General. But she was out in anticipating some dramatic change as a result of the courier's news. The Count pooh-poohed the alarm in Petersburg and roundly characterised his colleagues as a set of old women. Nevertheless, the Count understood better than any of them what the news of Napoleon's move meant. Realising that his days at Volnoya were now numbered, he decided that his explanation with Miss Smith would brook no further delay.

Passing through the upper hall later that morning, Sacha came upon a fair number of the servants hanging breathlessly over the banister.

The object of their interest was the raised voices clearly audible

F*

from the hall, where, with fine aristocratic scorn for the proprieties, the Count and Miss Smith had apparently chosen to conduct their epic encounter.

The domestics melted away at his approach. Sacha stopped only to enquire Miss Lise's whereabouts, before shamelessly settling himself down on an upper stair to eavesdrop.

To his relief Lise had been reported safely in the workroom; but after listening for a minute to the exchanges below, he reversed this opinion and swiftly rose to fetch her.

'Poppet, they're at it hammer and tongs, in the hall, of all places! Come quickly and eavesdrop with me if you don't wish to miss the battle of the century!'

Her troubled eyes as she rose to follow him told him volumes about what she imagined was being said. Sacha sent up a silent thanksgiving for botany, anthropology and the scientific method— those inexhaustible red herrings guaranteed to send Miss Smith flying off the scent.

He settled Lise comfortably beside him on the stairs in time to hear the Count say:

'. . . and I take leave to tell *you*, madam, that even my experience of English eccentricity leaves me room to question your motives! The loss of your fossils—'

'Plants.'

'Plants then, if you must, the distinction is otiose—'

'I beg your pardon, it is nothing of the sort! I would not travel a step for a fossil. The collection of such by an amateur in the field can best be described as *dabbling*. The anthropological aspect of botany, on the contrary, presents a scope—'

'Which you have extended beyond permission! And I tell you to your head, madam—'

'And I tell *you* to your head, sir, that I have heard enough! The courtesies extended to me during my stay here *had* influenced me to a better opinion of you Russians; but rest assured, sir, that I shall leave with every stricture upon the barbarism of your country amply, yes, amply confirmed!'

'If this is the price of your removal from Volnoya, madam, allow me to inform you that I hold it cheap. And let me beg you to feel no constraint in leaving. I will charge myself to make your excuses.'

'I would not dream of putting myself in your debt for any civility, sir,' came the glacial retort. 'And I have the honour to inform you that no action of mine is subject to your concern! As to our departure, *that* is already determined in my mind, since it would be a penance to any person of sensibility to remain in your company a day longer than necessary.'

The listeners upstairs heard the violent scrape of a chair and an approaching snort and hastily withdrew, just able to overhear his lordship's parting shot:

'I shall hold myself happy, madam, if any action of mine has so materially disrupted your scheming to—'

Sacha slammed the door of the workroom shut on the end of his father's sentence. Being able to read Lise's face like a book, he was tolerably assured that she had not caught its drift. In this he was right. Lise had retained nothing after the fatal words 'our departure is already determined'.

After a supper rendered conformable only by the obligation of good breeding, Sacha received his expected summons to wait on his father in the cabinet.

To his relief he found Graf Nureyn in attendance. His lordship finished dictating a dispatch and sent Nureyn off to make his copy, assuring that zealous young man that it would be time enough to send it off in the morning.

'Nevertheless, I must be off shortly, Sacha,' he said when they were alone. 'The Tsar needs all the heads we've got. This French business is boiling up. *My* task must be to see that we talk peace just long enough to wind up the Turkish affair. After that, if we can keep both the Emperor and our Germans out of the High Command, we should push through.'

The Count eased himself into a wing chair and took out his snuff box.

'I have written to His Majesty again about you,' he said, frowning slightly at the exquisite pastorale on its lid. 'The Governor has offered to write too, but—'

'If you please, sir, I would rather not be beholden in that quarter.'

'Your wishes are not in question. Ulanoff has some pretty things to say about not wasting your natural qualities as a fighting leader; but I told him it would not fadge. There's been too much gossip.'

His lordship gloomily contemplated the splendid figure presented by his son in evening dress.

'I wish it were possible for any part of your life to be conducted without a public scandal,' he remarked. 'Though I'll allow that this particular one is not entirely of your making.'

His son braced his shoulders against the high mantelpiece. The Count examined his well-kept nails.

'But I would not like to see you tied to a married woman's skirts for life, Sacha.'

Sacha stiffened, if that were possible, but bit down the hot rejoinder that rose to his lips. His father was looking at him with grim amusement.

'You are wondering at my—er—duplicity?'

'I would not permit myself to wonder at any action of yours, sir.'

'Admirable restraint. But you will allow that I know of what I speak.'

He rose abruptly and came across to Sacha. Their eyes met.

'I have not ever spoken to you of your mother. She was no Nina, and I think I loved her as much as it is possible for a man to love a woman. But even so it was a maimed thing for both of us. Do not let this be your lot; especially for the sake of a woman whom you only desire.'

Sacha shrugged.

'We suit,' he said curtly, 'and you will agree, sir, that in my present situation I cannot offer marriage to any woman.'

The fierce eyes on a level with his own glanced at him keenly.

'Would you do so otherwise?'

'I did,' replied Sacha with a flicker of a smile that lit his moody face with sudden sweetness. 'To Lise, if you recall, sir, after I had abducted her.'

The Count in his turn gave a faint shrug and returned to his chair.

'I was not speaking of your obligations as a gentleman.' He took snuff and sneezed irritably. 'Well then, since it is not in your power to make the girl happy, you will but be doing her a kindness in sending her away. I presume you realise the child is head over ears in love with you? But her precious "aunt" must bear the blame for *that*, in keeping her dangling here to try and fix your interest. This I told Miss Smith at the outset of our talk, before she went galloping off at a tangent about her infernal fossils. However, I flatter myself I finally convinced the lady of the desirability of their departure.'

Sacha suppressed a grin at this diplomatic version of the memorable tête-à-tête. He also came to an impulsive decision.

'Just so, sir. I imagine that Miss Smith may have in any case

formed such a design—unless of course she means to accept the
General—since I myself will shortly be leaving Volnoya.'

The Count gripped the arms of his chair. His eyes lit up.

'What's that? You have heard from Petersburg? The Tsar has
responded to my appeal? Why was I not informed at once?'

'Your pardon, sir, I have had no news from Petersburg. What I
propose—with your permission of course—is to join the French
army.'

For the first time in his life Sacha had the unfilial satisfaction
of seeing his parent put out of countenance.

The Count sprang to his feet.

'You propose *what*?' he roared, before he perceived the trap. Then
he took in his son's gleeful eyes and dealt him a genial buffet
that would have felled a less wiry physique.

'Damn your impudence!' he barked. 'Well? Explain yourself.'

Sacha righted his exquisitely tied cravat, disarranged by the
strength of the parental arm. When he raised his head all the lazy,
moody nonchalance with which he normally surveyed the world
was wiped from his face. A hard, tight smile curved his mouth;
above it his eyes blazed with the wild and dangerous brilliance
his father knew only too well.

'I believe it might answer to earn my freedom, sir,' he said softly,
'*if* the intelligence I brought back to our lines were of importance
and reached the right, important quarters. It is my hope that I may
depend on you for that.'

The Count did not immediately reply. Every natural feeling
clamoured in him to forbid the mad scheme; but looking at Sacha
his cool brain perceived two things: first, that the dangerous young
man before him was capable of making it succeed; second, that no
power on earth would stop him attempting it.

'You'll be depending on me for *rescue*, and earlier than that,' he
growled nevertheless. 'You young fool, how far do you think
you'll get if you cut and run from here?'

'To the first French pickets, as soon as the *Grande Armée* marches
into Russia,' replied Sacha calmly. 'You do not doubt that this is
their present destination? As for getting clear of here . . . Well,
things are bound to be a little confused; by the outbreak of
war. Also every man-jack of 'em here on the estate will cover
up for me to the last and the Governor has intimated—tacitly of
course—that he will turn a blind eye to my flight for as long as
possible.'

'The Governor? What has he to say to this harebrained start? Are you telling me that he is privy to it?'

'Well, in a sense—'

'In the sense that he would not be averse to your removal from here, I'll be bound! That's understandable.'

The Count threw himself back in his chair and gave a very creditable imitation of one of Miss Smith's snorts.

'Well, let's have it. The whole story, if you please.'

Sacha's eyes danced.

'The *whole* story is a trifle delicate,' he murmured. 'Let me put it this way: it was damned awkward for me to have Nina turn up here as the wife of my official keeper. From your own experience you'll agree, sir, that under these circumstances it is essential to have something to talk about with the husband, since one is such a frequent house-guest . . . The Prince and I talked about Russia.'

'Original,' commented the Count drily.

Sacha stiffened.

'It might be as well for our country, sir, if it were a more common subject of discourse—in official quarters! All Europe knows which way Napoleon's eyes have been turned for the past year, ever since our agreement with England left his famous Continental System in shreds. For months his vassal states and France itself have been squeezed dry for men, money, arms, transport. And all of it, all 60,000 men of the new *Grande Armée* are on the march to Russia. The Governor told me that this figure was furnished to Petersburg by no less an authority than the Prince of Benevento*—and of traitors!—himself.' He made an angry gesture of impatience. 'No doubt some clerk at our War Ministry has filed the information away for future reference! While our pen-pushing Germans in the High Command compile learned papers on military law!'

'Tol-lol, but I'd be glad to see their energies confined to that,' said the Count with a grimace.

Sacha had gone over to the console where a cellarette of brandies had been set out. He poured two glasses of cognac and carried them across to his father's chair.

'What will you wager, sir, that I'll nevertheless be making my report to General Kutuzov at Headquarters, before the year is out?'

'I'll drink to it; but there are too many bridges to be crossed—'

'Never fear, sir; the French advance will burn most of 'em for

* Talleyrand's title

you! And perhaps I can help to fire one or two in my rôle of Napoleon's most zealous recruit.'

The Count frowned, staring down into his glass.

'Tell me,' he said heavily, 'is it your design to present yourself to the French as yourself—a fugitive from exile, turned traitor in revenge?'

'No, sir. I had considered it, as the obvious course; but it might prove—embarrassing.'

Sacha had strolled back to propping up the fireplace. He said gruffly, looking anywhere but at his father:

'It—it was in my mind, sir, that if I do happen to get caught and shot, I would not like you to live with the stigma of a traitor son.'

He drained his brandy, swiftly refilled both their glasses and tilted back his own with a grin of pure mischief.

'Besides, it is going to be much more amusing the way I am planning it. Thank God, sir, you had a Cossack groom give me my first riding lessons here. Oh, a famous scheme! Almost as good as Lise and Nicky's Escape Plan for me. I am sorry that I cannot share it with either of them. Nicky, of course, would be wild to come too; but it might have served to distract Lise from her sorrow at leaving Volnoya.'

'I doubt it,' retorted the Count drily. 'But . . . How old is she? Sixteen—seventeen? She'll get over it.' His fierce eyes softened. 'A staunch child, as I recall, and schooled to disappointment. But even so, I'll be surprised if she does not make some push to save her happiness. You'd best be ready to resist a tearful eleventh-hour appeal.'

'I hate to let her go,' replied Sacha carelessly. 'Mme de Montargis sounds not at all the thing; and truth to tell, sir, I shall miss my little playmate excessively! But—' he hesitated, gazing down into the fire at a dozen jostling, bitter-sweet memories. 'But . . . Oh the devil! You're right. She must go.'

The eleventh-hour appeal arrived in Sacha's hand at midnight on the eve of Lise and Miss Smith's departure, four days later.

Lise had not planned such dramatic timing for her plea. The responsibility lay with time itself, which, after standing still for all the enchanted year, had suddenly, terrifyingly, speeded up. No time at all seemed to have elapsed between her aunt coming to her bedchamber to tell her that their departure was irrevocably fixed, and herself standing alone in that same bedchamber four nights later and realising that in the morning they would be gone.

Forever. Never to see Sacha again. Never to wake again to her beloved, familiar room, to the quiet river beyond the neglected garden, the rioting orchard, the dark, dreaming woods. Never to ride through them with Sacha again. Never to see Sacha again.

Her head throbbed with it. She pressed her forehead to the cold window-pane, staring huge-eyed at the moonlit landscape. And with some other part of her mind she was thinking: this is the first night it has been clear of snow. Soon it will be spring. Tomorrow Sacha and I will ride to that clearing in the woods where I found the snowdrops last year . . .

A sort of desperation seized her at the thought that instead she would be sitting in a closed coach and being borne away from Volnoya as fast as post-horses could carry her. She had no more tears left to cry. Dry-eyed, shivering, she re-lit her candle and flung herself down on the bed to write to Sacha.

He came upstairs at midnight. All the house was quiet when, having dismissed attendance, he stood at his dressing table looking down at the folded sheet addressed simply to 'Sacha', and thinking that he really did not need to open it. All the forlorn guilelessness of its appeal was there in the one word 'Sacha' in that careful, schoolgirl script.

Still, he owed it to her to read what she had written. He carried the letter over to the bed, stretched out and held it nearer to the bedside candle.

'Sacha, do not send me away. I know I said I only wished to get to my mother in London after that night in Vilensk. But now I know how to love you, so Why must I go away and leave you? Please Sacha let me stay with you Always. I love you so much that I know I could make you Happy. Please do not send me away. Lise.'

He let the sheet fall as if it had burned him. Guileless? Forlorn? Childish? Innocent? His first angry impulse was to damn the little innocent for a brazen hussy who knew only too well how to make a man's pulses throb with her prattle. On cooler reflection, he perceived the full injustice of this and took himself straitly to task for reading the child's foolish note in the same spirit as he would have scanned a passionate love-letter from Nina. The comparison was as absurd as it was odious; but of all the discomfiting thoughts it aroused in his mind, uppermost was a vision of Lise addressing another such naïve effusion to some gazetted rake in London who would not scruple to take advantage of her innocence. Sacha found his hands clenching at the thought of it, and fell asleep upon a firm resolve to send her off protected against her natural folly.

One of the benefits conferred by an iron constitution is the ability to wake at dawn, clear-eyed and refreshed, no matter in what state one has ended the evening.

Sacha rang for Danilo at six o'clock.

'Get me shaved at once. And have Miss Lise's maid get her dressed and tell her to join me on the terrace in half an hour.'

No vanity detained her; but, early as she was, he was there before her, lounging on the overgrown balustrade with his back to the house, gazing moodily into the faint mist hazing the river. He turned at the sound of her light footsteps; but Lise wondered, on a strangled giggle of nervousness, whether it was not the sound of her chattering teeth that had reached him, as he said crossly:

'Never do you seem able to appear suitably dressed! Here, take this, or you'll be sneezing in a minute.'

He stripped off his coat and placed it round her shoulders.

'And I'll vouch for it that you've chosen your thinnest slippers for walking through the wet grass.'

She had dreaded and longed for this meeting that would decide her fate. It was a long way down from these heights to the question of her footwear. She swallowed, trying to achieve a normal tone.

'No, truly Sacha. Look—' she lifted her skirts to display the red Cossack boots which she had donned as a sort of talisman.

'Well, that's something. Come on.'

He handed her down the terrace steps, and as on so many morning rambles, they turned down the rough-cut grass to the river.

But how different from their usual companionable silence was the silence that stood between them now! Even had she found the words she needed, Lise could not have broken it for the constriction in her throat. She swallowed convulsively to clear it. For now she had to speak, because here suddenly was time again starting to rush past her like some huge, silent wind, sweeping Volnoya away.

They had reached the first trees of the river bank. She stopped, as if by stopping she might arrest the relentless wind.

'Sacha—'

'No.'

He stopped too, frowning slightly as he looked down into her lifted face. She had instinctively held out her hands, displacing his coat round her shoulders. Sacha re-settled it around her and felt her tremble under his hands. He dropped them and stepped back.

'Lise, you wrote to me—'

He found it exceedingly difficult to continue in the vein he intended under the scrutiny of a pair of anxious dark eyes brimming with love and trust. Fixing his own on the tree behind her, he cleared his throat and made another attempt at the unfamiliar rôle of preaching decorum.

'Poppet, you are not really to blame,' he told her. 'My keeping you here all this year was probably an even worse folly than running off with you. At least I'll engage that your letter brought it home to me! Why, a year ago you would not have even known the words you use so ignorantly now! A year ago, for all my step-mother's faults, her chaperonage would have guarded you against such flagrant want of conduct. That is to put it at its least, leaving aside the dangers which I am persuaded you are blind to. My poor silly child, what do you know of love or men? Or of the *carte blanche* your letter so innocently offers me? There—you do not even understand what that means, do you?'

Dumbly she shook her head.

'Well, no matter. And, as *I* understand that innocence and neglect alone has betrayed you into this folly, I'll not enlarge on it—except to thank heaven that you'll soon have better guardianship than mine and Aunt Hon's! Come, we'll walk on.'

He put out a hand to take her arm, but it was submerged in his coat; he threw his arm companionably round her shoulders instead and hugged her to him.

'So now that's settled and we may be comfortable again. Shall we walk down to the bank and take a parting look at your favourite haunt? And what do you say to champagne for breakfast? Oh poppet, do not look so woebegone or I shall succumb to a flat melancholy too—for think how empty Volnoya is going to be without you!'

The small, silent ghost beside him came abruptly to life.

'Then *why* may I not stay? I don't give a fig for conduct! I do not want to go to England! I shall know nothing but misery there! I do not want my mother, I want you!'

'Rubbish!' snapped Sacha more roughly than he intended.

She shrank back.

'Listen to me,' he said between his teeth, 'I have tried speaking gently, but now I'll speak plain. Once before I was drunk and mad enough to take you at your foolish word. It's your good fortune, my girl, that I know you now—and I am not drunk. But neither your youth nor innocence might save you from another man. Damn your innocence! You little fool, do you not realise how you invite a man to use you? Like this—!'

He was not drunk; but for a few moments he was shaken enough to send crashing all the barriers he had carefully erected between them.

Lise emerged from his embrace dishevelled, gasping. She found herself obliged to grope for the support of the tree trunk. Her other hand crept up to finger her bruised mouth. In silence, Sacha picked up his coat from where it had fallen on the grass.

'I'll not apologise,' he told her grimly. 'Let that teach you a lesson in propriety until you are ready for such kisses. *And* show you how well rid you are of me!'

He turned on his heel and strode off; but had not gone more than a few yards before his stride faltered. He gave a small, exasperated shrug and retraced his steps.

Lise was standing where he had left her. She saw his approach through a blur of tears which were bringing no relief to the wildly confused emotions assailing her. Sacha slung his coat over a branch, produced a fine handkerchief, wiped her face, invited her to blow her nose and then proceeded to make a swift, experienced job of re-pinning her tumbled hair. Lise submitted docilely to these ministrations, being past all surprise and lacking, as Sacha had pointed out, any instruction as to how a young lady should behave under these trying circumstances. But the ex-leader of the Petersburg fast set could not but be conscious of the oddity of his conduct and felt it incumbent upon him to offer some explanation.

'You have had enough of a lesson without taking cold as well,' he grumbled, wrapping the coat snugly round her again. 'Now that you are presentable, we can go back. You are quite safe to take my arm. The lesson in propriety is finished; and thank God, poppet, that you'll soon have your mother to teach you how a lady must behave!'

She had allowed him to take her arm and had fallen into her usual two-steps-to-his-one beside him; though she had not yet ventured to look up. But at these words Sacha abruptly found his arm rejected and Mlle de Montargis drawn up to her full height, with black eyes flashing fire.

'My mother will know better than to teach me that! She is a Rohan; and whatever I do, I am a Montargis. It was how *we* chose to behave that set the tone for the *beau monde* you all copy in Russia—and I will make it do so again!'

Astonishment and a cool approval gleamed for an instant in Sacha's eyes. Then he swept her the most elegant of bows, only slightly marred by his shaking shoulders. However, his face was perfectly grave again when he straightened up.

'*Mes hommages, mademoiselle!* May I hope that the future arbitress of the *ton* does not disdain breakfast? And will grant a mere Russian the inestimable privilege of escorting her in?'

Lise haughtily surrendered her arm, her head held high and a hot glow of indignation and pride sustaining her and keeping at bay the hollow desolation inside her. Sacha too found himself holding on to the diversion her injured pride had provided. The thoughts lurking round the edge of his amusement were too disturbing.

They walked on. Ahead of them, the overgrown white house seemed already a place remembered, while their separate futures loomed close and comfortless; though only he dimly foresaw the cataclysm that would divide them. Lise, with all the resilience of femininity and extreme youth, was already planning her sweet revenge.

Part Two

Part Two

CHAPTER I

At dawn on the 1st of August 1812, the thirty-ninth day of Napoleon's advance into Russia, a small detachment of Dragoons of the King of Naples' command were making their cautious way along a wooded ravine above the Dvina river, in the vicinity of Vitebsk. The caution was enjoined by the healthy respect in which the *Grande Armée* had already learnt to hold the ranging Cossack patrols; so that when the sergeant in charge heard shouts and a flurry of hoofbeats ahead he had no need to exhort his men to alertness.

They emerged from the narrow defile they had been following, into a clearing: to be confronted by a scene that confirmed all they had heard about the savagery of their Cossack opponents.

A half dozen wild-haired ruffians, armed with the cruel *nagaikas*, were apparently too engrossed in wreaking their vengeance upon their prisoner to have noticed the French approach. Him they had tied spreadeagled by the arms to the branches of a tree. He sagged against its trunk, stripped to the waist, and his young, muscular back was already crossed by two cruel weals from the attentions of his captors.

Their bloodthirsty yells, which had so imprudently attracted the attention of the Dragoons, continued till these were upon them. Then, presumably seeing themselves outnumbered, the barbarians scattered to their hidden horses and vanished into the forest, leaving the French with their prisoner.

The sergeant's first care was to dispose a screen of look-outs. Meantime two of his men had cut down the prisoner. He slumped into their arms, well-nigh insensible after his ordeal; nevertheless it was obvious to them that he was not French.

Sergeant Mercier examined him curiously, for this was the first Cossack he had seen at close quarters without imminent personal danger. But was the young man a Cossack? His sweat-matted, dark-streaked, blond hair was cut long in the Cossack style and his breeches and boots were of the dark green and the soft, matt leather worn by Cossack regiments. But stripped as he was of all badges of rank, everything about him still proclaimed the aristocrat. Sergeant Mercier scratched his head.

'But then after all, sergeant, there may be princes amongst these heathen for all we know,' one of the troopers offered.

Another had meanwhile discovered the prisoner's horse. To their experienced cavalry eyes, one glance at his mount settled all doubts. No such prime bit of blood could belong to anyone less than a prince. The unlikelihood of such a prize being abandoned by any Cossack, even in flight, might have aroused their suspicions had they not been too busy arguing as to whom the loot should fall. It was agreed to dice for the animal.

The prisoner somewhat abruptly regained consciousness and sat up.

One of the men pointed this out to the sergeant, who reluctantly returned his attention to him, but to no advance in understanding. The young Cossack did not command a word of French.

'Well, we'd best get him down to the lieutenant. *Parbleu*, what ails him?'

'Probably thinks we're going to finish him off, sergeant, like his own savages were set to do.'

But the prisoner's trouble turned out to be no more than the loss of his clothing, to which, however, he appeared to attach inordinate importance. Pointing to the sergeant's uniform, he demonstrated in rapid dumbshow the cause of his concern. There had been something . . . Money? A document? Ah, a letter! A secret letter concealed in his belt.

'*Da! Da! Lettaire. Napoleon.*'

The magic name galvanised his audience.

'Can he stand up? Then he's fit to ride. Bring his mount over here.'

'But, sergeant, you said—'

'Look sharp now! Do you want him complaining to the Emperor that the Dragoons are a set of horse-thieves?'

The same thought preserved the prisoner's mount to his use after his delivery to the Advance Guard's Headquarters; and just as he was being led away he had his second piece of luck.

A flurry of trumpets and a swirl of dust announced the arrival of the King of Naples and his suite on an inspection of the advance posts. Joachim Murat, the Emperor's brother-in-law, had started life as a Gascon inn-keeper's son, but on horseback he had never cut less than a splendid figure. In this campaign he had elected to wear Polish dress, and now cavorted in all the magnificence of befurred green velvet, embroidered yellow boots, gold shoulder-knots, and long black curls streaming out from a shako whose white plume was studded in gems. Beneath it, his countenance was set in solid gloom. Here too there was nothing to report. There was still no trace of the main Russian armies. How much further into their trackless forests would they have to pursue these *sacré* Russians?

The Cossack prisoner was produced as a diversion. A Polish interpreter was available, and the prisoner's story stood its first test.

Undoubtedly his picturesque dishevelment helped to gain it credence. Three hours' hard riding under a broiling sun had greatly added to the discomfort of his scarred back; but even as he cursed the demands of verisimilitude, he could not but be aware of the favourable sensation he was creating.

Russian prisoners were still a rarity to the *Grande Armée*. Of Cossacks there had been a total dearth: the Cossacks left no wounded.

But as the King of Naples examined their prize, he was thinking of an even more exalted need which the young Cossack might fulfil.

From the moment he had crossed the Niemen into Russia, Napoleon had been awaiting the familiar deputations from the enslaved peoples who should be looking to him as their liberator. Six weeks and many weary leagues later, in Vitebsk, he was still waiting.

'Do you think I have come all this way to conquer these huts?' he had exclaimed in disgust to his Staff on entering the deserted city; and any one of the Kings, Princes, Dukes, Marshals and Generals attending His Majesty would have given much to be able to produce just one brace of bearded *boyars*, just a single Cossack, to supply the great man's need of conquest.

Here, ready to Murat's hand, was the single Cossack.

The cautions of his staff were royally waved aside, and the prisoner's importance gained in measure to the King's own.

'You say his name is Volnoy, meaning "free"? *Comme c'est à propos!* And he is the son of a Hetman—what is that? Ah, a chieftain, a prince then, of the Don Cossacks, come with a letter—a petition of course—to His Imperial Majesty, from his father? But *naturallement* to beg His Majesty's help in the liberation of his people from the Tsarist yoke! And he was captured, robbed of his letter and tortured, he says—*nom de Dieu, mais ça se voit!*—when he was almost within reach of our lines? No matter, he shall convey his father's words to the Emperor in person, under my patronage; and his people shall not find us deaf to such a plea! Also it will help to keep the Emperor amused,' added His Grace thoughtfully.

In the inactivity of Vitebsk, this task had assumed a formidable importance in the eyes of the Emperor's entourage. On entering the Imperial Headquarters in Vitebsk, Napoleon had thrown his sword down on to a table covered with maps, exclaiming:

'Here I stop! I want to collect myself, rally my forces, rest my army and organise Poland. The campaign of 1812 is finished. The campaign of 1813 will do the rest.'

Which still left some five months of 1812 to be occupied.

The needs of the army engaged the great man's attention for a little while. Hospitals, remount depots, stores were organised. Thirty-six bread ovens were set up to produce twenty-nine thousand loaves a day. The streets rumbled with the endless columns of commissariat, ambulances, artillery and pontoons which had been dragging after the *Grande Armée* across the Lithuanian sands.

Nor were the elegancies of life neglected. Some stone houses spoiling His Majesty's view across the Palace square were being torn down by the Guard. Thought was given to winter pleasures. Actors and actresses were to be bespoken from Paris for the theatre. Eligible feminine company would be supplied from Warsaw and Vilna. But none of this was enough to occupy the energies of genius.

Murat's picturesque captive kept the Emperor amused for a full half-hour of quick-fire questioning that left the self-appointed representative of the Don Cossacks slightly shaken.

But at the end of the audience the Emperor pulled his ear—most coveted of familiarities—and bade the interpreter tell *'l'enfant du Don'* that he was welcome at Imperial Headquarters.

Most of the restraints put upon him were thereafter lifted and he was told to consider himself a guest of the aides-de-camp's Mess.

He did not test his new status beyond prudence; but it enabled him to introduce a flat-faced Kalmuk he picked up in the town, to serve him as a sort of batman, and to procure a dashing Cossack uniform which *l'enfant du Don*—child of nature that he was— delighted to parade. It had been made slightly wide for him and it was his hope that it would pass muster on his servant for a vital few hours when the time came.

Meanwhile he was happy to indulge his hosts with displays of Cossack riding. They, in their turn, attempted to teach him French; but in this his progress was negligible and inclined them the more to speak freely in his presence.

The Emperor himself was apt to use him as a dumb audience. The sweltering heat and inaction lay heavy upon Napoleon. All his orders had been carried out. No proposals from Alexander arrived. There was nothing to do . . . except to decide the fate of Russia and the *Grande Armée*.

He could be seen wandering about his apartments as if haunted by some dangerous temptation. He was unable to keep in one place, walking aimlessly up and down, asking what time it was, remarking about the weather, humming a snatch of song, and then resuming his restless pacing.

In this state of perplexity he spoke a few disconnected words to whomever he chanced to meet; and he was not displeased when his Cossack hostage formed his audience, feeling himself then in the presence of Russia itself.

'Well, what are we going to do?' he would demand of him. 'Shall we stay here? Shall we advance? How can we stop now on the road to glory?'

With some effort Russia remained inscrutable, and the Emperor would move on without waiting for an answer.

One sweltering morning found the Emperor stretched out on a cot he had had brought in to his chambers, and wearing only light under-garments. In this manner he spent the great part of his days at Vitebsk. But with his body at rest, his mind was all the more active.

'How many reasons have I for going on to Moscow at once!' he exclaimed. 'How can I bear the boredom of seven months of winter in this place? Am I to be reduced to defending myself—I who have always attacked? Such a rôle is unworthy of me . . . I am not used to playing it. It is not in keeping with my genius.'

Suddenly he sprang to his feet and rushed over to the maps which showed him Smolensk and Moscow; great Moscow, the Holy City of the Tsars. Over and over again he repeated these names. His voice hardened, his eyes glittered, his expression became fierce. The members of his Staff and Household present drew back from him in mingled fear and respect. The young Cossack effaced himself in a corner. Addressing himself to his aide-de-camp, the Comte de Ségur, the Emperor cried:

'Bah, I've made my Generals too rich! All they dream of now is flaunting their elegant carriages in Paris. I suppose they've lost their taste for war!' And swooping round on a luckless General of the Guard he barked:

'You were born in a bivouac and in a bivouac you will die!'

A grave civilian personage, whom the Cossack identified as the Minister for War, ventured a protest. The Emperor promptly rounded on him.

'There's been no blood shed as yet and Russia is too great to surrender without a fight,' he told him. 'If necessary, I'll seek that decisive battle in their Holy City itself, and I'll win it! Peace awaits me at the gates of Moscow. If Alexander still holds out, I'll negotiate with the *boyars*.'

In his corner, the young Cossack blinked. *Boyars* had been abolished since Peter the Great; but he quickly returned his fascinated attention to his host.

'. . . or even with the large and enlightened population of the capital,' the Emperor continued, with an expansive gesture. '*They* will understand what is in their best interest and know the meaning of liberty.' After a moment he added pensively: 'Besides, Moscow hates St Petersburg. I will benefit from this rivalry. Why, the results of such jealousy are incalculable.'

Turning to Marshal Duroc, who was expressing his disapproval by a cold silence, the Emperor exclaimed:

'Of course I see clearly that the Russians only want to lure me on! Nevertheless I must extend my line as far as Smolensk. Smolensk is the key to two main roads, one to St Petersburg, the other to Moscow. We must take possession of it.'

Unobtrusively, the young Cossack slid out. His mission, although the Emperor was unaware of it, was concluded. He knew the final goal of the *Grande Armée*: Moscow, and its immediate objective: Smolensk.

His freedom and the Tsar's pardon would be purchased cheap for such a price.

'Your route through the town is pretty well laid, your honour; but I've still to lay hands on your disguise. Best if you went in one of their French uniforms, since you'll have to break cover outside,' Danilo deposed.

'Get your thieving hands on one fast, then. My news won't brook delay. Tonight?'

'I'll do my best, sir.'

'Good. What about you?'

'I'll be on view here, drunk and snoring on your honour's cot. With your clothes and hat on, and face-down, I should pass muster.'

'Drunk if you will, but *not* snoring. And then?'

'When your honour's got a good start, I'll slope off. These Frogs don't know a Kalmuk from a Dnieper peasant, and I've got a brace of fat geese against emergencies.'

The evening, however, brought a check to these promising plans. An Imperial aide arrived to require M. Volnoy's attendance at supper. An important mission from liberated Poland had arrived at Head-quarters and the Emperor wished to show off his Cossack aspirant to freedom.

L'enfant du Don accepted the honour without enthusiasm, straightened his sash and followed the adjutant to the saloon where a glittering bevy of uniforms were already assembled. His own seat was indicated at the centre, facing the entourage of the Polish magnates. He took his place behind his chair, glanced across the table and found himself looking into the eyes of Prince Adam Ralensky.

The Emperor left the supper table early. At a little after midnight Prince Adam let himself quietly into Sacha's room.

He was still wearing the resplendent full-dress regimentals of a lieutenant of the Polish Lancers. Sacha, lounging on his cot, rose. The two friends faced each other in the light of the single candle.

'Sacha, what are you doing here?'

'Spying,' said Sacha calmly. 'Going to denounce me?'

'Don't be a fool. But how—what—'

'For that matter, what are you doing in this *galère*?'

The boy's dark, unhappy eyes flashed.

'The Emperor Napoleon is the liberator of my country, and every true Pole must—'

'Napoleon is the invader of mine, and every true Russian must fight him by every means. *Especially* if it's going to help him out of disgrace with his own beloved Emperor. My poor Adam, don't look so downcast! I've never aspired to your alt of patriotism. But now to business. If you're not going to denounce me, what *are* you proposing to do?'

'I—I don't know.'

Sacha glanced across at the boy with more than a touch of compunction.

'It's the devil of a pass for you, ain't it? If it will salve your honour I'll gladly fight you.'

'You'd knock me out,' said Prince Adam practically. 'You always did.'

'Of course. That's the point. And leave you here trussed and senseless whilst I make my getaway.'

'You're escaping?'

Tonight. And I warn you, Adam, that neither you nor the whole dam' French army is going to stop me.'

Prince Adam grinned.

'When you look like that I don't suppose the devil himself could stop you. It's how you looked when I last saw you. You remember—when you took it into your head to carry off that girl with you into exile.'

'Would that you or the devil had stopped me *then*! I was sorry enough for it when I sobered. Still, she should be safely with her mother in London by now . . . I must try to get news of her when I get to Petersburg—No, I must not.'

'*When* you get to Petersburg? Sacha, this whole town is an armed camp and Headquarters bristles with guards. You've really got a plan?'

'A route; but so far Danilo's been unable to rustle me up the French uniform I want as a disguise. Well, I'll contrive to bluff my way out one way or another, and once clear of the town—'

'You've got tonight's password?'

'Yes, "Warsaw", in your honour.'

'But do you know that the sentries also have orders to check the credentials of everyone going in and out of Headquarters? That's in our honour too—they don't trust us above half.'

'The devil! Well, I'll push through. Now be off, dear boy, I must make ready.'

'Damned if I'll go and leave you to walk into a death trap!' cried Prince Adam with fine Polish illogic. 'Let me think. What's wrong with you leaving here as a Lieutenant of Polish Lancers?'

Sacha dismissed the notion with some regret. Morning would

see the whole Headquarters seething with enquiries; he could not
risk it for the boy.

'What's wrong with it?' he drawled. 'But everything! I've already
suffered exquisite agony wearing Cossack regimentals cut too
wide for me. Now you ask me to be seen in a Polish Lancer's rig
that'll be at least three inches too short. Pray consider my reputation!
Ah, that'll be Danilo now. Off with you, Adam, and—thanks.'

Danilo slid in, starting at the sight of Prince Adam whom, however, he quickly recognised.

'It's all right, Danilo. His Highness is *au fait* with my plans,' said
Sacha. 'What's that you're carrying?'

'One of the Frog Generals' uniforms, your honour. Best I could
do. The stuff was in the valets' quarters to be brushed. With this
dratted double guard, I couldn't get down into town to lift something from the clothing commissariat.'

'No matter, I shall now go in style. But these Hessians you're
forcing on me are torture! I presume it would not do to have a
French General of the Guard sporting Cossack boots?'

'Definitely not, your honour.'

'Sacha, are you sure there is not something I can do?' said Prince
Adam unhappily at the door.

Sacha hesitated. Then he said slowly:

'Yes. If I don't come through and you do ... When this is all over,
give my love to my father. And dance with Lise in London.'

Ex-Sergeant Mercier, newly created a lieutenant as a result of his
fortunate capture, found that his new dignity did not exempt him
from the dawn patrol. This morning their route was of the kind
he held in particular dislike. A recent storm had felled two great
trees across the wooded track ahead of them. Lieutenant Mercier
cursed and pulled his mount round, urging it up the steep hillside.
Yet another detour.

Once over the brow, his troop found themselves in a scene whose
wild grandeur would have inspired a more poetic taste. The
Dragoons were only concerned with their breakfast. This receded
rapidly as they wound further and further into the rocky defiles.
Presently they came to a dispirited halt.

'It's no good, *mon lieutenant*. We shall have to go back and
shift those —— trees.'

The lieutenant considered the uninviting width of the ravine barring their progress and reluctantly turned his horse. His men cursed. About halfway back, they halted at a stream to water their horses and get their bearings. One of the troopers had keen ears.

'Hoofbeats, *mon lieutenant*. Coming up fast on our right flank.'

They wheeled; but it was only a single rider, to whom, now that he was safe in the hills, speed had appeared a more paramount need than caution. He crashed out of the thicket on the steep slope above them—and Lieutenant Mercier was amazed to recognise at once a General of the Imperial Guard and his late prisoner.

The recognition was mutual and Sacha did not wait on explanation. Pulling Galant round on his haunches, he flung him across the troop's rear, roughly in the direction from which they had come. The Dragoons threw themselves back in the saddle and thundered in pursuit.

Galant had been ridden hard over wild country since well before dawn; but his breeding and his great heart still told over the troopers' horses. Several of their riders had discharged their pistolets in the first rush, harmlessly enough; but now some more carefully aimed bullets came whistling uncomfortably close past Sacha's ears. He flattened himself against Galant's neck, knowing there was no need of the spur to urge him to all the speed left in him. The pursuit dropped back and in a few minutes Sacha was surprised to hear the drumming hooves behind him fall away altogether. Then he saw the ravine ahead and knew why the pursuit had halted.

He reined Galant in and swept his eyes over the wild landscape for some way round the chasm; but in his heart he knew it was hopeless. The French would not be taking their time to re-form and load unless they knew they had him trapped. He sat, absently patting Galant's steaming neck and considering the ravine with a grimly measuring eye.

It was too wide.

Faintly, up the hillside behind him, he heard the renewed drumming of hooves. He smiled, a hard, tight smile, gathering up the reins.

'Well, Galant *mon brave*, we've never done it sober . . .'

CHAPTER II

Exactly three months and ten days after leaving Volnoya, Miss Smith and Lise stepped ashore in England at Plymouth.

Few of the major mishaps of sea travel had attended their progress but every minor inconvenience had been theirs, of which the latest was to find themselves setting foot on British soil practically penniless.

'Well, we'll not be making a piece of work of it, Lise,' said Miss Smith. 'But take our pot-luck at some hostelry suited to our reduced circumstances, until I can raise some funds. I shall desire the sailor unloading our baggage to procure us a handcart and some stout fellow to push it to the nearest such inn.'

The stout fellow was forthcoming and presently volunteered the intelligence that if Missus be boun' furr Lunnon, Royal Devonshire urr be 'bout due t'leave from urr Half Moon inn in Ole Town.

This Miss Smith was obliged to translate to Lise, who had not understood one word of his broad Devon.

'So come, child, with a push we can be on it. And I mean a *push*, for we'll not do it at our present pace. Let us two take a handle between us. Now, all in step, and off we go!'

Lise was sufficiently depressed by her arrival in England without finding that she could not understand the natives and being obliged to trudge behind a handcart through the streets. Miss Smith glanced at her shrewdly.

'Dear child, your expressive eyes must always defeat your good manners. Take heart, I am persuaded that the stage coach cannot prove as trying as when we were cooped up in our cabin with those three excessively plump ornaments of the Smyrna pasha's harem. Oh, and Lise—the headland to the left of us is Plymouth Hoe.'

'Where your Admiral Drake played his game of bowls as he awaited the Spanish ships?'

'The very spot.'

'Nicky and I were forever getting Mr Tickell to tell us the story!

Oh, how I wish—but you know that the Countess wrote forbidding me to have any further intercourse with Count Nicolas?'

Miss Smith compressed her lips, but bracingly assured Lise that such a determined character as Nicky's would surely triumph over all obstacles to their continued acquaintance. Cheered by this and the beautiful summer morning, Lise stepped out briskly and they arrived at the Half Moon Inn in time to detain the coach. Miss Smith quickly disposed of the guard's scruples about the obvious overloading entailed by their baggage and convinced their fellow-passengers that squeezing Lise and herself between them saw them all snugly settled.

Lise, wedged between an onion-scented farmer and a stout woman with a basket of pies on her lap, saw little of the countryside as the coach lumbered on, except when any important hill required the descent of all the passengers to walk.

Then she was able to look around. How small everything was after Russia! But she could not help being struck, like every visitor, by the neatness and propriety as well as the beauty of the countryside. The hedgerows of the deep Devon lanes through which they drove were full of shepherd's rose, honeysuckle and all sorts of wild flowers; the uplands were blue with hemp or flax, golden with corn, or provided lush green pasture to fat cows and sheep. All this landscape was constantly enriched by fine timber; and when Lise was not exclaiming over the beauty of the leafy glades, she was delighting in the sturdy white farmhouses and beamed cottages, with their rose and jessamine-festooned porches, their bright gardens full of wall-fruit and their well-stocked rickyards behind, telling of abundance and order.

Her raptures and her pretty French accent evoked slow grins from her fellow-passengers. Miss Smith, deep in horse-talk with her farrier neighbour, also gave vent to an occasional snort of sleepy content as she gazed out over her homeland.

'Ay,' she nodded, 'and you've only to look at these cottage gardens to know what sort of people our English labourers are, as Mr Cobbett has truly said.' And to Lise's incomprehension but the huge delight of their fellow-travellers, she proceeded to recite:

> 'The race is not always got
> By them wot strive and for it run
> Nor is the battel to them peopel
> Wot's got the longest gun

'—as Boney's marshals are finding in the Peninsula, eh? What's in the latest bulletins?'

They were able to give her the good news that Lord Wellington was across the Agueda, brought to Plymouth by fast frigate. But the farrier, recently in London, could make no such encouraging report of the war in the East, where Napoleon was reported to be sweeping all before him into Russia.

Lise's strained attention at the mention of Russia yielded her the gist of this, and thereafter her interest in the countryside waned.

It was dark when, on the second day, the slow coach began to rumble over London cobbles. Miss Smith pointed out various famous landmarks but Lise was too jolted and fatigued to note them.

'Come, child, if Paris was worth a Mass, Westminster surely rates a crick in the neck.'

'Yes, Aunt Hon. I'm sorry; it's just that—'

'Tut, I know. I vow every bone of me is rattled to death too. Never fear, our penury shall not endure beyond a hack to convey us to our hotel. I do not believe I now have even the price of a hack on me, but Poulett's can settle for it. My credit will stand it, I'm sure.'

Lise wished she could be sure of it too, when the hackney set them down at the imposing entrance of Poulett's hotel off Piccadilly. A series of powdered flunkeys conducted them to a luxurious suite on the second floor, where one of them proved himself human by lending a hand with the obstinately jammed lock of Lise's valise.

A fire, made welcome by the chilly evening, was kindled in the saloon where two waiters set out a copious supper.

Lise was too uneasy to do justice to the repast, but her aunt insisted upon her taking some soup and a glass of wine before the fire. Miss Smith raised her own glass.

'A toast, Lise; to England, home and beauty, and your new life!'

It was so like an echo of Sacha that she regretted it the moment it was out. Lise choked down a small sob. Miss Smith snorted.

'Your new life,' she repeated deliberately. 'And you'll not go botching it at the outset by repining over Sacha Arloff!'

Lise sat up with a jerk.

'Repining? Pray let me tell you, Aunt Hon, that I do not care if I never see him again! And that the next time Sacha Arloff hears of me it shall be as a leader of the *ton* with *dozens* of eligible suitors. *Then* perhaps I shall admit him to my presence,' she conceded grandly. 'Just to see his face—Oh, just . . . to know he's safe—'

Fatigue, the wine and the pictures in the dancing fire combined to break down all resolution. The small sob recurred, swelled and dissolved into a flood of tears on Miss Smith's shoulder.

Miss Smith let her weep her fill, administering an awkward pat now and again to her tumbled hair.

'There, child, there. I promise you he will come through safe and sound,' she murmured, not even troubling to question Lise's assumption that one way or another Sacha would have contrived to get into the fighting.

Lise woke late next morning to find her aunt gone out, and a billet on her dressing table warning her not to expect her return until after noon.

At first Lise was perfectly content with her solitude. Restored to the familiar comfort of luxury, she could not help feeling more at home in England. Her traditional vision of London shrouded in a perpetual fog, which her mother's letters had supported, also required adjustment to the fine though chilly morning outside. However, fires glowed softly in all the marble grates of the suite and a delicious smell of coffee and hot buttered toast was wafting to her through the open door of the saloon. She settled happily to explore the breakfast dishes under their silver covers, occasionally wandering to the windows.

Below her, the fashionable street had woken up. She listened lazily to the unfamiliar note in the street cries and the different clatter of horses and carriages over London cobbles, borne up faintly to her luxurious eyrie above it all.

But presently her very well-being began to fret her nerves. How was it possible for them to afford such a suite of apartments? A vision of the suave major-domo below having them summarily ejected by the very flunkeys who had bowed them upstairs, rose all too vividly before Lise's eyes; so that she jumped like a startled kitten when one of these, receiving no answer to his soft scratching, inched open the saloon door.

'Beg your pardon, miss. It was thought as how you might like to peruse the papers.'

He laid the Gazette and the Morning Post on a console and

hovered softly, having been directed to proffer every attention.

'Would there be anything else, miss? If miss will permit me—some fresh coffee and muffins. I'll have them up directly.'

'Oh no, I do not want for anything. Pray do not trouble—' stammered Lise, stricken with the thought of a double breakfast bill.

'It is a pleasure, miss.'

He sounded kind and Lise had now identified him.

'You were the man who kindly helped with my valise lock last night, were you not? What is your name?'

'Yes, miss. Jeeams, miss.'

'Jims?'

'No, miss. Jeeams.'

'Oh, you mean Jams,' cried Lise, pronouncing it French-fashion.

'That's right, miss,' responded her companion imperturbably, 'J, a, m, e, s, Jeeams.'

They looked at each other and burst out laughing. On this human footing, Lise felt emboldened to enlist his aid on the most pressing of her problems.

'Well, Jams, could you—that is, would you please—' she hesitated and then blurted, 'Would you please tell me the cost of these chambers? You see, it is so difficult. My Aunt—that is, Miss Smith—has been away from her native land for so long, and she—it is possible that she hasn't—that this suite is quite beyond our means, and—'

Her new friend burst into a guffaw that would have earned him instant dismissal if heard above stairs.

'Ho, ho, if that don't beat the band! If I may say so, miss, that's a corker, that is! The Honourable Honoria Devereux Smith not able to pay her shot? That's a turn-up for the book! Now you just set your mind at rest, missie, if that's what's worriting you. Why, miss,' he cried, slapping his thigh. 'His Grace, Miss Honoria's nephew, *owns* the best part of this neighbourhood—just as a sideline as you might say, for I believe most o' the Malvern land is up in the Midlands. Thousands of acres he's got there and collieries besides, as well as—'

Lise lost track of the Malvern inheritance. Her confusion clamoured for elucidation on just one point.

'Do you mean—you said "His Grace"—do you mean Miss Smith's nephew is really a Duke?'

' 'Course he is, miss. The Duke of Malvern. Succeeded his father a year ago. Ay, and I've seen his brother, the young Marquis here too—him as was the heir till he was killed in the Peninsula. A regular goer he was! Top o' the trees, and one of the Corinthian set; but not a bit high in the instep with it all. An open hand and a smile to warm your heart.'

'Oh, but I've heard of him!' exclaimed Lise. '*He* must have been the boy who climbed the tower.'

Her companion looked at her in puzzlement, but Lise had forgotten him. Her chin sunk on to her clasped hands, she was recalling the sunlit room at Volnoya and her Aunt's fierce tone and gentle look as she spoke of the boy who climbed the tower in faraway England. Lise's lips formed the half-remembered words.

'. . . another of your gay blades who're no good to anyone . . . like Sacha. And now it is his younger brother who . . . lives in the house with the tower.'

'Well, I dunno about a tower, missie,' said James. 'His Grace resides at Malvern Castle, and he was certainly the younger brother. But I dunno about any towers . . .'

'Aunt Hon,' cried Lise accusingly, hardly giving that lady time to remove her hat. 'You *are* a Duke's aunt!'

'Certainly, child, unless some sudden mishap has befallen him; but his butler reported him quite stout at Malvern when I called at his house in Grosvenor Square this morning.'

'But—' Lise bit her lip, flushing. Then she flung her arms about Miss Smith and went off into peal after peal of her enchanting laughter.

'Oh, I shall die! And there were Sacha and I trembling every minute to have you exposed as an imposter by the Count! Why didn't you *tell* us?'

'But I did,' replied Miss Smith tranquilly, disengaging herself. 'As I recall, on the first evening of my meeting with you at the posting house. I collect that my vagabond ways did not commend me to you as a person of *ton*? Dear me, what high sticklers the young are!'

'Oh no! Why, Aunt Hon, Sacha told me that even the Count allowed you to be a lady. A lady adventurer,' she added mischievously.

'I'll engage he amended it from "adventur*ess*", in the old Tartar's mouth! But since it has made you laugh, I'll forgive the pair of you. I have not heard you laugh like this since—for too long. And particularly because I have some vexatious news for you. I sent a servant from Devereux House to apprise your mother of our arrival, and he found the house in Highgate shut up. A neighbour informed him that Sir Barnaby Potts' household have removed to Yorkshire for the summer. That is your brother-in-law's name is it not?'

'Gone away?' echoed Lise in dismay. 'Oh, but then my mother cannot have had my letter which the frigate captain in Malta promised to remit to her. The family will have gone to Rigby, I expect, ma'am. That is the name of Sir Barnaby's house in Yorkshire, at a place called West Riding.'

'H'mm. The West Riding is somewhat vague as a direction. Never mind, we shall narrow it down and write at once to discover how you may join them. But even so it will take a week or more—'

'Could I not await the reply at the house in High Gate?' offered Lise, sensing some awkwardness.

'Highgate, all one word,' corrected Miss Smith mechanically. She took a few irritated turns about the room.

'No, you cannot go to the house. I have told you it is shut up. No, child, do not look so worried. It is nothing—or only a minor *contretemps*. You see, I had planned on going up to Edinburgh as soon as I have done my duty by my sister at Malvern. There is a Dr Robinson at the University there with whom I have corresponded these many years. I wanted him to have the first sight . . . Well, anyway, I have this morning sent off an express to him, as well as a man from Grosvenor Square to tell my sister to look for me at Malvern directly. Well, well, I cannot leave you, so that's that. And now we shall plan a continuous, dizzy round of pleasure, as Sa—as we were used to. Let's see, Astley's Amphitheatre for a start, and then perhaps to the Vauxhall Gardens for supper?'

But Lise was growing up. Astley's Amphitheatre could not divert her mind from the knowledge that she had become an embarrassment to her benefactress.

Next morning, however, brought a letter on which Lise was delighted to recognise her mother's hand.

Mme de Montargis wrote from Rigby. Her letter was to Miss Smith with an enclosure for her daughter, and the girl looked up from reading it with such a forlorn look that Miss Smith hastily wiped all her own dissatisfaction off her face.

'You are disappointed, of course, child, having looked to be re-united with your mother at once,' she told Lise. 'But a couple of weeks is no great thing after your years apart. One must respect your mother's scruples about exposing you to the fatigue of more travel and the risk of infection from a nursery full of—what is it?— ah yes, measles.'

'But my mother knows I have had the measles!'

'No doubt she forgot that circumstance when she wrote,' snorted Miss Smith. 'Tut, Lise, don't be childish. It is patently obvious that Mme de Montargis finds it ineligible to receive you in Yorkshire. She has many obliging things to say about my *bonté* in taking charge of you, and I promise you that my *bonté* will not be strained by another se'nnight or so! I shall send at once to the Duchess to tell her I am bringing you.'

Their journey into Worcestershire was accomplished in style. The Duke sent one of his London carriages to convey his aunt: a stately, gleaming barouche-landau. With it went four beautiful high-stepping greys—traditional to the House of Devereux—and coachman, footmen and outriders in the Malvern livery. The stir called forth by this equipage at the Inns might have compensated Lise for their pauper's progress to London, had she not so keenly felt herself an intruder on these gratifying scenes.

The late Duke had been used to keep his own horses at all the main posting-houses *en route* to his principal residences, and this extravagance continued unchecked by his successor's retired mode of life. Miss Smith snorted at it, but as they rolled through Malvern park the morning after leaving London, she was obliged to confess to the comfort and expedition it ensured.

Lise's discomfort had increased with each fresh evidence of Malvern's grandeur. Yet it was not its splendours that oppressed her. Great houses, deer-cropped parks, lawns rolled to green velvet, massed flowers, fountains, ice houses, conservatories, orangeries, whose opulence it took armies of servants to maintain, were no novelty to her; nor her own lot of being on sufferance in them. She mumbled a civil and colourless little remark about it being very grand. Miss Smith snorted.

'Grandeur's the least of it; and as you see the house is a fine jumble, having been built on by almost every generation. Dubrovnoye is a far more classic pile. But what distinguishes our English stately houses from it, Lise—from Malvern down to the smallest manor—is their tradition. They are the repositories of our unbroken centuries of civilisation—as yours were in France.'

'You mean that Sacha—that people like the Arloffs are not civilised, ma'am?'

'My dear child, the Arloffs were barbarous *boyars* murdering their Tsars when your forbears were the patrons of Ronsard and du Bellay.'

'And yours, ma'am?'

'Oh, they were engaged in rebelling against their Kings,' said Miss Smith, joining heartily in Lise's laughter.

Lise had barely time to regain her discomfort before the carriage turned into a small walled court and drew up before the side-door invariably used by the Family on private occasions.

Their arrival coincided with the return of some of the house party from a stroll in the rose gardens, and Miss Smith was at once surrounded by their welcome and a milling of servants. Lise, standing a little apart, was diverted to notice another outsider: a tall, angular, colourless young man, who cast a hasty glance round and seemed disposed to beat an unobtrusive retreat through the door in the garden wall. His glance encountered Lise's eyes. He stopped, straightened his rather narrow shoulders and came across to her, saying in a pleasant, soft voice with just the suspicion of a stammer:

'You must be Aunt Hon's friend, Mademoiselle de Montargis. How do you do? I—I hope you have had—'

'Ah,' boomed Miss Smith, coming up to them. 'I see you have made yourselves known. How are you, Francis? Lise, my nephew, Malvern.'

As Miss Smith was wont to put it, her sister Caroline had inherited all the looks of the family, leaving her to rub along with the brains and energy.

The loss of an adored elder son, shortly followed by the sudden demise of the fourteenth Duke, had removed from the Duchess the last incentive to exertion. Her younger son had been a totally unforeseen imposition and his survival proved a dubious consolation. The daily spectacle of his inadequacy under the weight of his new

G*

lands, titles and dignities had almost caused Her Grace to face the fatigue of removing to one of her son's other seats.

'The Dower House I could not contemplate; but Fontwell or Plessey might serve. Once I have Francis suitably married, I shall certainly think about it,' she told her sister as soon as their greetings were over. 'And I believe I have that well in train. We will talk of it later. Now tell me about your travels,' the Duchess commanded, having a sort of shuddering interest in her sister's arduous mode of life. She dipped a plump white hand into a silver dish of pralines beside her and settled herself more comfortably on the cushions of the day-bed in her boudoir. Miss Smith removed the sweets.

'Caro, you are getting fat. I shall have to take you in hand; and this time, my dear, I shall trouble you to read about my adventures! More of that in a minute, and of my plans. But first I must solicit your hospitality for my little protegée until I can hand her over to her mother.'

'Oh yes, you wrote. The little émigrée. Will you wish her to sit at table with us?'

'My dear Caro, the girl is a Montargis.'

'Oh, then of course she must. I have not their acquaintance, but I believe one of them made a *mésalliance* with some terrible Cit.'

Miss Smith frowned.

'It's known, is it? Lise has told me of course. Name of Sir Barnaby Potts. I gather that Mme de Montargis was prepared to swallow him for a son-in-law as a nabob, but finds him singularly hard to stomach as a half-plucked pigeon.'

'These émigrés!' said the Duchess with a faint shudder.

'Tol-lol, Caro, she'll not be the first woman of consideration to try to rivet her daughter to a fortune; only unfortunate in lighting on a bubble-merchant in the attempt.'

'Well, saddled with such a connection she'll have a push to get the younger one eligibly settled,' shrugged the Duchess. 'But you always return from your travels with some oddity, Honoria! By all means keep the girl here as long as you wish. I am persuaded she cannot cause as much disturbance as the tiger cub you brought home from India.'

In this surmise the Duchess was eventually proved wrong; but at her introduction to Malvern Castle Lise had no thought except to make herself as inconspicuous as possible.

At first all seemed familiar. Like Count Arloff in Russia, the late Duke had lived at Malvern *en prince*, seldom sitting down less than forty to dinner, with his household orchestra in attendance. Now, since the Duchess claimed to be living in strict seclusion, the orchestra had been dispersed, and the party assembled when Lise entered the Green Drawing Room that evening numbered no more than sixteen persons.

However, that want of decision which Miss Smith so deplored in the present Duke, caused many of his parent's oppressively pompous habits still to linger. Lise, partnered by a young gentleman in knee breeches and silk stockings, presently found herself passing in to dinner in strict precedence, through files of powdered footmen, and sitting down before an overpowering array of gold and silver plate.

Neither its splendour nor the women's jewels could astonish her after Russia; though both, in the opinion of the younger guests, were quite gothic for an intimate dinner in the country. Nor should Lise have been put out of countenance by resuming the humble rôle to which she had been accustomed in Petersburg. But in between there had been Volnoya and her resolve to become a leader of the *ton*, to which this could not be held an auspicious beginning. So that it was with dejection and a faint stirring of rebellion that she took a remote seat when the ladies adjourned to the drawing room.

Her host could not know this. He merely saw that the little girl in the ugly purple dress was being sadly neglected; and fellow-feeling as much as duty caused him to go over to her.

Miss Smith had gone straight to the whist table. Observing Lise about to be subjected to her nephew's tongue-tied civilities, she briskly recommended him to show Mlle de Montargis the portrait gallery.

Several of the younger guests drifted there too; and being all related or intimately connected, held themselves licensed to tour the walls commenting frankly on the shortcomings and scandals of their common ancestors. When this palled, three of the young gentlemen set out to prove a wager that with a sufficient pyramid made of the furniture, one of them could attach himself to the hanging chandelier at the centre of the gallery.

'Perry! You will certainly succeed in breaking your neck,' said a stately, good-humoured looking young woman who had joined Lise and the Duke. 'Are not younger brothers a trial, mademoiselle?

He is only just over breaking his collar bone last season. I wish you will stop him, Malvern!'

The Duke mumbled something, and the young woman, whom Lise had now placed as a Lady Agnes Somebody who had been much distinguished by the Duchess, smiled and said something to him in a low voice. But Lise noted the humorous look that passed between them and the warm squeeze of his arm which encouraged the Duke to advance on the contestants and swiftly put an end to their dangerous pastime. The small incident, so eloquent of long-standing friendship and easy intimacy, made Lise feel her isolation the more; but it put her more in charity with Malvern than all its magnificence.

In the morning she found Malvern transformed.

When she came down to breakfast, guided by the Groom of the Chambers through a maze of saloons and corridors, all the splendour had vanished. The troops of liveried servants, the glitter of plate, the silks and jewels, were all gone. The Duke, in a rough frieze shooting coat, sat at the head of the table buried behind a newspaper, and the papers or their post engaged most of the other gentlemen present, whom she had some trouble to recognise in fustian and hobnailed boots. The women were equally transformed in plain, round morning dresses and the simplest of caps.

Miss Smith was reported to be breakfasting with the Duchess in her private apartments. Lise felt quite unequal to seeking her there when the party dispersed after the meal, the men to go flapper-shooting, the ladies to make themselves invisible until luncheon. Trailing after the others upstairs, Lise rounded a bend of the staircase in time to hear an unintentionally penetrating voice say:

'Montargis? Which of the émigrés is that—the one who makes ices or the one who plaits hats? Has she solicited your custom yet?'

Lise's face flamed. She turned and ran blindly down the flight, all but colliding with a lady making her leisured way up it.

'Oh—I beg your pardon, I—'

'Not the least need, I assure you,' replied Lady Agnes good-humouredly. 'But—Good God, Mlle de Montargis, is something amiss?'

'No, no, it is nothing. I—please excuse me.'

'That I will not while you're in such distress. Are you unwell?' and, as Lise dumbly shook her head, 'then we shall go somewhere where we may be private, and you shall tell me how I can help you. Come.'

She shepherded Lise across the upper hall into a charming small parlour hung in Chinese silk, and sat her down on a sopha beside her.

Lise need not have worried about parrying questions. Good nature and a managing habit alone had prompted Lady Agnes to concern herself; and she had been told enough of Lise's situation to look no further for the cause of the little waif's tears. So she set herself to speak most cheerfully of life in London, and added the amiable hope that their acquaintance might continue there.

'Do you live in London then?' asked Lise, eagerly catching at the thought of having a friend in the strange city.

Lady Agnes' high colour deepened a fraction.

'In general my parents are used to remove to Town for the Season, and so of course have I since I came out. But I do not know about next year. It may be that—but my Aunt Malvern has often spoken about the desirability of re-opening Devereux House,' she ended with apparent irrelevance.

Lise's feminine instinct at once jumped to the correct conclusion that Lady Agnes had every expectation of being married to the Duke by the following spring, and fixed at Malvern unless she and his mother could prevail upon him to brave London Society. Thus diverted from her own troubles, she caught Agnes' hand and said impulsively:

'Oh, I am so glad! You have both been so kind to me—'

She found she had outrun British reserve.

'Thank you, but I have no cause to solicit your congratulations and must ask your pardon if what I said led you into any improper conjecture,' was Lady Agnes' chilling reply.

Lady Agnes was then assailed by an equally inherent sense of fair play, and added more warmly:

'Indeed you are not at fault. It is no secret that our parents have desired a match between us since we were in leading reins. Perhaps that makes me speak more freely than I ought. Come,' she went on, rising, 'what would you like to do until the men return for luncheon? Malvern has an excellent library. May I show it to you?'

Lise also rose, too mortified for the second time that morning to be susceptible either to *amendes honorables* or kindness. The icy formality of her thanks to Lady Agnes had all the glitter of her forbears insulting a rival at Versailles, and her exit would have been more suitably accomplished in panniers and a powdered wig than in an ugly purple morning dress and her own uncurled hair.

At two o'clock, a profusion of cold meats were set out on small tables in another dining saloon and everyone came in for a sort of lounging half-meal.

In the course of it, the Duchess honoured Lise with a question. 'What did you do in Russia?'

Lise saw several glances turn towards her and her chin came up.

'I was living in St Petersburg, madame, as the companion of my lady Arloff.'

The Duchess's own companion, an ageless, wispy spinster known as Cousin Emily, said kindly:

'So interesting! And for the young, such opportunities! Dear Honoria's travels—accompanying her to Turkestan!'

'No, mademoiselle, I only met my Aunt Hon—'

'Your what?' said the Duchess blankly.

'—Miss Smith, on her way back to England,' stammered Lise.

She was too stricken to notice the one look of sympathy directed at her. It came from the Duke, who knew only too well what it was to make a public gaffe.

After luncheon parties were made up for riding and driving. Lise might have been left standing but for her host's murmured intervention, which procured her a place in a carriage with a gay foursome and Lady Agnes's brother Peregrine up on the box.

The Duke saw his guests disposed and excused himself to go off to his daily ordeal with his bailiff and steward.

It was a glorious afternoon and Malvern's stately vistas of terraced lawns, water and park offered a prospect to dispel the most settled melancholy. Lise's spirits were sensibly revived. If only she could have been greeting the sunshine in the delicate embroidered cambric or tamboured muslin of the two young ladies with her, she might have allowed England some merit.

Along the main avenue they met Miss Smith driving the Duchess in a pretty curricle put to two cream ponies. Both ladies waved and Miss Smith called a kindly wish that the girls might not find themselves overset by their cowhanded coachman.

'I quite dote on Aunt Hon,' that young gentleman remarked imperturbably. 'She disappears for years into the back of beyond, and then bobs up again and begins abusing you where she left off.'

'But you *are* cowhanded, Perry.'

'I'm improving,' replied the Honourable Peregrine with perfect good humour. 'Drive to an inch compared with last year. Watch me take that gate.'

'Not for the world! Turn down the other avenue, for God's sake!'

'Don't be frightened, Mademoiselle de Montargis,' said one of the young ladies kindly. 'Perry is not as dangerous as he looks.'

'Is he not then! A public menace.'

'Nothing so vulgar. A *private* danger if you like, Georgina—'

'Perry! You will put me to the blush,' protested Lise's pretty neighbour, showing no signs of it.

'But I tell you of one person who is not rejoicing at Aunt Hon's coming,' the irrepressible Perry went on, 'and that is my sister Agnes; since the mere sight of Aunt Hon is enough to send Malvern flying to cover. *Just* as he seemed at last to have nerved himself up to offering for her.'

'Perry!' reproved the other young woman—it seemed an almost mechanical form of address from the young gentleman's friends. She indicated Lise's presence with an expressive lift of her eyebrows.

'Nonsense,' said Perry. 'Not being blind or deaf, Mlle de Montargis cannot continue many days at Malvern without becoming aware that the match is the dearest wish of us all. And do you not agree, mademoiselle, that when a man is a Duke and no longer obliged to marry *well*, as the common saying goes, he should marry to oblige his friends?'

'*Perry!* You will oblige *me* by a little more conduct! You will be giving mademoiselle an odd notion of the freedom of our manners. I am sure she met with more decorum in Russia.'

Mademoiselle, whose thoughts had flown to one vastly free-mannered Russian, mumbled a polite disclaimer. After civilly waiting for her to say something else, they returned to their own concerns and continued to discuss the match without further restraint.

Her son's future was also exercising the Duchess.

'I wish Malvern would offer for Agnes,' she said to her sister in her flat way.

'Which one is Agnes?' asked Miss Smith, disposing her ample

form into an open chair opposite the Duchess' sopha, on their return from their drive.

'Do not be so provoking, Honoria. You have known Agnes any time these twenty years. Our cousin Stour's second daughter. She would not have done for Guy, of course.' The Duchess sighed. 'But she is all I could wish for Francis.'

'H'mm. Does Francis think so?'

'My dear Honoria, how should I know? It is enough for *him* to know it is my wish, to disoblige me! His shyness, his reserve are but the disguise for a most obstinate self-will—as we all saw when nothing would serve but he must go rushing off to the Peninsula after Guy was killed, although he might have known it would be the death of his father.'

This was too much for Miss Smith's robust sense of justice.

'Nonsense, Caro. Malvern broke his neck in the hunting field. And going off into the army was possibly the only action of of Francis's life to have gained his complete approval. But as to this marriage—'

The Duchess shrugged.

'Yet it may well be that his shyness alone is the mischief. I can well believe that he does not propose to Agnes for sheer lack of address!'

'Then let her ask him.'

'I beg you will be serious, Honoria! Agnes is a young woman of character.'

'Well, it's either that or she must forfeit a little of that strong character. Francis always had a penchant for lame ducks.'

'Speaking of lame ducks,' said the Duchess. 'I hope you may not regret your kindness to your protégée, Honoria. Take care, or you will have her whole indigent tribe round your neck. You have no conception of the encroaching ways of these émigrés.'

Lise, with no suspicion of the encroaching ways of her kind, was discovering Francis's penchant for lame ducks.

Observing her, a few days later, wandering in the gardens without company or employment, he came out and joined her, being as mindful as his mother could have wished of his duties as host.

In this instance, he was not intimidated by their object. He civilly offered to conduct her on a tour of the principal rooms.

'Thank you, but—Pray do not trouble, sir. I was just . . . it is so lovely out—'

It was obvious to Francis that the girl was wretchedly afraid lest she ought not to be in the gardens; that he might think her angling for attention by advertising her neglect. Such embarrassments were well known to him, and with real kindness he set himself to dispel them, forgetting to be shy.

Lise rewarded him by chattering at least half as freely as she used to beguile Sacha on their rambles round Volnoya. They strolled at random across the cedar-shaded lawns, obtaining different prospects of the house.

'The whole original castle was ordered to be razed by Cromwell, but they skimped on the gunpowder,' Francis told Lise, 'and only the Banqueting Hall was thought worth preserving after the Restoration. So you see we are quite in fashion, for the remaining tower gives us our Gothic ruin to hand without need of building one. Even Perry, who would have me demolish all but Kent's modern wing, allows that our Folly is equal to anything at Chatsworth.'

The very word 'folly' held hateful memories for Lise. She said quickly:

'Oh, I wonder if it is the tower my—Miss Smith told me about? The one you and your brother climbed?'

'Yes, that is the one. But it was only my brother who climbed it. I tried to follow him but I've no head for heights.'

Lise heard the echo of a still-unburied grief in his voice and said warmly:

'But you followed him into the war in Spain, and that must have taken far more courage than climbing a tower.'

Hearing his exploit described as anything but the grossest of self-indulgence was so novel to Francis that he glanced at his companion with some suspicion. He encountered nothing but a glow of friendly sympathy in the lustrous dark eyes whose beauty he had not noticed until then.

From then on Lise's situation improved. The Duke was far too shy to give her consequence by openly distinguishing her. But in several unobtrusive ways he found means to show her attention. He would have done as much had she been only small, poor, ill-dressed and neglected; as she was young, engaging, possessed of fine eyes and a magical laugh, he made several efforts to come upon her alone again.

Success unexpectedly came his way in the third week of Lise's sojourn at Malvern. He was riding home through the park from a particularly trying visit to one of his tenants, when agitated voices apparently in the trees overhead, arrested his attention.

'I can't!' came a shrill wail from somewhere in the high branches. 'I can't missie, not for ever so—'

'Yes, you *can*. Just lie along the branch and wriggle. Don't look down, you foolish boy! Oh, dear—very well, just hold still till I can get at you . . .' and Francis was horrified to recognise the rescuer's voice as the little emigrée's.

He leapt off his horse, threw its bridle over a branch and ran for the tree. In the fork of one of its high branches he could now distinguish a purple skirt and the frill of a petticoat. Craning his neck as he ran, he also caught a glimpse of her problem—a small urchin whose pale blur of a face peered fearfully along the limb which Lise was now gingerly beginning to negotiate.

In an agony of indecision Francis came to a halt at the foot of the tree, dreading to startle either of them by shouting, unable to stand there and do nothing. Fortunately, just at that moment his horse neighed, and Lise alone looked down.

Her horror at being discovered up a tree by a gentleman of the house party yielded to relief as she saw it was the Duke.

'Stay where you are,' begged Francis in an urgent, lowered voice. 'For God's sake stay where you are.'

He cursed his habit of dismissing all attendance and looked round desperately for someone to send for rescue.

'It's all right,' called Lise. 'He's one of your gamekeepers' children. He got stuck going after a bird's nest. I can get to him,' and she inched herself out further along the limb.

This was too much for Francis. Forgetting all his dread of heights, he hurled himself up the tree. His greater reach made short work of it and he arrived at the fork in time to relieve Lise of her weeping burden, as she regained its safety.

The boy transferred his limpet grip to Francis's neck and clung there without a word during their descent. Once set down, however, such understanding as he possessed returned. Recognising his august rescuer, he gave a howl of terror and took refuge in Lise's skirts. In the end the Duke was obliged to dismiss him with a shilling for his iniquity.

'And I trust his father *will* give him the thrashing he deserves! Are you sure you have taken no harm?' he cried. 'That abominable child! You might have been killed for your heroism. A little thing like you to climb that great tree—'

'And you—with your fear of heights!'

They both laughed at that, but Francis' kind grey eyes still looked worried.

'You are *sure* you have taken no hurt?' he persisted, hovering over her as if she were a piece of Dresden he expected to come to pieces in his hands.

'Only to my appearance,' Lise examined the damage. 'Both my flounces torn, my petticoat hanging, smears *all* the way down—Oh, please sir, could you show me some back way to my room, for I must look a perfect hoyden and anyone meeting with me might well suspect I have been climbing a tree!'

'I would be proud to tell them so; and of your courage.'

She gave a little shrug of impatience. Sacha would have scolded her roundly and done something about her scratched hands and bruised knee, instead of extolling her heroism.

'I have had plenty of experience of small boys and trees,' she said a little tartly. Then seeing the Duke still concerned, she regaled him with anecdotes of Nicky until they reached a small side door in the kitchens' courtyard.

Tiptoeing their way through a warren of passages and back-stairs, hand in hand like guilty, grubbied children, warmed Francis with memories of similar returns in the wake of his adored elder brother. He attended Lise to the door of her bedchamber and there seemed at a loss for how to leave her or surrender the hand still warmly clasped in his.

'You are sure, really sure, you have sustained no injury? I'd never forgive myself—'

'For my imprudence?' laughed Lise, whom his awkwardness had relieved of all constraint. 'No, truly the only sufferers are my slippers and my clothes. Now pray let me go, sir, to attend to these before someone comes—'

'Oh, I beg your pardon!' he stammered, dropping her hand as if it had grown red hot.

The irritation of several splinters caused her to clasp it round its fellow, but not before Francis had seen the scratches across the small, begrimed palms. The sight brought such a warm, confused rush of emotion to his throat that he quite forgot to be awkward. He bent and kissed each small palm, holding her hands to his lips in both his own. Then his shyness returned in full force. Bereft of speech, he left her with an embarrassed bow.

So little did Francis correspond to the image of romance indelibly fixed in Lise's mind, that she indulged in none of the reflections open to a young lady whose hands have just been warmly kissed by an unattached Duke. The only satisfaction she derived from the incident was the passing thought of how much it would have annoyed the Duchess and Lady Agnes.

She was interrupted, but already at a respectable stage of her toilette, by Miss Smith, hastening to tell her that the post had brought a letter from her mother.

'The Marquise writes that the family count on being installed at Highgate by the end of this week, Lise; and though she is good enough to beg me not to cut short your sojourn at Malvern, I am sure you will wish to be united with them as soon as may be; and so I told the Duchess.'

This was a tactful version of the assurance Miss Smith had given Her Grace.

Nevertheless, Miss Smith felt it incumbent upon her to deliver Lise personally into her brother-in-law's protection, and the two of them set out for London at the end of that week.

The Duke was not sorry to see Lise go. The tumult of his feelings since the incident outside her bedchamber had made it difficult for him to meet her with ordinary composure. Morbidly sensitive to ridicule, his chief concern was to have no one notice his emotion, and he welcomed the prospect of being able to put her out of his mind.

CHAPTER III

At the age of fifteen, young Barnie Potts had followed his father into the employ of the East India Company.

India, as Sir Barnaby was wont to put it in later years, was a honeypot for a fly 'un; and young Barnaby dipped deep. His depredations were on such a heroic scale as to command respect. At thirty-five he had put himself in a position to retire, with a knighthood, his fortune made and a handsome tribute of jewels from various native potentates to mark their gratitude for the occasion.

The youthful nabob thus found himself in a position to fulfil the ambition of many better men: a triumphant return to his birthplace and the purchase of the Big House, which young Barnie Potts had viewed only at a safe distance when poaching pheasant chicks on the estate.

Rigby Park, in the county of Yorkshire, had then lacked a tenant for some sixteen years; but no amount of mildew and dry rot could dim its glory in its new owner's eyes.

Several of their acquaintance thought it served him pretty well in securing the hand of the elder daughter of the late Marquis de Montargis; and his new mother-in-law for one declared his fortune to be a small recompense for her becoming Louisa Potts. Even Potter—or Pottaire, as Mme de Montargis pronounced it—would have been more eligible. Marie-Louise Pottaire *might* be borne for the income from £30,000 invested in Funds. But the first of her standing grievances against her son-in-law was his withdrawal of his money from this security. Her second was his refusal to be anything but Potts and to address his wife as other than Louisa. Herself, to her annoyance, he termed Lady Mountargeese, which, as she virulently pointed out, was neither her name nor her title.

During the first years Louisa usually contrived to restore the peace, or at any rate to divert her mother's attention to the material advantages of their present situation. Unfortunately, Sir Barnaby's affluence did not long survive their removal to the Metropolis.

For this, his gentle wife was all unwittingly responsible. Marriage to a lady both undermined Sir Barnaby's assurance and awoke in him a wistful yearning to prove himself in her eyes. The resultant mixture of bluster and inner humility proved fatal to his business acumen.

The land at Rigby was the first to go; though fortunately no buyer was found for the house. Next, at her own insistence, it was Louisa's pearls, her saddle horse and the second carriage. Finally, the necessity was faced of reducing their whole establishment by removal to a district where a simpler style of living could still maintain gentility.

This descent was accomplished with the maximum of inconvenience when Louisa was daily awaiting her lying-in with their fifth infant. The new house, in the village of Highgate, left much to be desired, and her accommodation in it provided Mme de Montargis with years of well-grounded complaint.

What Louisa thought of it, or indeed of her marriage, she kept to herself. No doubt she would have done so even if anyone had troubled to ask her. Her nursery and schoolroom were her refuge and her chief care; for the rest, the business of her life was keeping household, its solace was her children and its bane the running battle between her mother and her husband.

Mme de Montargis felt, and frequently said, that she had sacrificed enough when she had accepted Sir Barnaby's offer for her daughter. Only her obdurate reluctance to avow that her son Armand had been right in his opposition to Sir Barnaby's suit kept her from admitting that her sacrifice had been a vain one and hazarding herself to the primitive evils of America.

It may be imagined with what mixed sentiments the family awaited the arrival of the daughter whom Mme de Montargis had so confidently declared lost to her.

However, the circumstances of her child's return in the company of the Duke of Malvern's aunt, and the actual sight of her daughter's slight figure being helped out of the Duke's travelling chaise by two powdered footmen, could not help enhancing a mother's natural feelings. It also acted powerfully on Sir Barnaby, home for the great occasion.

Lise was looking her worst. Pale, sick with apprehension and so rigid with nerves that it robbed her movements of all their natural grace, she advanced hesitantly towards the thin, high-nosed, elegant personage in mauve armazine, who watched her curtsey with a critical eye before enfolding her in a scented embrace.

'Maman!' sobbed Lise.

'Mon ange!' exclaimed Mme de Montargis, disengaging her lace from Lise's impetuous grip, 'Mon enfant bien aimée! Restored to her mother at last to console my unhappy lot! Ah, let me look at you—' and straightway turned to make her bow to Miss Smith.

Lise, left standing, was quickly embraced by the faded, gentle-looking woman standing behind her mother. Then she submitted to a port-laden peck from a short fat man in a yellow waistcoat, who informed her she must call him 'brother'.

'So this is the amiable Mees Devereux Smeeth to whom I owe the restoration of my precious angel!' Mme de Montargis clasped a delicate white hand to her bosom and closed her eyes. 'Ah, mademoiselle, if her homeless mother's prayers can repay you for your care of cette pauvre enfant, rest assured they are yours.'

'Now then, Lady Mountargeese, prayers ain't called for when we're all privileged to see the Hon Honoria looking so stout,' put in Sir Barnaby bracingly. 'Ay, privileged, ma'am,' he turned with a courtly bow to Miss Smith, 'for I protest my household is monstrous gratified at such affability as you have shewn. To come in person, to distinguish me and Lady Potts with such a mark of civility—'

'Lise,' barked Miss Smith, 'you may make your mother and sister known to me.'

Only Miss Smith's affection for her charge extended the acquaintance to Sir Barnaby. The party passed into the drawing room, where Miss Smith coldly refused to 'wet her whistle' with his best Madeira.

The mother was not much more to her taste; for Miss Smith was not of those who find affectation and folly any the less odious for being practised by a member of the haute noblesse. Louisa's self-effacing habit made her barely noticed as usual; but Miss Smith was also displeased by the tone of the obviously straitened household. Shabby gentility she could have respected; but the furnishings were a monument to Sir Barnaby's heyday. The uneasy pretence at elegance, no less than Sir Barnaby's simple vulgarity, showed Lise an aspect of her chaperone which she had never yet encountered.

Stiff-necked, icily polite, Miss Smith sat bolt upright on the pretentious gilt sopha, barely condescending to acknowledge Mme de Montargis' recital of her woes, and disdaining even that notice to Sir Barnaby's civilities.

Louisa's kind heart ached for Lise. No wonder the poor child

looked almost green with pallor after a year in the intimidating care
of this haughty dame, to whom her new-found family must now seem
in a conspiracy to expose themselves. Louisa could not know, and
Lise did not suspect, that her kind Aunt Hon's gelid façade hid her
dismay at abandoning her charge to such care. She rose and brought
the visit to an abrupt close, bestowing a peck on Lise and dividing a
frigid bow between the rest of the company.

The family attended her to her carriage.

'One does not need to ask oneself why that one has been left
single,' shrugged the Marquise, as they watched the chaise out of
sight. She turned to Lise.

'Well, *mon enfant*, you have not inherited my looks I'm afraid.'

'No, maman.'

Louisa said quickly:

'But Lise has our father's eyes, maman. Just like your nephew, my
little Charles Edmond, Lise. Beautiful eyes,' she smiled, watching
them blink back tears.

'We must hope they'll do as well for Miss Eliza as your ma's did
for you, eh Lady Potts?' rumbled Sir Barnaby with heavy gallantry.
'I'll lay you a pony there's a beau or two left smitten at Malvern right
now, eh, Miss Eliza? Or why not the Duke himself for that matter?'

Lise, barely recognising herself as Miss Eliza, instinctively drew
closer to Louisa, who said quietly:

'Maman, have you ever seen our roses look lovelier? Later I will
show you all the garden, Lise my love. Do you dine at home, Sir
Barnaby?'

Her husband mumbled a disclaimer and turned into the stables,
leaving Mme de Montargis gazing thoughtfully after him.

The four elder children had been barely restrained to peering at
their new aunt through the upstairs banisters. So for a time there was
amiable employment in rummaging through Lise's big valise for
their presents. Then there was the rest of Lise's baggage to be unpacked upstairs and subjected to her mother's minute scrutiny.

'You have inherited my taste as little as my looks, it seems. These
lamentable purple dresses! And surely this cannot be all you have
received in presents from Russia? Not a single memento from the
Arloffs? No jewels? My friend, Lady Cory, says the Misses Wilmot
returned from their stay with Princess Dashkow *laden* with diamonds, besides a handsome—'

'Maman, you forget the—the circumstances in which my sister
parted from the Arloffs,' Louisa put in gently.

'*Certes*, I do *not*; and considering Amélie Arloff's lack of care in permitting her stepson to run off with you, Lise, I think the least she could have done would be to—but there, no one is so ungenerous as the rich, as I know too well by now. And I must always be grateful to Amélie for putting you in the way of encountering the Honourable Smeeth.'

Lise was too relieved to wonder at Mme de Montargis's apparently wholesale acceptance of Miss Smith's bland version of her flight. Louisa, who had never accepted it and had known many sleepless nights over what had really befallen her sister, was relieved too; and not only at Lise's escape from the ordeal of questioning.

One look at the girl had been enough to convince Louisa that her sister's innocence was intact; perhaps in her own good time Lise would tell the rest. She said diffidently:

'None of Lise's life in Russia can have been happy, maman; and I do not suppose that being an enforced guest at Malvern can have afforded her much pleasure, whatever its splendours. Let us forget it all. We have her home at last. Now if only we get our dear Armand back too, we can want nothing to make us happy. Dearest Lise, do you know he has written many times of how well he has prospered? Only the present hostilities* have held up his coming to England.'

'I'll believe his prosperity when I see it—or him,' retorted their mother. 'And as for sailing off to join him in some wretched log cabin—*ah, ça non*! Better the devil I know. . . . But I beg you will not distract me, Louisa. Lise shall not repeat your error if I can help it, and her connection with Malvern can be of inestimable value. Who knows, if she created a favourable impression there, that the Duchess herself might be persuaded to frank her sister's protégée! But I would doubt it,' she added gloomily. 'No one could create an impression in these disastrous garments. *Mon dieu*, if I had but known the *tenue* you would appear in at Malvern—! Well, never mind; it can be set right on your next visit.'

'But I am very sure I shall not be asked again, maman, and I was unhappy—well, most of the time there. The Duchess did not say above five words to me, but I know she took me in dislike. Oh, how I wish we could forget it all as Louisa says!'

The Marquise smiled thinly.

'Émigrés cannot be choosers, *ma fille*. Now you may attend me to my dressing room, for I wish to hear all the particulars of your visit before we write our letters of thanks to the Duchess.'

* War between England and America had broken out again in June 1812.

Lise re-entered her rumpled room with a little start of annoyance at the sight of the mess. How careless of the maids not to have finished her unpacking! Then, with a bigger start, she recalled that there would probably be no maids here to do such service. She looked round the chamber: Louisa had done her best with flowers and fresh linen, but the chipped jug of roses only recalled Volnoya's luxuriant bouquets. The threadbare linen, as she threw herself down on the bed, only brought back the very feel of the verbena-scented pillows that had cradled her in such security at the only house she had called home.

Never, never would she think of this ugly house and hostile England as home! Never could she be happy here! All that remained to live for were the empty conquests that would dazzle Sacha at two thousand miles. To this end one wrote effusive letters to hateful Duchesses. And Sacha might be lying dead or wounded in one of the forests they had driven through together. . . .

'Lise! Oh my poor little sister, what a homecoming!'

Lise gladly sought the comfort of her sister's arms. Presently the happiness of knowing such comfort for the first time in her life had its effect. Raising a drowned face from Louisa's shoulder, she was able to assure her that she was merely crying for joy.

'Little liar,' said Louisa affectionately. 'Dear Lise, I could cry too. You cannot know how often I have planned your return—and then to have it turn out like this! And after you have had more than a year at the mercy of that dragon!'

'Dragon? You mean Miss Smith? Oh no, you quite mistake the matter, Louisa. Nothing could have equalled her kindness to me always. Her manner today . . . well, it was perhaps a little forbidding, but. . . .' She trailed off.

Louisa flushed painfully.

'I understand,' she said. 'Forgive me. . . .'

She stood silent a moment, clasping and unclasping her thin hands. Then she said in a low, hurried voice:

'Lise, you must never forget that maman intends nothing but your good; and that Sir Barnaby has given you the protection of his home.'

Lise threw her arms round her.

'For *your* sake I'll not forget it. But— Oh, Louisa, one day, you will see, I shall be so grand and rich that none of them can touch us. It was my intention for—for another reason; but now I shall redouble my efforts, because then you and the children can come and visit me forever, and—and maman too of course.'

Louisa was still taking in this bold declaration when Mme de Montargis came in carrying her completed letter. Lise was obliged to confess that she had not started hers.

'*N'importe*. On reflection I have decided that it is of no moment—a mere observance of civility. I will compose it for you. But *you* shall write where your thanks may be of value—to the Duke.'

'But, maman—'

'Maman, you cannot mean Lise to do so! She has no occasion to thank him, since she was the guest of the Duchess. And to receive such a letter from a young girl—maman, I beg you will consider what an idea it will give him of her and her family.'

'Bah! Do not be so missish. These great men like to be flattered, and I hope a Montargis may be acquitted of toad-eating,' retorted the Marquise. 'Besides, Lise herself has told me that the Duke showed her many kindnesses.'

'All the more reason why we should not presume on them,' cried Louisa, angered out of her timidity. 'Madame, if you must lay siege to the Duke, address him yourself and in as few words as possible.'

Mme de Montargis gave a little resigned shrug with which Lise was to grow familiar.

'Very well. To hear you, one would suppose that I do not put myself to this trouble solely for Lise's advancement. You, Louisa, might be content to have me a mother like Solange de Lastic, who is happy to peddle embroidered dresses all day, and to laugh over their misfortunes in the evenings with Counts and Marquesses turned hairdressers and fencing masters. Yes, and to have her guests discreetly drop three shillings into a vase for their dinner. Well, so am not I! Turning back by candlelight to what we used to be at home will not restore us to Versailles; but if my plans are not thwarted by the pair of you, I shall yet see Lise make her curtsey at St James's.'

'Indeed, maman, we both realise—'

'Let maman write to the Duke if she so pleases,' interrupted Lise with a little smile. She spread her hands and her beautiful eyes narrowed down on to her palms. The scratches were completely healed. She shrugged. 'But I do not think her letter will make any difference. Men,' she announced, with a cynicism born of an acquaintance with Sacha, 'should have *no* reliance placed upon their past sentiments.'

CHAPTER IV

Mme de Montargis's letter to the Duke of Malvern elicited a cool acknowledgement expressing his obligation for her permission to call but regretting that his movements would not allow him to take advantage of the honour, and remaining hers etc.

Since his letter coincided with the publication of the first bulletins of the battle at Borodino, it is doubtful whether Lise was even aware of its arrival. All her energies were devoted to scouring every newspaper she could lay hands on; all her efforts to coaxing her mother to wait on the Countess Lieven, the wife of the new Russian Ambassador. Her ladyship was an acquaintance of the Arloffs in Petersburg and might have news of the only participant in the battle whose fate concerned Lise.

Madame Lieven, whose simple boast it was that 'It cannot be fashionable where I am not' was not usually at home to impoverished widows; but a remembered hint of scandal about the daughter, and a morning devoid of more amusing callers, led her to have them admitted.

Her expert eye at once summed up their clothes as elegant make-overs—but one had to avow the French had taste! And the girl, with no real beauty but her eyes, was something out of the common run. Her ladyship decided that with the right franking the little Montargis might take.

'So you are the ward for whom Amélie Arloff was fortunate enough to secure Honoria Devereux's patronage? And in the nick of time, I surmise? How did you fare with that most august of bluestockings?'

'Countess Arloff confided my daughter to Miss Devereux Smith's care with my full concurrence, madame,' riposted the Marquise. 'And Lise can give you very present news of her chaperone with whom, on her arrival in England, she passed many pleasant weeks as a guest at Malvern.'

The Countess raised pencilled eyebrows.

'My felicitations, madame. Dull though Malvern has grown under poor Francis, in England a Duke is a Duke.'

Decidedly the little Montargis might take with such franking.

'Am I to collect that the Duchess will actually bestir herself to sponsor mademoiselle? Devereux House would make a splendid setting to launch her début.'

Mme de Montargis tinkled with laughter.

'Dear Countess, *ma petite* Lise has had her head quite sufficiently turned at Malvern. I entreat you not to encourage her dizziness!'

Lise took advantage of the ensuing pause to intervene, and begged to know whether her ladyship had any news 'of—of my friends in Petersburg who may have been in the present battle.'

'I take you to mean either Count Paul or Sacha Arloff. H'mmm. Sacha, to be sure. Well, from the last intelligence I have, he at any rate should be thanking heaven for the war. Pardoned, restored to favour, given a command, making Petersburg ring with his exploits as a guerilla leader—and of course with his other conquests, you may be sure! As I said to Alvanley the other day at Sally Jersey's rout, our Russian women . . .'

For Lise the rest of the visit passed in a joyous blur of relief. Sacha not only alive and whole, but restored to the Tsar's favour and given a command! It was only when they emerged into the bleak autumn morning outside, that she became sufficiently rational to take in the last item in the Countess's inventory of Sacha's triumphs.

'Odious woman,' said Mme de Montargis, as they jogged home. 'And what is all this about the younger Arloff, Lise? Am I to understand that you are harbouring a *tendre* for him?'

'N-no, maman.'

'In our circles,' said Mme de Montargis, absently picking at a hole in the threadbare squabs, '—I refer to our circles in France before our calamities of course—marriage was an alliance between great Houses, arranged by our parents. It was considered perfectly eligible to enter into such an alliance with a decided preference for another man. In this deplorable country, I have noticed the bourgeois habit of marrying to suit some fancied attachment spreading fast among the aristocracy, and even affecting some of us of the *ancien régime*. I trust, however, that I shall never see a Montargis succumb to it.'

'N-no, maman.'

Her mother laughed and patted her cheek.

'*Allons*, Lise! I was entirely happy with your father, after fancying myself vastly in love with another man up to the morning of my wedding. And in your case such fancies are a luxury we can ill afford. I am not wearing myself to the bone to persuade Adela Cory to sponsor your début, only to have you discourage any eligible *prétendant* who is not already repelled by entering a connection with Sir Potts. *Mon dieu*, they will be few enough!'

Nevertheless, Mme de Montargis unsparingly continued her siege of Lady Cory. Long-standing friendship and the circumstance of bringing out her own second daughter that year, inclined Lady Cory to oblige her; but she was a mother first, and had Lise presented any threat to take the shine out of Miss Sophia, no claims of friendship would have weighed with her ladyship. But Lise, though greatly improved by her emancipation from the purple uniform, continued to resist all Louisa's efforts to put colour into her pale cheeks and fill out her new, attenuated growth.

'I declare I do not know how to fatten you up, my love,' sighed Louisa at dinner a few weeks later, helping Lise liberally to a second round of the raised apple pie.

'Nothing wrong with Miss Eliza's appetite that *I* can see,' grunted Sir Barnaby. 'Now if she was to have *my* liver—'

'We must account it among our few blessings that she has *not*,' snapped the Marquise. 'And I would remind you, Louisa, that although Lise has the misfortune to inherit the Montargis lack of complexion, in her delicacy of bone she undoubtedly favours me. At Versailles I was known as The Sylph.'

'And you still could be, maman.'

'Privation,' said Mme de Montargis, gazing with scorn at the pie, a cheesecake and a soft pudding before her, '*years* of privation, at least enable one to keep one's figure. And there is nothing wrong with Lise that a really good Paris dressmaker, coiffeur and *modiste* could not turn to advantage.'

'I tell you what, Miss 'Liza,' cried Sir Barnaby, 'if Canny Lou wins at Newmarket on Saturday, I'll stand you a bang-up rig to put all your ma's Cory noses out of joint. How's that, eh?'

All of which afforded Lise a surprising satisfaction for one who anticipated no further happiness in life.

Certainly the present offered few material prospects of it. Canny Lou's defeat by several lengths was the first of a series of reverses.

The war news from Russia was calamitous. And her Aunt Hon seemed to have dissolved into some Scottish mist of erudition.

None the less, as she settled into it, life in Highgate proved less bleak than its beginnings.

Lise's sharp, seventeen-year-old eyes noted that Sir Barnaby was much kinder to Louisa when her mother was not by. He could not help being vulgar; his mother-in-law made him boorish. Away from her baleful eye, he made many clumsy efforts to show his pride in Louisa and his fondness for his children. Lise also observed that Louisa was by no means always unhappy; a puzzle which she rightly shelved as one of the mysteries of the married state.

Most mornings saw Sir Barnaby set off for the city, with great show of business and importance. But one rainy Monday, Lise found that Sir Barnaby's business had taken him no farther than the yard of the Gatehouse tavern. He was standing in a puddle, rather forlornly watching the bustle around a coach. He saw her and came across to her straightway, asking if aught was amiss?

'No, I'm only to get some liniment for Julia's chest. Her cough is troublesome and we've none in the house. But I thought you were gone into London, sir?'

'Ay, well, so I was, to be sure. But something was said at breakfast —well, Miss 'Liza, to make no bones about it, it sounded to me like Lady Mountargeese might be off to spend the day at the Corys. So I just thought I'd hang on a bit and see. . . .' His small eyes shifted under her gaze. 'There's nowhere much for me to go in the city, you see.'

Lise stared at the portly, vulgar figure in its many-caped greatcoat, yellow boots and high crowned beaver. It had seldom evoked anything but a shudder in her before.

'But do you not go to the Cocoa Tree or the coffee houses?' she demanded.

'Costs money,' said Sir Barnaby briefly.

To his surprise, he saw his sister-in-law's expressive eyes glint with tears. She touched his arm.

'Well, today there's no call to go anywhere in this cold and rain, when you can be snug at home. Maman has bespoken the carriage for eleven o'clock. . . .'

From that day on, it became an unspoken pact between them that Lise should tip him the office, as Sir Barnaby put it, whenever the Marquise planned to sally forth. Sir Barnaby returned the favour by making his presence about the house felt as little as possible, and by bringing Lise offerings of newspapers whenever he went into the city.

Lise had not the heart to tell him that she had acquired a far more valuable source of information about the progress of the war in Russia. This was the Rev. Henry Cossett, a retired clergyman who eked out his pension by coaching Charles Edmond and a few other boys for Highgate School.

Military strategy and cats were Mr Cossett's twin passions. His sliver of a cottage in Southwood Lane was a magpie's nest of maps, bulletins, journals and broadsheets, many of which harboured un-expected kittens, fish heads and saucers of milk, until Lise took them in hand.

Mr Cossett was delighted to discover a fellow-enthusiast. To be sure, Lise's interest in the campaign was a trifle narrow, but he did not despair of broadening her scope. A staunch Whig, he took a generally pessimistic view of the war, and especially of English adventures on foreign soil.

'Take this fellow Wellington, my dear. Nothing but a Sepoy General, with an army of cut-throats enlisted for liquor and cavalry that dashes after the enemy like a field of fox-hunters. I tell you, Miss Lise, our English business is at sea, and we'll never have Boney beat until we stick to it! Mark my words, you may rejoice to have him in retreat from Moscow, but he'll come about. And a fine pickle we'll be in, when he turns up with the *Grande Armée* in the Peninsula.'

'But he will *not*,' asserted his fellow-strategist, sweeping a tabby kitten off the vital part of the map. 'Only look, sir, at the vastness of Russia before him. Oh, you do not know how immense it is! And silently, out of the forests, our Cossacks and—and bands of resolute men under a born fighting leader, will fall upon his line of march—'

'Irregulars,' grunted Mr Cossett.

'Oh no, sir, Sacha was a regular officer of the Tsar's Own Black Hussars till he shot that silly fat Prince.'

Not even this reassurance could shake Mr Cossett's scepticism. However, he generously shared Lise's rejoicing in the glorious bul-letin of Christmas Day, in which the Tsar proclaimed that not one enemy soldier was left on Russian soil. If the Fellows of his own College at Cambridge could greet the news by leaping on the Com-mon Room tables, singing, dancing and hugging one another, Mr Cossett could permit himself the mild indulgence of partnering Lise in an impromptu jig round Sir Barnaby's drawing room.

And for Lise the wonderful news was shortly eclipsed by a single paragraph in the reports; because among those distinguished by His Majesty was listed the youngest Colonel in the Russian Army, who had become something of a legend as a Cossack guerilla leader under the *nom de guerre* of Sacha Volnoy; and who was now honoured by the title of Count under that name.

For quite a month this news rendered Lise valueless to Mr Cossett. All her concern was switched to Mme de Montargis' campaign for the début that would whirl her to international fame and Sacha's notice.

Eventually, however, Mr Cossett's training told, and she registered with dismay that forty thousand war-weary Russians were trudging on into Germany to continue the war.

'Oh, why cannot the Tsar be content to halt at his own frontiers?' she cried to Louisa. 'It's none of Sacha's business to liberate Europe!'

But the war everywhere dragged on, and Mr Cossett saw no end to it. At home, Mme de Montargis despaired of Lady Cory, abused Miss Smith and scolded Lise for want of attention to her patroness.

'A paltry letter a week, and you wonder that a *grande dame* has ceased to interest herself in you! Never mind, you must write again. *Mon dieu*, these English eccentrics! Just when she could be of use to us to sway Lady Cory. But from the first moment I saw her . . .'

Fortunately, the wooing of Lady Cory took the Marquise much from home. At these times the household relaxed; and at all times for Lise as well as Louisa, cheerfulness was at hand with the children.

Coming upon a spirited representation of Uncle Armand's entirely apocryphal routing of the Cherokee Indians in the schoolroom one February afternoon, Louisa identified her sister behind some fierce Cherokee war-paint and threw up her hands in dismay.

'Lise, your complexion! After all the oatmeal and Denmark lotion maman has lavished on it! My love, I beg you will go and wash off these chalk smears at once.'

'But, mama, my Aunt Lise is the Chief of the tribe and I have *captured* her.'

'Yes, my treasure, but now you will release her, will you not, if mama asks you? Indeed Lise, you must go. Maman will be sending for you directly to speak to you about her news.'

'If it is to tell me that I am to have the felicity of dining with her at the Corys next Friday, I know it already from Sophia Cory, who hastened to assure me that it will only be the Jacksons and a dull, family party.'

H

'I wish it were that. Julia, *mon chou*, not in your mouth, I beg— No, Lise, it is not the Corys, at least not directly; but maman has it from Lady Cory that the Duchess of Malvern is expected at Devereux House, and she has determined to call on her with you.'

Lise made a fearsome Cherokee grimace.

'Willingly. In my war-paint, which will confirm Her Grace in her worst expectations of émigrés! Besides, I have no need of her now to get some word of Aunt Hon. I was coming after our game to tell you *my* news. Louisa, I have had a letter from her! Rudd managed to give it to me privily, bless him, for you know how maman would have fussed. Oh, Louisa, I am so relieved! Aunt Hon writes that the wretched Edinburgh damp has brought on her rheumatism—at least, I am not glad of that of course, but she says it makes writing a tribulation to her and that has been the cause of her silence. She has been forced to resort to dictating to Dr Robinson's sister whose "braw Scots" she can barely understand. And she is so droll about it all! It seems that Dr Robinson gave her a lowering scold about frittering her time away on her book, when she had her scientific notes to develop. He has offered her the run of his library and his hospitality, "hastening"— Wait, I have the letter somewhere here in the wigwam— Yes, "hastening to assure me that my modesty will be preserved by the presence of his sister!" Then she goes on: "Naturally, I have jumped at the chance of working under his aegis—no mean distinction for a female, I would have you know! My only grumble is that it puts it out of my power to have you visit me as I intended. Never fear, Lise, I shall beg your mother to spare you to me as soon as I come South; for I miss you, child, more than I can say." There! And I had thought. . . . But she has *not* forgotten me, nor been set against me by those odious people at Malvern. Charles, *mon brave*, if I gave you my parole, may I go and wash my face now? For—oh *yes*, dear Louisa, I'm going down to maman at once, and I shall be *infinitely* pleased to pay the Duchess a morning visit and give her *all* the latest news of her sister.'

The next day's papers duly carried the intelligence that Caroline, Duchess of Malvern was arrived at Devereux House. One zealous Society chronicler had it from a reliable source that the object of Her Grace's visit to the Metropolis was to honour with her presence the ball being given by the Earl of Stour to mark the twenty-fourth birthday of his second daughter, the Lady Agnes Chepstow. The first circles of the polite world were far more interested in the strong rumour that the recluse Duke of Malvern was also to attend the ball. The long-awaited announcement of their betrothal was cordially expected.

This *on-dit* was naturally not shared by Lady Cory and Mme de Montargis. Fearful lest the Duchess' energy might not survive the first London fog, Lise and her mother paid their call the following morning.

In the event, Mme de Montargis need not have worried about the weather and Lise could have gone in her Cherokee war-paint instead of Louisa's best pelisse. The Duchess of Malvern was not at home to émigré widows.

In the carriage going home, Lise saw tears in her mother's hard, faded eyes, and threw her arms round her in fierce affection: the first she had felt for her.

'Madam, one day, I promise you, I *promise* you—'

'What, *chérie*? In Society there is only one way to repay an insult. And that is with interest. Now . . . well, Adela Cory will not be slow to ask me how the dear Duchess received her sister's protégée.'

'You will tell her, maman?'

'I shall tell her that Her Grace's manners would not have got her past a *valet de pied* at Versailles. You and I, *chérie*, will do ourselves the honour of ignoring the whole episode.'

CHAPTER V

But it is one thing to stiffen one's spirit with aristocratic disdain, quite another to wake up next morning knowing that one's life is over.

Her début had been the essential door to the glittering future and Sacha; indeed, as Lise now bitterly realised, to *any* future beyond the confines of Highgate. With a couple of careless words the Duchess had slammed that door in her face. And to make matters worse, Highgate was shrouded in dismal white fog.

Lise sat up in bed, hugging her knees and staring out at the fog. But her imagination refused to indulge her with visions of an exquisite riposte, delivered from some dizzy eminence to a discomfited Duchess. Instead it presented her with a very clear notion of the revenge open to her by the simple exertion of writing to Miss Smith about her sister's cruel conduct.

The picture was not an attractive one. Lise wrinkled up her little nose at it and jumped out of bed, her pride salved and the tone of her mind materially restored.

At breakfast, encouraged by the absence of his mother-in-law, who breakfasted in her room, Sir Barnaby offered to take Louisa up in the carriage to Islington for the market. Such a treat was not to be missed by the children. So Roger, Julia and Armand were packed in among the baskets, while Charles Edmond departed grumbling to Mr Cossett in Lise's care.

The fog had cleared by her return and a thin, cold sunlight was trickling through the windows. Lise had not far to look for employment. Louisa's mending basket stood bulging as usual with the children's stockings and small clothes. The daunting prospect of spending the rest of her life bowed over such gave her a few bad moments. But she recalled that her future of domestic toil would at least be interrupted by a sojourn with Miss Smith; and something of that lady's robust common sense suggested that her present drudgery might be more comfortably tackled before the fire in the breakfast parlour.

It thus came about that she was the only member of the family downstairs when the remaining footman hoarsely announced the Duke of Malvern.

Lise had established herself in moderate comfort on the hearthrug. She also considered her brown merino round dress, though simple, to be tolerably becoming. But to Francis's eyes, the picture she presented crouched over her humble toil, made Cinderella's home life appear pampered, and a startled exclamation escaped him at the sight.

Francis had come up to London with the firm intention of offering for Agnes Chepstow. Instead he found himself calling on Lise de Montargis. If the mystery of such conduct could be explained there would doubtless be fewer ill-assorted marriages; but equally fewer young ladies and their mamas would be gratified by visits from eligible Dukes.

Lise, however, appeared anything but gratified. Scrambling to her feet, her eyes flashing, she demanded to know how dared he present himself in High Gate?

'I—I beg your pardon,' he stammered. 'Indeed, I desired your man to discover if it was convenient—but I did not suspect—having your mother's kind permission to call . . .

'Given before she suspected to what insult she would be subjected by *yours*! If you are come to offer apologies, let me inform you, my lord Duke, that they will only be acceptable from Her Grace in person!'

'Apologies? Insult? Good God, Mlle de Montargis, what has happened? What has my mother done?'

Lise whirled round on him.

'Why, nothing it seems! Turning a couple of émigrés away at the door must be too normal a practice in English first circles to warrant my lord Duke's notice. But I'd have thought that common delicacy would have prevented a *gentleman* from—'

'My mother had *you* turned away from my house? What is this you are telling me? There must, indeed there must be some misapprehension.'

'Yes, on our side! For *madame ma mère* considered it her—her *obligeance* to call on the Duchess to thank her for the hospitality I received at Malvern. Hospitality! Your mother's haste to repudiate my acquaintance could not have been greater if she had given houseroom to the monkey her sister was set to bring home from Gibraltar! So perhaps I should account myself fortunate in having been bidden to sit at table with my lord Duke, and—'

'Will you stop calling me my lord Duke!' cried Francis, goaded out of all shyness. 'My God, "bidden to sit at table with us"!' A few agitated strides took him across the room to her. 'My darling—when I have longed to—oh, my darling!'

Lise's outraged squeak as his arms went clumsily round her brought him abruptly to his senses.

He fell back, aghast alike at the impropriety of his conduct and the impulse that had prompted it. No conscious thought of being in love with Lise had so far entered his head; he had simply been unable to get her out of it. And of course, everyone including himself had known forever that he was going to marry Agnes Chepstow. The impossibility of reconciling this course with his present overmastering desire to pull Lise back into his arms, made his brain reel. Had Mme de Montargis not chosen that moment to make her entrance, he would have probably taken refuge in abject apology and flight.

Barred from both by the presence of the injured Marquise, he was obliged to pull himself together and beg Lise to present him to her mother.

'So that I may offer Mme la Marquise the explanations due to her for the unfortunate misunderstanding when she called at Devereux House.'

Mme de Montargis's frozen hauteur melted slightly at this and she nodded permission for Lise to introduce their august caller.

Lise performed the office abstractedly. Her experience of men had not encouraged vanity, and blank astonishment had been her only reaction to the Duke's extraordinary conduct. But now she was wholly entranced by the vista it opened up before her.

How amply would the insult to her mother, and every slight at Malvern to herself be repaid, if the Duke were seen to be at the feet of the penniless émigrée! And then let the polite world see if they could shut their doors in her mother's face!

Not since the great Escape Plan had there been such a famous scheme. But there was a difference: the difference between sixteen and eighteen. And this time as she launched herself on her unprincipled course, Lise had a fair inkling of the fire she played with.

The prospect delighted her. It only remained to attach the Duke. She glanced at him under her lashes. Francis, floundering to a standstill over the fatigues of travel and the delicacy of his mother's constitution, looked as sheepish as only a very shy young man divided between infatuation and the conviction that he has made a fool of himself, can look. Common humanity required of Mme de Montargis to accept his discomfort as an apology and bid him sit down.

Thus encouraged, Francis went on to apologise for his intrusion, for the vagaries of the British climate, for the slowness of Lord Wellington's advance and the dirt of the Highgate roads. Then he ventured one more look at Lise, and was rising to take his leave when a commotion outside announced the return of the shopping party.

Excitement had made Julia's nose bleed as usual, and Louisa had rushed the sufferer upstairs before the footman succeeded in conveying the news of their noble caller. So Sir Barnaby alone straightened his cravat and rolled into the parlour, determined to show his little sister-in-law that she could count on him to further her interests. . . .

By the time Francis regained Grosvenor Square, the confused emotions and discomforts of his visit had resolved themselves into simple anger. He stormed up to his mother's apartments, pausing only to fling a curt order for his packing and horses, in a tone that vividly recalled his late father to the butler and several startled footmen.

A shattering half-hour later, the Duchess had also been forcibly reminded of Francis's parentage.

Cousin Emily completed her discomfiture by presently running in with the report that His Grace had departed for the country, leaving no direction.

'But he cannot go away on the eve of Agnes' birthday ball! What am I to say?'

Cousin Emily wrung her hands.

Pollock, the Duke of Malvern's valet, was possibly the only retainer at Malvern who did not consider his master a poor substitute for his brother. Consequently, the household at Plessey, the Duke's hunting box in the county of Leicestershire, were deprived of the intriguing reason for His Grace's sudden descent on them, and equally in the dark over his abrupt departure a week later.

Pollock was glad that His Grace had so far regained his senses as to see the absolute necessity of an explanation with Lady Agnes.

Francis set out for his ordeal in London with rather more apprehension than he had faced the French guns at Almeida. When Lady Agnes received him exactly as usual, he was far too distracted to feel any relief. Staring straight before him, he launched at once into the tortured speech he had spent the week preparing.

Fortunately it petered out halfway through under the bracing check of Lady Agnes' uncontrollable laughter.

'Forgive me!' she choked. 'But really, this solemn harangue. . . . My dear Malvern, I am not the House of Lords! ". . . .the magnitude and heinousness of the offences which you may justly lay to my charge". . . . If this is your style of apology for missing my party—'

'You know it is not that.'

'Dear Francis, *I* know that there is only one way in which you have offended me; and that is in withdrawing from me the confidence of an old friend. Did I field your and Guy's cricket balls and tie up *revolting* bait for your rods, to be now treated *en forme* because you find you do not wish to marry me? That is to be hard on me indeed!'

'Agnes, I—I am so miserable.'

'Well, I am not precisely in whoops myself; but I am persuaded we shall not improve matters by cutting off our friendship to please the gossips. Let 'em dine off us this Season if they so choose! I shall go on being just the same to you as I've always been. Now tell me about Plessey. Did you get any cubbing?'

After a wondering look at her, Francis collapsed into a chair and laughed for the first time in weeks.

'No, I did not. To tell you the plain truth, I spent the chief of the time in rehearsing my speech to you. Oh Agnes, you are a *dear*! Are you fixed in Town now for the season? But you'll come to Malvern as usual for the daffodils? When I was leaving for Town—' he flushed, recalling the destination of that visit, '—Morecambe said to be sure to tell her la'ship that we've never had such a crop. You *will* come?'

'I am very fond of gardens,' responded Lady Agnes mechanically, feeling her faculties reel a little.

Her own wishes as much as the Duchess's pleas for patience had guided her unconventional response to being virtually jilted; but she was unprepared for Francis to take it quite so literally that nothing was changed between them. Prudence forbade her to let his invitation flatter her hopes. But prudence had little chance against the joyful leap of her heart. Nothing was over. The little émigrée's dark eyes may have bewitched Francis, but *she* would not be strolling by his side through the golden harvest of spring at Malvern.

Lady Agnes, to whom poetry lay in a garden, acceded to the Duke's request, subject to her mama's consent, and felt distinctly more sanguine about her blighted love now that it could flourish out of doors.

CHAPTER VI

After the Duke of Malvern's descent on Highgate, Lady Cory was empowered to exercise all the benevolence she pleased for her old friend's daughter. Not in their wildest dreams could the Misses Cory hope to attach the Duke themselves, so they only stood to gain by association with someone who might—for Mme de Montargis rightly refused to admit of any reason for his call other than the prompting of passion.

From then on her sole object became to see Lise provided with a suitable wardrobe to receive his august addresses.

Louisa ripped and sewed with a heavy heart.

'Maman, I beg you— After all these years in the emigration, you *must* know that whatever we were in France, here we are nobody. The Duke of Malvern would no more contemplate marriage to Lise—'

'Are you insinuating that he would dare offer a *carte blanche* to a Montargis?'

'No, maman, of course not! I do not know what quirk prompted his visit. I choose to think that it was the response of a generous heart to his mother's cruel act. But if you must have him attracted to Lise, he is merely flirting with her.'

Mme de Montargis laughed.

'*Ma chère Louise*, you have not seen our gangling hero. *Le vrai type Anglais maladroit*. He would not know *how* to flirt.'

In this assumption the Marquise was wholly correct. Francis had never flirted with a girl in his life. His few excursions into the muslin company, in the wake of his rake-hell brother, had been brief and to the point. For the rest, his steady affection for Agnes and the assumption that he would eventually marry her, had sufficed.

And never had she seemed so fitted for that position as during the weeks of her spring visit to Malvern.

The Duchess, utterly bewildered, had followed Cousin Emily's advice to recuperate from her recent trials at Bath. Her Grace's absence and Lady Agnes's tact freed the house party from much tedious ceremony and made Francis a much better host. His guests enjoyed themselves. The sun shone. The gardens had never looked lovelier; and with each agreeable day Francis felt the hold of his recent madness wane.

By the end of the third week he was able to ride past Lise's rescue-tree without a tremor, and accounted himself cured.

But of course he owed Mlle de Montargis a profound apology. Just what form could cover his loose-screw behaviour to her defied his imagination. A letter? Cowardly: besides, what in God's name could he say in it? No, he finally decided, the only honourable course was to wait on mademoiselle in person. And at the thought of seeing her again—just *once* more—the fever coursed through his blood again, and he no longer saw or cared how admirably Lady Agnes would fill her rôle as Duchess of Malvern.

It had been settled that Lise would remove to the Corys' on the day of the Hon. Mrs Hautboy's rout party, which, as regularly as the Royal Academy's Summer Exhibition, signalised the opening of the Season.

The Cory barouche came for Lise at midday and was soon filled with the boxes containing her re-furbished finery and the ample form of Betsy, the under-housemaid, promoted, willy-nilly, to the role of her abigail.

The whole household saw Lise off to her début into the great world.

'Be happy, darling,' whispered Louisa.

'Come back soon, Aunt Lise,' chorused the children.

'Success, *chérie*!' enjoined Mme de Montargis.

'Write to us about the lions you meet,' urged Mr Cossett.

'Knock 'em for six!' bellowed Sir Barnaby, as the carriage receded down Highgate Hill.

Betsy sniffed.

'Well, miss, a fine start-off this is to our junketing, to be sitting there crying your eyes out. And in the mistress's best pelissey too!'

Lise's spirits on her arrival in Manchester Square had not far to sink to zero. This descent was swiftly accomplished when she turned from Lady Cory's greeting to face a battery of curious eyes from the party assembled in the drawing room. The Jacksons, engaged to dine with the Corys before proceeding to the rout, had not seen Lise since she became an object of interest. It hardly needed Sophia's whisper of 'Well, what news of our noble suitor?' to bring home to Lise the considerations that had procured her début.

'What a sly-boots you are, Lise,' she said, as the ladies went upstairs to dress. 'Unless, as I was saying to Sukey Jackson, you've not all that much cause to be conscious? For you've not heard any more of him, have you?'

Lise would have been less than human if she had not there and then vowed to show Miss Sophia the hateful Duke squarely down on his knees before her. But as she sat at the dresser in the comfortable chamber allotted to her, with Betsy curling her hair and Louisa's embroidered sarsenet laid out ready on the bed, she only longed to have the odious pretence of her début over and be allowed to return to the obscurity of Highgate.

It would be safe to vouch that no one invited to Mrs Hautboy's rout anticipated less pleasure from the evening than Lise. An hour later, wedged behind Sophia in the press of guests struggling up the staircase to be received, her expectations looked to be justified.

The rout had already all the hallmarks of success. Six hundred people were crammed into a house meant to hold three hundred. The glare of two thousand candles was blinding; the heat was overpowering; the noise deafening. The flowers in the ballroom had already wilted. The ice for the champagne was melting rapidly; and several ladies' headdresses and trains were knocked and torn in the crush.

When their party attained one of the less overcrowded saloons, Sophia's was found to be among the casualties. Lady Cory withdrew with her younger daughter to repair the damage, recommending Lise to await her return by Mrs Jackson.

Lise stationed herself behind that lady's chair. Presently, the lessening of the crush enabled her to look round the company. One glance sufficed to show her that however becoming the sarsenet had looked in Highgate, it fell lamentably short of the toilette required for a London ballroom. Every woman but herself seemed to be shimmering in satin and lace and a-glitter with jewels. Everyone was talking, laughing, promenading, flirting, greeting their friends. Even the toothy Misses Jackson had found acquaintance. Imprisoned

in silence, ignored, ill-dressed, Lise felt herself repaid for every impertinent hope of conquering London Society. Her eyes smarted with
the shame of her isolation. If Francis could have crossed the room
to claim her at that moment, he might have had her hand and heart
from sheer gratitude; but instead she heard herself hailed in the hunt-
ing-field tones of English first circles, and looked up in surprise and
thankfulness to see the Lady Agnes.

'Mlle de Montargis! What a pleasant surprise! Such a shocking
squeeze, is it not? You will recall my brother Peregrine? And Colonel
Eliott and Lady Sarah? And this is our cousin, Selbridge. Perry *will*
have us brave the crush in the ballroom. If you will indulge him, he
has no need to look for a partner. Is that your chaperone? May
he—'

Lady Cory, returning into the room, was somewhat startled
to find it in the power of her protégée to introduce her to the Lady
Agnes Chepstow. The Honourable Peregrine, obedient to a glance
from his sister, was also made known to Lady Cory and won her
ready assent to dance with Lise. Once on the ballroom floor, he was
rewarded by Lise's graceful performance: and from thinking himself very ill-used in bestowing his fashionable notice on an obscure
débutante, decided she did him so much credit that he invited her
to waltz with him after supper.

The Chepstows' supper table was constantly interrupted by
acquaintances; but Lady Agnes seated Lise beside herself and was
tireless in seeing her eligibly entertained. Lise, suspicious but gratified, found herself being returned to her chaperone at the end of the
rout only on her firm promise to ride with Lady Agnes in the park
the following day.

'You will be doing me a kindness, mademoiselle, for I fell in love
with the prettiest bay filly at Malvern—I told you I was visiting there
lately, did I not? and nothing would do for Francis but to make her
my Easter present! But she is not up to my weight, is she, Perry?'

'Nor's mademoiselle,' signalled her brother's speaking look.

On their return home he lost no time in cornering his sister.

'Aggie,' he accused. 'You're up to something. I'm shot off to do
the pretty by some dab of a girl. All our acquaintance commanded
to distinguish her. She'd do you a favour by exercising your new
mount. . . . Doin' it rather too brown, m'dear. Especially,' he added
frankly, 'as no Chepstow ever had the wit to dissemble anything.
Remember when you tried to pretend you weren't as proud as
Lucifer of Malvern going off to Spain?'

'Perry, that's just it,' cried Lady Agnes, abandoning all further attempt at dissembling. 'No, I don't mean Spain, you lackwit! I mean Malvern. He is in love—or he fancies he is in love, with Mlle de Montargis.'

'He must be mad,' decided Perry after due thought. 'No, I mean, dammit, Agnes, a little nobody franked by a Lady Cory—! Well, dashed awkward for you, of course, but at least you can rest assured he won't marry her. Aunt Malvern won't permit him. Not to speak of Aunt Hon.'

'I wish you will not talk as if Francis had no mind of his own,' snapped Agnes. 'He shall marry whom he pleases.'

'As long as it's you, eh? But making much of your rival seems a corkbrained way of setting about it to me.'

Lady Agnes folded her capable hands.

'It must seem so; but I have two strong motives for doing it.' She smiled a little bleakly. 'And I beg you will not tell me they are contradictory! You see, I believe that Francis—that his infatuation with this girl springs largely from chivalry. There she was, dumped amongst all of us at Malvern, I declare I pitied the little waif myself! We all seemed so big and fortunate beside her. But now when Francis sees her in London—'

'Is he coming to Town then? I thought he told Bob Elliott he was fixed at Malvern for the summer?'

'So he believes. But I think I knew the exact moment when his thoughts turned to seeing her again.' Lady Agnes rose and closed her fan with a snap. 'Well, I am determined mademoiselle shall *not* present him with a lonely little figure blinking back tears across a ballroom floor. I cannot make her fashionable, but I can see her provided with eligible company. And you can find her enough partners to make sure that we have her dancing every dance. No girl can look pathetic waltzing with one of your set, Perry.'

'Waltzes like a dream,' murmured Perry abstractedly. 'M-mmm. Beg y'pardon, Agnes. Well, it's too deep for me, but count on me o'course. It's at least no hardship to dance with mam'selle. Light as a feather.'

He stifled a yawn.

'Well, I'm for bed. But wait though, you have not told me your other motive for your deep doings.'

'I think I won't after all. Off to bed with you, little one.'

'Well of all the shabby starts—! Not so much as a country dance will I stand up with your protégée. And I shall write to Aunt Hon.'

'If I thought that would do any good—! Oh, very well then. But you will not laugh?'

Perry's sleepy eyes opened wide at such a plea from his stately sister. However, she went on composedly enough:

'You know that I—I am very sincerely attached to Malvern. If I am wrong in my surmise . . . That is, if he truly loves this girl, I would not wish him to marry a—what did you call her—"a nobody franked by a Lady Cory". Her birth is as good as ours: and in my hands she can be introduced to good society and—and fitted for her future position. Perry! I forbade you to laugh at me!'

But the Honourable Peregrine was beyond reach of admonition. 'Women!' he managed to gasp out between paroxysms.

CHAPTER VII

It was as well that the housekeeper at Devereux House had been alerted by Pollock to keep His Grace's rooms ready. The Duke arrived without warning and in the shortest of tempers, having spent three solitary weeks at Malvern wrestling with his conscience, his duty to his position, his common sense and his shyness.

None of these had prevailed against his craving to see Lise again. With this single end in view, he set out for Highgate at an unfashionably early hour next morning.

Faced instead by Mme de Montargis, the purpose of his visit was quickly made plain to him. He left Highgate a trifle dazed, with her full permission to pay his addresses to her daughter.

When the Marquise made her triumphant entry into the Cory drawing room, Lise was not yet returned from her ride with Lady Agnes, which had become a standing engagement. That day, the beautiful weather had tempted their party out to Richmond, but in the afternoon the heat became a little oppressive. Lise had complained of the head ache and Lady Agnes solicitously insisted upon escorting her home. It was the merest ill-luck, however, which caused her to accept Lise's civil offer of refreshment and to accompany her into the drawing room where Mme de Montargis was rehearsing for the third time the splendours that awaited her daughter. At the sight of Lady Agnes, the Marquise's eyes snapped.

'*Chérie*,' she exclaimed, embracing Lise. 'The most exciting news has brought me! I have been soliciting Lady Cory's permission for you to receive a *particular* friend here. He arrived in London late last night and rode out to Highgate—*mon Dieu*, at dawn!—to beg leave to call on you. *You* will know of whom I have the happiness to speak.'

Lise's raging head ache blurred the import of her mother's words. Lady Agnes was startled to see her grow perfectly white and take a stumbling step forward.

'Maman, you cannot mean—? But—how would he know where to find me in London—?'

'Exactly, dear child. Malvern had no notion that you were fixed in Town for the Season; but I ventured to engage that Lady Cory—'

'La, ma'am, I believe Lise is going to faint,' broke in Sophia. 'Well, I must say, so would I,' she added frankly.

'The heat,' said Lady Cory, with a repressive glance at her daughter. 'It is really quite unseasonable for April. Some hartshorn—'

'Open the windows, quick! We'll lay her on the sopha.'

'Here, *chérie*, my smelling salts—'

'No, please . . . Indeed, maman, I am perfectly well. It was just you saying . . .' Lise hid her face in the cushions.

Lady Agnes rose.

'I will go. Pray do not trouble to escort me, madam. Lise, I think you should lie down for a while. Perhaps our gallop this morning was too fatiguing on such a warm day.'

'*Chère* Lady Agnes, I was *sure* you would understand,' murmured Mme de Montargis. 'The dear child's constitution is *not* robust. Perhaps it is as well that she will now have little time for such exertion.'

Miss Sophia spent the next three days glued to the drawing room windows. Her vigil yielded not so much as a glimpse of a ducal hat, and she was gradually persuaded to resume a more rational mode of life, declaring that she would not be surprised if it was all a hum.

Sophia was mistaken. Once it had been made clear to him that he wished to marry Lise, Francis was as ardent to win her as Mme de Montargis could have wished. The sheer relief of having all his perplexity summarily settled dispelled most of his doubts. The rest melted away at the thought of holding Lise in his arms. In short, few of the considerations that push a diffident man into a rash marriage were lacking.

But no one had ever accused a Devereux of lacking the courage of his convictions. Determined to make amends for the ramshackle manner of his courtship so far, Francis posted down to Bath to apprise his mother of his coming alliance.

The Duchess did not spare herself the exertion of falling into strong hysterics at the first mention of it.

Cousin Emily, though reduced to complete incoherence by the

crisis, commanded her powers sufficiently to get off an express to Miss Smith.

By the end of the week Francis was no nearer his goal.

'Your father would turn in his grave,' asserted the Duchess, with the weight of twenty-eight years dependence on her lord's boundless energy. 'First Spain, now this! It is beyond anything. And after I had told Emily I did not think even you mad enough to contemplate *marrying* the Nobody—'

'I would beg you to remember, madam, that Lise is—'

'Please do not interrupt me, Francis. I recall her telling me that she was some sort of governess in St Petersburg. And her brother-in-law is Sir Somebody Potts. You must be mad.'

The trouble was that Francis could not wholly dismiss this conjecture.

He returned to London divided between defiance and apprehension. The latter was fully justified when he encountered his Aunt Honoria in the hall at Grosvenor Square.

He had rallied a little by the time he presented himself in the apartments kept to Miss Smith's use whenever she descended at Devereux House. His aunt was directing the unpacking of two large corded boxes of books for what looked ominously like a long stay.

'My baggage,' she explained, waving the footmen out. 'Well? So you fancy you want to marry Lise?'

'I do not *fancy* it! I love her and I have her mother's permission to—'

'Doubtless,' snapped Miss Smith. 'But not *your* mother's I collect.' Her eyes narrowed. 'And what of Lise herself?'

'I—I have not approached her yet, but Mme de Montargis's assurances permit me to dare hope—I was naturally anxious for my mother's approval; but I warn you, aunt, if need be I shall do without it!'

'What a charming wedding yours will be,' mused his aunt. 'Your family unrepresented, conjecture rife among your guests, and Sir Barnaby Potts to give you away a bride whose own affections are engaged elsewhere.'

Francis blenched visibly; but to his aunt's surprise replied with steady dignity:

'If mademoiselle's affections are already engaged, no doubt she will so inform me herself.'

'Francis, don't be a fool!' exploded Miss Smith, voicing the fear that had brought her post-haste from Scotland. 'Recollect who you are, and ask yourself how may the girl refuse you? You have seen her family's wretched circumstances; that *ancien régime* harpy of a mother . . . A child of barely eighteen! Every feeling must be revolted—'

Francis strode agitatedly to the windows.

'If—if I thought she was being constrained—' he stammered.

'At least give me time to find out,' barked Miss Smith. 'Lise will be open with me as to that and—other matters.'

Taking his silence for consent, she went on in a calmer tone:

'And now you will sit down and we shall talk rationally. You are mistaken if you think I share your mother's views, as I shall presently inform her. The match is unequal; but if I thought there was the possibility of a genuine attachment . . . But I will *not* have her pushed into it by her mother's ambition. I am very fond of the child, Francis, and I promised someone in Russia to care for her.'

Francis had obediently taken a chair and was staring gloomily at the carpet. He looked up.

'Who?'

'No one you need consider if you can win her love. I hope at eighteen one is entitled to a change of heart! But give it time. Good God, a scant three weeks in each other's company and you prate of marriage! Come and tell me in a year that you are still of the same mind: let me be satisfied that she goes to you freely, and I will be your first advocate with your mother and the Family.'

'A year to wait—' cried Francis in dismay. 'No, it cannot be.'

'A *full* year,' boomed his aunt inexorably. 'And you may leave me to deal with her mother. Dear me, in a year I shall be rising fifty-three; but I must trust that I shall still have the use of my limbs to dance at your wedding. Or perhaps at *both* of your weddings,' she added with a baleful grin.

With this parting shot undermining what was left of his confidence, Francis went away to consider his next move.

The Duchess had to be content with Miss Smith's assurance that Francis would do nothing precipitate. She ordered Cousin Emily to write back immediately, imploring her sister not to abandon her post.

No arrangements could have suited Lise better.

She had her dear Aunt Hon restored to her months before she had looked to see her. She was abruptly freed from her mother's importunities—for Miss Smith lost no time in waiting on the Marquise. And even without the spur of revenge, it would have been a lofty turn of female mind that found no satisfaction in the attentions of the biggest and most despaired-of prize on the Marriage Mart.

For her sake the holland covers were removed from the splendours of the ballroom at Devereux House. For her benefit a dashing, high-perch yellow phaeton and a silken-mouthed black colt were added to the stables, and the Malvern box occupied at the Opera. To please her Francis swallowed his nervous horror of fashionable drawing rooms. There was nothing to be done about his awkwardness on a dance floor; but as dancing was the breath of life to Lise, he submitted cheerfully to the absolute necessity of spending night after night in the heat and crush of the Season's ballrooms.

Some of it he enjoyed. Away from Malvern and the daily reminders of his own inadequacy, the Duke's eyes were agreeably opened to the advantages of great wealth and position, of which he had so far only felt the weight.

It was surprisingly enjoyable to fill his house with guests of his own choosing. The Duchess's wrongs, freely circulated among the innumerable Devereux connections, were the talk of the town; but only a few gothic dowagers could resist an invitation to Devereux House—and the chance to see the Nobody for themselves. The Season was at its brilliant height. Only the glitter of scarlet and gold on the ballroom floors served as a reminder of the war. London was full of agreeable company, bent on pleasure; and none with more wide-eyed relish than Lise.

Lady Agnes, biting on the bullet, stuck to her Trojan resolve to make Lise a conformable bride for the Duke.

'And is it not odd, Louisa, that of all the people I have met lately,

I would rather have her my friend than anyone?' confided Lise to her sister on one of her now rare visits to Highgate.

The day was Sunday. Lise had arrived without warning, to find her mother not yet returned from the French Church in Somers Town. Sir Barnaby had taken the elder children to watch cricket on the green. Louisa's bees hummed drowsily among the roses and a placid Sunday peace enwrapped the house and garden. Lise, basking in the sun on a rug beside baby Letty, leant back against Louisa's knees and indulged in philosophic reflection.

'Is it not strange how things turn out?' she mused. 'How little did I think I'd ever find England agreeable or want Agnes Chepstow, of all people, for my friend! Or that she should wish to distinguish me.' She sat up and giggled. 'A last straw, I hope, for the dear Duchess, to hear who is my staunchest adherent—apart from the Duke of course.'

'Lise, I cannot like your tone. My dear, in your situation—'

' "The notice I attract must be distasteful to true refinement"? Louisa, what nonsense! Of course I realise I'm invited everywhere because people are curious to see the émigrée who's fixed Malvern's interest. But what of it? I assure you it's *infinitely* more agreeable to be fêted in the first circles than to stand pushed in a corner behind Sophia Cory, or spend a ball picking up *ma tante*'s fan as I was used to in Petersburg. Oh Louisa, it is such fun to be of consequence! When *I* dropped my fan at the Devereux House ball, you might have seen half a dozen of the best names in England start forward to retrieve it. And the Duke of York asked Countess Lieven who the chit with the eyes was? Oh, if only she'd be inspired to write to Warsaw about it!'

Lise met her sister's questioning eyes with a small, cat-like smile.

'Did I not tell you about Madame Lieven's gossip from Petersburg?' she murmured. 'It seems that all the *ton* are flocking to Warsaw where the Grand Duke Constantine holds a constant round of fêtes and balls and reviews. La Lieven took particular pleasure in informing me that the Princess Nina quite outshines the Polish beauties, according to Mme Arloff. Her ladyship herself was off there directly, to visit her younger stepson who is on the Grand Duke's Staff.'

'Your Sacha—Count Volnoy—is in Warsaw? Then he was not involved in this heavy fighting at Bautzen? I am glad for you, Lise.'

Lise turned reproachful eyes on her.

'Did you think I could be enjoying myself like this if I did not know him safe? I have known it these six weeks. Mr Cossett made a special journey into Town, bless him, with the *Gazette* after the battle at Lutzen. Sacha was mentioned in the dispatches and appointed to the Grand Duke's Staff in Warsaw.' She grimaced. 'A city which the Princess Nina just *happens* to feel she must grace with her presence. Without her husband, Madame Lieven says. As if that made any difference to Nina!'

'Lise!'

'Louisa, you will startle the baby. There! Hush, sweetheart, come to your Aunt Lise. Mama does not mean to scold us.'

'But I do, I must. My love, it borders on indelicacy for a young girl even to know about such things.'

Lise snapped open the elegant fan Francis had given her and retired behind it.

'Dear sister, I am sunk beneath reproach. But, alas, what chance would any female of delicate principle have against a Princess Nina? Oh Louisa, don't look so shocked! I am not proposing to have Malvern set me up as his mistress to rival her.'

'Dearest, I know you are only funning; but such sentiments even in jest—'

Lise rose with a defiant swish of her skirts.

'Oh, I'd say it in earnest if I thought it'd accomplish anything. But I am persuaded it will gain me more *éclat* if Madame Arloff reports me in Warsaw as having the prize of London's marriage mart at my feet.' Baby Letty, chewing Lise's hat ribbons, gurgled. 'Look, Letty agrees with me. And I am having such fun bringing him there.'

It only ceased to be fun when she found herself alone with him. Looking into Francis's troubled grey eyes she was much more apt to see him as the awkward young man who had been kind to an unwanted guest at Malvern. And Francis was rigidly loyal to his tacit undertaking to his aunt. Lise should neither be constrained nor dazzled into accepting him. A coarser-grained man might have been blinded by Lise's perfect willingness to dance and ride and flirt with him. Francis merely willed himself into believing time would cure her manifest indifference. Meanwhile he went on spoiling her and sought comfort with Lady Agnes.

CHAPTER VIII

Miss Smith summoned Lady Agnes to breakfast in her rooms at Devereux House.

Lady Agnes had dined there the previous evening, in company with Lise, before going on to the Opera to watch Francis watching Lise. Her appetite was a trifle impaired.

'You may feel more like sampling some of these excellent kidneys when you've heard what I have to say to you,' Miss Smith told her. 'Now attend me. I'm off; being tolerably satisfied that none of you will be any the worse for this folly of Malvern's. Lise is so young that I had wondered— But there is no change there; and I flatter myself I have scotched maman's design to push her into accepting him. In your shoes, I'd stick to it. Give Malvern six months—'

'Your pardon for interrupting you, ma'am, but I cannot agree with you about Lise's sentiments. I still believe *his* feeling for her to be mere infatuation; but it makes little odds, since she will have him. I happened to be present when her mother virtually informed her that Malvern had applied for her hand.' Lady Agnes took a gulp of coffee and blew her nose. 'I would be happy to "stick to it", as you put it, Aunt Hon, if I did not have the melancholy conviction that all it will ensure me will be a card to Lise's wedding.'

'It may, but not to Malvern. I don't know what you saw; but I know what *I've* observed during these two months of junketing,' snorted Miss Smith. 'Heaven knows, I've often been tempted to put missie across my knee; but when I think of her life up to now . . .' Her eyes softened, 'Tol-lol, Agnes, Cinderella can't resist going to the ball! But I promise you that your Prince is quite safe from her as long as— Oh, ever after, to be sure.'

'That's not what you started to say, ma'am.'

'Fairy tales aren't my forte,' grunted Miss Smith. 'In any case, I doubt if there's one about a Russian Younger Son who might one day come to prefer his loyal Cinderella to his mistresses; *if* he doesn't stop a French bullet meanwhile.'

Agnes took a little time to digest this. Then she wrung Miss Smith's hand.

'*Thank* you, Aunt Hon. I shall *pray* for his safety. And I shall be delighted to continue—er—escorting Cinderella to the ball.'

'Good girl,' said Miss Smith, laying down her napkin. 'So now that's settled, perhaps my sister Malvern may be persuaded to rise from her death-bed in Bath and I can get back to Scotland and get on with my work.'

Relieved of the chief of her anxiety, Lady Agnes was surprised to acknowledge how much she enjoyed her rival's company.

'She said to me last week how much she had always wished for a younger sister instead of a brangle of boys,' Lise reported eagerly to Louisa. 'And she has introduced me to her elder sister, Lady Frensham. She is quite old of course, past thirty,' Louisa smiled, 'and she was widowed in the Peninsula so she lives retired in the country. But she is very good *ton*, and so kind! And at least I need have no pangs of conscience about being friends with *her*.'

'As you have about Lady Agnes? Oh, Lise.'

'Well, a trifle,' admitted Lise. 'But less so now that Malvern is not my only admirer. As Madame Lieven says, there is nothing like a Duke to set one off! And she is essential to my plan, so—'

'Dearest, this tone, these sentiments— What plan?' asked Louisa in alarm.

'Oh, nothing,' muttered Lise. 'The point is Lady Frensham doesn't find me as reprehensible as you do, and if maman agrees we are all to go and stay with her when the Corys remove to Kent.'

'I know I must seem to be forever scolding you; but I cannot help being uneasy! Who is comprehended in "we" for this house party, Lise?'

'Why, Agnes and I and Perry and the Elliotts and George Alvanley and Stepforth and—oh, a host of agreeable people.'

'And Malvern?'

'Of course,' purred Lise.

Frensham Priory was a sprawling Tudor house sadly in need of repair, since Lady Frensham's lawyers saw to it that not one penny of her jointure went to its upkeep under the odd arrangement by which she continued to occupy it.

Lady Frensham was a dark, quiet woman whom her family were accustomed to refer to as 'poor dear Mary'. After her husband's death she had prepared to remove to her Dower House with her two little girls; but the new heir, a cantankerous and miserly Scottish peer, had other ideas. His lordship had hit on the novel scheme of leaving her as a sort of unpaid housekeeper in her own home and planting his motherless offspring on her to bring up.

'And Mary sees nothing wrong with this iniquitous lot!' cried Lady Agnes, as she and Lise collected their hostess to go down to dinner during the first week of their stay. Her sister laughed.

'You must not allow my family to bore you on the subject, Lise. Indeed I am well content, since it enables my daughters to grow up in their father's home; and with my own life over, what more could I ask? To be sure, I could wish that my cousin-in-law were a little more openhanded about the house; but as long as our shabbiness does not put off my friends—'

'May I hope that absolves me for having put my foot through the breakfast parlour floor?' said Francis with his shy smile, coming up.

'Oh, you have been licensed to do so for years. It is Lise I am concerned with. You *will* say if any rain comes through the bad patch in your ceiling, Lise? I count on your mother sparing you to me again for a really long stay.'

'I should like it of all things,' breathed Lise, meaning every word.

Lady Frensham had taken as instant a liking to her sister's odd rival as Lise to her. To Lise she was a livelier, less harassed Louisa, but blessed with a sense of humour—which had been vastly tickled by the situation unfolded to her by her sister Agnes.

She was further diverted when, towards the end of the visit, the Duke also laid his troubles before her. His immediate dilemma was where to go next.

'Agnes is promised to the Colchesters and I am invited there too; but dash it, Mary, *I* can't well write to my host asking him to include Lise in his invitation.'

'I collect your nice sense of propriety equally forbids you to ask Agnes to do so? And the Duchess is embattled at Malvern? Poor Francis! But pray why are you dependent on the Colchesters? To my certain knowledge you own four large country houses, apart from

Malvern. Can they have escaped your notice? Or the fact that Lise has a home and family?'

'N-no. But Mary, I am persuaded that she is not happy in High-gate. If you could have seen her there as I did—'

'Crouched over the cinders?' murmured Lady Frensham irre-pressibly; but she was instantly contrite and charged herself with the task of getting Lise included in the Colchesters' house party.

The party broke up in November, when estate and County business would no longer brook the Duke's absence from Malvern. There was nothing for it but to restore Lise to her family, under his own escort, which did much to reconcile Mme de Montargis to her daughter's return.

The Marquise took the opportunity to have a brief, private talk with the Duke.

The interview sent her with added zest into the battle over the renewal of Lise's wardrobe.

The battle was truly joined two days after Lise's return. Soon after breakfast, a smart delivery gig deposited a pile of beribboned bandboxes embossed with a single, expensive name and the simple legend 'of Bond Street'.

'But why *shouldn't* maman accept credit for me from Celeste? Or Madame Rose and Pinet's and the rest, when they are positively *pressing* it on us?' pouted Lise. 'I have not asked for it. Oh, why cannot I have some pretty, *new* dresses for once in my life?'

'Miss could do with such,' contributed Betsy from behind a cloud of silk paper. 'Regular pushed I've been to have her turned out proper with what we've got.'

'Hush, Betsy. Dearest, I don't grudge them to you!' cried Louisa. 'But you must see for yourself how improper, how wrong it would be—'

'I see nothing improper in these tradespeople soliciting Lise's custom,' said the Marquise at her most haughty. 'The *petit bourgeois* habit of paying one's tradesmen on the nail was undreamt of in our circles.'

'Stuff you get on tick has to be paid for in the end,' deposed Sir Barnaby, from gloomy experience. He shot a shrewd glance at Lise. 'Wouldn't maybe care to have the bills sent to the Duke to settle?' he mumbled, with another, apprehensive, glance at his mother-in-law.

Her wrathful response was all he feared; but as far as she was concerned the mischief was done. Lise sent back the gowns.

To distract her, Louisa performed miracles of refurbishing. Sir Barnaby pawned his fobs to hire her a hack. The children initiated her into their new game, depicting the arrival of their Uncle Armand attended by a retinue of captive Indian chiefs. Mr Cossett, not to be outdone, refought for her benefit the whole of the battle of Leipzig on his maps.

Safe in the knowledge that Sacha was three hundred miles away from the scene of battle, Lise paid little heed. Happily for her peace of mind, she did not consider how quickly such safety would have palled on a natural fighting leader, nor what resource he could bring to wangling himself back into action.

Mr Cossett recalled her straying attention to the fact that the three terrible days at Leipzig had sent Napoleon in full retreat leaving the whole Eastern frontier of France open to the Allied advance, but at such a cost that they must hesitate to invade.

Lise yawned.

'But everyone's saying that peace is only a matter of weeks now,' she offered, recalling the exalted gossip at the Colchesters'.

'Typical of Tory judgement! Boney won't give up his conquests that easy. No, Miss Lise, it will be a long hard grind, taking every man the Allies can muster to bring him to his knees.'

'Oh sir, do not say so!' cried Lise in dismay. 'Not *every* man!'

Her fears quietened as the peace negotiations dragged on through the festive season, which everyone prophesied would prove the last Christmas at war. The only part of the Duke's letters Lise read attentively presently carried the news that Lord Castlereagh himself was off to see Great Britain properly represented in the negotiations.

'My sole dependence is on his lordship,' announced Mme de Montargis. 'The Tsar is a mad Slav. The Emperor of Austria is Bonaparte's father-in-law. The King of Prussia is a sot. But Great Britain will surely never countenance a peace that leaves the Usurper on the throne of France!'—a sentiment which for once left her in perfect accord with her son-in-law.

Even Miss Smith was moved to a cautious optimism. Lise was more interested in the joyful news that she might shortly look to make her long-promised visit to her Aunt Hon, whose rheumatism was to benefit by a stay at Harrogate Spa.

CHAPTER IX

Harrogate's sturdy Yorkshire patrons were not to be put in a flutter by the mere arrival of a Duke's aunt in their midst. But when she was found to be not above her company and heard to declare Yorkshire cooking and climate the best in the Kingdom, she and her charming young companion were generally pronounced a valuable addition to the Winter Season.

Only the lingering unease left by Mr Cossett's reference to 'every man' marred Lise's contentment. The swaying fortunes of the resumed fighting gave ominous weight to Mr Cossett's prophesy. If Miss Smith had harboured any doubts about Lise's unchanged heart, they would have been resolved by the devotion with which her charge scoured the newspapers for any mention of Russian regiments.

She was at this daily task at breakfast one morning, when Miss Smith looked up from her post to snort:

'It seems we are not to be left long in our tranquillity. Malvern is coming to Harrogate.'

Lise was frowning over the report that Napoleon had caught Blücher's Russian corps in flank and rear at Champaubert.

'Is he? I wonder—Ma'am, you know that the Duke has many connections at the Horseguards. Do you think *he* could discover which Russian regiments are involved in the present battle?'

Miss Smith threw up her hands.

The Duke's intention had been to travel post and rack up at an hotel as privately as possible; but he had inadvertently mentioned his design to visit Yorkshire to his steward, and from then on the inexorable machinery of His Grace's establishment had taken over.

Several household dignitaries descended on Harrogate. The largest of the vacant mansions in the vicinity was hired and an army of maids were set to scrubbing it from attics to cellar. Meanwhile, a convoy of wagons rumbled across country from the nearest of His Grace's seats, loaded with furnishings, linen, plate and a lovingly-bedded consignment of claret. This was followed by the head groom from Plessey in charge of His Grace's own mount and a string of hunters. Finally, a huge travelling chariot brought an array of upper servants and a footman in charge of His Grace's writing desk and shaving stand. After all of which, as his aunt remarked, the Duke's own arrival could not but present an anti-climax.

She was alone in this opinion. All Harrogate except Lise was cast into a pleasurable flutter. Francis took refuge in his bedchamber. He had come to Yorkshire in a sufficiently troubled state of mind, without providing a spectacle for a set of gaping provincials. He quickly proceeded to justify every worst expectation of himself as a moody and toplofty recluse. But to Mme de Montargis, the news of his visit brought unmixed satisfaction, all of which she expressed in a long letter to Lise. She added a postscript:

'You will be amused to learn, *chérie*, that your London Triumph has even had its effect in Petersburg. I have had a letter from Amélie Arloff, complimenting me on your future Distinction and having the Effrontery to claim that you will owe it largely to her careful upbringing! The Count joins her ladyship in sending his compliments to you, as does Count Paul. As she writes, they still have no news of Count Sacha, who commanded a Cossack brigade at the battle of Leipzig. Your former playmate, Nicolas, must have him off on another secret Exploit. She says you would find Count Nicolas much grown—'

Her mother's elegant script wavered before Lise's eyes. Francis, who was breakfasting with them, sprang to his feet.

'Lise, what is it? You have had bad news? Good God, what is wrong? Only tell me—'

'Hush, Francis. What's happened, child? Is someone taken ill?'

'No, wounded, prisoner, killed!' wailed Lise and ran out of the room, brushing past Francis as if she had never seen him before.

His aunt's brusque gesture restrained him from following her. Miss Smith's rubicund complexion had lost some of its colour. She hesitated and then reached across the table and picked up Lise's letter. A rapid perusal confirmed much less than her worst fears. She poured herself more coffee, saying to Francis:

'No call to put yourself in a taking. No disaster has befallen. The occasion of her distress is, alas, a common one in wartime.'

'Then—I collect her concern is for "someone in Russia"?'

'Yes.'

The Duke took a few hasty turns about the small parlour, coming back finally to sit staring at his neglected breakfast.

'Her mother has spoken to me of him. She could have spared herself the trouble of trying to reassure me. I have told myself a hundred times I am a fool to hope; but it makes no difference.'

'It will,' promised his aunt absently. 'Francis, when an officer is missing after a battle— Bah! this is to be as foolish as Lise. There are a dozen good explanations.' She rose. 'I will go up to Lise. She really must learn not to make such a piece of work over the natural hazards run by a born daredevil.'

This, however, turned out to be only the half of it.

'I am well served for my wickedness!' sobbed Lise. 'How *could* I—when he was in danger . . . Oh, you don't know how scheming and heartless I have been—'

'Well, I've a fair idea, but am I to collect now—'

'No, no, you cannot know the whole! If Sacha is killed it will be a judgement on me! I always knew it was wrong in me to encourage Malvern! I saw how miserable it was making Agnes! Louisa warned me, begged me not to let maman procure me that odious début! And it was all towards my stupid, *wicked* plan to be revenged on the Duchess and become a leader of the *ton* and —and show Sacha . . . Oh, if only God will let him be alive and safe, I will never even try to see him or the Duke again. I'll beg Agnes to forgive me, and the Duchess too. I'll stay quietly in High Gate all my life—'

'Now that is the outside of enough!' exclaimed Miss Smith. 'I am willing to grant you a Borgia of iniquity if you wish, but that you are turned into a saint before my eyes I cannot and will not believe! Now if you will moderate your transports and wash your face, I shall endeavour to allay your guilty fears.'

Lise raised a drowned, set face from the pillow.

'Ma'am, I am going back to London.'

'And pray what will that accomplish?'

'I—I shall get news of him somehow. I shall apply at the Russian Embassy. I shall besiege the Horseguards. I shall entreat the Duke of York to exert his influence—'

'I can depend on your mama to forbid you do anything so unbecoming! Maybe York is not such a bad idea; but *I* will enlist His Highness's good offices, and maybe Emily Castlereagh's as well.

Castlereagh will be in a position to do much at the Allied Head-quarters.'

Lise cast herself on Miss Smith's neck.

'You will? Oh ma'am. Oh Aunt Hon, how can you be so good to me? Oh Aunt Hon—!'

'So I am become Aunt Hon again, am I? Drat the child, you have taken all the starch out of my stock! Well now, we shall make an early start in the morning, and I think you may begin your reformation by refusing Malvern's escort.'

CHAPTER X

All Countess Arloff's rational explanations for Sacha's silence failed of their effect with her husband and the Princess Nina. Nina gave way to hysterical and public distress. The Count departed for Germany.

His agents there had drawn blank at the military hospitals, and an intermediary could get no news of Colonel Count Volnoy among the prisoners taken by the French at Leipzig. But Nicky's dangerous surmise quite needlessly added its mite to his father's anxiety. Now that he had his regiment, Sacha was no longer interested in cloak-and-dagger activities.

He had borne a perfectly open part in the battle at Leipzig, terminated abruptly by the bullet of a well-hidden sharpshooter.

He woke up in a jolting wagon moving slowly in a convoy of wounded and prisoners. There had been no time to sort them out, for all order had gone by the board in the chaos of the French retreat. The convoy's sketchy escort had been hastily mustered from Marshal Ney's rearguard.

This Sacha ascertained from his companions in the wagon. He also registered the comforting fact that he had the use of his limbs; although an exquisite agony shot through him at each jolt of the wagon. He rolled himself up in his cloak and went to sleep.

His next awakening was to far greater discomfort from his wound, and to the awareness of some intense activity along the convoy.

He must have slept through the night, for the light was now of a grey dawn and showed the convoy to be halted along an unappetising, rutted road between rain-soaked woods. Under the orders of a cursing staff officer, the inmates of the carts were being summarily tipped out, prisoners and wounded pell-mell.

'Push them into the ditch, you *crapauds*! And sort the officers out, in case the Emperor wishes to inspect them *en passant*.'

Unlikely though this was with his Imperial army in full retreat, Sacha felt all the undesirability of inviting another meeting with his late host under present conditions. The guard were putting their shoulders to the bogged wagon. He therefore took the opportunity to inch himself out of the ditch and melt away into the trees.

He was obliged to stop within ten paces, dizzied with the exertion. The front of his tunic was unpleasantly sticky, and some unregarded sword-graze was dripping blood into his eyes. However, he was presently able to press on until he found a cosy hollow beside a stream, where he decided to lie up and promptly fainted.

There he was discovered a couple of hours later by a straying and extremely malodorous pig and the woodcutter's daughter who had come out in search of it.

Here Sacha's luck gave out. She was decidedly unattractive. Consequently, his stay at the family's cottage was not prolonged. He waited only until his injuries had responded a little to Gretel's rough but devoted nursing, before he set about rejoining the Army.

Sacha strolled into the Imperial Russian Headquarters at Langres on the morning of January the nineteenth, a se'nnight before Lise was vowing to renounce all designs on him if God would only let him be safe, and four days after Count Arloff reached Langres at the end of five exhausting weeks of scouring every garrison town in western Bavaria.

His lordship's feelings on being confronted with his errant son, brown as a berry and apparently in the best of health and spirits, were at first too deep for words. Then he called on heaven to inform him what he had done to deserve the affliction of fathering such a scapegrace? Interpreting this to signify his father's joy in having such offspring restored to him, Sacha enfolded his parent in a warm embrace before turning to be thumped and congratulated by the dozen or so officers present. The thumping caused him to wince sharply, eliciting the tale of his wound. His father abruptly cut the welcome short and haled him off to the Tsar's own doctor.

That worthy ordered Sacha straight to bed, declining to stake any part of his reputation on the continuance of the miracle that had so far preserved his patient from gangrene.

There followed the most painful week of Sacha's life. It was only relieved by the restoration of Galant and Danilo, the former causing widespread havoc by mounting the stairs to his master's bedside and refusing to be removed. Sacha was also honoured by a call from a very august visitor. His father's old acquaintance, Lord Castle-reagh, accompanied by Prince Metternich, had arrived in Langres to pay his respects to the Tsar and, if possible, to undo the wholesale surrender of British interests his predecessor had permitted in the peace treaty currently being offered to Napoleon.

Lord Castlereagh had already learnt that there was an even more urgent task. Informed opinion in London had been what Lise heard at Society dinner tables—that Napoleon was already beaten and peace could be concluded any time. Prince Metternich's forecast was as chilling as Mr Cossett's. Many arduous battles still lay ahead. The first essential was to re-establish the shaky Grand Alliance, strained to breaking-point by the jealousies and dissensions of the Generals, and bedevilled by the Tsar's obsession with Poland.

'You'll need the patience of Job,' remarked Count Arloff. 'We distrust the Austrians and Prussians almost as much as they distrust us. Our Germans are at the throat of their Germans in the High Command. And you'll find His Imperial Majesty at his most sphinx-like over what to do with France—let alone with those infernal Poles! *I* have not been able to get a decision out of him even on the minor matter of Finland.'

Castlereagh sighed.

'Nevertheless a basis for agreement exists, as you'll allow. The Tsar must be as anxious as any of us that, having reduced France by our union, we do not re-establish her authority by differences among ourselves.'

'H'mmm. Well, what influence I have with His Majesty is of course at your disposal. Not that I'm here in my official capacity, as you know, having had the whole of this wild-goose chase foisted on me by my rascal of a son.'

'How is he?'

The Count smiled.

'A trifle sorry for himself at the moment. Well, it won't hurt him to live at something less than his usual pace for a couple of months; which he shall do, if I have to take him home bound and gagged! If your lordship can spare a half hour from your duties, I'd be honoured to present him to you.'

Castlereagh spent an hour at Sacha's bedside being regaled with the tale of Napoleon's Cossack guest.

A couple of weeks later, he was reminded of the incident by a postscript in one of his wife's letters, asking him to have one of his staff enquire about a young Russian officer whose welfare was exercising her friend, Honoria Smith.

His lordship found time amid a dozen grave preoccupations to send a few lines himself by the next courier. The gist of it Lady Castlereagh straightway relayed to Miss Smith, now back in Harrogate.

CHAPTER XI

With Lise back in Highgate and Malvern departed home, Miss Smith had nothing to do but drink the waters and wait for news of Sacha.

The war news offered the only hopeful prospect. With Russia, Austria, Prussia and England at last all in the field together and fighting on the soil of France, the end could not be long delayed. Then, if Sacha had been taken prisoner in the shambles of Leipzig . . . Miss Smith was roused from her plans of touring the French prison fortresses by the entry of the footman with the post.

She fell upon Lady Castlereagh's letter first. Having read it, her relief found its first expression in falling to her rheumaticky knees to thank God, and its second in sending for a bottle of champagne.

Glass in hand and beaming benevolence, she proceeded to read her other mail.

'Dear, dear Aunt Hon,' wrote Lise. 'I know you have tried Everything, but do you not think I might apply again to the Russian Embassy? It does not matter about my Reputation. Maman says I am finished in the Polite World anyway. You must know that Malvern came here last Thursday and asked me to Marry him. I have refused him and begged him to forgive me for the Pain I have caused him by my wickedness. He was so very kind and obliging and said No, no, it was his own Folly in thinking that such a Stick as himself could attach me, and I must not feel any reproach. So I said that I *did*, because he and Lady Agnes and all of them had been so good to me and it had been like some Wonderful Dream to be one of them. And he gave a sort of groan and said Oh my little waif, how do I learn not to love you? And ran out of the house, forgetting his hat and not even taking leave of maman in the hall.

'Dear Aunt Hon, if you knew how miserable I am! Maman says my wanton selfishness will see us all Starving in the Gutter. At least, she does not exactly say it to me, because she has declined Ever to Address me Again. Poor Sir Barnaby is in the basket too. John coachman is turned away and Betsy and cook are owed their wages.

252

Now there is talk that we may remove to Rigby altogether, because living is cheaper there. *I* do not care. If only I could know Sacha safe—'

Miss Smith downed two glasses in rapid succession.

'Poor chicken!' murmured Miss Smith on a hiccup. She hastily despatched an express reassuring Lise, before picking up the letter with Malvern's imposing frank on its cover.

'My dear Aunt,' wrote Francis. 'I write to beg your kind offices for Lise, since I fear she may have incurred her mother's Grave Displeasure. Aunt, she has refused my suit, and I cannot be blind to the Worldly Consequences for her. If only I am allowed to protect her, I can ask Nothing More. Of my own feelings I will not speak. I must have known all along that I had Nothing to offer her but my title and possessions. I must always Honour her for being uninfluenced by them.

'My mother cannot know how she wounds me by her Unjust Strictures on Lise. I wish I could go away. I cannot face my friends at present—'

'Ha! Agnes,' grunted Miss Smith.

She laid the letter aside, poured herself another glass and slowly twirled it, considering the future through its winking bubbles. The future took on a roseate glow for all her protégés. She toasted each of them in turn. Dansh—*dance* at all their weddings yet, despite the doctors, mumbled Miss Smith belligerently. With Mirnoff, she decided on a hiccup. It seemed a pity not to finish the bottle. Miss Smith did so, crashed her glass over her shoulder with Russian abandon, subsided on to the sopha and began to snore delicately.

Waking up in a mood of more sober elation, she rang for a servant to sweep up the broken glass and sat down to consider in a more realistic light the four young futures she was determined to disentangle.

The first move was obvious. She went to her desk and, fingering Lady Castlereagh's note like a talisman, wrote to a highly-placed acquaintance at the Horseguards, suggesting that some fairly simple, honorary mission might be found to require the Duke of Malvern's services to his country abroad.

CHAPTER XII

Now that Lise was not admitted to her mother's presence the task of carrying in the Marquise's breakfast devolved on Louisa. She bade her mother 'good morning', set down the tray and took a deep breath.

'Maman, forgive me, but will you not reconsider your refusal to let Lise accept Lady Frensham's invitation? I am persuaded a change of scene would benefit her.'

'Enough. I have already said—and anyone but a simpleton like you would realise—that Lise must not take up her giddy life again. What can it confirm to Malvern but her indifference? He is heart-broken. He will renew his suit. And he will find Lise *here*. Or in that hole at Rigby. Not waltzing in some other man's arms.'

'But Lady Frensham lives quite retired—'

'I have always deplored your literal mind, Louisa. Pray do not let me detain you from your marketing. Do not let Sir Potts neglect to borrow Mr Cossett's *Gazette* for me.'

'Indeed not, maman,' cried Louisa, grasping at a glimpse of cheer. 'Mr Cossett came yesterday especially to show us the bulletin saying that the Allies are within sight of Paris. Oh maman, only think that perhaps after all you may see France and our home again!'

'France.'

Mme de Montargis's hard, faded eyes misted. Then she straightened her rigid back again and gave her little resigned shrug.

'Maybe. But not *my* France, or our home again, I think. I was listening to them yesterday at Solange de Courcelles', prating as if it only needs the Allies to get to Paris for us all to step back into Versailles. Bah!'

'But if our King is restored—'

'I'll vouch it will not bring back our lands and châteaux to us who sacrificed all in the Royal cause. No, *ma fille*, to be restored to what we were one must be rich; and but for Lise's gross selfish-ness—'

Louisa fled.

She collected Julia and the shopping baskets and descended to the
hall where they found Sir Barnaby gloomily contemplating a king's
ransom of hothouse roses from the Duke.

'She will not accept them?'

'Just glanced at the card and went on crying.'

'Oh dear . . . Perhaps I should stay and sit with her—'

'Now Lady Potts, you know it's no manner of use. All she wants
is to see me off to the post.'

In the breakfast parlour, Lise raised her head as the front door
shut. Then she resumed her mending of Charles Edmond's nightshirt and her weeping.

Her tears were in part involuntary. The unswept chimney was
making the fire smoke abominably. For the rest, she was crying
over Sacha and life in general, most immediately because of its
latest blow in denying her the comfort of a sojourn with kind Lady
Frensham.

And she had not even been allowed to reply herself. Lady Frensham would certainly never ask her again. And none of Miss
Smith's enquiries had yielded any word of Sacha.

Lise dropped her face on to her mending and wept in earnest.
Through her sobs she became vaguely conscious of horses and
bustle outside. But what could it matter to her? She did not lift
her head until the door flung open and a perfect stranger, dressed
in a travel-stained, drab benjamin, burst into the room, shouting:

'*Bon dieu*, what a welcome! Where *is* everybody?'

His dark, snapping glance swept over her, and before she could
speak he caught her up in his arms.

'Lise? Yes, it must be Lise!' Holding her out at arms' length, he
gave a shout of laughter. 'And you don't even know me! But
where's maman and Louise? Never tell me you've not had my
letters?'

'Armand!' shrieked Lise, casting herself back into his arms. 'It's
really you? Oh, Armand—!'

'At last. *What* a welcome! Faugh, this smoke! Is that why you
are crying? What the devil are you doing sitting here darning shirts
anyway?'

'Because I dislike stockings worse, and Louisa is doing the
marketing, and they must be done.'

Armand's black brows snapped together. He glanced at her sharply. Then his eyes flickered around the room.

'Ah, just so,' he drawled. 'And a kitchen slattern *must* open the front door, and the chair seats *must* be threadbare, and the chimney *must* smoke for want of sweeping. A pretty nabob maman caught for my sister! Dear God, if I had known—'

'But did you not, sir? Why, poor Sir Barnaby has had his pockets to let for years! Surely maman must have told you in her letters?'

'Well she did not,' he said grimly. 'Not one word of anything going awry. The Rohan obstinacy is of truly heroic proportions, and I fear that you and Louise have been paying dearly for it. For my share of it too, in not coming until I had a fortune at my back.' An impish grin lit his sombre face. He caught her hands. 'Ah, but *how* I'm going to make up for it to you both, *petite*! Everything in the world. Tell me, what is it you want most in the world?'

The lustrous dark eyes that were a mirror of his own, gazed up at him wonderingly and then filled with tears.

'A letter.'

'Oho! So you're old enough to be in love? Take care, Lise; I intend to prove vastly hard to please over any man aspiring to my new-found sister. Now run and break the news of my arrival to *madame ma mère*, bless her mulish heart!—whilst I see if I've any odd bars of gold in my valise to convince her of my prosperity. *Nom de dieu*, what's that racket?'

A series of joyful bellows was announcing the breathless arrival of Sir Barnaby, who had run all the way from the post with Miss Smith's express.

He roared into the parlour, Julia and the three boys close on his heels and Louisa not far behind. For a few moments the urgency of his mission to Lise prevented Sir Barnaby from taking in the fact of his long-lost brother-in-law's arrival. When, however, the import of Louisa's transports penetrated his understanding, his exclamations, his wonder, his cordiality more than made up for any previous neglect. The clamour brought Mme de Montargis down to enquire if the house had caught fire—to be swung off her feet in her son's exuberant embrace.

Lise took no part in the joyous confusion of greetings and explanations. She sat perfectly still in the middle of it all, Miss Smith's letter clasped in both hands and a beatific smile on her face. Glancing at her, Armand was left in no doubt that the single sheet of paper in her hands encompassed all she wanted most in the world.

CHAPTER XIII

Such undemanding bliss cannot endure long in a fallible world.

'But I want of all things to go to Lady Frensham,' Lise was saying, a mere three weeks later.

She looked towards her brother as she spoke, having acquired a well-founded belief in his ability to work any miracles she required. His coming had brought Miss Smith's letter. The past three weeks had seen their translation to a luxurious house in Park Lane, the abdication of Napoleon and Sir Barnaby's appointment to a lucrative post with The Indies Mercantile Marine Company, where Armand had connections. If Lise did not actually ascribe the overthrow of Napoleon to her brother's powers, it was a near thing.

The house was a gift to his mother; Sir Barnaby's employment to Louisa; and Napoleon's downfall—had Armand but known it—to Lise, who now luxuriated in the knowledge that Sacha could not run into any further danger.

Park Lane had gone some way to convince the Marquise of her son's affluence, although she was still subject to relapses; as now, when she had been scolding him roundly for indulging Lise's passing fancy for a delicious parasol whose ivory handle was a snake with diamond eyes. Since the Marquise's own shopping that morning disclosed an ermine-lined carriage rug and a silver-gilt travelling service, Armand shouted with laughter in which his mother ruefully joined.

'But both are essential if our journey home is to be accomplished in tolerable comfort,' she hastened to point out. 'I am told that the inns between the coast and Paris are sunk in squalor, and they are probably even viler from Paris to the Loire.'

She said it with a touch of defiance. Armand sighed. Now that émigré London was frenzied with rumours of a Bourbon restoration, their return to France had become her sole preoccupation. He himself was eager to see Paris, and only awaited his passports to set out there to prepare their home; but he viewed a return to their ruined and gutted château in the Loire with less enthusiasm.

To his mother it was the core of her homecoming. For her,

Napoleon's fall and Armand's return with a fortune had but one divinely decreed purpose: to restore the Montargis inheritance to all its former glories.

The Park Lane house, in whose elegant withdrawing room this discussion was taking place, had become as odious to her as Highgate. Louisa might have it with her goodwill, and Lise could stay on with her, since she appeared deaf to everything but the calls of pleasure with her English friends! The Marquise was going home.

Lise tactlessly chose this moment to bring up the question of Lady Frensham's renewed invitation.

'Well and why not, *madame mère*?' smiled Armand. 'I could tool Lise down in my new curricle. I confess to a curiosity about this milady whom Lise mentions at least once a day.'

'Armand, you are a great deal too indulgent to your sister. She is becoming thoroughly spoilt,' began Mme de Montargis, but Lise's trained ear detected a note of weakening.

She guessed that she owed this complaisance to a letter which had arrived for her by diplomatic bag from Madrid that morning, on the heels of the Duke's regular tribute of her favourite dark red roses. These continued attentions had quite reconciled Mme de Montargis. Absence, she considered, in the case of such a dull suitor, might well make a girl's heart grow fonder of his Dukedom.

She smiled at her daughter. Really the child repaid elegant dressing! And this was not yet Paris . . .

'Very well, *chérie*, go to your country mouse if you must, until Armand's return from Paris. But it is out of the question for him to escort you. Armand, you know very well that I daily await your Command to Hartwell to be presented to your future King.'

Armand groaned.

'Knee breeches, powder and all? Madame, only for your sake! I am grown too American to relish such pomp. Lise, I'll send my man Tobias with you, and you'll take Betsy of course—unless you'd prefer my lovely Eulalie?'

'Armand! To offer that shameless creature to your sister—'

'Quite right, maman, I cannot spare her.'

'But I'd like her, Armand. I never knew that a slave—'

'Lise—!'

'Very well, I engage to have her with me when I come to fetch you.'

He was as good as his word, and the ravishing mulatto, perched up beside the coachman, was the first object to greet Lady Frensham's eyes as she and Lise crossed the lawns to meet his carriage.

The black footman ('No, miss Lise, Ah ain't no slave; Ah'm the Marquee's pussnal prop'ty') let down the steps and Armand descended. He saw coming towards him a brown-haired, heavy-browed woman, with a generous mouth and laughing eyes that lit up her plain face. She was sturdily built and wore a faded blue round dress that did not become her. It was evident from the earth smears on her hands and gown that she had been gardening in earnest.

To Armand's exacting, Frenchman's eye, she was neither handsome nor elegant. He judged her to be about thirty. He also knew that here was the woman he was going to marry.

This revelation came to him somewhat obliquely. He became aware that she had been stooping too long and it was making her back ache. She had no business to be carrying that heavy trug, while Lise tripped along with a posy of violets. And what was she doing without a shawl in the chill breeze? It was all he could do to stop himself scolding her for it and remember that the usages of civility demanded at least an introduction before he could marry her.

The dark Frenchman bowed formally over her hand. Lady Frensham saw that he had his sister's fine eyes, and they were looking at her with an intentness that made her drop her own in unwonted confusion. She chided herself for such foolishness at her age. She passed into the drawing room, where both ladies settled down to ply him with questions about the sensational developments in Paris.

'Did you see the Tsar? And Prince Metternich? Is it true that the Empress Marie Louise has turned against Napoleon? Are there really Russian troops encamped in the Champs Elysées? And what about—'

'Pray sir, is our Lord Wellington arrived in Paris? And what is to happen to that poor little boy of Bonaparte's—him they call the King of Rome?'

'I heard he's with his mother, the Empress, ma'am; and she— well, she is a Hapsburg first, in all things—'

'But what about the divorced Empress, the Creole, Josephine?' cried Lise. 'Is it true Bonaparte has not ceased to love her? Is she as fascinating as they say? And did you go to the Opera? And—and did you meet any of the Russian officers?'

I*

'Whew! What a list. Yes, to most of it, and I truly don't know what I found most fantastic. You must know I arrived with the Comte d'Artois—the only Bourbon Prince Talleyrand could lay hands on in a hurry—to face a wild reception. White sheets out of every window, doing duty for Bourbon flags, the ground before us strewn with white flowers. Shouts, embraces, tears—for a man they'd hardly heard of the day before! Poor Artois was completely overcome. He kept saying, "I am so happy, M. de Talleyrand, come along, come along! I am so happy." This was held to be insufficiently eloquent for a Prince of the Blood setting foot on the sacred soil of Paris after twenty years of exile. So in the *Moniteur* next day, we had Monsieur saying: "Nothing is changed in France. There is merely one Frenchman more."'

'Marquis, we shall suspect you of being tainted with American republican sentiments! But tell us about M. de Talleyrand—'

'Did he remember you?' demanded Lise. 'Mary, you recall I told you he was once Armand's patron? But is it really true he has changed sides again and is now for the King?'

'Tut, Lise, to the Prince of Benevento treason is a matter of dates. His only loyalty is to M. de Talleyrand—and, oddly enough, to France. Yes, he received me most kindly, once he had assured himself I require neither a pension nor employment; for his ante-room is besieged by indigent émigrés demanding that the clock be turned back to 1789. By the by, Lise, we cannot have the *hôtel* Montargis back. The Marshal in possession also changed sides just in time. But I have acquired the elegant house of a banker who did not. You will be delighted with the oval salon, copied from Josephine's at Malmaison. It only lacks her to grace it, as I told her when—'

'Armand! *You* waited on the Creole?'

'Certainly, and in very good company; all Paris flocks to Malmaison, led by the Tsar of All the Russias. He has fallen completely under her spell. And the Grand Duke Constantine—'

'Never mind him. Pray tell us how she looks?'

'Little and dark. Bad teeth. Growing a trifle plump. And still the most elegant woman in Europe. Like you, Lise, she never had any real beauty but her eyes; but there is something more potent—a languor, a grace, an instinctive seductiveness that informs her lightest gesture—' he threw up his hands. 'Ah, *diable*, in short, she has the art of pleasing men.'

To Lady Mary his every word was sounding a knell. She rose.

'I must go up to hear the children's lessons. You will excuse me until dinner?'

Armand bowed and held the door for her, wondering dismally what he had done wrong. She gave him a small rueful smile and went out, saying:

'We keep country hours here. Lise, my love, you will show your brother his room?'

But Lise made no move to do so, being riveted to her chair by a lightning flash of surmise.

'Armand, you *did* say the Grand Duke Constantine was in Paris?'

'Yes, what about him?'

'With his Staff?'

'A regular court of wild young bloods,' he replied absently. 'Oh, the devil! Lise, did I say something to displease your friend?'

'Is Mary displeased? I did not notice. Oh Armand, *please* let us start for Paris at once!'

'Fired by my traveller's tales, are you?' he grinned. 'Well, I confess I can't wait to get back myself. For a little while,' he amended, in deference to his drastically revised plans for the future. 'But never fear, pet, you shall have your full fling and subdue the heart of every glittering Lancer and Dragoon on the General Staff. Provided maman does not drag you off to reclaim the ruins of our ancestral home.'

Within a few days of their arrival in Paris this proved to be Mme de Montargis's fixed intention.

But Lise had now tasted a year of getting her own way, both at Francis's hands and her brother's. She took one look at the gutted grandeur of the Château de Montargis, stamped her lilac kid slipper and flatly refused to be consigned to this gothick exile when she could be in Paris. Armand tactfully intervened to remind his mother that Lise had been accorded a rendezvous with the great Leroy, on the Empress Josephine's own recommendation to that prince of couturiers.

'She shall keep it,' said Mme de Montargis absently. She sighed. 'Neither of you knew the Château as it was.' She walked across to the huge, empty fireplace and reached up her hand to touch the Montargis arms carved on its great stone hood. 'This hall was always draughty. But I shall always remember it as I saw it the night

your father first brought me here. It was in mid-winter and snowing
hard, but we stepped inside to find all this vast hall in bloom with
flowers from the hot-houses. Carnations, lilies, azalea, lilac, and
roses—oh, such roses! And the light of the fire was so bright that
we had them put out the *flambeaux* and supped by its light down
here, because I could not bear to be parted from the flowers.'

'Madame, I swear you shall see it restored, hothouses and all.'

'Will I, Armand? I know you think it a selfish old woman's whim;
but this is the home of your ancestors and one day you will wish to
bring your wife here, for all your wild talk of settling in America.'

'Did I say that? I must have been mad. America is much too
far from England.'

'From *England*? What can you intend, Armand? Why England?'

'Nothing, maman, nothing,' he hastily assured her. 'The important
thing is to see the château restored to *your* use. But how can we
leave you here? There's not a comfortable inn in the vicinity.'

'I shall be entirely content to rack up at the gatekeeper's lodge,'
declared the Marquise with uncharacteristic disregard for her comfort. 'It will be the more convenient for me to supervise the masons
and carpenters. You may expect me in Paris when I am ready to
order the furnishings. Aunt Solange de Rohan can act as Lise's
chaperone.'

Monsieur Leroy did not normally visit any client below the rank
of royalty; but the Empress Josephine had been his greatest patron.
So, on the morrow of the Marquis de Montargis's and his sister's
return from the Loire, Leroy's elegant caleche drew up at the
Marquis's house in the rue St Honoré.

Lise received him with full honours and then suggested a move
to her boudoir upstairs. There, monsieur introduced his *directrice*,
Madame Rose, and in a holy silence, slowly circled his new client.

'The *taille* is a trifle thin, and the *porte de tête* requires correction.
The hair is a disaster. Duplan must be called in. Mademoiselle must
learn to keep her hands still. The line of my toilettes is not to be
disturbed by fidgetting. The eyes—*magnifique*!' he kissed his
fingers. 'As for the lack of complexion—well, we shall make that
a virtue. Pallor, unrelieved pallor shall be the new mode.'

He cast himself back in a chair and closed his eyes.

'Yes, I can see it,' he announced finally. 'We shall have much to do, but mademoiselle has the essentials—youth and the illusion of beauty, which is so much more interesting than beauty itself.'

Lise learnt it with modified pleasure. Sacha was not among the Grand Duke's suite. But she smiled at M. Leroy.

'You smile, mademoiselle, you think it is an idle compliment? *Mais c'est moi qui vous parle*; I, Leroy, who have dressed all the great beauties of the Empire—and made the black-toothed Creole outshine them all. I take it mademoiselle *wishes* to become a reigning belle?'

Lise sighed. Once, childishly, it had seemed a passport to Sacha.

'I suppose so. One must do something.'

M. Leroy and Madame Rose exchanged glances.

'Not bad, eh? The negligence; the *dégagé* air! So rare in a debutante, so essential for a *succès mondain*! Now to work. May I ask if mademoiselle is partial to the colour she is wearing?'

'Oh yes. It is called pomona green and it is all the rage in London. Betsy, show monsieur the outfits I commanded from Chimène. But first desire his lordship to step up here if he is free.'

M. Leroy accorded the Marquis a bow as elegant as his own. He then examined Mme Chimène's creations through his glass and gave a faint shudder.

'May I enquire without impertinence whether *M. le Marquis* is very rich?'

'Tolerably,' said Armand, amused. 'And quite prepared to foot your ruinous bills for my sister's toilettes.'

'*D'accord*. Then mademoiselle will do me the kindness of ordering these deplorable garments to be thrown out of the window.'

'But—but I have a large wardrobe from London!'

'Burn it. Give it to your maid. Distribute it to the poor. *Nom de dieu*, must *I* suffer for the excesses of the émigration? And do me the favour of having your maid divest you of these layers of petticoats. I create on the female form, not on a cocoon of frills.'

His ascendancy thus established, the Master relaxed, accepted a cup of chocolate and declared himself ready to launch his new client on her career of conquest.

CHAPTER XIV

'One of the few occasions when I agreed with Bonaparte, was when he used to say that a woman needs six months of Paris to learn what is due to her and to understand her own power. Mademoiselle has accomplished it in as many weeks.'

His Excellency bowed, Mademoiselle de Montargis curtsied gracefully.

'Monseigneur is too kind to me.'

'You repay it. You have restored my faith in our old aristocracy. I had begun to despair of finding a single young, pretty, fashionable woman in the whole returned émigration.' Monseigneur raised his quizzing glass to take stock of her sleek bared shoulders, rising out of a cloud of diamond-powdered tulle. 'Ravishing. Leroy, I collect? You are said to have quite consoled him for the loss of Josephine. But what am I doing detaining you with my gossip, when I observe a vastly romantic-looking Polish Lancer waiting to beg you for a dance—and to run me through, I fear, if I monopolise the belle of the ball much longer.'

His Excellency bowed over her hand and limped off, bestowing a nod of encouragement on the louring young man.

'But I do not know the gentleman—' began Lise. Then something about his wan, dark good looks struck a disturbing chord in her memory. 'Prince Adam!' she cried.

'What's left of him,' he bowed, with a grimace at his empty right sleeve. 'I dared not hope you would remember me, mademoiselle, for I had some trouble in recognising you—but with better cause! I am afraid I cannot ask you to dance, but—'

'Now why ever not?' smiled Lise. 'I recall that you had the extreme goodness to dance with me in Petersburg, where no one else bothered to distinguish me. So you shall not refuse *me* now. Do you come from there? Oh, there is so much I long to ask you! Come, you shall hold me with your left arm and we shall deal famously.'

'*Ma chère*,' cried Princess Ralensky to the dowager beside her. 'My poor Adam is actually dancing. Oh, I knew Paris would do him good! You must know I have had the boy to every doctor in Europe this past year, since the Tsar pardoned his rash adherence to Napoleon. All to no use.' She sighed. 'His arm, of course; but more than that, a settled melancholy that has made us fear a decline. The trouble I had to coax him here tonight! Who is the young woman?'

Her neighbour raised her lorgnette on to the brilliant dance floor. '*Voyons*, you are behindhand! He has captured The Troika Belle —Lise de Montargis who's breaking all their hearts this season. She is usually seen with an escort of the Tsar's Cossacks, so Paris has dubbed her The Troika Belle. A *trifle* fast, but impeccable *ton*. The brother made a fortune in America. Ah, Excellency, we were just talking about the success of your young protégés.'

His Excellency bowed.

'*Chère* comtesse, their secret is simple and I claim no credit for it. They are young, gay, elegant and very rich. One should always try to be at least two of these things, they are the most amiable of the virtues.'

The possession of all four of these desirable attributes, plus the Marquis's American contempt for the fusty ceremony that stifled the Court, was rapidly making his lavish house the meeting place of all that was gay, brilliant and fashionable in Paris.

Lord Wellington came, imperturbable as ever in his plain blue coat. M. de Talleyrand brought the Tsar, on the assurance that 'here Your Majesty may see the prettiest women in Paris'. And His Majesty expressed himself especially pleased with his young hostess. 'Your little Troika Belle who is so partial to my Cossacks.'

For of all the scarlet and gold, black, silver, blue and white regimentals who arrived to dazzle and be dazzled in the oval salon, none found as much favour with their hostess as the dark green and silver of the Cossack officers. The Don Cossacks' Mess drank Lise de Montargis till their drunken tongues could no longer form the foreign syllables; and there was some talk of staging a review in her honour—until Mme de Montargis returned on a flying visit, to put a summary stop to such a scandalous scheme.

'Your conduct in general is grown quite unbecomingly free,' she scolded. 'I cannot think what Aunt Solange is about. The King looks to people like us to set an example . . .'

Lise burrowed deeper into her sea of lace pillows. She was still abed at eleven o'clock, having come home at dawn. 'But I *do* set an example, maman. My toilettes are copied everywhere, and at least two Duchesses have tried to emulate my Cossack escort.'

The just expression of her mother's wrath was diverted by the mention of Duchesses.

'And that's another thing. When, pray, did you last hear from the Duke?'

'*Which* Duke?'

Her mother boxed her ears, and Betsy announced the Marquis.

'Well done, maman,' he observed, eyeing the Troika Belle's discomfiture. '*Quite* time mademoiselle was brought to book. But now she is suitably chastened, will you not relent over my taking her to London for the Tsar's visit? She has given me no peace for weeks; indeed, with all the Allied Sovereigns coming, the Victory Celebrations should make a show not to be missed. And we shall see Louisa and—er—all our English friends,' he added a little consciously.

It was not the promised splendours that drew Lise. She had had her fill of these in Paris. But currently in London was a lady on whom she now pinned her dearest hope. The Grand Duchess Catherine, the Tsar's favourite, wayward sister, had preceded him to England where she had already managed to antagonise practically everyone of importance.

Lise had been privileged to hear that the Grand Duchess took a marked, personal interest in the newest regiment of the Russian Army and its Colonel. The possibility that he was included in Her Highness's large suite had been enough to make Lise besiege her brother to attend the London celebrations.

Prince Adam was her sole confidant, promoted to that honour ever since he had told her of Sacha's injunction to him 'to dance with Lise in London'. Informed of Lise's departure there, he smiled.

'You are very constant, Lise, for all your flirting. But—forgive me —if Sacha *were* in London now—'

'He has only to enquire among a dozen people to discover my direction and come here? I know that.'

'Poor Lise.'

'No! There was enough of "poor Lise" in Russia. Believe me, Adam, Sacha shall not now find in me a worshipping ninny to teach his singular notion of decorum!'

CHAPTER XV

The Tsar's London visit was an unmitigated disaster, disappointing more public hopes than Lise's.

As Miss Smith said, the English resented anyone but themselves insulting their Monarch; and this, egged on by his intolerable sister, the Tsar contrived to do in every possible way—from patronising the Regent's rabid political foes, to snubbing his latest mistress.

More serious, if less spectacular, was the mischief done by the acrimonious festivities to the urgent business of re-settling Europe. Lord Castlereagh had cordially hoped to have most of the major questions of the Peace Treaties settled in London, leaving only a few weeks' business for the Congress which was to meet in August at Vienna. Instead, the havoc of the wasted month in London was crowned by the Tsar's irritable refusal to set foot in Vienna before October. It was his parting shot. His sister's farewell gesture of stopping her carriage at Hastings to shake hands with the astonished peasantry paled beside it, merely causing Princess Lieven to take to her bed.

No one was more indignant in their condemnation of the Grand Duchess than Lise; perhaps unfairly, since the absence of Colonel Count Volnoy from her entourage was not Her Highness' fault. Nothing would have pleased her better than his inclusion in her train; but not even her whim could wean him from the sterner duty of garrisoning Occupied Poland.

There, thanks to a chance-met acquaintance in Warsaw, he learnt of Prince Adam's whereabouts and presently wrote to him in Paris.

The posts had somewhat improved with the ending of hostilities. It took but four weeks for his letter to reach Paris, in the same packet as a note from Lise at Rigby, now rendered almost comfortable by Armand's lavish improvements.

Prince Adam smiled as he contemplated the two letters lying side by side on his bureau. If Lise could know—! But the most careful perusal yielded only one phrase to raise her hopes in Sacha's letter.

'Did you ever get to London and see Lise, I wonder?' he wrote. 'I was within an ace of assisting at the present junketings there myself, being now on the rota of H.M.'s aides. But I suppose *my* turn of duty will fall to some dam' progress through one of our more Godforsaken provinces. Meanwhile, you are well out of Poland. Nothing could be more insipid than the drawing room intrigues and plottings in Warsaw. By God, though it's my task to sit on their necks, I swear I have more time for the hotheads who resist our Occupation in the provinces. To be sure, I hang a couple of 'em every week, *pour encourager les autres . . .*'

Prince Adam read the rest, his thoughts aflame. At dinner he informed his mother that he was returning to Poland to take part in the struggle for the independence of their native land.

His distracted parent sent for his doctors. Prince Adam threatened to throw them downstairs with his remaining arm. His mother wrung her hands and dashed off a frantic appeal to his grandmother in Vienna, where that formidable *grande dame* had made her home since the demise of her fourth husband and ninth lover, aged seventy-nine and eighty-two respectively.

A reply by special courier recommended Princess Ralensky not to be more henwitted than God made her, and to stop fussing the boy. For Adam there was a blistering postscript pointing out that as the fate of Poland was being decided at the Vienna Congress, he could more profitably serve his country there than firing hayricks in Galicia. To which end he might come and stay with her ladyship, as long as he did not bore her with his heroics.

None of her progeny had ventured to disobey Countess Anna for some fifty years. Adam set about his departure, quite forgetting his decline.

He also forgot to write to Lise; and once in Vienna, he was too preoccupied to send her more than two lines about Sacha, at the end of three pages of boring her with the wrongs of Poland.

Lise, back in Paris, stamped her foot with vexation. It was wonderful to have some direct news of Sacha; but where did it get her, unless Prince Adam made a push to recall *her* to his volatile notice? And she could scarcely *ask* Adam to do so.

It was all on a par with the low ebb of life in general. Her maman was back. Paris was dull and thin of company. Everyone who was anyone was flocking to Vienna.

All Lise's favourite cavaliers, from M. Talleyrand to her dashing Cossack outriders, were gone there. Talleyrand to manoeuvre France back to a place among the Big Powers, the Cossacks to cavort at the magnificent Peace Review staged for the entertainment of the six Sovereigns, the princes and notables past number and the seven hundred diplomats attending the greatest gathering Europe had ever known.

Only Lise de Montargis, their toast, the belle of the season, was condemned to sit watching the rain in Paris, or worse still, be dragged round interminable furnishing warehouses by her maman.

An unexpected relief was afforded her by a glimpse of Miss Smith and Agnes, who stopped off in Paris on their way to Vienna and Baden, where Miss Smith was to take the cure.

'Not that this is my sole purpose in Baden,' she confessed a trifle coyly to Lise. 'My old friend, Mirnoff, is coming from Russia to meet me there.'

'Ma'am, the General! Oh, how does he go on? And Annette? I heard that Zacharovo was burnt in the war—'

'He writes that it is being rebuilt and—er—urges me to come and see it. Failing which, he proposed to venture to London. However, now that my book is finished I am footloose again, so I suggested Baden, where I may conveniently proceed after our stay in Vienna. The cure will benefit him too. His spleen—'

Lise's attention had strayed to Agnes, dutifully sorting patterns for the Marquise at the far end of the salon.

'How lucky Agnes is to be going with you to Vienna,' she sighed. '*Everyone* is gone there. Dear Aunt Hon, could you not take me too?'

'The whole world with his wife—and mistress!' said Miss Smith brightly, ignoring Lise's plea. 'Never was there such a circus, it seems, and I confess to the liveliest curiosity to see it. Malvern has hired us an apartment; a *house* is not to be had for love or money. You know he is in Vienna, attached to the Austrian General Staff for Lord Wellington?—drat it, I cannot get used to calling Old Douro Duke! He growled to me that Francis had made himself quite useful in Madrid, which is more than I engaged him for, I can tell you! I will not disguise from you, Lise, that I have every hope of having matters between him and Agnes settled before the year is out. Seeing you in London this summer proved a slight setback; but he shows encouraging symptoms of recovery.'

'I do not see why you should have to describe it so,' complained

Lise. 'I am not some sort of disease! And I beg you will not tell maman. But I am glad for Agnes. It would be famous if they could make it a double wedding with Armand and Mary. And *then* could I come and stay with you?'

'Better. I'll take you to Warsaw.'

She snorted with laughter at Lise's face.

'Oh yes, I have my sources of information too. But Agnes first, or I'll have no peace from my sister.'

Lise was still building on this promise several weeks later.

The afternoon was conducive to dreaming, with the pouring rain outside, a bright fire and nothing to do but yawn over Mme de Staël's new novel. Lise curled herself into a ball on the cushions of the chaiselongue and stared into the dancing flames. Her imagination readily transposed the driving rain into the soft snowflakes brushing against the windows at Volnoya, and the elegant rose and grey salon into the charming rusticity of Volnoya's quiet rooms. It was growing dusk. Sacha would be too lazy to ring for candles. . . .

She frowned at the noise of a carriage drawing up below; but sat up eagerly when the footman announced Prince Adam Ralensky.

'All alone, Lise? I am fortunate indeed.'

'Adam, I am so pleased to see you! You cannot conceive how stupid and flat Paris is grown. And you look so much less hagged! Are you newly arrived? But how could you bear to leave Vienna?'

'Only because I am to return there directly. Wait till I tell you! And I have some news for you. But first of all, the important thing. Lise, Poland is to get her Constitution!'

'How—how nice. News for *me*, Adam?'

'It is all in train,' Prince Adam swept on, striding excitedly about the salon. 'The Tsar has sworn to Prince Czartoryski that he will restore Poland if he has to go to war to do it! Czartoryski is given the task—the honour—of drafting the Constitution. And, Lise, he has admitted *me* to his junior staff—'

At any other time Lise would have been diverted by the mention of the legendary Prince Czartoryski: patriot, hero, romantic friend of the Tsar's idealistic youth and rumoured consoler of the Tsar's neglected wife. But Adam had news for her.

'—it is to be known as the "Principles of the Constitution of the Polish Kingdom",' Prince Adam was saying exaltedly. 'I have helped to draft Clause 29 A.'

Feeling that some answering rapture was called for, Lise clasped her hands to her bosom, exclaiming:

'A whole Clause! How exciting for you! But Adam *dear*, my news—?'

'To be sure. Forgive me. Lise, the Arloffs are in Vienna.'

'Adam! *Not*—?'

'No. Just her ladyship and Nicky; she's in attendance on the Russian Empress. But the Count is expected. And so is Sacha.'

'Oh, Adam! When—?'

'Do have a care for my cravat,' begged Adam. 'Well, I do not know precisely. His step-mother, from whom I had it, says he is due for a furlough before he takes up his turn of duty as one of the Imperial aides-de-camp. But, Lise—'

It was then that Prince Adam failed in the higher duties of friendship. Countess Arloff had also intimated to him that Sacha was not expected in Vienna alone. But Adam's tender heart shrank from dousing the radiance in the dark eyes fastened on his face.

'In my reply to Sacha's letter I mentioned that you were living in Paris,' he mumbled. 'So perhaps . . .'

Lise gave a crow of her glinting laughter.

'You'd not have me place my dependence on that? No, I must get to Vienna.'

'I—I hope you may not be disappointed, Lise,' muttered Adam.

The minute he had gone, Lise sped downstairs to whirl into Armand's cabinet with the news that he must straightway escort her to Vienna.

'My pet, I've told you "no" a dozen times already.'

'Yes, but now I *need* to go there. I will stay with Miss Smith, so maman can have no objection. All you need to do is escort me there. Oh, Armand, *please*.'

'So important? Which of the dashing Cossacks or Lancers is it? Write him a billet and he'll come galloping here. No, puss. And it is useless making big eyes at me. I cannot take you if I would. As soon as my present business is finished I am going to England—to Stour,' he added, colouring. 'I was coming to inform you anyway.'

'Oh Armand, to offer for Mary?'

'Have I been so obvious in my intentions? Yes, if you must know.'

'Oh I am delighted! And if you will but take me to Vienna—'

'*No*, Lise. The Stours are expecting me. I was coming to settle what to do with you in my absence. You could join maman at the château—'

'I am going to Vienna.'

The Marquis's black brows snapped together.

'That you are not! You may go to maman, or if you wish you may remove to Aunt Rohan. Take your choice.'

'No!' cried Lise. 'You cannot be so cruel and disobliging when my whole happiness *depends* on being in Vienna.'

'Don't talk such foolishness. Last week your well-being hung on having the topaze set. Maman is right. I have thoroughly spoilt you, and your pretty head's so turned by admirers that you think your lightest whim is law. Now that is enough. Let me hear no more of this start.'

'I'll go to Vienna if I *walk* there!' stormed Lise. 'I don't care what you say! You *will* not stop me!'

Armand lost patience.

'And *you* will not use that tone to the head of your House! Go to your rooms and stay there till you have my permission to leave them. A little solitary reflection may mend your headstrong ways.'

Lise's incarceration was not prolonged beyond the cooling of Armand's own hot temper. She emerged to spend a busy week in conclave with Messieurs Leroy and Duplan, the genius in charge of her hair. The Marquis made no reference to their cause of contention until the end of the following week, when he sent for her to say that he was leaving for England the day after the morrow.

'And little though you deserve such consideration, puss, you may come with me. I will allow that the choice of rusticating with maman or Aunt Rohan may have got you blue-devilled. I shall set you down in London with Louisa. There!'

'Thank you, Armand, but I am resigned,' sighed Lise. 'I shall go to maman, if you please.'

She curtsied and withdrew, presenting a picture of demure resignation until she was outside the door. Then she danced upstairs and sent off her page with an urgent billet begging Prince Adam to wait on her privately.

'You must have taken leave of your senses,' was his blunt verdict on her request. '*Me* take you to Vienna?'

'Certainly. You have told me you are ready to return there, so it can put you to no inconvenience.'

'Put me to no— My poor girl, are you deranged? I never heard of anything so scandalous. Why—why, people will think—at best!— that I've eloped with you.'

'Well, it will be the first elopement chaperoned by a maid and a hairdresser,' retorted Lise. 'Oh do not be so gothick, Adam! I am only asking your escort; Adam, you *cannot* fail me when you know that it will bring me to Sacha. He would do it for you.'

'Yes, and probably have the girl in love with *him* by Vienna! Did you say "hairdresser"?' demanded Prince Adam faintly.

'The drollest little man. You will like him excessively. M. Duplan has lent him to me. His name is Sigismond.'

Adam groaned. 'I shall probably take him in strong dislike. Does he frisk?'

'Only a trifle. Oh Adam, you blessing! Now sit down and listen to my plan of escape.'

CHAPTER XVI

The apartments Francis had secured for Miss Smith and Agnes in Vienna were on the first and second floor of a decayed palace in the Bauernmarkt, built round a cobbled courtyard which, even in mid-winter, was freely used as a market and meeting place to exchange the day's gossip of the Congress.

The morning of January the fifth found the courtyard further enlivened by a strolling one-man band and a puppet show with a fiddle and flute. Out of their breakfast parlour window, Agnes was enchanted to observe that in Vienna even such humble music was dispensed perfectly in tune. She never tired of watching the colourful pageant below and hoped Francis would arrive to breakfast in time to see the puppets.

The crisp, clear morning had brought the courtyard population out in force to watch them; but their volatile attention, like her own, was soon transferred to a travel-stained, luxurious berline, put to six horses, which dashed up with a clatter to the doorway directly below her.

It seemed to be an equipage of some consequence. When the steps were let down, an extremely personable young man in a furred greatcoat jumped out, followed by a lady's maid in a close bonnet. But then there emerged an extraordinary personage in a lavender cloak and a state of violent agitation. Agnes craned out, earning an impatient snort from Miss Smith at the breakfast table.

'I declare you now gape at a raree show like any Viennese. What is it this time, a juggler?'

'No, much more droll. Someone out of the coach. Ma'am, he is exactly like my Aunt Malvern's curled poodle! And his antics are causing milord to clutch at his hair in the most distracted fashion! As for milady—'

'Well? What's she clutching?'

'An elegant sable pelisse,' said Agnes in a colourless voice. 'Aunt Hon, I collect we are about to have a visitor. Milady is Lise.'

Prince Adam was too relieved at having his harassing charges off his hands to notice the ominous nature of Lise's welcome. He departed after the briefest civilities, leaving the three ladies standing in the breakfast parlour.

Lise, who had noted the charged atmosphere, chose to ignore it. She tossed off her hat and stretched luxuriously.

'Oooh, I'm stiff! Agnes, what a becoming gown; you should always wear blue. How good to see you both again—oh, and real English buttered toast! Are you not going to offer me breakfast, Aunt Hon?'

'Certainly,' said Miss Smith cordially. 'And a nuncheon and dinner, since it will probably take me all day to make the arrangements. Tomorrow morning I am sending you back to France.'

Lise choked on her toast.

'Aunt Hon! You cannot mean it, when I *told* you as soon as I came in that Sacha is coming to Vienna.'

'I do not care if he is coming to Jericho! You are not staying here. If you recollect, *I* told you in Paris why it is ineligible for me to have you. Agnes, pray do not stand there being well-bred! Go and stop that lavender mountebank sending all the servants into hysterics. I will deal with mademoiselle.'

'Ma'am, you mean my good, I know, but I would not wish—' began Agnes in a strangled voice.

'Fiddle. This is no time for nobility. Off with you.' She closed the door on Agnes's scruples and advanced on the breakfast table where Lise was hastily fortifying herself with some coffee.

'Now, Lise, when you have quite finished your breakfast, we will have a few explanations if you please! Am I to collect that you have travelled from France in the company of that unfortunate young man?'

'Well, yes. But it is quite unexceptionable. Adam is *au fait* with everything, and when Armand would not let me come to Vienna—'

'Lise,' said Miss Smith in awed tones. 'Did you inveigle Prince Ralensky into *abducting* you from Paris?'

'No—that is, yes, I suppose so. But *pray* do not be troubled, ma'am. I waited until Armand had left for England, and I wrote to maman explaining that I was going to you, and taking Betsy and Sigismond.'

'After a sight of M. Sigismond I can well believe that his attendance would daunt the most determined seducer,' snapped Miss Smith. 'But how we are to stop the scandal . . .' She sank into a chair and gulped some coffee. 'You graceless little *wretch*, Lise!

It would serve you right if I let you be ruined by this mad escapade. Running off with the first young man to hand—'

'He's not. He's a friend of Sacha's—'

'Sending your mother wild with anxiety—'

'But she knows I'm with you, ma'am—'

'Coming here when you are well aware what mischief your presence can bring to Agnes—'

'It's not fair! Why should my life be blighted just because Malvern chooses to— Ma'am, you know I only want Sacha.'

'Exactly. So conduct, decency, consideration can go hang, as long as you— Yes, and pray what became of your vow to renounce all thought of him if only he were preserved?'

'Lord, did I say that? How childish one is at eighteen. But that was before—'

'You grew into the spoilt, selfish hussy of nineteen I see today! And you may save your tears, miss. I shall send you back with the first respectable Englishwoman I can find.'

'No! You *cannot* be so cruel—'

Just indignation had caused Miss Smith to raise her voice and anguish had lent a highly penetrating quality to Lise's wails. Their breakfast guest raised a startled eyebrow at Lady Agnes in the hall. She hesitated and then gave a resigned shrug and ushered him into the breakfast parlour.

'Francis—oh, the *devil*!' breathed Miss Smith, recollecting the breakfast invitation.

'Malvern!' wailed Lise, casting herself on his chest. 'Oh Malvern, please, please don't let Aunt Hon send me back!'

By the afternoon Miss Smith's wrath had cooled.

'Try to understand there's not an ounce of malice in the little fiend,' she growled to Agnes. 'She simply saw Malvern to hand, so she used him; as she will use anything to get her heart's desire. Well, what do you want to do? Advance our removal to Baden?'

'I am not given to running away, ma'am,' replied Agnes with a flash of battle in her eye.

'Good girl. I promise your ordeal will not be prolonged. Malvern looked distinctly sheepish. Meanwhile I suppose I must make a push to salvage ma'mselle's reputation. I think it will be as well if she appears with us at Countess Zichy's tonight. Seen under my wing, it may stop a few tongues wagging. We cannot hope that her exploit is not all over town by now.'

Miss Smith's forecast was based upon two months' acquaintance with Congress Vienna and proved entirely correct.

Liveliest curiosity attended Lise's entrance to Mme Zichy's *redoute parée*. As she made it in Leroy's breathtaking snow-white gauze and black pearls, Vienna's raised eyebrows were quickly topping a goggle of lorgnettes raised in avid speculation. How would the dazzling outrage be received by the dozen or so personages whose actions decided the verdict of the *ton*?

Her sponsorship by the English Duke's Aunt was duly noted— not to speak of the attendance of his Grace himself. But all still hung in the balance as she walked slowly in Miss Smith's wake down the length of the brilliant room, expressing from the top of her coiffure to the tips of her satin slippers a true Parisienne's disdain for the opinion of any other Capital.

Her progress was arrested as all the lorgnettes swivelled upon the entrance of the Tsar. He provided a far greater sensation by making it on the arm of M. de Talleyrand, whom it was the current Imperial whim to distinguish in the hope of annoying the English.

The Frenchman's eye was naturally caught by Leroy's masterpiece. He murmured to the Tsar and paused in his limping progress through the bowing groups to welcome his Paris protégée to Vienna.

The Tsar, pleased with another chance to demonstrate his Francophile mood, also halted to bestow a few gracious words in his squeaky but admirably carrying voice, on '*ma petite Cossack parisienne*'.

It was enough. Lise rose from her curtsey established.

Vienna was soon affording Lise every gratification except news of Sacha. Not even her joyous reunion with Nicky had yielded her any certain intelligence of his arrival.

Count Nicolas had made an instant conquest of Agnes and Miss Smith. Thereafter, pending his mama's return from Baden where the Count was restoring nature with the waters, Nicky virtually transferred his residence to the Bauernmarkt, where his cheerful presence did much to relieve the gloom of the Duke's constant attendance.

But if there was one issue that united all Miss Smith's household it was their determination that she should not fail at her rendezvous with General Mirnoff in Baden.

How she was to keep it without leaving the two young ladies unchaperoned formed the subject of constant debate between Lise, Francis and Agnes. Since the difficulty lay in Lise's overt and Agnes' tacit refusal to budge a step from Vienna, some constraint in their discussions would have been understandable. Fortunately, however, all their vagaries could not quite prevent the three of them being friends; and the inclusion of Count Nicolas in their councils finally excluded all undercurrents.

However, his proposal that Lise and Lady Agnes should take up residence at the Arloff mansion during Miss Smith's absence earned the Duke's peremptory veto. A more acceptable solution was offered by the hospitality of Prince Adam's grandmother; though 'offered' hardly does justice to her ladyship's imperial edict.

'*Voilà*, so that's settled,' she informed Miss Smith, summoned to the Orenbourg palace to hear the Ukase. 'Now you may go off to your General with a quiet mind. The girls will be under my eye here and one of my *dames de compagnie* shall attend them when they go outdoors. My grandson has his own wing, so there's no risk of having their modesty affronted by bachelors' parties.'

Countess Anna retained the etiquette as well as the morals of the Court of Catherine the Great. An elopement attended by a maid and a hairdresser, and Lise's rapid establishment as a Congress belle, were exactly calculated to commend her to the scandalous *grande dame*. Here, she had promptly decided, was the very girl to distract her grandson's melancholy. By the end of Lise's visit she would have them betrothed.

'It is vastly obliging in you, madam, but I have by no means decided—' began Miss Smith.

'Well, I have,' snapped the autocrat. 'Your Agnes shall exercise my English. As for Lise, her grandfather was my lover in '73—or was it '75? So that makes it practically *en famille*.'

No scruples could hold out against such reassurance. Miss Smith packed her bags for Baden. The following day saw Lise and Lady Agnes installed at the Orenbourg palace and struggling in vain to open a window in the sumptuous quarters assigned to them.

'Try climbing up on a chair, Sigi, maybe it will move from the top,' urged Lise.

'My hands, mademoiselle! I beg you will ring for a footman.'

'Oh don't be so prissy! It's probably as much as their place is worth. Betsy, go ask someone for a ladder.'

'Lise, do you think we should?' said Agnes. 'To be sure it is excessively hot in here—'

'Are you trying to let in a breath of air?' asked Prince Adam, arriving to pay his respects. 'Don't waste your efforts. Grandmère made Napoleon himself shut the windows at the Hofburg when he occupied Vienna. If you want to breathe, you'd better come and visit me. I've had 'em unseal all the windows in my wing. It's the big door across the court, or there's a passage through the servants' quarters. I'm always in,' he added gloomily.

'Well, you should not be,' scolded Lise. 'I am persuaded that your mooching on a sopha cannot benefit Poland.'

M. Sigismond, who had been much moved by Prince Adam's louring stance, emitted a squeak of protest, and then hastily retired under His Highness's astonished eye. Lise giggled.

'Poor Sigi thinks you are so romantic.'

'Ugh.'

'Well then, relax. Come with us to Schönbrunn for the ice fête this afternoon. We are to be driven there in thirty sleighs and it will be the prettiest spectacle imaginable. All the ice of the lake and the façade of the Palace will be lit by flambeaux—'

'Do come, Prince Adam, the fresh air will restore you,' put in Agnes bracingly. 'We are to see a performance of Cinderella, and a young countryman of mine will give displays of skating—'

'Imagine, he is to trace the monograms of chosen ladies on the ice,' cried Lise. 'Every woman in society is wild to see if she'll be included. Oh, and Nicky says Cinderella's coach is being fashioned entirely of frozen sugar by the Palace pastrycooks.'

Prince Adam clutched at his dishevelled curls.

'Sugared coaches—while Poland is dismembered at England's bidding!'

'Partitioned,' said Agnes coldly.

'Talking of frozen sugar, I am sure the divine Dorothea will be there,' murmured Lise, taking his arm. Prince Adam's melancholy at the Tsar's scuttle over Poland had lately been deepened by his unworthiness of an Angel known on this earth as Dorothea Von and Zu Haustaffenburg. He laughed hollowly.

'Yes—to observe me arrive in your train!'

But he went to the fête just the same, confirming his grandmother's impulsive decision that Lise was the very wife for him.

The distinction of having her initials traced out in the skater's dazzling turns confirmed Lise's arrival among the gazetted Congress Beauties. It also served to fire her and Nicky with the ambition to emulate young Mr Tyler's skill on the ice. Their plans suffered a check in Countess Anna's immovable prejudice against the perils of fresh air, so the two of them were obliged to confine their sessions with Mr Tyler to a secret hour before breakfast.

This clandestine arrangement had been in force for a week, and Lise declared all her tumbles worth while for the delight of skimming over the sunlit ice. Then came the triumphant day when she finally achieved an S. and L. entwined. Flushed with exercise and achievement, she settled into the homebound sleigh beside Nicky.

'Oh, that was good! But I had not realised it was so late. You'll have to set me down, Nicky, and no time for a *kaffeeklatsch* at Hügelmann's today I'm afraid.'

Nicky pulled a face.

'But I am *starved*. And I don't want to go home. We had a visitor arrive last night and ten to one I'll be hauled down to do the pretty by her. She calls me her "little page" if you please. Don't know if she thinks it will commend her to Sacha.'

Lise sat up.

'To Sacha? Nicky, tell me instantly who is this person?'

'Princess Nina Ulanoff. Lord, you remember her, Lise. The Beauty Sacha was forever dangling after in Petersburg.'

'Yes, yes, but— She is *here*?'

'Lord, haven't I just told you? She has descended with us on her way to Paris. Anyway that's what she said at first. Ten minutes later she has countermanded her horses and says she wants to stay in Vienna. A more henwitted female you've never—but you must've known her at Volnoya. And she's worse still since she was widowed.'

'Wi—widowed?' faltered Lise.

'The Governor succumbed last year. But I don't see why she didn't marry Sacha in the first place if she's so set on it, do you?'

Lise had turned perfectly white.

'Oh no,' she whispered. 'Oh, *no*.'

'Well, I don't like it above half either,' said Nicky judiciously. 'But Danilo heard my father tell Count Paul that we must resign ourselves to it after the open scandal of Warsaw. Whatever that means.'

'But—but the Countess has not said anything. Nor Prince Adam or any of Sacha's friends here,' stammered Lise, clutching at straws.

'No? Well, I daresay it is all a hum,' said Nicky easily. 'I say, Lise, you do look green. I don't wonder. I'm *faint* with hunger myself. I suppose you wouldn't—?'

'Nicky,' Lise sat up, staring straight before her with hard, glittering eyes. 'Tell the man to drive to your house. Fast. I am coming in with you.'

'Well of all the shabby starts, when you will not come to—'

'Nicky, if you are my friend, you've got to help me.'

'Well of course I will, silly. But what do you want me to do?'

Lise gave a slightly hysterical giggle.

'Poison Princess Nina's breakfast coffee for me. Oh, don't be so stupidly *masculine*! Just help.'

Count Nicolas rightly took it that his plea required him to

attend Lise into the breakfast parlour and abet her pretty start of surprise at finding the Countess entertaining a guest.

The Princess Nina, in the act of sipping her coffee, set down her cup with such abruptness as to spill some drops over her gown. She waved away a proffered napkin and went on staring at Lise as if she had seen a ghost. A ghost made doubly unwelcome by being ravishingly dressed in sable-trimmed apricot velvet, Roman boots and a sables shako, and much improved in looks.

The Princess glanced swiftly at her own reflection in one of the wall mirrors. It confirmed her husband's parting comfort that she would be suited to admiration by her widow's weeds. She relaxed a trifle. The Countess had also rallied.

'My dear Lise, let me give you some coffee, and pray do not apologise,' she smiled. 'Your intrusion—if you must term it such—comes most happily to afford you a glimpse of an old friend. Our dear Nina is to be with us so briefly before proceeding to Paris.'

She said it a trifle more emphatically than the case warranted; Lise's entrance having interrupted a stormy passage between the two ladies on this very point.

The Countess's sense of propriety had militated strongly against Nina's impulsive descent on her house. She was even more opposed to Nina's present intention of awaiting Sacha's arrival and confronting him with the various injuries a concluded love affair is apt to leave. And while she was willing to believe Nina that the rift was as temporary as their others had been, she had no intention of placing her home at Nina's disposal for a reconciliation. The mere thought of the Count's reaction made her ladyship shudder. She said brightly:

'Dear Nina is simply aching for a sight of Paris after all these years. But we all are! Were you not yourself my informant, Nina, that Sacha proposes to spend the chief of his furlough in Paris?'

'Yes, but that was before we—' began Nina incautiously.

'Paris in the spring!' urged the Countess.

'Once I've got matters arranged here—'

'With Paris in view, who would linger in Vienna? I am persuaded Sacha will only descend here briefly to see his father, and that need not detain Nina, when Paris presents so much more *suitable* a venue for her purpose. *Ma chère* Lise, you must be her guide as to the best of the new *modistes* and warehouses.'

The notion of the Countess's little émigrée guiding her taste at first deprived Princess Nina of any adequate response; but a closer inspection of Lise's toilette induced not only respect but inspiration.

'I should be pleased to have the name of your dressmaker, mademoiselle,' she drawled.

'I am dressed by Leroy,' said Lise simply.

'Indeed? I might have guessed it. Anyone who could do so much for you *must* be a genius. I am sure Sacha would be happy to have me order my trousseau from him. You know of course that this is the chief object of my visit to Paris?'

'Your trousseau?' echoed Nicky, solidly busied with his breakfast until then. 'Oh Lord, Lise, what did I tell you?' He swallowed the last of his eggs and stood up.

'Will you excuse me, maman? Au 'voir, Princess.' He turned at the door. 'We skate tomorrow, Lise?'

Lise spared a shudder for male insensibility that could envisage skating in a shattered world. The Princess Nina clasped her hands.

'Sweet child! Volnoy is quite devoted to him. You must promise me to spare him to us for a *long* visit, Countess.'

But her ladyship had had enough of having her breakfast table turned into a battlefield. Coldly bidding both young ladies to take their time, she found business outside.

Lise rose too. Her voice controlled by the courage of despair, she said:

'Do I collect you are engaged to marry Count Volnoy, Princess?'

It was Nina's moment and she made the most of it.

'My dear mademoiselle, such delicacy does you credit! But you must have now been in Society sufficiently to realise . . . In short, in such a recognised connection as exists between myself and Volnoy, a formal engagement is superfluous. Naturally my recent bereavement enjoins a certain delay to the public announcement . . .'

A certain delay from which, by the end of a sleepless night, Lise hoped for nothing but the time to get her own formal engagement announced as publicly as possible.

To whom did not greatly weigh with her.

In the unlikely case of her surviving Sacha's wedding, her plans were unformed. The only aim left in life was to meet him with the unconcern which only a brilliant commitment elsewhere can bestow. With a fresh access of woe, she recalled that this had once been her childish pledge for her next encounter with Sacha. The

K

Troika Belle wailed aloud and cast herself face down into her wet pillow. Very well, she thought with almost Slavonic fatalism, they shall all see me fulfil it! To admiration. Starting tomorrow.

Towards dawn she had sobbed herself to sleep; to dream of Sacha who was at that moment dreaming of nothing but a bath as his chaise splashed through the slush of the Vienna suburbs.

Some two hours later, leaving the Princess Nina in strong hysterics and the Countess with the thankless task of restoring her *amour propre*, Sacha's chief need was still a bath and breakfast. Both were forthcoming at Prince Adam's, together with a cordial invitation to stay as long as he wished and to treat Adam's quarters as his own.

His host, flushed and animated with pleasure, saw him comfortably bestowed and went off whistling to instruct his butler and round up a select company of young blades for a dinner that evening in Sacha's honour.

'Oh, and I'll stop off at the Palace to procure you a card for the ball tonight,' he called at the door. 'The Hofburg balls are pretty flat, but you'll see everyone who counts there.'

Sacha, draped in a towel, emerged on to the mezzanine landing.

'Thanks. I'm for the Palace myself directly, for I have to report to the A.D.C.'s quarters to make my number. Furlough or no furlough I'm apparently to hold myself on call for duty with His Majesty. *Never* get yourself seconded to the Staff! Hey, Adam, speaking of seeing everyone, her ladyship tells me that Lise—'

But Adam was off to arrange his party.

CHAPTER XVIII

In the small ormolu and gilt salon used by Lady Agnes and Lise to receive their personal guests, an open fire à l'anglaise added to the steamy heat of the palace. Francis ran a finger round the inside of his shirt collar, sure that it was wilting. Though normally indifferent to a fault about his appearance, tonight it piqued him to cut a creditable figure.

All day, ever since Prince Adam had called on him with an invitation to his dinner, Francis had been trying to track down the elusive Count Volnoy. His quest had proved fruitless and he had returned to his rooms with barely time to assume evening dress before he was due at Prince Adam's. Lise's summons to wait on her privately before escorting her to the Hofburg ball, had arrived as he was struggling with his neck-cloth, which the irritation of his nerves had caused him to wrest from Pollock's capable hands.

He examined the botched result in the mantel mirror. The limp muslin with his long-jawed, Friday face above it, served to deepen his gloom as he wondered for the tenth time if he owed this rendezvous with her to Volnoy's arrival. Miserably he rehearsed in his mind the words which would at once put an end to his revived hopes—and bring him a certain relief.

If once I *know* that I cannot have her, he thought—and looked up to find her standing before him.

For a full minute the Duke stared at her, too sunk in his depressing thoughts to turn his tongue round the civilities of greeting. She was in full ball-dress; to Francis's dazzled eyes merely a rivulet of glitter, but in fact one of Leroy's most daring inspirations, perfectly set off by the diamonds in her high-piled hair and encircling her slender throat and arms. M. Leroy had never intended this toilette to serve as a battle uniform, but that was what it had become.

She stood perfectly still, one exquisitely gloved hand playing with her fan. There was scarcely a trace of the forlorn, ill-dressed intruder he had befriended at Malvern. Only her eyes were the same;

but that little waif would not have known how to look at
him with this faintly mocking lift of her extravagantly arched
brows.

'Well, Malvern, finished your inspection?'

'F-forgive me! I fell to thinking of something and—and did not
realise how unmannerly I must be staring at you.'

'*Fi-donc!*—when I was persuaded that your riveted gaze was a
tribute to my toilette. So you were deep in thought about . . .
Wait, I shall divine it. About the dry rot in the tower at Malvern? Or the minutes you must draft for tomorrow's session of
Ministers?'

'I was thinking how much you had changed.'

'Oh, completely! But how dull if one did not! And just to show
you *how* much I have changed, I will become engaged to you—if you
still wish it, of course.'

'Lise—!'

'*Mon dieu*, what a frown! You have thought better of it? Or
are you shocked by my boldness?'

'I—I . . . Lise, are you serious?'

He started forward. She swayed out of reach, setting her diamonds
a-glitter.

'*Voyons*, one must always be serious about an engagement then?
No, I am not serious. I am the most *volage*, frivolous, gazetted flirt
in Vienna, with a fancy to be an English Duchess. There. Does that
satisfy you? Now do you wish to marry me?'

Instinct and reason alike prompted him to return the obvious
answer to this proposal. His brain told him coldly that in some
obscure fashion he owed the honour solely to the arrival in Vienna
of an unknown Russian officer. A vestige of common sense clamoured
for consideration.

But there before him stood the object of two years' longing, his for
the taking; and for the first and last time in his life the Duke of
Malvern lost his head. Seizing Lise hungrily in his arms, he covered
her face and neck with clumsy kisses.

Mlle de Montargis displayed all the answering enthusiasm of a
Paris-dressed wax doll, and freed herself with an angry little shake
that reminded Francis forcibly of a bristling kitten. He fell back,
his ardour abruptly damped. Lise turned to pat her curls back
into place in the mantel mirror.

Watching her, Malvern was visited by the lowering suspicion that
this was how his Duchess would receive his embraces in their mar-

ried life. He dismissed it as unworthy, kissed her hands and apologised humbly for his roughness.

'I shall post to Paris straightaway to obtain your brother's consent,' he cried. 'And then there's your mother and mine, and of course Aunt Hon to be apprised, and all the relations and my people at Malvern and the rest. And the notices for the *Gazette* and the *Moniteur*—'

'No!'

The public aspects of becoming the Duke of Malvern's bride in his homeland and hers, had not so far entered Lise's consideration. The miserable hours since courtyard gossip had informed her of Sacha's arrival, and of his early call on the Princess Nina, had reinforced her melancholy conviction that no plans beyond his wedding were required. But sitting down at her escritoire to acquaint Leroy with her intention to be buried in white, she did give fleeting thought to the void of the future, should heartbreak not prove mercifully mortal at nineteen.

Her thoughts had ranged from pursuing some remote botanical quest with Miss Smith, to marrying anyone but Malvern and becoming as scandalous as Countess Anna. In either case, the temporary nature of her requisitioning of Francis had gone some way to quiet her conscience over Agnes. She glowered at him, pleating a fold of her glittering skirts between nervous fingers.

'I—I mean Armand is in England, so it is quite useless for you to go to Paris.'

Feeling the inadequacy of this, she added imperiously: 'In any case, I want you here.'

For some reason the Duke did not find this comforting. He continued to watch her with troubled eyes.

'But you may let *everyone* here know I am engaged to you.'

'But my darling, we cannot—'

'Yes, we *can*. Otherwise it is all off.'

Tears of guilt and misery trembled on her fringe of lashes. They had their effect.

'Very well, my dear torment, it shall be as you wish,' he said helplessly. 'But you will grant that Aunt Hon must be informed?'

'And Agnes,' said his beloved with a doleful sniff.

He stiffened.

'I shall tell Agnes myself, Lise.'

The tears on her lashes splashed down her cheeks and more followed them.

'Oh, Francis,' she wailed, completing the ruin of his neck-cloth, 'Oh, dear Francis, I am so miserable.'

Prince Adam had chosen to receive his guests in Russian style, in honour of Sacha. The *zakouski* and vodka stage was prolonged beyond expectation by the tardiness of the guest of honour, and the party passed noisily to table with him still missing.

Francis had never formed one of the set of young bloods round the table; and tonight, cold sober and seething with confused emotion, he was farther than ever from sharing their exuberance.

Count Volnoy's entrance, just in time for the green duck, was greeted with howls of execrance and riotous welcome. A penalty for his tardiness was demanded and noisly settled. The silver *épergne* centrepiece, filled to the brim with claret, to be drained at a draught.

'At one draught, mind, Sacha.'

'Standing up on the table—'

'Without displacing a single glass—'

'And no heel taps—'

'Followed by a *full* account of the ladybird who kept you so late—'

A shout of laughter greeted this sally and a dozen eager hands pulled Sacha on to the table. Francis, who had taken no part in the general upsurge, leant forward to obtain at last a clear look at the shadowy 'someone in Russia'.

Colonel Count Volnoy, shouting with laughter, elegantly dishevelled and more than a trifle drunk, was a disconcerting ghost. Francis also found himself uneasily eyeing the perilous proximity of two blazing candelabra to Count Volnoy's slightly swaying form. Unobtrusively, he edged forward, ready to snatch them out of danger.

His position, his concern, touched an aching chord in his memory. How many times, as a callow, adoring younger brother, he had fulfilled this anxious rôle at Guy's revel-routs; then as now sitting solemn and sober among the gay blades he would have given so much to emulate.

The crash of the emptied *épergne* to the floor and a yell of approval round the table, disrupted his thoughts. He grabbed at the candelabra just in time, as Sacha leapt down to collapse laughing into his seat beside Prince Adam.

The dinner proceeded on its riotous course to the toasts. Malvern edged up to Prince Adam.

'What? Word with whom? By all means. Let's all have lots o' words later. But now have some more champagne.'

'Thank you, but—if it were possible, a private word with Volnoy before we leave.'

'Lord, Malvern, you'll get no sense out of him tonight! Tell you what, have some more champagne,' urged Prince Adam as one who has been struck by an original notion.

Francis gave it up. Thanking his host, he excused himself, pleading his engagement for the Hofburg ball.

'Good God, so'm I, and what's more, so's Volnoy. Hey there, Sacha! On your feet! We're off to the ball.'

'To hell with the ball!'

'Oh come, dear boy. Royal command and all that y'know—'

And indeed a number of the young gentlemen present, engaged for the Palace, were pushing back their chairs and scattering to their waiting valets.

They reappeared, spruce and sobered, to receive their cloaks and dolmans in the vestibule. The Duke's carriage was at the door when Prince Adam detained him.

'Were you not wishing to speak with Volnoy? Let me take you up with us then. Unless your matter is private?'

But Francis felt quite unequal to a tête-à-tête with Count Volnoy in the state that gentleman had left the dinner table. He accepted a seat in the carriage with mechanical civility. He found, however, that he had under-estimated his rival's iron head.

Sacha emerged from Danilo's hands looking precise to a pin in the full glory of the Volnoy Irregulars' black with azure facings and sash, silver lace and shoulder knots, and jingling with medals. He appeared to be entirely sober and only in such decorously high spirits as became a Colonel of the Imperial Staff about to grace a Royal ball.

The three young men took their places in the barouche which presently joined the long line of carriages bound for the Palace. Sacha was a shade put out to have the company of the English Duke, since he had had it in mind to question Adam about Lise. However, the morrow would serve; and he availed himself of the opportunity to ply Malvern with questions about Wellington in the Peninsula.

They were among the last of the guests to make their way up

the flower-decked staircase. After four months of Congress entertainments, the ingenuity of the Master of Festivals was understandably beginning to flag. All that his over-taxed fancy could devise for that night's ball was a lavish draping of the imperial salon in white silk, lit with wax tapers, and the re-upholstery of all the seating in gold-decked velvet.

Sacha and the Duke passed through this décor without comment, but by no means unremarked themselves. The youngest Colonel in the Russian armies was naturally the focus of most feminine glances. The *on-dit* quickly spread that the black, blue and silver splendour of his regimentals had been designed expressly to match his eyes by the Grand Duchess in person. The English Duke in his sober Court dress, crossed only by the ribbon of the Bath, was a more familiar figure; but the rumour, already current, that he was the successful suitor of The Troika Belle gained him a new measure of interest.

In the drawing room Prince Adam noted an over-curled flaxen head beside a forbidding dowager and left them with a muttered excuse. Sacha raised his eyebrows.

'Good God. Serious?'

'I—I am afraid I am not sufficiently in Prince Adam's confidence; but it would seem—'

'It would, wouldn't it? Never cared for pink sugar-plums after the age of ten or so myself. Well, shall we proceed?'

A pillared gallery gave access to the ballroom. The stairs were kept busy with traffic to and from the dance floor. Sacha and the Duke paused on the balcony to let the press disperse.

The dancing awaited the arrival of the Sovereigns, so the floor was given over to the gossip, parade, intrigue, flirtation and manoeuvre that was the other business of a Congress ball. Sacha smiled, savouring the taste of being back in the swim of the great world. The two young men lounged against the balcony rail, quizzing the celebrated faces and the oddities in the glittering throng below.

Presently there was a stir in it, a murmur and a turning of plumed and jewelled heads marked the entrance of M. de Talleyrand escorting a dark, slender young woman in shimmering white through the double doors at the far end of the ballroom.

His Excellency might remind Mr Crocker of an old, fuddled, lame, village schoolmaster, and his disability certainly lent him an odd, tottering walk, but no one's escort could bestow such a *cachet*.

In the present case, however, it was evident that his young companion was an object in herself; for her unhurried progress was attended by the sort of stir that alone sets the seal of success in the polite world.

She made her curtsey to a bejewelled dowager enthroned on one of the gilded sophas, and was at once surrounded by a press of uniforms; although M. de Talleyrand jealously retained his station at her side.

Can it be—but no, it cannot be her, thought Sacha, leaning over the balustrade. Yet her eyes— But what nonsense! My foolish poppet in her clumsy purple dresses . . .

His companion was saying something to him, nodding at the crowd below. Sacha collected himself.

'I beg your pardon. I was not listening. Tell me, Duke, who is that young woman over there, in the white gown, talking with M. de Talleyrand?'

It was then that Francis understood whom his graceless betrothed had meant by 'everyone here in Vienna' to be informed of their engagement. An expression that linked him unmistakably with his more pugnacious ancestors crossed his Grace's mild countenance.

'It is plain you have not been long in Vienna, sir.'

'Granted; but who is she?'

'My affianced wife.'

After the smallest pause, Sacha said coolly:

'Indeed? My felicitations. For a moment I had fancied that the lady was—'

'Mademoiselle de Montargis.'

'Lise?'

'You know her, I collect?'

'Know her? Any time since she was in leading strings! Never would I have believed—but pray take me to her so that I may offer an old friend's congratulations.'

Francis's hollow triumph knew a slight check.

'The engagement is a private one for the present,' he said stiffly. 'Well, not precisely private but—er—unofficial, until such time as mademoiselle's brother and parent make the public announcement. But of course—'

'But *of course*. Well, take me to her anyway to present my compliments. And is her Aunt Hon—that is, a Miss Smith—with her in Vienna by any chance?'

'*My* Aunt Hon, sir. Yes, she is, though at present visiting Baden.'

K*

'Good God,' cried Sacha. 'The ducal nephew! Malvern, I owe
you an apology for entertaining the liveliest doubts of your existence!
But has your aunt never spoken to you of me? She enlivened *my*
existence for over a twelvemonth.'

'Oh yes,' said Francis grimly. 'I know all about you. Come, I'll
conduct you to mademoiselle.'

The two of them, topping by a head most of the crowd, made
their way through it, pausing to give way to M. de Talleyrand
who was being borne away by an Imperial equerry. His passage
afforded Lise an early view of Malvern and his companion.

She froze. She had been steeling herself for her first sight of
Sacha to be with the Princess Nina on his arm. That he should
re-enter her life escorted by her betrothed was the final mockery
of fate. Her look of anguished appeal at her chaperone met with
a stony glare. Countess Anna, informed of Lise's precipitate engagement, had flown into a rage and declined to further such
folly, except to predict that Sacha would make the Duchess of
Malvern an admirable lover in, say, three years' time. Lise's cheeks
still grew hot at that recollection—now, when nothing mattered
except to meet Sacha without betraying herself.

Someone—a bemedalled blur—was speaking to her. She smiled
and murmured she knew not what, as she turned to meet Sacha's
eyes.

The Duke stepped between them to kiss her hand.

'My d-dear,' he said rather loudly, never having called her 'my
dear' in public before. 'Here is a friend of yours, newly arrived
in Vienna, who wishes to be among the first to felicitate us.'

Fourteen generations of ice stiffened Lise's spine as Sacha bowed
over her hand.

If she had trembled or turned pale, succumbed to tears or vapours,
even swooned, she would have found Sacha prepared for it; and
even prepared to forgive such indecorum, since he was put to
it to master his feelings himself. What he was totally unprepared
for was the perfect calm with which the Duke's bride looked at him.

Search her face as he might, he could discover no trace of his
artless poppet in the glittering Congress belle confronting him. As
in a dream, he offered her his congratulations on her betrothal. She
smiled faintly and asked him if he was pleased with Vienna and
intended a long stay? Then, learning from Francis's mumble that he
and Count Volnoy had met at Prince Adam's dinner, she turned
gracefully to her chaperone and begged her permission to present

'a friend from Russia' to 'Prince Adam's grandmother and my kind hostess'.

Behind them, a fanfare announced that the sets were forming for the first quadrille. A brilliant uniform clicked heels before Lise. With a languid glance of apology, Mlle de Montargis laid her exquisitely gloved hand on the Duke's arm.

'You will forgive me, Malvern? I have been promised to His Excellency this age.' The Duke bowed and effaced himself. His Excellency bore off his prize. Sacha found himself raked by a pair of coal-black old eyes snapping with malicious amusement.

'Well, young man? Inherited your father's temper as well as your mother's looks, I see! No call to glower at me, though. I don't like this engagement of hers any more than you. *I* had intended her for my grandson.'

Sacha detached his strained attention from the dance floor.

'Mademoiselle appears to be surrounded by unsuitable *prétendants*,' he snapped. 'Your ladyship must forgive my astonishment. Three years ago when she left—er—Russia, she was still a child.'

'And you do not relish the change in her, *ça se voit*.' The old lady nodded rapidly in response to some interior calculation. Sacha, his eyes riveted to the dancers, frowned.

'It is news to me that Adam is to be numbered among her suitors. Am I to collect, madame, that Mlle de Montargis preferred the Englishman?'

Countess Anna had just perceived that all was not lost for her darling project. She said blandly:

'By no means. But you modern young people . . .' She shrugged. 'Incurably *volage*. She eloped with Adam from Paris—'

'She *what*?'

Her ladyship favoured him with her blistering views on modern young people's manners. He apologised for his interruption.

'Well, it is understandable that it comes as a shock to *you*,' purred the Countess. 'But rest assured I saw to it that her credit was unimpaired; for *no* one could have contrived an elopement more fashionably. Imagine, the minx took her personal hairdresser in attendance!'

'Charming,' rasped Sacha.

'Precisely. Oh I assure you that your former—er—protégée's *ton* is quite the rage. The Tsar calls her his "*petite Cossack*".' She paused to relish the dangerous flash in Count Volnoy's stormy eyes. 'But the mischief is that my stupid Adam suddenly takes it into his head to fancy himself vastly smitten in another direction. The Ralenskys,' said her ladyship severely, 'have always had deplorable taste in women. His grandfather—my third husband—*zut*! His mistresses were so unworthy of me that I was obliged to leave him. And now Adam prefers a pink German pudding to Lise! So naturally she ripostes with this beanpole of a Duke.'

A movement of the dance brought Sacha an unimpeded view of a slender, glittering figure swaying with languid grace down the set. The little girl who had scarcely dared to breathe when he had danced with her at the Governor's ball. The Tsar's *'petite Cossack'*. He said between his teeth:

'Doubtless she will enjoy being a Duchess.'

'Fiddle-faddle! With an English stick who will bury her in the country and ruin her figure with innumerable children? Not to be thought of! Now Adam can give her just the sort of fashionable establishment she needs to launch her, for *au fond* she is a very *mondaine* creature,' confided the Countess, well-pleased with her effect. 'And having caught the Tsar's eye . . .'

Catching Count Volnoy's eye, her ladyship allowed herself to be thankful she was not a man. But it was some thirty years since she had permitted anyone to ruffle her composure. She wagged a jewelled claw at him.

'Mind now, I shall depend on you to exert your influence with Adam; since I perceive you to have such a *warm* interest in Lise's welfare.'

This happy thought was all Sacha needed to fire his temper. He said furiously:

'I beg you will hold me excused, ma'am! Mlle de Montargis—' The quadrille had been succeeded by a waltz. He glared at her drifting by, far too closely clasped in some popinjay's arms. 'Mlle de Montargis does not look to need any help towards a modish establish-ment—nor the licence that goes with it!'

His glare at the dance floor brought into view the Princess Nina, magnificent in black velvet, slowly descending the staircase into the ballroom. Favouring the dowager with a curt bow, he crossed the floor and drew Nina familiarly into his arms for the waltz.

Sacha ended an eventful four-and-twenty hours totally unable to sleep. The exquisite discomfort that kept him wakeful was quite unfamiliar—except in cursing himself for the idiocy of getting embroiled with Nina yet again. But no previous adventure in love had occasioned him his present turmoil, let alone interfered with his sleep. He re-lit his bedside candle yet again and counted the hours until he could see Lise and recover his silly, loving poppet in the glittering Congress belle inflaming his senses.

Morning, however, brought Nicky; and, within a half hour of his arrival, the urgent necessity of a further explanation with Nina, since she presented herself on Prince Adam's doorstep—where she was duly observed by the courtyard and reported to Lise. As Adam remarked, life with Sacha was seldom dull.

Their combined efforts eventually dislodged both the visitors; but Sacha only crossed the courtyard to Countess Anna's in time to witness Mlle de Montargis' departure for her airing in the Prater, attended by a hatchet-faced duenna and squired by two dashing Hussars of the Guard.

In the week that followed he was privileged to watch her dance, dine and flirt, win a jewelled *bonbonnière* from the Tsar's hand at Princess Radziwill's tombola and take a prize at a masquerade in the Apollo Hall. He was permitted to hold her bouquet and fan at the balls, to stand behind her chair in Countess Anna's box at the Opera, occasionally to anticipate Malvern in placing a ransom of furs around her shoulders. He could take his turn to ride beside her carriage in the Prater, and of course to figure among the glitter of uniforms always in attendance on a gazetted belle. None of which rôles suited Colonel Count Volnoy's consequence or temper.

Nor did he derive any satisfaction from his former protégée's public triumphs.

Lounging against a pillar at the Empress's soirée of *tableaux vivants*, he moodily watched Lise's sensational presentation of Cupid returning in triumph with Peace (Princess Esterhazy) in the train of Allied Victory (Mesdames de Périgord, von Furstenburg and de Langes) to crown Valour (Count Auguste de la Garde-Chambonas). Cupid's exiguous costume, and especially the little gold, winged boots, vividly recalled to Sacha the Smolensk *bania* where he had seen her even more scantily attired. That the little girl who then had sobbed out her penitence for displeasing him should now be leading him this dance was beyond endurance. With rage in his heart and a dangerous light in his dark blue eyes, the spoilt darling of the Petersburg fast set moved off to punish her.

He came up to the outskirts of the circle crowding round to

congratulate her at the end of the tableau. She had thrown a ruffled gauze cloak around her bared shoulders—a garment designed to veil rather than conceal its wearer's charms—and only Malvern of the gentlemen around her looked displeased. The crowd parted to admit the felicitations of a very August Personage. The passage cleared for his withdrawal brought Lise into direct line with Sacha's smouldering gaze.

She clasped the cloak a trifle more tightly round her. The gold boots tapped a nervous tattoo and then advanced towards him.

'Well, Volnoy, did not my performance earn your approval? You have not added your congratulations to His Majesty's and these gentlemen's.'

'Mademoiselle's performance was as polished as any I have seen her give on more private occasions,' he said silkily. He saw her hands clench on her gauzes and followed up his advantage. 'But I cannot say the same of mademoiselle's costume—' He grinned, and capturing one of the small clenched hands, said for her ear alone: 'Never forget, Lise, that *I* can recall seeing you even more scandalously clad in a rather small towel and Cossack boots. One of my more treasured memories.'

'How *could* he, how *dared* he!' raged Lise to Betsy on her return home.

The abigail was her sole remaining support, Lady Agnes having barricaded herself behind a screen of glacial good manners and Countess Anna remaining unmollified. Nicky and Adam were wholly taken up with Sacha, and even Sigi, after one look at Count Volnoy, had perfidiously gone over to what Lise now regarded collectively as the enemy camp. She had it on courtyard authority that he had twice sneaked off to dress Princess Nina's hair. As for Miss Smith, an ominous silence was her sole response to the news of her nephew's engagement.

Betsy had taken to her rôle of confidant with her usual robust independence.

'Well, I dunno about saying it to your head like that, miss,' she sniffed. 'But if *I* was to have any man see me near enough without a stitch, me Ma would've had the banns called afore the week was out. And so 'ud yours I dessay, Quality or no Quality.'

'Well yes, I expect she would have,' agreed Lise, preparing to cry again at the thought of how simply her happiness might have been attained. 'But what has that to say to anything? It is too late now. He will marry Princess Nina just the same.'

Betsy sighed and tucked in the bedclothes disarranged by her mistress's agitation.

'Dunno about that, miss. Look at the way 'is Russian lordship 'as been dangling round you ever since he arrived—'

'Yes, to mortify me as he did tonight! Because now that *I* am fashionable it piques him to add me to his conquests!'

Lise dashed a couple of tumbled silk pillows to the floor.

'Oh Betsy, you are so stupid! Don't you suppose I'd end this hateful pretence tomorrow—yes, and beg Malvern's and Agnes's pardon—if I thought it would do any good?'

'Can't tell what you can do till you try, me Ma used to say. Better than going on the way you are,' remarked Betsy with feeling, bending down to retrieve the pillows.

There are a number of irreproachable ways to let a gentleman know that his addresses are welcome. Few of them, however, are open to a lady who happens to be the bride of another, unless she is ready to incur the odium of Society. And little as Lise cared if the salons labelled her Fast, it was another matter to find Sacha apparently subscribing to these opinions.

By now Sacha had firmly convinced himself that he had come to Vienna solely to reclaim his poppet. Instead he had found the Troika Belle, and he reacted to her timid advances with all the perversity of a man violently in love.

One of the most mortifying aspects for Lise was to surprise the glance of rueful understanding that occasionally passed between him and her betrothed.

Their duties as well as their amorous pursuit frequently threw the two young men together. Sacha had had the ill-luck to arrive in the midst of one of the Tsar's military moods, when His Majesty declared 'I am a soldier! I am never happy unless I am surrounded by soldiers!' Colonel Count Volnoy's disgust at the resulting encroachments on his furlough found a patient audience in the Duke, as they kicked their heels in Congress ante-rooms.

Lounging together through the tedium of a Hofburg levée, the Duke abruptly mentioned his removal from Vienna for the next couple of days, as his aunt had requested his attendance on her in Baden. Good manners forbade him to add 'leaving you a clear field'. Sacha, after a moment's pause, grinned. 'Damned if I don't come with you to pay my respects! Had my fill of this dam' hothouse for a while.'

Their departure next morning left the three ladies chiefly concerned with an empty two days to consider their unhappy situations. Each of them came to a fateful decision.

Lady Agnes waited on Countess Anna to announce her departure for England, in the company of the 'respectable Englishwoman' Miss Smith had once designed as an escort for Lise.

The Princess Nina thanked Madame Arloff charmingly for her hospitality, but feared she could no longer delay her departure for Paris, and ordered her packing.

Lise decided to put an end to her misery, entreat Malvern's pardon and seek an explanation with Sacha.

None of these eminently sensible aims were achieved. The fault, however, lay far outside the scope of the young ladies concerned; and many grander designs than theirs foundered in the critical days that followed Napoleon's escape from Elba.

CHAPTER XIX

In a calm, sunlit sea, the French cruiser *Zephyr,* patrolling from Toulon, hailed a brig flying the Elba flag and demanded her destination.

Her signalman, stammering slightly, replied that she was the *Inconstant*, bound for Genoa from Elba, where, he added, the Emperor Napoleon was wonderfully well. For this he had no less authority than the Emperor himself, standing concealed on the *Inconstant*'s deck and watching the two ships closing in across the smooth sea. Another few yards would undoubtedly show the *Zephyr*'s look-outs the fifty Grenadiers whom he had ordered to lie flat on the deck; and the *Inconstant*'s gun ports open for action.

For a few sickening heartbeats everyone aboard her held their breath.

The *Zephyr* bade them a cheerful 'Godspeed' and sheered off. The *Inconstant* sailed on for France and a hundred days of chequered glory.

Varying degrees of panic seized the authorities around Elba. Sir Neil Campbell, the English Commissioner, muttering that he was well aware how much 'the improvidence of nations would be left to my charge', departed to call out the British Mediterranean Fleet and to send urgent warnings to Genoa, Sicily, Paris, Vienna and London that Napoleon was at large.

The Austrian Imperial and Royal Consul-General in Genoa seized a pencil and the first piece of paper to hand—a torn-off sheet from a ruled commercial notebook—to scrawl a confidential despatch to Prince Metternich. He subscribed it 'Express' and 'Urgent'; but even so the Imperial courier did not reach Vienna until dawn on Tuesday, March the seventh.

There, everything was proceeding as usual. On the previous Saturday, when Sacha and Malvern had left for Baden, Count Zichy's weekly redoubt was slightly enlivened by the *on-dit* that the English Duke had challenged Count Volnoy to a duel; a rumour given credence by The Troika Belle's wan looks. By Monday morning she was in a fair way to believing the rumour herself.

The young ladies breakfasted in their boudoir. Lady Agnes vouchsafed two gelid comments on the weather and retired to supervise her packing. Lise fidgeted disconsolately round their quarters for a while and then picked up her skirts and whisked through the green baize door of the servants' passage leading to Prince Adam's wing.

It was gothick to be thought to require chaperonage for a coze with an old friend. Nevertheless she was annoyed at having to ask directions of startled domestics in the dark maze of passages. She emerged into the sunlight of Adam's upper hall a trifle ruffled and out of breath—to come face to face with Sacha.

Both he and Malvern were due on duty that Monday, so they had ridden from Baden at dawn to give themselves time to change into uniform. A footman was in the act of handing Count Volnoy his shako and gloves. At the sight of Lise he jerked his head at the man and tossed both down on to a console.

'The most unexpected of pleasures!' he remarked, advancing upon her and taking her hand. 'Never tell me that I am at last to be honoured by a few words in private with mademoiselle? Dare I hope that this was your object in coming here?'

His lips formally brushed her fingertips, but his hold on her hand did not slacken, nor did the hard intensity of his gaze at her. Lise backed away.

'I—I came to see Prince Adam.'

Sacha's brows shot up.

'Alone, unchaperoned, by a privy passage? Adam is privileged indeed! But perhaps such favours are only to be expected after an elopement. In that case, should not I also—?'

'Don't be so odious!' snapped Lise. 'Adam is my *friend*. As for coming here unchaperoned, I—'

'Whatever your views on decorum, my girl, *I* do not wish them shared with every servant in this establishment. In here—'

Lise found herself in the smallish salon off the hall, alone in far more dangerous company than Adam's, and with the door firmly shut behind them. Since this had been her sole aim for three years, it was surprising to feel nothing but acute apprehension. She said coldly but a little breathlessly:

'Now pray will you have Prince Adam informed that I am here?'

'No, by God I will not! Come here.'

Mlle de Montargis retreated behind a sopha.

'And don't start playing off maidenly airs on me. Let me tell you they hardly become a Congress belle visiting a bachelor establishment. Especially when she happens to be betrothed to another man —poor devil!'

Rage and tears equally choked Lise's utterance. But it is more practical to rage at a man across a sopha than to cast yourself weeping into his arms.

'How *dare* you!' she spluttered.

Sacha laughed.

'Decidedly unoriginal. But I will tell you precisely how I dare. Because I came here to—' a certain fundamental honesty intervened. '—Well, I came here anyway. To find you turned into a gazetted flirt! Engaged to a man for whom you don't care a button, just for his consequence! How dare you play me such a trick?'

'Play *you* a trick? When you yourself— Really, Volnoy, this tone is one you are entitled to use to Princess Nina, but not to me!'

'Nina? What's she to say to anything?' demanded Sacha furiously. 'She's not my intended wife and no one's accusing you of being Malvern's *mistress*!'

He rounded the sopha in two strides and loomed over her.

'And that puts me in mind of another thing. How come you to have the Tsar term you his *"petite Cossack"*? Have you *no* sense? A man of his libertine propensities—'

'Now that is the outside of enough!'

With the blessed words 'not my intended wife' singing through her head, Lise was enchanted by his jealousy. No girl of spirit could resist playing on it a little after so many years of unrequited love. She said demurely:

'It is most improper in you to speak so of your Sovereign. Why, His Majesty's favour made me the most envied girl in Paris! And it proved *invaluable* in establishing me here.'

'So Aunt Hon let out to me. Only a gazetted blue-stocking could be so innocent! Your present chaperone is not so deluded as to where such favour leads, even if you are! Or do I underestimate the ambitious Mlle de Montargis? Perhaps, having married your Duke, you aspire to succeed the Princess Naryshkin in His Majesty's affections?'

This was no longer a gratifying jealousy.

'Perhaps you would prefer me to succeed Nina Ulanoff in yours?' flashed Lise.

'You little fool, I'm going to *marry* you, God help me!'

It was not how he meant to say it; nor in her worst nightmares could Lise have imagined herself responding 'Oh, *are* you!' in a voice shaking with rage, to Sacha's proposal of marriage.

'—but I collect you imagine no woman could resist such an obliging offer from you! Especially if she is betrothed to another! Having now insulted me in every possible way—'

She stopped for want of something to hurl at him. Unfortunately, instead of a handy vase, memory supplied her with a more deadly missile.

'In any case, yours are not the qualities one looks for in a husband,' she drawled with Countess Anna's own worldliness. 'Though I daresay you might make one an admirable lover in, say, three years' time.'

She saw his face and gave a gasp of fright, never before having unleashed this side of Sacha's temper. Until now, for all his rancour, his adult brain had been telling him that he was making a fool of himself. But no tenderness, no memories, no adult sense softened the cold fury with which he turned to deal with one of the high-born hussies he knew too well.

'Why wait three years?' he said smoothly. 'Since we now understand each other so well . . .'

He passed a practised arm around her rigid shoulders and drew her to him.

'Let me go!'

'But why? No circumstances could be more inviting. There is an alcove through those *portières* over there— But I am persuaded you know it already.'

Mlle de Montargis slapped his face. Sacha laughed and caught her up in his arms. His mouth found hers in a kiss that lasted all the way to the alcove.

For its duration it drove all rational consideration of her position out of Mlle de Montargis's head. Bemused by the happiness of being in Sacha's arms, she was so far lost to decorum as to respond warmly to his embrace, regaining her disordered senses only when she found herself flung down on the cushions of the day bed, with Count Volnoy unfastening the sword-belt of his uniform above her.

She had opened her mouth to scream when Prince Adam's worried voice at the door of the salon called:

'Sacha? I was told Lise was here with you—?'

Sacha rammed back home the buckle of his belt and parted the alcove curtains.

'Mademoiselle found herself oppressed by the heat,' he said expressionlessly, 'I have persuaded her to seek the repose of the couch.'

'Er—yes, of course,' stammered Adam, coming up to the alcove.

From the foot of the day-bed the two young men surveyed their sobbing guest, huddled on the cushions and looking in her distress exactly as she had looked at other crises of her acquaintance with Count Volnoy.

By grim effort he schooled his face to its habitual nonchalance. Brought abruptly to his senses by Adam's interruption, he was now a prey to a variety of discomfiting emotions; chief among them an anguished tenderness which belated regard for Mlle de Montargis's reputation forbade him to express. He was also plagued by the ill-timed levity of the thought that surely by now he should have learnt that Mlle de Montargis's virtue was safe from him!

He met Prince Adam's eyes with a gratitude tinged by exasperation, knowing exactly what addlepated notions of his duty as a man of honour were passing through Adam's romantic head. A challenge from a one-armed firebrand is all I lack, thought Sacha. He retrieved some scattered hairpins and said with an authority he was far from feeling:

'There now, my child, you are quite restored, are you not? With your abigail to support you, I am sure you'll feel equal to regaining your rooms.'

'Yes, yes indeed! Pray let me ring for her to be fetched at once,' burbled Adam.

'No!' Lise made a clutch at her tumbling hair and strove to rise.

Both gentlemen sprang forward to assist her. She rejected their proffered arms, and brushing past them, fled sobbing out into the hall and across the courtyard to her rooms.

'She did not come down to nuncheon or dinner. She will not speak to me or even allow Betsy to attend her. I *cannot* leave her in this state,' said Lady Agnes worriedly to Malvern.

The Duke was looking even more worried, having just been tearfully informed by his betrothed that she was the greatest Beast in nature, proposed to spend the rest of her days in the Antipodes, and begged his pardon for all the trouble she had caused him. Would he please tell Agnes? She had then stripped off his ring, laid it sorrowfully on his knee and run sobbing out of the boudoir where he and Agnes were now conferring in lowered voices outside her locked bedroom door.

'But what has happened?' cried Francis. 'What could have plunged her into such distress?'

'Sh-shhh,' admonished Agnes. She rose and motioned him to follow her out into the petit salon.

Malvern, with vivid memories of his last tête-à-tête there, avoided the sopha and went over to the windows, mechanically parting the curtains in the hope of a breath of air.

'Can you not tell me what has happened?' he said again.

Lady Agnes resisted the temptation. Sensational rumours of Mlle de Montargis's morning activities were flying all over the palace; but *noblesse oblige*. She shook her head.

'All that has reached me is servants' gossip. You of course have a right to know Lise's concerns,' she went on, staring fixedly out of the window. 'But in the present case she has doubtless told you as much as she sees fit herself. I believe, however, that I may inform you I felt it my duty to send for Aunt Hon. Excuse me now, Francis, I have requested to speak to Countess Anna.'

The Duke said to his boots:

'It is good in you to stay with Lise. I—I must not conceal from you that she has ended our engagement. She—she charged me to inform you.'

A trembling *dame de compagnie*, quietly having hysterics in the ante-room, admitted Lady Agnes to the Countess's presence.

Her ladyship, in full evening rig and jewels, dismissed the huddle of weeping servants before her and turned to Agnes.

'Well, I suppose you are come to give me *your* version?'

Agnes curtsied. 'No, madame. Merely to inform you that I have sent to Miss Smith. With your permission, I have also decided to postpone my departure.' Indefinitely, sang her heart. She repressed its exuberance and said calmly:

'Perhaps it would also be as well to send for Lise's mother.'

'A precious lot of use all three of you will be!' rasped her ladyship.

'*I* have sent for Volnoy. Unfortunately the Tsar has taken it into his head to attend the meeting of Ministers tonight and Volnoy's in attendance. I will see him in the morning. His future wife,' said

the Countess blandly, fixing a beady eye on Agnes, 'will doubtless
be improved by a night's sleep. Meanwhile I would remind you
that we receive at ten and you are not dressed. When you are
Duchess of Malvern you will learn that no private crisis justifies
keeping one's guests waiting.'

No hint of the impending *public* crisis disturbed the normal acri-
mony of the Ministers' meeting that night in Prince Metternich's
rooms at the Kaunitz Palace. The meeting broke up at three in the
morning, and the Prince had forbidden his valet to disturb his rest.
In spite of this prohibition, the man ventured in at six, with an
express despatch marked 'Urgent'. Upon its cover the Prince read
'From The Imperial and Royal Consulate General at Genoa.' He
was not impressed; and having enjoyed but two hours' sleep, laid the
despatch aside unopened upon the table beside his bed.

But once disturbed, he was unable to rest again. At about seven-
thirty he resigned himself to opening the troublesome despatch.

Prince Metternich, that dandy of dandies, later described himself
as having dressed in a flash. At any rate, by eight o'clock he was
with his Emperor. His Majesty read the despatch with that perfect
calm which not only his enemies ascribed to lethargy. But for once
there was the light of energy and decision in the pallid eyes he
lifted to his chief Minister.

'Go at once and find the Emperor of Russia and the King of
Prussia; tell them that I am prepared to order my armies once
again to take the road to France. I have no doubt that the two
Sovereigns will join me in my march.'

At 8.15 Metternich was with the Emperor Alexander who used
the same language as the Emperor Francis, several more sonorous
phrases occurring to him only after Metternich had bowed himself
out. At 8.30 the King of Prussia gave Metternich his assurance of
solidarity. At ten, Wellington joined the gathering of Ministers in
Metternich's cabinet. At the same hour aides-de-camp were flying
in all directions, carrying to the several Army Corps who were
returning to their homelands, the order to halt.

In this way War was decided on in less than an hour.

Among the speeding aides-de-camp, on his way to Poland, was
Colonel Count Volnoy.

CHAPTER XX

Vienna woke next morning to a changed world.

'A thousand candles,' mourned Comte Auguste de la Garde Chambonnas, 'seem in a single instant to have been extinguished.'

But few of the glittering figures who had waltzed the nights out beneath them had time to regret the deserted ballrooms. The Vienna mood was of natural apprehension; people gathered in anxious groups in the street and snatched the news-sheets off the presses. But all were heartened by the amazing unity and despatch prevailing among the Allies.

Less exalted persons than the Sovereigns also felt all the urgency of settling their problems in a rational manner.

The Princess Nina, caught by the news halfway to Paris, turned back for Petersburg and her second splendid marriage.

The Duke of Malvern, under orders to leave for London with urgent despatches for the Cabinet, snatched a half hour from his preparations to hurry to the Orenbourg palace.

Lady Agnes came into the *petit salon* from the boudoir where she, the Countess and Miss Smith took it in turns to sit with Lise.

The Duke took her hands.

'Agnes, I am under orders to leave for England on the instant. Will you come with me?'

She had said: 'Yes,' before either of them realised the enormity of such a proposal.

Suddenly Francis roared with laughter, earning a swift 'Sh-shhhh' with a glance at the boudoir door. It was powerless to repress his spirits.

'My love, I'll hold this over you whenever you feel bound to inflict our stuffier relations on us at Malvern! Oh Agnes, would you have really come? Say so and I will countermand the respectable Mrs Robinson I've been at such pains to procure as your chaperone.'

'Malvern, I beg you will be serious! I did not mean— Yes,
I did! Rather than lose you again . . .' She trailed off and then,
being a courageous young woman, looked him squarely in the
eyes.

'Francis, you *are* sure . . . ?'

He returned her look.

'Yes.'

Holding her hands like a talisman, he groped for words to
explain how a man can be in love with one woman while truly
loving another. Not surprisingly, none came. Lady Agnes touched
his cheek.

'I think you will always love Lise with the part of you that cannot
resist a lame duck—or the charm of your Etruscan figurines. I
undertake not to be jealous of it. Poor Lise, she's in too sad a case
to warrant anything but our friendship. I must see her before we
leave—did you really mean "on the instant"?'

The Duke shook himself out of his thoughts.

'Indeed I do! I require you packed, ready and waiting within
the hour. Make my farewells to Aunt Hon and—and Lise. Aunt Hon
will have to miss our wedding.'

'Yes, but—Oh Malvern, we might arrive in time to celebrate it
with Mary's! I have but yesterday had a letter—'

'Tell me as we go,' he called over his shoulder.

Colonel Count Volnoy was rather less fortunately placed than
Malvern to take the rational way out of his predicament.

Seated on a bench outside a peasant's hut in Pomerania, whilst his
horse was shod at a smithy across the muddy road, he propped his
old campaign message pad on his knee and tried, for at least the
tenth time, to write to Lise.

But that morning he was too saddle-weary to seek for the impossible words to set everything right between them and to torment
himself with the thought that she might be married to Malvern, or
whisked off somewhere in disgrace, or hating him enough to become
what in an insane moment he had thought her. Instead, he wrote
rapidly, from his heart, the pencil scrawl straggling a little down
the page as the tablet moved on his knee.

Allowing for their differing circumstances, his letter was a fair
transcription of Lise's tear-stained note which, if he did not still

precisely cherish it, was at any rate lurking *somewhere* among his papers at Volnoya.

He set his seal to it without re-reading what he had written and went off to hurry the smith. The next town was only an hour's ride, and with any luck he might intercept a courier for Vienna.

CHAPTER XXI

'Lise, dear child, if you *will* not drive out, I insist that you step into the garden. Yet another week without stirring from this hot-house will make you really ill. Look at you, worn to skin and bone—'

Countess Anna glared at Miss Smith.

'And catching a rheum will hardly speed her recovery! Now Lise, attend me; a perfectly quiet dinner at the Saxe-Coburgs', practically *en famille*. With Adam as your table partner. Come, *petite*, you cannot stay shut away from the world forever, you know!'

On this one point the two ladies were united. Miss Smith nodded vigorous agreement, saying:

'Dear child, you are much in Countess Anna's debt for seeing to it that no word of scandal about you has circulated. The consequences of your innocent folly—'

'She has Bonaparte to thank more than me, if there are none,' shrugged the Countess, '*I* only stopped the servants' mouths. *He* gave everyone in Vienna something else to talk about.'

'He did indeed!' Miss Smith leant forward. 'Tell me, Countess, is it true Old Douro has found matters in a sad way in Flanders? I had it on good authority that the Saxon regiments—'

'Mutinous,' snapped the Countess. 'And the Prince of Orange's Corps a mere ragbag of Dutch, Belgians and bobtail. I have it that Wellington took one look at the troops and said . . .'

The Countess's towering turban and Miss Smith's severe white capote nodded together over Vienna's new line in *on-dits*. Lise slipped silently away to her bedchamber.

Sacha had no luck with his courier. His letter finally reached Lise only a week before he himself, by dint of moving heaven and earth, was on the road back to Vienna.

So she had a mere two weeks of re-reading it, crying over it, sleeping with it under her cheek and generally becoming accustomed to happiness. It was shared by all her well-wishers, now augmented by General Mirnoff from Baden, and Malvern on business from Brussels, where, with Agnes gaily installed, he was attached to Wellington's Headquarters.

To be in Old Douro's 'family', with his new-married wife at hand, was all any young Englishman could ask in the summer of 1815. And Francis posted back to Flanders with the added joy of knowing that Lise's happiness was secured.

He regaled the farewell dinner in his honour with a lively account of the gaieties of Brussels. Miss Smith compressed her lips; but to the General alone she later confided her anxiety for her nephew and her fear that Lise's expectation of lifelong bliss might also be subject to the drums beating again in Flanders.

'Poppycock, Honoria! Like to see both of 'em with the Colours; but as for young Arloff, we haven't so much as a Russian platoon within five hundred miles of Flanders: more's the pity. Wouldn't mind taking a lunar at Napoleon meself if I could but see a way to it.'

Miss Smith threw up her hands.

'Well, I shall see to it that Volnoy apprehends the full ineligibility of a bridegroom who vanishes into the smoke of battle,' she snapped. 'The minute he reappears in Vienna.'

Unfortunately she was still asleep when, riding through the night, Sacha reached Vienna in the light drizzle of a June dawn.

Brushing aside the domestics outside, and only demanding of a scandalised Betsy 'Which door?' he went straight into Lise's bedchamber, muddy-booted, cloaked and caked with dust as he was.

The pale girl, all eyes and tumbled hair, leaning on the window-sill to re-read a letter she knew by heart, was undeniably his poppet. But he could only stand silent before her, uncertain for the first time in his life of his reception at a woman's hands.

And she had grown so thin. With an aching and unfamiliar tenderness constricting his throat, Sacha reverted to the simple warmth of his mother-tongue.

'*Doushenka moya lubimaya* . . . Oh my little love, you have grown so thin . . .'

Lise, sobbing blissfully into his mud-splashed shoulder, saw nothing lacking in this as a declaration and contributed nothing but an ecstatic 'Oh, Sacha!' in reply. Few ladies of his previous acquaintance would have considered either adequate. All of them would have been flabbergasted when he abruptly loosened the arms fastened around his neck.

In the same moment, Lise became conscious of being clad only in a flimsy lawn nightgown.

'My darling,' said Sacha not quite steadily. 'I promise myself here and now that this shall be the last time I tell you to get some clothes on. Is this thing your *peignoir*?'

Lise gave a chirrup of laughter that broke on a sob. She caught his hands.

'Promise me something else. That nothing shall ever—'

'—part us again,' she finished breathlessly when he next allowed her the use of her mouth.

'Nothing and no one ever again, my love!' promised Sacha with fine romantic brio.

Then he found himself regarding his enraptured audience with a certain dismay.

'Except for . . . Sweetheart, you will not cavil at a mere bit of sightseeing around Flanders? I'll be back to you the minute we've sent Boney to the rightabout.'

Lise stepped back.

'Sacha! But—but there's not a single Russian regiment—'

'Well I know it! Having spent the past month battling to get 'em mustered again. But how do *you* know?'

'Betsy. John footman overheard the General telling Aunt Hon. Sacha, then you cannot have been *posted* to Flanders—'

'Well, no. I've—er—seconded myself, having some friends at Headquarters and being still officially owed some furlough—'

'And you've no better use for it *now* than to—'

'Dammit, poppet, you would not wish the battle of the century fought without a Russian representative, now would you?'

'Yes I would!'

'And you about to become a Russian yourself!'

'When, pray?'

'As soon as . . .'

Sacha gave it up.

'*Doushenka*. Come here—'

His intended gave him a cool cheek to kiss and went on surveying him in a fashion he did not relish.

'*Doushenka* . . .'

'Very well. But I come with you.'

'Do you, by God! Just the thing to commend me to your family, to go gallivanting off with you to Flanders. Don't be silly, poppet.'

The tolerant scrutiny he found so discomfiting became positively maternal.

'*Dear* Volnoy, if we are to deal charmingly together in our married life you must positively allow me to have grown up a trifle since our last elopement! I shall descend with Agnes in Brussels. She is married to Malvern now, so that makes it quite proper. And she writes that Brussels is so gay! *All* my ball dresses; but I can be packed within the hour. A soldier's bride must grow used to marching orders! I shall take Betsy and Sigi—'

Sacha, grappling with this foretaste of his married life, and sternly dismissing some delectable possibilities of gay Brussels, came abruptly out of his thoughts.

'Not Sigi. Adam may have been fool enough to put up with his frisking, but I won't. Oh, poppet . . . sunlight on diamonds. How many men have succumbed to that laugh of yours?'

'Dozens. So I'm to come?'

Instead of answering he took her provocative little face between his hands, examining it with a touch of grimness behind a gaze that set Lise trembling.

'So you are quite grown up now, are you? And I, as I pointed out to you once before, am only human. So . . . Yes, you come. But only if Aunt Hon comes with you.'

'Oh Sacha, just like to Volnoya—'

'Not precisely.'

He frowned. But with Miss Smith there to whisk Lise off at the first smell of danger, his 'sightseeing' gave him fewer qualms. And the dark eyes that closed under his kisses brought home to him another aspect of his need of Miss Smith.

'Not precisely, no,' he grinned. 'This time, my black-eyed darling, you are going to need a strict chaperone every minute until our wedding. Think we can persuade her again?'

Still flushed poppy pink, Lise gurgled with that glinting laughter.

'Maybe—if we were to enlist the General too . . . Sacha, she has permitted him to call her Honoria!'